Columbia

THE LAST CIRCLE

Books by STEPHEN VINCENT BENÉT

Published by Rinehart & Co.

ROSE

The Beginning of Wisdom
Young People's Pride
Jean Huguenot
Spanish Bayonet
James Shore's Daughter
The Devil and Daniel Webster
Thirteen O'clock
Johnny Pye and the Fool-Killer
Tales Before Midnight
America

POETRY

Five Men and Pompey
Tiger Joy
Heavens and Earth
John Brown's Body
Ballads and Poems
Burning City
Young Adventure
A Book of Americans
(with Rosemary Benét)
Nightmare at Noon
They Burned the Books
Western Star

SELECTED WORKS

Volume One: Poetry
Volume Two: Prose

LIBRETTO

The Devil and Daniel Webster

RADIO SCRIPTS

We Stand United and Other Radio Scripts

The posthumous poems and stories in this volume will be included later in the works of Mr. Benét as they are re-edited and re-published by Rinehart & Co.

The Last Circle

STORIES AND POEMS BY

STEPHEN VINCENT BENÉT

"You drop a stone in a pool and the circles
spread. But on what far shore of the pool does the
last circle break?"
From *As It Was in the Beginning*

FARRAR, STRAUS AND COMPANY

New York · 1946

CONTENTS

INTRODUCTION

As I re-read these stories and poems, there seems to be in them a premonition of death. I do not know that the facts entirely bear this out, and I think that should be said, as he used to say, "for the record." If ever anyone was struck down in the midst of life, it was Steve. Though he suffered for many years from a slow, chronic malady, arthritis—a condition which he accepted with his usual philosophy, fortitude, and humor—the heart attack which killed him was as unexpected as a bolt of lightning. I was told by the doctors to try to think of it as an accident inside instead of an accident outside, for that is what it was.

All good work deals with life, love, and death. The human pattern in the life of the author is bound to coincide with the written word in such work at some time. Then we think of it as being prophetic. When I try to rationalize this way, there are two facts over which I stumble . . . that he always told me he would not live to be old . . . that he was working on a piece about the Resurrection when he died.

On the other hand, if I had been looking for such intimations earlier, in his first book of collected short stories, published eleven years ago, there is "A Death in the Country," in the second volume, there is "Johnny Pye and the Fool Killer," both preoccupied with death. "If This Should Change," perhaps the most truly prophetic of all his work, was written as long ago as 1939.

The poem "Little Testament" he put away deliberately.

He wrote it in June of 1941, when he decided to re-make his will. He said he wished to make another will—of intangible, not tangible, things—picking up that legal phrase, "the tangibles." He laughed and said he would leave it to speak for him after he died. But I think he thought it would be a long time.

No, the mind did not know. The heart may have a different perception. One cannot argue with the spirit . . . The spirit has a sense of time all its own, that is not ours: another measuring-rod, another hourglass.

Rosemary Benét

PART ONE

And there it is and could be worse,
With notes and preface and the rest
And every kind of teacher's aid
To harry schoolboys into learning
The unpremeditated verse,
Written because the heart was hot
With quite a different kind of burning.
And that is the revenge of time
And that, they say, the workman's pay,

It may be so, I wouldn't know.
I wrote it poor, in love, and young,
In indigestion and despair
And exaltation of the mind,
Not for the blind to lead the blind;
I have no quarrel with the wise,
No quarrel with the pedagogue,
And yet I wrote for none of these.

And yet there are the words, in print,
And should an obdurate old man
Remember half a dozen lines
Stuck in his mind like thistle-seed,
Or if, perhaps, some idle boy
Should sometime read a page or so
In the deep summer, to his girl,

3

And drop the book half-finished there,
Since kissing was a better joy,
Why, I shall have been paid enough.
I'll have been paid enough indeed.

THE BISHOP'S BEGGAR

*I*t seems that in the old days there was a bishop of Remo, and he was a heedless and proud young man, though of good intentions. Now, that was possible in those days, when the fire and light of the new learning had spread through Italy, and men drank, as if intoxicated, at a new spring. There were bishops who cared less for the Word of God than for their own splendor, and cardinals who were rather men of the world—and of no good world—than sons of the Church. I do not say that our bishop was as idle and self-seeking as some of these; I do say that he was a child of his time. He would have liked to be a lord, but his eldest brother was the lord; he would have liked to be a soldier, but his second brother was the soldier. So he went into the Church, for there, too, a man who bore a great name could rise. He was clever, he was ambitious, he had great connections. Now and then, to be sure, he asked a disquieting question, but the Baldis had always been original. The path that is rugged for many was made smooth for him from the first. When he was made bishop of Remo at an early age, the fact did not surprise him. Since he was to be neither lord nor soldier, he found that pleasant enough.

All went well for him, at first. They were glad to have a young and handsome bishop at Remo, for the bishop before him had been old and ill-favored. It was a pleasure to no one to kiss his ring, and he frightened the children with his peering eyes. With the coming of our bishop all this was changed.

There was a great to-do and refurbishing of the bishop's palace; the smells of good cooking drifted again from the bishop's kitchens; when the bishop drove through the city, men threw their caps in the air. There were fine new frescoes in the cathedral, a new way of chanting in the choir. As for sin and suffering—well, they are always with us. The people of Remo liked to sin pleasantly and be reminded of it as little as possible.

Nevertheless, at times, a grayness would come over our bishop's spirit. He could not understand why it came. His life was both full and busy. He was a friend to art, a host to the gay and the learned, a ruler of men. He did not meddle in things which did not concern him; he felt in his heart that there was no prize in the Church which might not be within his grasp. And yet, at times, there was a grayness within him. It was singular.

He could not show that grayness before the world, he could not show it to his secretary or the witty company that gathered at his table. He could wrestle with it in prayer, and so he did. But he found it no easy task. Had the Devil appeared before him with horns and a tail, he would have known what to do. But a grayness of spirit—a cool little voice in the mind which said to him now and then, "What do you in these robes, at this place, Gianfrancesco Baldi?"—that was another matter.

He came to find by experience that motion in the open air helped him as much as anything. When the grayness oppressed him too severely, he would summon his coach and drive about the countryside. So one day, as he drove through a small country village in the hills beyond Remo, it happened. It was nobody's fault; the bishop's least of all. He saw to it that he had a skilful coachman and good horses as he saw to all such matters. But when a tall, gangling boy darts across the street right under the nose of the horses, the most skilful coachman cannot always save him. There was a cry and a scream and a soft jar. Then, where the coach had passed, the boy lay writhing in the street.

The bishop always showed at his best in emergency. When he got out of the coach, the angry shouts of the crowd died away to a respectful murmur. He lifted the boy into the coach with his strong arms and drove back with him to Remo. On the way he talked to him soothingly, though the boy was in too much pain to pay much attention to this graciousness. When they got to Remo, he had the boy carried to a servant's room in the palace and doctors summoned for him. Later on he gave instructions about cleaning the coach.

At dinner his secretary recounted the little incident, and all men praised the kindliness of the bishop. The bishop passed it off pleasantly, but, at heart, he felt a trifle irritated. He had not felt particularly drawn toward the boy; on the other hand, he could not have left him lying in the road.

By the next day, as such things do, the story had gone all over Remo, and there were unusual demonstrations of good will as the bishop passed to the cathedral. The bishop received them with dignity, but his irritation remained. He disliked ostentatious shows of virtue and distrusted the fickleness of crowds. Nevertheless, it was his duty to see the boy, and he did so.

Washed, combed, and rid of his vermin, the boy looked ordinary enough, though somewhat older than the bishop had thought him. His body was slight and emaciated, but he had a well-shaped head and large liquid eyes. These stared at the bishop with some intensity; indeed, with such intensity that the bishop wondered, at first, if the boy might not be an idiot. But a little conversation proved him sound of mind, though rustic in speech.

His name was Luigi and he was an orphan, living as best he could. In the summer he tended goats; in the winter he lived with his uncle and aunt, the tavern-keepers, who fed him and beat him. His age was about nineteen. He had made his Easter duty as a Christian. He would never walk again.

Such were the facts of the case, and the bishop thought them over clearheadedly. He wondered what to do with the boy.

"Luigi," he said "would you like to go back to your village?"

"Oh, no," said the boy. "It is a very good village, but now that I can no longer herd goats, there is no place in it for me. Besides, one eats better in Remo—I have had white cheese twice already." And he smacked his lips. His voice was remarkably strong and cheerful, the bishop noticed with surprise.

"Very well," said the bishop patiently. "You need not go back if you do not choose. You are now, in some sense, a ward of the Church, and the wings of the Church are sheltering." He looked at the boy's legs, lying limp and motionless under the covers, and felt, though against his will, the natural distaste of the hale man for the maimed. "You might learn some useful trade," he said thoughtfully. "There are many trades where the hands do all—a cobbler's, a tailor's, a basket-weaver's."

The boy shook his head joyfully. "Oh, no, your lordship," he said. "Trades take so long to learn and I am very stupid. It would not be worth the expense; your lordship would be embarrassed."

"My lordship, perhaps, is the best judge of that," said the bishop a trifle grimly. He kept thinking of the boy's remark about white cheese; it must be a spare life indeed where white cheese was such a treat. "But we are reasonable," he said. "Come, what would you be?"

"A beggar!" said the boy, and his dark eyes shone with delight.

"A beggar?" said the bishop, astonished and somewhat revolted.

"Why, yes," said the boy, as if it were the most natural thing in the world. "For ten years my father begged on the cathedral steps. That was before your lordship's time, but he was an excellent beggar and a master of his craft. True, he was subject to continual persecutions and jealousies from the honorable corporation of the beggars of Remo, coming, as he did, from outside the city. It was that which caused the ruin of our fortunes, for, in the end, when he had begun to fail, they threw him down a well, where he caught a bad cold and died of it. But in his good days he could outbeg any two of them. If your lordship would care to have me demonstrate his celebrated fainting fit, when his eyeballs rolled backward in his head—"

"I can think of nothing I should like less," said the bishop, shocked and disgusted, for it seemed to him an unworthy thing that a sturdy young man, though a cripple, should think of nothing better than beggary. "Besides," he said, "these other beggars you speak of—if they persecuted your father, no doubt they would persecute you."

"Me?" said the boy, and laughed. "Oh, once they understood, they would not dare touch me—not even Giuseppe, the Hook. I would be your lordship's beggar—the bishop's beggar!" And a light as of great peace and contentment spread over his countenance.

The bishop stared at him for a long time in silence. "That is what you wish?" he said, and his voice was dry.

"That is what I wish, your lordship," said the boy, nodding his head.

"So be it," said the bishop with a sigh, and left him. But when his coachman came to him the next morning for orders, it was all he could do to keep from reviling the man.

The bishop was not the sort of man who liked beggars.

Indeed, were it not for custom and Christian charity, he would long since have cleared them from the steps of his cathedral. He could not very well do that; he knew what an impression such a move would make. Nevertheless, when he passed among them, as he must at times, he saw to it that his almoner made a suitable distribution of small coins, but he himself did his best to see and smell them as little as possible. Their whines and their supplications, their simulated sores, and their noisome rags—these were a fret and a burden to him.

Now, it seemed, he was to have a beggar of his own. He would have taken it as a suitable humiliation for pride, but he did not feel himself to be a proud man. Nor could he think of the accident as anything but an accident. Had he deliberately trodden the lad beneath the hoofs of his horses— but he had not. He was well liked, able, decisive, a rising son of the Church. Nevertheless, he was to have a beggar— every day he must see his beggar on the steps of the cathedral, living reproach, a living lesson in idleness and heedlessness. It was a small thing, to be sure, but it darkened his dinner and made him sore at heart.

Therefore, being the man he was, he put a mask upon his face. He meant to speak of the thing, so it should be known —at least *that* might ward off ridicule. He spoke of it to his secretary; the secretary agreed that it was a very seemly and Christian idea of his lordship's, while the bishop wondered if the man laughed at him in his sleeve. He spoke of it to others; there were compliments, of course. Each time he spoke of it, it turned a small knife in his breast. But that did not keep him from speaking of it, nor from seeing that every care was given Luigi.

Nevertheless, he dreaded the day when Luigi would take up his post on the steps of the cathedral. He dreaded and yearned for it, both. For then, at last, the thing would be done. After that, like many things, it would become a custom, and in time Luigi himself would fade into the mass of whining beggary that haunted the steps of the cathedral. But things were not to be quite that way.

He admired, while he detested, the thoroughness with which Luigi prepared himself for his profession. He heard the whine ring out from the servants' quarters—"Ten scudi for Luigi!"—he saw the little cart and the crutches Luigi had made for himself. Now and then he heard his own servants laugh at the beggar's stories. This was hard enough to bear. But at last the day of parting came.

To his disgust, the bishop found the boy neither clean nor well-clad, as he had been since his accident, but dirty and dressed in tatters. He opened his mouth to reprove the boy, then he shut it again, for it seemed pitifully true that a beggar must dress his part. Nevertheless, the bishop did not like it. He asked Luigi, coolly, how he meant to live.

"Oh, your lordship's secretary has found me a very suitable chamber," said Luigi eagerly. "It is on the ground floor of a rookery by the river and it has room for crutches, my gear, and my cart. He will move me there tonight. Tomorrow I will be at my post on the steps of the cathedral." And he smiled gratefully at the bishop. "That will be a great day," he said.

"So," said the bishop, who could not trust himself to say anything further.

"Yet before I go," said Luigi, "I must thank your lordship for his kindness, and ask your lordship's blessing on my work. That is only suitable."

The bishop stiffened. "I may bless you, Luigi," he said, "but your work I cannot bless. I cannot give the blessing of the Church to the work of a man who lives by beggary when he might live otherwise."

"Well, then, I must go unblessed," said Luigi cheerfully.

"After all, your lordship has already done so much for me! The bishop's beggar! How my uncle and aunt will stare!"

Now, of all the vainglorious, self-seeking, worthless, rascally sons of iniquity—and to think that I stand your sponsor, said the bishop, but, fortunately, he did not say it aloud. Silently he extended his ring and Luigi kissed it with such innocent reverence that the bishop was sorely moved to give him his blessing after all. But he summoned up his principles and departed in silence.

The bishop slept ill that night, tormented by dreams of Luigi. He dreamed that, for his sins, he must carry Luigi on his back all the way up the steps of the cathedral. And as he mounted each step, the weight upon his back became more crushing, till at last he woke, unrefreshed.

The next day he went to the cathedral in great state, though it was an ordinary Sunday. Yet he felt the state to be, in some measure, a protection. When he passed by the steps of the cathedral, the beggars set up their usual supplications. He sent his almoner among them; it was over quicker than he thought. He did not look for Luigi and yet he felt Luigi's eyes upon him as he stood there for a moment, splendid in robe and miter. Then the thing was finished.

In the cathedral that same day, he preached passionately against the sins of idleness and heedlessness. Seldom had he been so moving—he could feel that from his congregation. When Mass was over he retired to his palace, exhausted. Yet it was pleasant for him to walk about the palace and know that Luigi was not there.

It was just after vespers when his secretary came to him and told him that a man called Giuseppe, self-styled provost of the company of the beggars of Remo, requested an audience. The bishop sighed wearily and ordered the man brought before him. He was a squat fellow of great strength and an evil cast of countenance, for one side of his face had been so burned in a fire that it was as if he had two faces, one of them inhuman. Also, his left arm terminated in an iron hook.

"This is Giuseppe, the beggar, your lordship," said the secretary with repugnance.

"Giuseppe, called Double-Face, also called the Hook, provost of the honorable company of the beggars of Remo," said Giuseppe in a rusty voice, and plumped on his knees.

The bishop raised him and asked his business.

"Well, your lordship, it's this new fellow, Luigi Lamelegs," said Giuseppe. "I've got nothing against him personal —I wouldn't hurt a fly myself in a personal way"—and he grinned horribly—"but there he is in a good place on the steps, and your lordship's servants put him there. Well, now, if he's your lordship's beggar, that's one thing—though, even so, there's fees and vails to be paid, for that's the custom. But if he isn't your lordship's beggar—and your lordship paid him no attention this morning—"

"Stop!" said the bishop with anger. "Do you mean to tell me that the very steps of the cathedral are bartered and sold among you? Why, this is simony—this is the sin of simony!"

"Your lordship can call it hard words," said Giuseppe stolidly, "but that's been the way it's been done ever since there were beggars in Remo. I paid twenty crowns for my own place, and fought old Marco too. But that's beside the point. Your lordship has a right to a beggar if your lordship wants one—we're all agreed on that. But the question is: Is this man your lordship's beggar or isn't he?"

"And supposing I said he was not my beggar?" said the bishop, trembling.

"Well, that's all we'd want to know," said Giuseppe. "And thank your lordship kindly. I had my own suspicions of the man from the first. But we've got him down by the river now —Carlo and Benito and old blind Marta; she's a tough one, old blind Marta—and once we're through with him, he'll trouble your lordship no more." And sketching a clumsy salute, the man turned to go.

"Stop!" said the bishop again. "Would you have the guilt of murder upon your conscience?"

"Oh, your lordship takes it too hard," said Giuseppe, shuffling his feet. "What's one beggar more or less? We're not rich folk or learned folk to bother a mind like your lordship's. We breed and we die, and there's an end. And even at the best, it's no bed of roses on the steps of the cathedral."

The bishop wished to say many things, but he could think of only one.

"I declare to you that this man is my beggar," he said. "I stretch my hand over him."

"Well, that's very nicely spoken of your lordship," said Giuseppe in a grumbling voice, "and I dare say we can make room for him. But if the man's to keep a whole skin, your lordship had best come with me—old Marta was talking of ear-slitting when I left her."

So they found Luigi, bound but cheerful, in his first-floor chamber by the river, guarded by the persons Giuseppe had described—a hunchback, a dwarf, and a blind woman. The window which gave upon the river was open, and a large sack, weighted with stones, lay in one corner of the room. The bishop's arrival produced a certain consternation on the part of all but Luigi, who seemed to take it as a matter of course. After the boy had been unbound, the bishop addressed the beggars with some vivacity, declared that Luigi was his beggar, and gave him a piece of silver before them all, in token. This seemed to satisfy the company, who then crept away in silence.

"And yet have I done right? Have I done right?" said the bishop, striding up and down the chamber. "I greatly fear I have condoned the sin of simony! I have spent Mother

Church's substance among the unworthy! And yet, even so, your blood may be upon my head," and he looked at Luigi doubtfully.

"Oh, your lordship need not take it so hard," said Luigi, rubbing his arms. "All is safe enough now. I arranged about the dues and vails with Giuseppe while your lordship was discussing her state of grace with Marta. He's an honest fellow enough, and his point is reasonable. One should not take a good place without money to keep it up. Had your lordship given me alms with your own hand this morning, our little difficulty would never have arisen. That was my fault—I assumed that your lordship knew."

"Knew?" said the bishop. "What should I know of such things? And yet, God forgive me, I am a priest and I should have knowledge of evil."

"It is merely a difference in knowledge," said Luigi gently. "Now, your lordship, doubtless, has never been in a room quite like this before."

The bishop stared at the damp walls and the mean chamber. He smelled the smell that cannot be aired from a room, the smell of poverty itself. He had never doubted his own experience before—when he had been first made a priest, he had gone on certain works of charity. Now it seemed to him that those works must have been rather carefully selected.

"No," he said, "I have never been in a room just like this one."

"And yet there are many of us who live in such rooms—and not all beggars," said Luigi. He changed his tone. "That was a fine rousing sermon your lordship gave us on idleness and heedlessness this morning," he said. "Hey, it brought the scudi forth from the good folks' pockets! An admirable sermon!"

"I am grateful for your encomiums," said the bishop

bitterly. He glanced around the room again. "Is there nought else I can do?" he asked unwillingly.

"No, thank your lordship," said Luigi, and his eyes were smiling. "I have a woman to cook my dinner—it is true she is a thief, but she will not steal from a cripple—and soon, with your lordship's patronage, I shall be able to afford a charcoal brazier. Moreover, my friends seem to have left me a sack. So, after dinner I shall say my prayers and go to bed to refresh myself for tomorrow's labor."

I shall say mine, too, for I need them, said the bishop, though he did not say it to Luigi.

So that was how it began. Soon enough, the bishop's beggar was a familiar figure on the steps of the cathedral—one of the admitted curiosities of the town. He was well-liked in his trade, for he always had a merry word or a sharp one for his clients—and it passed around until "Luigi says" became a byword. The bishop became used to him as one becomes used to a touch of rheumatism. Other men had their difficulties; he had his beggar. Now and then it seemed odd to the bishop that he had ever thought of the beggars on the steps as a vague and indistinguishable heap of misery and rags. He knew them all by now—blind Marta and Carlo, the dwarf, Giuseppe Double-Face, and Benito, the hunchback. He knew their ways and their thoughts. He knew the hovels where they lived and the bread they ate. For every week or so he would slip from his palace to visit Luigi's chamber.

It was necessary for him to do so, for to him Luigi represented the gravest problem of the soul that he had yet encountered. Was the man even a Christian? The bishop was not sure. He professed religion, he followed the rites of the Church. Yet sometimes when he confessed him, the bishop was appalled. Every sin that could ravage the human heart was there—if not in act, then in desire—and all told so gaily!

Sometimes the bishop, angrily, would tax him with wilful exaggeration, and Luigi, with a smile, would admit the charge and ask for still another penance. This left the bishop confused.

Yet through the years there grew up between the two men a singular bond. The bishop may have been heedless, he was not stupid. Very soon he began to realize that there was another Remo than the city he had come to first—a city not of lords and scholars and tradesmen and pious ladies, but a city of the poor and the ignorant, the maimed and the oppressed. For, as Luigi said, when one lay all day on the steps of the cathedral one heard stories, and anyone will talk to a beggar. Some of the stories struck the bishop to the heart. He could hardly believe them at first, yet, when he investigated them, they were true. When he was convinced they were true, he set himself stubbornly to remedy them. He was not always successful—pleasant sinners like the Church to keep its own place. Now and then he discussed his efforts with Luigi, who listened, it seemed to the bishop, with an air of perfect cynicism. His attitude seemed to be that it was all very well for a man like the bishop to concern himself about these things and, if other folk starved and died, it was none of his concern. This irritated the bishop inordinately and made him more determined than ever.

Gradually, he noticed, the composition of his table changed. There were fewer courtiers and scholars; there were more priests from the country, smelling of poverty and chestnut bread. They came in their tattered cassocks, with their big red wrists; at first they were strange and ill at ease at his table. But the bishop was able to talk to them. After all, were they not like the old parish priest that Luigi talked of so often? When the ceremony of his table disturbed them he saw to it that there was less ceremony. Luigi mocked him for this and told him bluntly what his richer clients were saying. The bishop rebuked him for impertinence to his spiritual director and persisted.

It is strange how time flies when the heart is occupied. In no time at all, it seemed to the bishop, he was a middle-aged man with gray at his temples, and Luigi a man in his thirties. That seemed odd to the bishop; he did not know where the time had gone. He thought of it, one morning, with a sense of loss. He had meant to do many things—he was still ambitious. Now, when night came, he was often too tired to think. The troubles of many people weighed upon his heart—the troubles of the peasants in the hills, who lived from hand to mouth; the troubles of Domenico, the shoemaker, who had too pretty a daughter; the troubles of Tessa, the flower-seller, whose son was a thief. When he had first come to Remo, he had not had all these troubles. He picked up a letter on his desk—a letter that had lain there for days—and, having read it, sat staring.

The dreams of his youth came back to him, doubly hot, doubly dear. While he idled his life away in Remo, his brother and his friends had been busy. They had not forgotten him, after all. Cardinal Malaverni, the great, sage statesman whose hand was ever upon the strings of policy, meant to pass by Remo on his way to Rome. The bishop knew the cardinal—once, long ago, he had been one of the cardinal's promising young men. There was a letter also from the bishop's brother, the lord—a letter that hinted of grave and important matters. The bishop almost sobbed when he thought how long both letters had lain unanswered. He summoned his secretary and set himself about an unaccustomed bustle of preparation.

It often occurred to him, sorrowfully, within the next few days, how foolish it was to leave one's letters unopened. The preparations went forward for the cardinal's visit, yet it seemed to him that they went forward ill, though he could not put his finger upon the cause. Somehow he had got out of the way of the world where such things go forward smoothly; he was more used to his country priests than to entertaining distinguished visitors. Nevertheless, he botched together a few Latin verses, saw to it that the hangings in the guestchambers were cleaned and mended, drove his choirmaster nearly frantic, and got in the way of his servants. He noticed that these were no longer afraid of him, but treated him with tolerant patience, more like a friend than a master, and this irked him oddly. What irked him even more, perhaps, was Luigi's shameless and undisguised self-interest in the whole affair.

"Ah, your lordship, we've waited a long time for this," he said, "but it's come at last. And everyone knows that a great man like Cardinal Malaverni doesn't come to a place like Remo for nothing. So all we have to do is to play our cards well, and then, when we move on, as we doubtless shall—well, I, for one, won't be sorry."

"Move on?" said the bishop, astonished.

The beggar yawned.

"But how else?" he said. "I have been the bishop's beggar. When your lordship is made a cardinal I will be the cardinal's beggar. The post will entail new responsibilities, no doubt, but I have confidence in my abilities. Perhaps I shall even employ an assistant for my actual begging—after all, it is often drafty on the steps of the cathedral."

The bishop turned and left him without a word. Yet what Luigi had said caused trouble and disquiet in his heart, for he knew that Luigi often had news of things to come before even the Count of Remo had an inkling of them.

At last the great day of the cardinal's visit came.

Like all such days, it passed as a dream passes, with heat and ceremony and worry about small things. The Latin verses of welcome were unexpectedly well read; on the other hand, the choristers were nervous and did not sing their best. Two gentlemen of the cardinal's suite had to be lodged over the stables, much to the bishop's distress, and the crayfish for dinner had been served without sauce.

The bishop hoped that all had gone well, but he did not know. As he sat, at last, alone with his old friend in his study that overlooked the garden, he felt at once wrought-up and drowsy.

This should be the real pleasure of the day, to sit with his old friend in the cool of the evening and renew contact with the great world. But the bishop was used to country hours by now, and the feast had broken up late. He should be listening to the cardinal with the greatest attention, and yet those accursed crayfish kept coming into his mind.

"Well, Gianfrancesco," said the cardinal, sipping delicately at his wine, "you have given your old tutor a most charming welcome. Your wine, your people, your guests—it reminds me somehow of one of those fine Virgilian Eclogues we used to parse together. *'Tityre, tu patulae recubans—'* "

"The choir," said the bishop—"the choir usually is—"

"Why, they sang very well!" said the cardinal. "And what good, honest, plain-spoken priests you have in your charge!" He shook his head sadly. "I fear that we do not always get their like in Rome. And yet, each man to his task."

"They have a hard charge in these hills," said the bishop wearily. "It was a great honor for them to see Your Eminence."

"Oh, honor!" said the cardinal. "To see an old man with the gout—yes, I have the gout these days, Gianfrancesco—I fear we both are not so young as we were." He leaned forward and regarded the bishop attentively. "You, too, have altered, my old friend," he said softly.

"Your Eminence means that I have rusticated," said the bishop a trifle bitterly. "Well, it is true."

"Oh, not rusticated," said the cardinal, with a charming gesture. "Not at all. But there has been a change—a perceptible one—from the Gianfrancesco I knew." He took a walnut and began to crack it. "That Gianfrancesco was a charming and able young man," he said. "Yet I doubt if he would have made the Count of his city do penance in his shirt, for his sins, before the doors of his cathedral!"

"I can explain about that," said the bishop hurriedly. "The shirt was a silk one and the weather by no means inclement. Moreover, the Count's new tax would have ruined my poor. It is true we have not always seen eye to eye since then, yet I think he respects me more than he did before."

"That is just what I said to your brother, Piero," said the cardinal comfortably. "I said, 'You are wrong to be perturbed about this, Piero; it will have a good effect.' Yes, even as regards the beggar."

"My beggar?" said the bishop, and sighed.

"Oh, you know how small things get about," said the cardinal. "Some small thing is seized upon; it even travels to Rome. The bishop's beggar—the beggars' bishop—the bishop who humbles his soul to protect the poor."

"But it was not like that at all," said the bishop. "I—"

The cardinal waved him aside. "Do not hide your good works beneath a bushel, Gianfrancesco," he said. "The Church herself has need of them. These are troubled times we live in. The French king may march any day. There is heresy and dissension abroad. You have no idea what difficult days may lie ahead." He watched the bishop intently. "Our Holy Father leans much upon my unworthy shoulder," he said, "and our Holy Father is beginning to age."

"That is sore news for us all," said the bishop.

"Sore indeed," said the cardinal. "And yet, one must face realities. Should our Holy Father die, it will be necessary for those of us who truly love the Church to stand together—

more especially in the college of cardinals." He paused and with a silver nutpick extracted the last meat from the walnut. "I believe that our Holy Father is disposed to reward your own labors with the see of Albano," he said.

"The see of Albano?" said the bishop as if in a dream, for, as all men knew, Albano was an old and famous diocese outside the walls of Rome, and he who was bishop of Albano wore a cardinal's hat.

"It might have a most excellent effect," said the cardinal. "I myself think it might. We have clever and able men who are sons of the Church. Indeed. And yet, just at this moment, with both the French and the German parties so active— well, there is perhaps need for another sort of man—at least as regards the people." He smiled delightfully. "You would be very close to me as cardinal-bishop of Albano—very close to us all," he said. "I should lean upon you, Gianfrancesco."

"There is nought that would please me more!" cried the bishop, like a boy. He thought for a moment of the power and the glory, of the great, crowded streets of Rome and the Church that humbles kings. "I would have to leave Remo?" he said.

"Well, yes, naturally, it would mean your having to leave Remo," said the cardinal. "Your new duties would demand it."

"That would be hard," said the bishop. "I would have to leave Luigi and all my people." He thought of them suddenly—the lame, the halt, the oppressed.

"Your people, perhaps," said the cardinal, "but certainly not Luigi. He should come with you by all means, as a living example."

"Oh, no, no, that would never do," said the bishop. "Your Eminence does not understand. Luigi is difficult enough as a bishop's beggar. As a cardinal's beggar, he would be overweening. You have no idea how overweening he would be."

The cardinal regarded him with a puzzled stare.

"Am I dreaming, Gianfrancesco?" he said. "Or are you declining the see of Albano and a cardinal's hat for no more reason than that you are attached to a beggar?"

"Oh, no, no, no!" cried the bishop, in an agony. "I am not in the least attached to him—he is my cross and my thorn. But you see, it would be so bad for him if I were to be made a cardinal. I tremble to think what would happen to his soul. And then there are all his companions—Giuseppe, the Hook, is dead, but there is still blind Marta, and Benito, the hunchback, and the new ones. No, I must stay in Remo."

The cardinal smiled—a smile of exasperation. "I think you have forgotten something, Gianfrancesco," he said. "I think you have forgotten that obedience is the first law of the Church."

"I am five times obedient," said the bishop. "Let our Holy Father do with me as he wills. Let him send me as a missionary to savages; let him strip me of my bishopric and set me to work in the hills. I shall be content. But while I have been given Remo, I have work to do in Remo. I did not expect it to be so when I first came here," he said in a low voice, "and yet, somehow, I find that it is so."

The cardinal said nothing at all for a long time.

Then at last he rose, and, pressing the bishop's hand, he retired to his own quarters. The bishop hoped that he was comfortable in them, though it occurred to him, in the uneasy sleep before dawn, that the chimney smoked.

Next morning the cardinal departed on his journey toward Rome without speaking of these matters further. The bishop felt sorry to see him go, and yet relieved. He had been very glad to see his old friend again—he told himself that. Yet from the moment of the cardinal's arrival there had been an unfamiliar grayness upon his spirit, and now that grayness was gone. Nevertheless, he knew that he must face Luigi—and that thought was hard for him.

Yet it went well enough, on the whole.

The bishop explained to him, as one explains to a child, that it did not seem as if God had intended him to be a cardinal, only bishop of Remo, and with that Luigi had to be content. Luigi grumbled about it frequently and remarked that if he had known all this in the first place, he might never have accepted the position of bishop's beggar. But he was not any more overweening than before, and with that the bishop had to be satisfied.

Then came the war with the French, and that was hard upon the bishop. He did not like wars, he did not like the thought of his people being killed. Yet, when the Count of Remo fled with most of his soldiery, and the mayor locked himself in his house and stayed there, shaking, there was no one to take over the rule of the town but the bishop. The very beggars in the streets cried out for him; he could not escape the task.

He took it with a heavy heart, under the mocking eyes of Luigi. With Luigi in his cart, he inspected the walls and defenses.

"Well, your lordship has a very pretty problem," said Luigi. "Half a dozen good cannon shot and the city will be taken by storm."

"I thought so, I feared so," said the bishop, sighing. "And yet my people are my people."

"Your lordship might easily compromise with the enemy," said Luigi. "They are angry with the Count, it is true—they thought they had him bought over. Yet it would mean but two score hangings or so, and a tribute, properly assessed."

"I cannot permit my flock to be harried and persecuted," said the bishop.

"Well, if your lordship must die, I will die with your lord-

ship," said Luigi. "Meanwhile, we might set the townsfolk
to work on the walls—at least it will give them something to
do. And yet, there may be another way."

So it was done, and the bishop worked day and night, en-
heartening and encouraging his people. For once, all Remo
was one, and the spirit and will that burned within it were
the bishop's. Yet it seemed no time at all before the French
sat down before Remo.

They sent a trumpet and a flag to demand the surrender
of the city. The bishop received the young officer who came
with the trumpet—a dark-faced man he was, with a humorous
twist to his mouth. The bishop even took him on a tour of
the walls, which seemed to surprise him a little.

"You are well defended," said the Frenchman politely.

"Oh, no, we are very ill defended," said the bishop. "My
good children have been trying to strengthen the wall with
sandbags, but, as you perceive, it is rotten and needs rebuild-
ing. Moreover, the Count was badly cheated on his powder.
I must speak to him of it sometime, for hardly a gun we have
is fit to fire."

The Frenchman's astonishment grew. "I do not wish to
doubt your lordship's word," he said, "but if those things are
so, how does your lordship propose to defend Remo?"

"By the will of God," said the bishop very simply. "I do
not wish my poor people killed; neither do I wish them oppressed. If needs must, I shall die in their stead, but they
shall go scatheless. Ere you hang one man of Remo, I shall
take the noose from around his neck and put it around my
own."

"Your lordship makes things very difficult," said the
Frenchman, thoughtfully. "My King has no desire to attack
the Church—and, indeed, the walls of Remo seem stronger
than your lordship reckons."

Then he was conscious of a plucking at his sleeve. It was

Luigi, the beggar, in his little cart, who, by signs and grimaces, seemed to wish the Frenchman to follow him.

"What is it, Luigi?" said the bishop wearily. "Ah, yes, you wish to show our friend the room where we store the powder. Very well. Then he may see how little we have."

When the Frenchman rejoined the bishop, he was wiping sweat from his forehead, and his face was white. The bishop pressed him to stay for a glass of wine, but he said he must return to his camp, and departed, muttering something incoherent about it being indeed the will of God that defended Remo.

When he had gone, the bishop looked severely upon Luigi. "Luigi," he said sternly, "I fear you have been up to some of your tricks."

"How your lordship mistakes me," said the beggar. "It is true I showed him three of my fellow-beggars—and they did not seem to him in the best of health. But I did not say they had plague; I let him draw his own conclusions. It took me four days to school them in their parts, but that I did not tell him either."

"That was hardly honest, Luigi," said the bishop. "We know there is no plague in the town."

"We know also that our walls are rotten," said Luigi, "but the French will not believe that, either. Men of war are extremely suspicious—it is their weakness. We shall wait and see."

They waited and saw, for that night a council of war was held in the French camp and the officer who had come with the trumpet reported (a) that Remo was held in great force and strongly defended; (b) that its bishop was resolved to die in the breach, and (c) that there was plague in the city. Taking all these factors into account, the French wisely decided, after some forty-eight hours' delay, to strike camp and fall back on their main army—which they did just in time to take part in the historic defeat of the whole French invasion a week later. This defeat sealed for all time the heroic defense of Remo; for, had the part of the French army occupied before Remo rejoined their main body before, the historic defeat might have been as historic a victory for the French. As it was, all Italy rang with the name of the bishop of Remo.

But of all this the bishop knew nothing, for his beggar, Luigi, was dying.

As the French moved away they had loosed off a few cannon shot, more in irritation than for any real military purpose. However, one of the cannon shot, heedlessly aimed, struck the steps of the cathedral, and you may still see the scars. It also struck the cart wherein Luigi lay directing his beggars at one task of defense or another. When the bishop first heard that his beggar was hurt, he went to him at once. But there was little that a man could do but wait, and the waiting was long. It was not until seven weeks later that Luigi passed from this earth. He endured, indeed, till the messengers came from Rome.

After they had talked with the bishop, the bishop went alone to his cathedral and prayed. Then he went to see Luigi.

"Well?" said the dying man eagerly, staring at him with limpid eyes.

"His Holiness has been graciously pleased to make of me the first archbishop of Remo, placing under my staff, as well, the dioceses of Ugri and Soneto," said the bishop slowly. "But I have the news from Cardinal Malaverni, and I may remain here till I die." He stared at Luigi. "I do not understand," he said.

"It is well done. You have stood by the poor in their poverty and the wretched in their hour of trial," said Luigi, and for once there was no trace of mockery in his voice.

"I do not understand. I do not understand at all," said

the bishop again. "And yet I think you deserve recompense rather than I, Luigi."

"No," said Luigi, "that I do not."

The bishop passed his hand across his brow. "I am not a fool," he said. "It was well done, to humble my spirit. And yet, why did you do so, Luigi?"

"Why, that was my great sin," said Luigi. "I have confessed many vain and imaginary sins, but never the real one till now." He paused, as if the words hurt him. "When your lordship's coach rolled over my legs, I was very bitter," he said. "A poor man has little. To lose that little—to lose the air on the hills and the springing step, to lie like a log forever because a bishop's coachman was careless—that made me very bitter. I had rather your lordship had driven over me again than taken me back to your palace and treated me with kindness. I hated your lordship for your indifferent kindness—I hated you for everything."

"Did you so, Luigi?" said the bishop.

"Yes," said Luigi. "And I could see that your lordship hated me—or, if not hated, loathed, like a crippled dog that one must be kind to without liking. So I set myself out to tease and torment your lordship—at first by being your beggar, then in other ways. I could not believe in goodness; I could not believe there would not come a moment when your lordship would turn upon me and drive me forth."

He paused a moment and wiped his mouth with a cloth.

"Yes, I could not believe that at all," he said. "But you were not to be broken, Gianfrancesco, my brother. The evil I showed you daily was like a knife in your heart and a burden on your back, but you bore the knife and the burden. I took delight in showing you how ill things went in your city—how, below the fair surface, there was misery and pain. And had you once turned aside from that misery and pain, I would have been satisfied, for then, bishop or no bishop, you would have lost your soul. Was that evil of me, Gianfrancesco?"

"Very evil in intent," said the bishop steadily, "for, while it is permitted to be tempted, it is evil to tempt. And yet proceed."

"Well," said Luigi, with a sudden and childlike stare, "it did not work. The more I tried to make you a bad man, the better man you became. You would not do what was ill; you would not depart from your poor, once you had known them —not even for a red hat or a count's favor. You would not do ill at all. So now we have defended Remo, the two of us, and I am dying." He stirred uneasily in his bed. "It is just as well," he said, with a trace of his old mockery. "I told my uncle I would live to be a cardinal's beggar, but I am not sure that I would have liked it. I have been the bishop's beggar so long. And yet, from the first I have loved you also, Gianfrancesco. Will you give me your blessing now, on me and my work— the blessing you denied me once?"

The bishop's face was wrung. Yet he lifted his hand and absolved and blessed Luigi. He blessed Luigi and his work in the name of the Father and of the Son and of the Holy Ghost. When that had been done, a smile appeared on Luigi's face.

"A very fine blessing," he said. "I must tell that to the Hook when I see him; he will be envious. I wonder is it drafty on the steps of heaven? A very fine blessing, your lordship . . . ten . . . scudi . . . for . . . Luigi." And with that his jaw dropped, and it was over. But the bishop knelt beside the bed with streaming eyes.

And all that, to be sure, was a long time ago. But they still tell the story in Remo when they show the bishop's tomb. He lies upon it, fairly carven in marble. But carved all around the tomb are a multitude of beggars, lame, halt, and misshapen, yet all praising God. And there are words in Latin which say, "It is not enough to have knowledge—these also are my sheep." Of the tomb of Luigi, the beggar—that no man knows. They say it is beside the bishop's but, in one war or another, it was destroyed and there is no trace of it now. Yet Luigi was an arrogant spirit; perhaps he would have liked that best.

THE CAPTIVES

. . . *It* WAS good to have news of you, my dear Charles
—you have no idea how eagerly we seize upon the mails from
Britain, in this exile. Even a six-months-old scrap of gossip
is chewed like a bone. I've no doubt the same is true of all
foreign service, but here, in the colonies of America, you
may take it for a fact. Indeed, sometimes I wonder whether
it is truly the year of our Lord, 1764, or if I but doze and
hibernate, as bears are said to, in the wilderness.

. . . My own budget will not repay yours, I fear. I cannot
tell you of Lord X's duel with Lord Y, recount the witty
things said by Mr. B—— at the coffee-house, or how the world
took Viscount Z's elopement to Gretna Green with the
heiress. You question me as regards the late campaign, and,
certainly, I shall do my best to inform you. To one who has
played his part—and a noble one—in such a victory as that
of Minden, our backwoods scufflings here must seem unworthy a true son of Mars. Nevertheless, there are certain
details you will not find in the newsletters, and it is for these
I crave your attention. To tell you the truth, this American
campaign has unsettled my mind in a way I would not have
believed possible, when we last spoke together. And the chief
reason for that unsettlement has nothing to do with either
strategy or tactics. Perhaps it is part of the vein of superstition
that you have ever claimed, though pleasantly, was a part of
my Scots heritage. Yet I think we see things as clearly at
Auchairn as you do in London, and perhaps with a deeper
vision. Well, well, to my tale.

As you doubtless know, our difficulties at the outset of the business were grave enough—the war having broken out so suddenly and with such unexpected violence over the whole American frontier. I believe it to be generally thought, in England, that a few thousand whooping and painted savages are little to tax the strategy of a British general—and this after Braddock!—but, I assure you, it is not the case. No doubt they would be easy enough to deal with on the plains of the Low Countries, but here, in these loathsome and scarcely penetrable woods, it is a different affair. You smile a little— you have seen the forests of Germany. But these are not woods, they are wilderness. The tree-boughs meet above, the underbrush has never known the axe. At night there is a darkness of darkness and small, crying sounds. I despair of showing you the difference, yet it exists, like a creature that has not been tamed.

I joined the regiment in the West Indies, just in time to get my first dose of fever and sail for the Pennsylvania Colony with the effects still upon me. My Highlanders had been riddled by the disease—it was pitiful to see their plight. There were clansmen of mine in the regiment and they depended upon me, as men will—I fear ineffectually, for the most part. Indeed, I will confess to you that there was a moment when I did not see what use we might be in an active campaign, even granting that we reached the port of Philadelphia alive. But I did not know our new commander, Colonel Henry Bouquet.

A Swiss, a free sword of the old adventurous stripe and a most sagacious soldier—he had served under Forbes in the previous campaign and, in truth, did most of that business, Forbes being an old man and ailing. He is a red-faced man and careful of his dress, but you see the look of true command in his eyes. My Highlanders grinned woodenly when they heard that he was to lead them. For myself, I was perturbed

at first, when I saw the exercises he put us to—for leaping
over logs and darting from tree to tree are not part of the
ordinary exercise of a soldier. There were those who thought
it an undignified proceeding—they should try to cut their
way through the wilderness of Pennsylvania. I can only say
that my own men took to it like ducks to water—it was the
way of fighting that we used at Preston Pans, if you will
pardon the analogy.

Well, I will not rehearse the events of the war. We beat
the savages soundly at Bushy Run—they had thought to
catch us there as they caught poor Braddock, but did not,
thanks to our commander. A small affair, for Europe, but,
I may say, fiercely contested. It is incorrect to believe the
savages will not stand fire—they charge with great dash and
spirit. True, if you break them, they will run—so will any
troops. You must fight them their own way, if you are to
succeed—not by set volleys of musketry. L—d J—f—y A—h—st
may be of a different opinion. I may say, and with no ill will,
that I would L—d J—f—y had been at Bushy Run.

Well, we relieved Fort Pitt and, next year, pushed on to
the Muskingum—it is a wide, flowing river. Now that is what
I wish to talk about—you will think me daft for doing so, yet
it weighs upon my mind. It was the question of the captives.
Again, I despair of making you understand.

They had been captives for years, through all the Indian
country. There were stolen girls who had grown to woman-
hood, there were men who had barely escaped the stake and
the fire, there were children who had forgotten the sound of
English speech. When we got to the Muskingum, the Indians
began to bring them in. You have doubtless seen prisoners
exchanged. This was not like that.

It was the season we call St. Martin's summer—a part of
autumn when, for a week or two, the warmth and the light
of summer return, before the snow. They call it Indian sum-

mer here, and it is a most beautiful time. More beautiful than in England, for the sky seems made of blue smoke and the trees turn bright red and gold. It is dauntingly beautiful, yet there is something fey about it. You would not think that a wilderness could look so fair and so peaceful. And yet the gold is fairy gold, and might vanish at a touch.

Now had we been but invaders—and, indeed, there were times when I felt strange enough—all might have been according to rule. But with us were the Virginia and Pennsylvania riflemen—and, many of them, come for that thing alone. It was their own blood and their own kin they sought to recover, not ours. That makes a difference. I shall try to describe them to you. They wear linsey shirts and leather breeches, they are tall, strong men. They are not rich in possessions yet they do not look like hinds or yeomen. They carry their rifles lightly and they walk with a long, springing step. You would know the likeness—you, who have seen our poor, proud clansmen in the Highlands. But these are Germans, Irish, English—God knows what they are, yet all walk the same and carry their heads high. I could understand it, at Auchairn—after all, we are all of the same stock there, and we cleave to the chief. But they have no chief and yet they have the pride. There is no one man among them who does not feel himself a man and the equal of any. They are difficult to command—yet I have seen them drive the head of a nail with a bullet at fifty yards. To be sure, they are both rough and rustic—it is a rough life they lead. Yet, somehow it is *their* country, rather than ours—I can put it no other way and yet I know you will smile and ask me what I mean.

I had speech with a number of them—they were laconic but humorous. They were not always respectful of the prowess of British arms, but they liked Bouquet. Most of all they were anxious for the captives—I shall tell you of that.

When the first eighteen were brought in by the Delawares,

I felt very appropriate sentiments, I can tell you. A pitiful troop they seemed, clad in skins like the savages themselves and so burnt by the sun as hardly to be distinguished from them. It was shocking to me to see those of my own kind and race reduced to such a condition. I expected to see anguish and horror writ clear upon every face. And yet, when the thing was accomplished—and it was not till after a deal of ceremonious speech-making—I saw a young, tow-headed Virginia rifleman step up to one of the wild figures.

"Well, Henry," he said with a drawl—they slur their speech in a manner I cannot reproduce—"You've kind of filled out in the brisket. But you're looking peart, at that."

"Thanks, Tom," said the strange, wild figure, in the same accent, "I reckoned if they sent a war-party, you'd be with it. Obliged to you. Say, have you got any Christian tobacco? I been smoking willow-bark all winter. Wasn't bad, excepting for that."

Then the two brothers beat each other upon the back, whooping and swearing strange oaths that I did not comprehend. A tall, painted savage watched them; it seemed to me, scornfully. After a moment the brother who had been a captive, turned.

"Oh, Tom," he said, indicating the savage, "this here's Little Bear. He's a friend of mine. His ma 'dopted me. Guess if she hadn't, they'd have burned me—they seemed to be fixing to. But him and the old lady stood up for me something handsome. Treated me right. Like you two to be acquainted."

"That so?" said the other brother. He raised his hand and made a sign—it was odd to see a white man do it with the slow dignity of a savage.

"What's their word for peace?" he said.

The other brother gave it and he repeated it. Not a muscle

seemed to change in the savage's countenance but now he, too, made a sign and began to speak.

"He's saying you're my brother so he's your brother," said Henry. "But you ain't to believe all he says—I helped him out in a pinch once, but why wouldn't I?" His tone was precisely the tone of an anxious collegian, introducing some new-found friend. "Where's that tobacco of yours? We'd better have a smoke on it. Say, that's fine."

It was then I began to understand a little of what goes on in these wildernesses. The man, Henry, was younger than I, yet to him captivity and rescue were part of the normal lot of life. That would be comprehensible in a soldier, but he was not a soldier. At the end, there was a ceremonious leave-taking between himself and Little Bear. Yet, when I had speech with him later, he talked to me as cheerfully of killing Indians as a man might of knocking over a hare. There was no inconsistency to it—he could not imagine a life lived another way.

I shall not describe all that I saw—it would take a better pen than mine. I have seen a woman dressed in skins give a wild high cry and run to the husband who had thought her lost forever. I have seen a woman from the pack-trains go endlessly up and down through the throng of captives, muttering, "A little boy named Jamie Wilson. Has anybody seen a little boy named Jamie Wilson? He wore a blue cap and is about ten years old." I have seen memory and recognition come back into a child's eyes, when, at first, he strained away from the strange, white faces and would have gone back to his savage foster-kin. There were women who had red husbands and red children. They were delivered over to us faithfully, loaded with the poor gifts of the woods, yet, before we had reached Fort Pitt, there were some who had slipped away and back to the bark lodges. We did our best to retain them —indeed, we bound one or two, though I thought that wrong

—but the forest had entered into their veins, and they would not stay. I shall tell you of one other woman and then my tale will have an end.

It was part of my duties to help make out a muster-roll of the rescued—and that is how I first saw her. She had come in with a group from the villages of the Shawnees, but, though with them, she was not of them—she always stood a little apart. That is how I shall always think of her—a little apart from the rest. A gray-eyed girl, slight but strong, with hair that the sun had bleached to a silvery-gold. She was dressed, like the others, in the gear of the savage and there was an old Indian woman with her who made much of her and howled when she was taken away. She was perfectly biddable and quiet, but none appeared to claim her from among our men and women. Well, there were others in that case, and yet, somehow, she was different. There are wild legends of women turned into deer. I could believe them, looking at her face.

When there was an opportunity, I questioned her, though the opportunity did not come till the evening. I then saw that she was younger than I had imagined—indeed, she could not have been more than sixteen. She answered my questions pleasantly and with dignity, though there was little she could tell. She had been captured, as I gathered, somewhere in Western Pennsylvania and she knew her name to be Mary. But of what her last name had been she had no recollection, though, she assured me, she had often tried to recall it. The cabin had been beside a stream, but to each name of a river that I mentioned she gravely shook her head. It was always called the river, to her remembrance—she could tell me no more.

No, she could not remember neighbors, but her father had worn a beard and her mother had had a red apron. There had been a little brother—she remembered the look of him very well. Then, one day, she had strayed into the woods, gotten lost, and fallen asleep. As she told it to me, gravely and sweetly, in her halting English, it was like one of our own old rude ballads of children stolen away to dwell in a green hill. For that was the last she saw of hearth and home. There were scalps at the belts of the raiding-party that found her—she thought one to be her mother's by the color and texture of the hair but she was not sure. This she told me with the unstudied, poignant matter-of-factness of a child. I gather, at the time, she must have been about six years old.

Why the Shawnees had spared her instead of despatching her I cannot tell—it is a thing that happens at times. Since then she had lived with them, not unhappily. From time to time she had seen other captives—so kept her English. There had been in particular, a woman named Margaret McMurtrie, a later captive and kind to her. She had tried to teach her something of white ways, though they did not always sound very comfortable. And now, after all of this, she was going back to a white world.

It may not seem logical, but I cannot tell you how forcible an impression her recital made upon me. It was not only the story but the circumstances—the girl's clear, candid face in the red light of the campfire—the great sky above us with its stars. I wondered privately to myself why she, unlike so many others, had no Indian husband. Then, looking at her, suddenly I knew. There was a fey quality to her—an unawakened simplicity. I queried her.

"Yes," she said in her careful English, "they thought I helped with the corn. It is very important to have the corn good. They did not wish to give me a husband till they were sure the corn would like it. Perhaps they will take me back again, but I do not think so. You are very strong people, you English."

"I am Scots," I said, "not English. But you are English."

"Am I?" she said. "Well then, I suppose I am. But I do not know what I am." And she smiled at the fire.

"And what do you think of me—of us—now you have found us?" I said, with a man's blundering.

She looked me over gravely and candidly.

"Why, I think you wear very pretty clothes," said she, touching my sleeve with a child's inquisitiveness. "You must have wonderful animals to give you clothes like that."

That was how we talked together at first—and yet, how might I have done otherwise? I wish you would tell me. It was part of my duty to make out the rolls—part of my duty to assist the captives. The child could not remember ever having seen a wheeled vehicle before she came to our camp. Would you think I could play the schoolteacher? I would not have thought so myself. Yet I taught her the greater part of her letters, on our way to Fort Pitt and beyond it, and she proved an obedient scholar. You will say it is the Scotsman in me, yet you would have done the same. I could not bear to think of her as merely childish or a savage, when she looked at me out of her gray eyes. The Bible, fortunately, she knew of—her father had been wont to read a chapter of it aloud in the evenings, and that good woman, Margaret McMurtrie, had been a professing Christian. We used to read a chapter of it aloud, by the campfire, and I would expound it to her as best I might. Now and then I would hit upon some verse that touched a chord of memory and a puzzled, rapt expression would come upon her face.

You see it was my thought—God knows why—that if, by any means, I could make her remember her name and more of her past history than she knew, the spell of the wilderness might be shaken from her. I do not know why I thought so—and, indeed, it will seem to you a matter of little import. What matter if she lived and died, unlettered and savage? There are many such, in the wilderness. And yet, it mattered to me. ⸂ knew how a man must feel whose bride has been, as we say, fairy-kist, and comes back to him out of the green hill, but not as she went away. Yet I did my best—you will laugh to hear what I did. By the time we had passed Fort Pitt, she could say the first half of her catechism very fairly. Yet, if I must be honest, it did not seem to me that she spoke with understanding. She would repeat her answers as well as any lass, but I could not feel that grace had penetrated her heart. Yet it was not a hard heart, nor a recalcitrant, as I should know.

The belief of the Indians is not easy to set down, yet, at the core, it is simple. They are not blind idolaters, like the pagans of old, and they worship a spirit or presence, though they name him differently. At least, that is what she told me. I should be glad to think she told me truly. It is hideous to think of whole nations consigned from birth to the pit or the flame, though John Calvin makes no bones of it. Yet she must have been baptized a Christian, even if she could not remember it. I keep cleaving to that.

I remember one night when we were talking and she told me of the devils in tree and water that her friends also believed in. At least they seemed like devils to me, though perhaps they were not. I could not bear to hear her and I groaned aloud.

"Why, what is the matter? Are you sick?" she said, with her candid stare at me and the light on her silver-gold hair.

"No, not sick," I said.

"If you are sick," she said, "why, that's easy, for a man. You will go to the sweat-lodge and feel better. But, I forget—you English do not use the sweat-lodge."

"Child," I said, very gently, "will a time never come when you say 'we English' instead?"

"I try to say that," she said. "But I forget." It maddened me, for some reason, to hear her say so without fear or shame.

"Woman," I cried, like any dominie, "have you no fear of God's judgments? Do you not see that every day you have spent in the wilderness has been a day without grace?"

"I do not know what you mean," she said. "Sometimes the sun shines and sometimes the snow falls. In the winter, we often go hungry but, in the spring, the hunters kill game again. And even in winter, there is much to do—the fire to be tended, the deerskins to be chewed and made soft."

"God gave you an immortal soul," I said. "Have you no feeling of it?"

She looked at me with her fey look—the look of a changeling.

"Now you talk like a medicine man," she said. She sighed. "They are very terrible and wonderful, of course. But a woman has other business."

"In God's name, what?" I said.

She opened her eyes wide.

"Why," she said, "to know how to work the skins and cook the food—yes, and plant the corn and the beans. You think that is hard work—but the English women I have talked to who come from the towns have harder. They live shut up in their towns like corn shut up in a pouch and they wear so many clothes the air never gets to their skin. They say it is a noble life, but I do not see how they bear it. We are often cold and hungry but, when there is food, we share it, and there is always the sky above and the earth beneath."

"But what is the end of it all?" I said, for it seemed to me she talked like a pagan or a child.

"Oh," she said, "to go to a man's lodge and lie by his side and bear his children. That is the end of it all."

"Would you have done that?" I said.

"Why, yes," she said. "Next year, perhaps. Not this year, for they were not sure of the corn." She flushed, faintly. "He was a strong man, though older," she said. "He had plenty in his lodge and he had killed many enemies."

The thought of it made me desperate.

"I do not understand women," I said in a groaning voice. "I think I do not understand them at all."

I rose and walked up and down in front of the fire.

"Why are you walking up and down?" she said in an interested voice. "Are you thinking of your own enemies? Be content—I am sure you will kill many of them. You are strong and quick."

"No, child, no." I said. "I am thinking of your soul and my soul and—" I stopped and sat down beside her again.

"There is an old song," I said. "It is sung in my country of a man who was led astray. I do not know why I wish to sing it to you but I wish it."

So sitting beside her, by the campfire, in the great woods, I sang her the rough old ballad of Thomas the Rhymer, or as much of it as I could remember—how he met the Queen of Elfland and she took him where man should not go.

" 'Now ye maun go wi' me' she said
'True Thomas, ye maun go wi' me;
And ye maun serve me seven years
Thro' weal or woe as chance may be.' "

I sang, and wondered, as I sang, if it were the eildon-tree that, in truth, we sat beneath—the tree that is on the border of another land than ours. But I when I reached the verse that says—

"It was mirk, mirk night, there was nae starlight,
They waded through red bluid to the knee"

—she nodded her head, and when I ended the song, she nodded again.

"That is a fine song," she said. "There is strong medicine

in it. He was a strong chief—yet he did not have to go with
her unless he wished it. It is so in some of our stories."

I could not speak but sat watching her. There was an intent and puzzled look upon her face. It seemed to me that
I saw her from a great distance.

"There is something in the song," she said. "I cannot remember." She put her hand to her head. "I cannot remember," she said again. "But there was something in the song.
I have heard it and another—another. The Queen was not
clad in green—she was clad in scarlet. Do you know of that?"

She looked at me pitifully and eagerly, while her brows
knitted, but I did not know how to help her. She struck her
hands together.

"The Queen was clad in scarlet
  Her merry maids all in green,"

she sang, "Eh, feyther, I ken
the tune—I'll not fail you."

I joined her in a low voice, greatly daring, but I do not
know that she heard me, her face was so rapt and content.

"Ride hooly, hooly gentlemen," she sang,
"Ride hooly now wi' me."

Then, for a moment, her voice stumbled and faltered but
only to come strongly and piercingly on the verse all Scotland knows.

"Yestreen the Queen had four Maries,
  The night she'll hae but three;
There was Marie Seaton and Marie Beaton
And Marie Carmichael and me."

Then she gave a great loud cry. "Carmichael—Mary Carmichael!" she said. "Hide yourself in the cupboard by the
door, Jamie—the Indians are coming and feyther's head is

all red!" And with the cry, her voice broke and she burst into a passion of tears. I held her in my arms, scarcely daring to breathe till it had passed for I knew that with that, name and recollection and Christian memory had come back to her.

Well, that is the wilderness-tale I have to tell you—a strange one enough, I think, though with no true sequel. I have talked since with a medical man in Philadelphia of much experience—he deems it probable that the sound of the Scots words and the lilt of the tune touched some hidden spring in the girl's mind and she knew, having long forgotten, that she was Mary Carmichael. It must have been a song that her father sang her oft.

I know myself that, from that moment, there was a certain change in her though I did not perceive it till afterwards. For the next day I fell ill of my fever again, and they tell me I was skin and bones when they brought me in to Carlisle.

When I came to myself again, and that was not for more days than I care to count, she was sitting by my bedside. I could not account for the difference in her at first—then I saw she was decently dressed in Christian homespun, no longer in the gear of the savage. I should have rejoiced to see that and yet I did not.

"You were singing, but I cannot remember the tune," I said, for those were the first words that came into my head.

"Hush," she said and smoothed my coverlet with her hand like any woman. "You have been very sick. You must rest awhile."

After I had grown stronger, I found from the woman in whose house I lay that she, Mary Carmichael, had come each day to nurse me. Also she had prepared certain draughts of leaves and herbs. I cannot remember drinking them but I fear they have entered forever into my veins.

She was not too changed, you understand. Even in the sad dress of the frontier, there was still a strangeness about her.

But the changeling look had gone. She was very calm and kindly, sitting by my bedside, yet I knew I could not keep her or hold her, though I would dream at nights of bringing her back to Auchairn.

When I was quite strong again and she brought in the man named Henry—the strong, yellow-haired youth whose friend had been Little Bear—I knew that that, too, was fitting. They were of a likeness and I was not of their likeness. When I had the barber in to powder my hair, I knew there was no likeness between us.

They were to be married next day, and they asked me to stand up with them, so I did so. The church, as it happened, was full, for the wedding of a captive caused great interest in the town. It is a plain, small church, but the minister was of the right persuasion.

Before that she thanked me very sweetly and civilly for teaching her her letters and for all that I had done. It was hard to bear, to have her thank me, yet now I am glad she did, for I shall remember it. The man thanked me also and wrung my hand. It was odd—he was shyer than she, in the church, though I had seen him friendly enough on the march. He had his rifle, his axe and a pack horse with some goods upon it. They were going to a place called the Forks of the Yadkin—it is many miles away in the rougher part of Virginia. From there, he thought, they might venture some day to the wilds of a new land called Ken-tuck-e—a land full of game and grass where few white men had ever trod. It was odd to stand beside that man and, though one day I will be Auchairn, to feel myself poor beside him. Yet I have a good conceit of myself, as a rule.

The minister—a good man—made them an excellent and searching discourse on Christian wedlock. She listened to it attentively, but I have certain fears that she would have listened quite as prettily to the heathenish ravings of a medicine-man. Then they set off together, he and she. The last glimpse I had was of the silvery hair, as they topped the rise and began to go down. It was a clear day, not yet cold. He had his rifle in the crook of his arm—she walked a little behind him, leading the pack horse. She did not walk like a lady, but freely, and you could not hear her steps though the ground was covered with blown leaves.

The adventure has left me confused—I thought it might help my confusion to write it down. You will say it is all simple enough—that I fell in love with a rustic beauty for a few weeks, behaved like a gentleman and a Christian, and was glad to see her married off, in the end. That is true, perhaps, and yet there is something more. Even now, I cannot get the thought of those two people out of my mind. By now, no doubt, they will have reached the Forks of the Yadkin, and he will be making his clearing—there, in the utter wilderness that to them is home. It is there that their children will be born—or in some even wilder land. Yet was she very much of a woman, when she took me by the sleeve and said I wore pretty clothes.

They are not English or Scots—they are not German or Irish—it is a new nation they are making. We are deceived by the language, and even that begins to change on their tongues. Oh yes, I have been graciously received in fine houses in Philadelphia, but that was an imitation, as Bath is a little London. It is different, in the wilderness—and our Lords in Council have not fathomed it. As for me, I have taken the King's shilling, and some day I shall be Auchairn. Yet were it not so—I swear I should like to see what this stream called the Yadkin is like—I should like to see what children came of such a marriage. Aye, even did it mean the abandonment of all I have been.

You will think me daft to have such thoughts in my head —it may be I am not yet wholly recovered of the fever. It may also be that I shall never recover. We hear that the Government intends to close the Western frontiers to settlement—no doubt for good reasons of policy. But these people are not to be stayed, and I have seen them fight. Had they a Bouquet to lead them—well, this is all speculation. Yet I still keep thinking of my changeling. Aye, even had all things been otherwise, I could not have brought her back tamed, to be lady of Auchairn. And yet, she had nations in her eyes.

THE MINISTER'S BOOKS

WHEN young Hugh McRidden was called to the old brick church at Titusville in the closing years of the past century, he felt that strong, slow leap of the heart which comes to all ambitious young men, no matter what their profession, who see their ambitions in a fair way of being fulfilled. Born in one of those small communities in the West Virginia mountains where the Scotch-Irish speech still lingers almost unaffected by Time, he could hardly remember the day when the ministry had not seemed to him the first of callings—and the hopes that had been placed in him made him eager beyond most young men. Tall, lean, and darkly handsome, he carried a fire within him—it had made him the marked man of his time at the seminary—and there was something very appealing about the grave earnestness of his voice. "All fire and bone and sinew," thought the leading elder, John Waynfleet, as he talked to him. "And those gray-blue eyes would face the Devil himself. We've made a good choice, I think—I like spirit in man or minister. Though no doubt he'll give us something of a shaking up—and all the better. Dear old McCullough was a saint but he let us get rather sleepy, in Titusville. I shan't take my mid-sermon nap as easily under this young man."

He chuckled a little internally—the older elders might say what they liked but he held them in the hollow of his hand and knew it—for thirty years he had been an unobtrusively important figure in the councils of the Church. Moderators

might come and go, but John Waynfleet remained a pillar—
and he felt drawn to this young man. "He'll go far," he
thought. "We must find a suitable wife for him. I'm glad he
didn't go into the mission-field—he has the spirit for it but
we need such men at home."

And indeed, for a time, it seemed as if all John Waynfleet's prophecies were in excellent train for fulfillment. Titusville was an old town, rather proud of itself and its red-brick
pavements, its quiet, long-settled wealth, and its fine Pennsylvania cooking. But religiously, as John Waynfleet said, it
had grown a little sleepy—and the new broom swept clean.
Not only did it do so, but people liked the sweeping, which
is a different matter. Dr. McCullough had been a saint and
a tradition—but Dr. McCullough, toward the end, had grown
very old. The young people came to church now with a
willingness they had not shown in Dr. McCullough's time—
the sick and the poor were visited with energy—the young
girls, seeing the grave, youthful face in the pulpit and hearing the rich voice, musical and sincere, had the thoughts of
young girls but with them a sense of the Spirit they could
not have explained. All in all, the town was happy in its
new minister.

As for Hugh McRidden, he did not think of himself as
happy, for that was not what he sought for in life, but he
found his days busy and new. More comfortable, also, than
he had yet been—for Titusville was proud of its manse and
kept it well. He need no longer deny himself the books he
coveted—indeed, he had been able to take over all Dr. Mc-
Cullough's library as well as most of his furniture at a
ridiculously low valuation. John Waynfleet was responsible
for that, as he was for Mrs. Breek, Hugh McRidden's house-
keeper, though Hugh McRidden did not know it. Mrs.
Breek had only one eye but she was an admirable cook, and
while Hugh McRidden seldom noticed what he ate, he was

better nourished than he had been in years. It did not spoil his ascetic look, though now and then it gave him nightmares.

Church and manse were alike to his mind, the townspeople very friendly though a little foreign in their ways. And yet, sometimes, he felt homesick for the West Virginia mountains in spite of it all, and that puzzled him. The Cumberland hills in the distance were softer and rounder—they were fair in their blue haze, yet he found himself wishing for sharper, clearer outlines, he did not know why. He knew as well as any man that his work was succeeding. And yet, when the first few months had passed, he still did not feel really at home in the town, and there was not the satisfaction in these things that there should be—the satisfaction of work well done. Sometimes he thought, a trifle wearily, that the people of Titusville, despite their civil manners, were like their hills—rounded and soft—yes, terribly soft like their copious feather beds. At first he put it down to his being a stranger, but the feeling increased instead of diminishing. Yes, there was a feather-beddiness about Titusville and its inhabitants. You could kick and punch them into any state you liked—but the feathers would rustle back into place as soon as you shook out the bed again. There was something almost stifling in so much comfort and quiet. Then he would think, remorsefully, that he was doing the godly wrong, and humble himself. And yet he was not overworking, as far as he knew. It was a queer state for a minister to be in.

He summoned his strength and preached a terrifying sermon on the secret sins of the heart. It created a sensation—and those whom he thought he had lashed in it came up to him afterwards and shook him by the hand. He reproved John Waynfleet sharply for unbecoming language at a meeting of elders—a bold thing to do, but John Waynfleet took it like a lamb and asked him to supper. There was nothing he could do that was not acceptable—and that in a small, self-centered community. And yet the higher he rose in their estimation, the less he joyed in his charge.

Sometimes he put the state of his mind down to the reading he did late into the night and resolved to give it up. And yet it was hard to give up—he had always been starved for books, and Dr. McCullough's library, while not very modern, was a curiously fascinating one. He would not mean to read, and then he would find himself by his study fire, bright and cheerful, with a book in his hand. He was familiar, of course, with the early persecutions of the Church in Scotland; the thing ran in his blood, and sanctified John McRidden had been shot before his own plow-stilts by no less a person than bloody Claverhouse himself. Yet, in these old calf-bound books, with their quaint type and browning paper, the scenes and personages of that persecution became singularly alive. They came out of the past as if to a hoarse skirl of pipes—he could see the blood on the heather and hear the wailing of the women. He told himself that profitable and searching examples might be drawn from this early church-history—yet that was not the reason he kept on reading.

There were other volumes too, and odder ones—old tomes on witches and witchcraft, from Glanvil to Mather. They were foxed and the bindings worn. Many of them bore a quaint bookplate—a crowded little woodcut of a number of persons in Puritan costume gathered together for prayer or conventicle in an open glade in the forest; below the scene was the motto, "Seek it and ye shall find"; and in one corner the initials of the artist or owner which seemed to be "J. v. C." These had been well read in their time, though not by Dr. McCullough, for the occasional notes in spidery brown ink on the margins were not in his hand.

Hugh McRidden felt a trifle contemptuous of his predecessor—obviously he had bought or inherited the library of some elder divine, set it up on the bookshelves of the manse, and paid little subsequent attention to it, for the books were not in good condition. Such things were done, as he knew— there were booksellers who made a specialty of fitting out clerical libraries. But he was a lover of books, and it went against his heart to see them neglected or misused. He repaired a few of the oldest—he was clever with his hands—and gave Mrs. Breek special instructions about dusting in the study. She did not seem to take very kindly to the idea—and, indeed, during the first few days of her ministrations, there was an odd smell in the study whenever he entered—a smell of dust and crumbled leather and something else that he could not quite identify, though it reminded him a trifle of churchyard yew. But it was not an unpleasant smell and he soon became used to it, though he found, after that, that it was hard to keep flowers in the room for longer than a day.

When the winter came, Hugh McRidden noticed a further change. It was not a hard winter—in fact sometimes the lax air made Hugh McRidden long desperately for the clean cold of his mountains. But a green Christmas makes a fat graveyard —and time after time, young McRidden was summoned to some old man or old woman's bedside to put heart into them for the last journey. That is part of any minister's duty, and he did it well—yet, though death is the joy of the Christian, it has its ugly aspects, and the faces and words of the dying come back to one's mind. Had he done all that he could for them—had he guided them as he should toward effectual grace? Here and there, there was one who would look at him in a daze—he could not rouse that one to a pressing sense of God's wrath and love—or so it seemed to him, and he reproached himself for it. One even, a stubborn old woman, turned her face to the wall when he began to pray, and said in a sort of whimper, "I'm wishing it was Dr. McCullough praying for me—there's a darkness about you, young minister." Hugh McRidden knew that such talk should not hurt him, yet it did.

What hurt him more was the growing feeling that, in some inexplicable way, he was losing his grip on his parish. It was the weather of course and the epidemic—if epidemic it were —it was hard to rouse enthusiasm when people felt sickly. Yet his Bible class waned, and there was coughing during his sermons. He felt anew as if he were fighting some invisible adversary. He had meant to make Titusville a burning and shining example, yet, when he looked around it, he seemed to have changed it but little. He took his difficulties to John Waynfleet and got what was meant to be comfort but did not console him. "An old town—settled ways—a sickly winter— he was doing as well as man might—the parish believed in him—"

It was a hard thing for Hugh McRidden to say but he said it.

"Tell me, Elder Waynfleet," he said, earnestly, "do I seem changed to you at all?"

"Changed?" said Mr. Waynfleet, slightly puzzled.

"At times I seem changed to myself," said Hugh McRidden, staring broodingly at the fire. "At times I feel as if what that old woman said were true, that there is a darkness about me. It is not pleasing."

Mr. Waynfleet took a look at his face, and exerted himself, as he could upon occasion. He made the young man stay to supper and gave him much sound, sensible talk. He did not speak of a wife, though he longed to—but he spoke of the advantages of horse-exercise and the dangers of over-study. He agreed that Dr. McCullough had been little of a reader and must have purchased his library in a lot from some enterprising bookseller, remarking that some of the volumes McRidden described were odd ones for a minister's shelves. But when McRidden began to talk of the early martyrdoms of the church, and the struggles of the saints against the Accuser of the Brethren, he fell silent and watched his companion keenly. At the end he put in some gentle, sensible words on the general subject of superstition—oddly enough, there had been quite a deal of witch-lore in Pennsylvania, and ignorant farmers still painted certain signs and marks on their barns against the hex. "But I never saw a witch could so much as sour a cream-pan—though I've met some queer cases in my legal experience," he ended with cheerful scorn.

He spoke with authority, but when Hugh McRidden took his leave, he looked after him thoughtfully. "All fire and bone and sinew," he muttered. "But that's the difficulty— and a Scotch-Irishman too. I wish I had a niece unmarried —'tis not good for man or minister to live alone. I thought he was a liberal, too, but, by my faith, when he talked of the martyrs, his eyes burned like a Covenanter's. And, as for the Accuser of the Brethren—he might have wrestled with him, hand to hand." He shivered a little and stared about the room. "Now where have I heard of a bookplate like the one he speaks of? There was some story or other—I wish I could remember it. I must do more for the lad."

It would have been better for all concerned had Mr. Waynfleet been able to carry out his resolution. But the following day he sickened, and, while the case was not grave, his doctor ordered him off for change of air as soon as he was able to travel. Like most men, he was deeply concerned with his convalescence, and he and Hugh McRidden parted as elder and minister with no further chance of intimate talk.

That was a pity indeed, for the very night after he had talked with Mr. Waynfleet, the desire to be at his reading again came upon Hugh McRidden with redoubled force. For a while he strove against it consciously—perhaps Mr. Waynfleet was right and he was neglecting his health for his researches. He would walk in the garden till he tired himself and go to bed early. But, when he pulled back the curtain, a chilly rain was falling and the garden looked glum and dismal. He could not stumble around it in the dark, and the study, with its fire, would be so snug and bright. He liked it better than any room in the house—he could smell its queer smell of leather and dust already. Even as he stood, irresolute, a gust of wind snatched the window shut, and he felt a weight lifted from his mind. He turned down the corridor.

The smell was unusually strong as he entered the study. For a moment he thought of ringing for Mrs. Breek and reproving her for neglecting her duties; then he let it go. He rather liked the smell, and the fire was laid—a good thing, for he felt chill. He lit the fire and pulled up his chair before it. Once or twice, while he watched the flames catch, he looked over his shoulder. Then the fire began to crackle merrily. There was a small brown book on the table beside him—he could not remember taking it from the shelves, yet he must have done so, for Mrs. Breek never touched the books except to dust them. He did not intend to read this evening —he would meditate over his sermon. Yet the only texts that came to him were fearful and gloomy ones: he needed distraction. He opened the small book idly, glanced at its curious title page, and began to read.

Some two hours later he was roused from his fierce concentration of reading by a loud and brawling voice outside. He shook his head impatiently and tried to resume his book, but the song was too loud. It was punctuated by heavy, wavering steps—he could hear them splashing in the puddles of the street. "Oh I'm a snolleygoster and we'll all jine the Union!" sang the raucous voice. "The Union forever, hurrah, boys, hurrah!" Hugh McRidden put down his book angrily. He knew well enough who it was—drunken Danny Murphy who lived in the shanty behind the grogshop at the end of town.

He had been a good carpenter once and a Civil War hero—
now his pension went to the grogshop and he was the town's
disgrace. The young town bucks would amuse themselves
by getting him drunk and mocking his windy stories, but the
older men still had him play the fife on Memorial Days, for
they remembered the Sergeant Murphy of Antietam. As for
Hugh McRidden, he had seen him in the gutters, snoring
like a beast, and his thoughts of him were not kindly.

"I'm a snolleygoster—" roared the voice. The wavering
steps began to come up the path. "Intolerable," thought
Hugh McRidden and went to the door.

The man was actually mounting the steps of the manse
when Hugh McRidden flung the door open. For a moment
they stared at each other in the sudden gush of light. The
veined and bulbous nose, the slack mouth, the unhallowed
white hair—oh yes, it was Danny Murphy, his clothes drip-
ping with rain.

"Bejasus, if I haven't come to the minister's!" said Danny
Murphy, in a stupefied voice. "Now why did I do that? I'm
a snolleygoster if I know!"

Then a gleam of wheedling intelligence lighted the broken
face for a moment.

"Ah, minister dear," said Danny Murphy, in a practiced
whine, "sure it's a poor man I am, and neither bite nor sup
in my mouth the livelong day, and the shanty destroyed with
rain. It was only a dry place to sleep I was searching—and a
cup of hot soup maybe—and to dry my clothes, if your
reverence'd be so kind—"

"You're drunk, Daniel Murphy," said Hugh McRidden
distastefully. "Why do you come here? Be off before I call
a constable."

"Sure, ye wouldn't turn an old man out in the rain—and
you a minister?" said Danny Murphy, advancing.

"You are not of my congregation nor my belief," said

Hugh McRidden, biting his lips. "There is no place for you here."

"Oh, it's that way is it?" said Danny Murphy, smitten with a sudden truculence. He advanced another step—his hot breath stank in Hugh McRidden's face. "Not a piece of bread in charity—and ye call yourself a man of the church. But I'll tell you what sort of minister ye are—and the black curse of Clare upon it! I'll tell you—"

Then he stared at Hugh McRidden, and beyond him, and the color left his face completely and in a moment. For an instant Hugh McRidden thought the man had died on his feet and stepped forward to catch him as he fell. But Danny Murphy backed away instead, and there was naked fear in his eyes.

"I beg pardon, your reverence," he muttered. "I'll not do it again, your reverence. I did not mean to disturb your reverence—nor your friends—"

"My friends, fool?" said Hugh McRidden, sharply, but Danny Murphy did not answer the question. He backed down the steps, mumbling that he humbly begged all their pardons, and at the bottom turned with a hunted look, and fairly took to his heels. Hugh McRidden watched him run—he ran swiftly for a drunken man and yet with a strained anguish of body as if he feared hands on his shoulder. "The wicked flee when no man pursueth," murmured Hugh McRidden, approvingly. As he shut the door, he heard a shout in which only the word "minister" stood out clearly. Later on, he thought it had been "I wish you luck of your friends, minister," or, "Keep your friends from me, minister," but which he could not be sure.

Nevertheless, when Danny Murphy came to him the following morning, wan and tremulous with sobriety, to offer his apologies, he accepted them. Indeed, though the man was not of his congregation, he even went so far as to spare him a five-minute discourse on the deep damnation of his drunken ways—a discourse to which Murphy listened with a white-faced, strained attention. Now and then his eyes strayed uneasily over Hugh McRidden's shoulder, but he kept perfectly still. Next day the word went through town that Danny Murphy had taken the pledge for the new minister— and Hugh McRidden won added glory. But by that time, Hugh McRidden was past caring.

He was past caring because he had read the book. It was a manuscript volume, bound like certain old diaries and written throughout in the spidery copper-plate hand with which Hugh McRidden was already familiar. It called itself soberly, *An Examen Into The Powers Of The Invisible World*, and it bore the familiar bookplate—but, as Hugh McRidden read it, the words seemed to enter his veins. The style was entirely lucid and reasonable—he could bring no arguments against it, though he tried. After he had finished it in the early morning, he felt entirely composed and better than he had in many days. So that was the way things were—it only remained to prove them. He must go and look at a barn or two in the country when he had the opportunity, and talk to some of the farmers—he knew what the signs and the marks meant now.

Nevertheless, such things are not borne without revulsion, and the next day he found himself praying alone in his church—praying like a frightened child till the tears ran out of his eyes. But that evening he went to his study again and looked at the bookplate under a strong reading glass. It was as he had thought—the figures were gathered together in the grove but for no innocent or Christian purpose. Under the glass, the faces were extraordinarily lifelike and vivid. As he gazed at them, they seemed to move a little. Then he knew that he was lost and opened the book anew.

The second attack of the epidemic was sharper than the

first—it even attained notice in the Philadelphia newspapers. They spoke of the heroic work of the local pastor; and indeed, throughout those weeks, Hugh McRidden was indefatigable. After the two doctors were stricken, he was the prop of the town and he seemed to need neither rest nor food. Wherever he went among the sickbeds, a white-faced and silent Danny Murphy followed him, performing the most menial offices with competence and care. They exchanged few words, but there seemed a strong bond between them— nor was it the least of the miracle that Danny did not touch a drop during all that time. "No, I'll not be offending the minister or his friends," he would say uneasily to the proffered glass, and whatever was made of it, men knew it was Hugh McRidden's work. He slept in the stable of the manse now, much to the disgust of Mrs. Breek—though she had to admit that he was quiet enough except for the crying at night, and then a word from the minister would always quiet him.

The epidemic waned at last; oddly enough, with only two deaths, and those long-expected. The town began to think of testimonials, and Mr. Waynfleet, at the Springs, began to think of coming home. The minister himself looked haggard and worn, as was to be expected, but he preached as powerfully as ever and with a strange fervor that moved his sparse congregation to their marrowbones. So must some of the martyrs of the Covenant have preached among the mists and the curlews—the men who knew sin like an enemy in their own hearts.

Then he would go back to his study, and his lamp burned late there. There were other books beside the *Examen*— soon he knew them by heart. The first steps in the knowledge were easy—after that they grew more taxing on the strength. He felt a certain contempt for the broomstick-rides and hexings of tradition—he had saved the child at death's door, though they had not asked him in whose name. There must be a price paid for it, of course. Well, let there be a price. He began to understand the fearful joy of the warlocks, who let themselves be put to the question and burned to ashes rather than abandon their power and their sin. Between good and evil there was a deep gulf fixed; there was a fearsome joy in crossing to the other side.

Yet let it be said to his credit that remorse walked with him often, and sometimes at night he would wring his hands in pain. And when the Spring began to come, sweet and daunting, the first breaths of air from the garden were almost more than he could bear. And yet, with the coming of the Spring, he knew something else must come.

He fought against the knowledge stubbornly—but one may not stand still in these matters. The shadow in the depths of the grove within the bookplate was darker and more tangible each time he viewed it—soon enough he would see the face. When the sun was hot, in May, there would be the meeting of the coven—he did not know where or when, but doubtless he would be shown. But first there must be a sacrifice. And that sacrifice would be the man, Daniel Murphy. Hugh Mc-Ridden knew it well enough, in spite of his prayers and tears.

On the whole, it speaks well enough for the remnants of his character that it was this soul and no other that he selected. By any rule of life, Danny Murphy was a scoundrel and a wastrel. He had been scared into righteousness for a moment, but, left to himself, he would sink to the gutter again. The world would be well rid of him indeed; and yet it was a fearful thing to contemplate. But there were things more fearful still, and they were becoming impatient—he knew it by the look of the books. It was the last night of April that he called Dan into his study, having sent Mrs. Breek away.

There were glasses and a decanter on the table, and the

fire was very bright and clear on the hearth. The old man's eyes looked longingly at the decanter.

"Come in, Dan, and sit down," said Hugh McRidden with cheerful heartiness. "There's something I want to say to you."

"Your lordship—your reverence, I mean—won't be entertaining your friends tonight?" said the old man, timidly. "Faith, I wouldn't want to disturb them."

"Nonsense, Dan," said McRidden, still cheerfully though with altered color. "Besides, what other friends have I but you?"

"Oh, your reverence has many in the town," said Danny Murphy. "Well—thank you," and he sat down on the edge of a chair. He wetted his lips a little, staring at the liquor and the glasses.

"Yes, Dan," said Hugh McRidden, and his eyes were dark. "It's for you. You've served me well through this epidemic— and I've kept you rather strictly. Now you shall have your reward."

Some time later, Hugh McRidden wiped the sweat from his brow with a handkerchief. He felt soiled and sick at heart. The old man was snoring in his chair now—he would not wake for hours, even at the prick of a knife. But it had been a lengthy business, sitting there and watching a man grow maudlin. Danny had been, by turns, boisterous, bellicose and pathetic—he had told the interminable tale of his bravery at Antietam and wept dishonorable tears for his lost youth. Yes, it had been like watching a soul take on corruption—a soul with not one white spot left upon it—a soul where no grace might grow. Hugh McRidden thought of his own soul and shivered, but it was too late to turn back, now.

He made his preparations—they took time, and a glass of the liquor in the decanter would have steadied his nerves, but he did not take it. He was about to commit a mortal sin but he would not break his rule. When all was ready, he stood and listened. The house was entirely quiet, the smell in the study had never been so strong. He picked up the long knife and looked at the sharp blade. It would all be over in a moment, he knew just where to strike. Then at last he would see the countenance of the shadow in the grove, not as in a picture but face to face. He wondered, idly, just how and when it would appear. Dark and comely, with the beauty of a ruined angel, or hideous yet compelling? It was hard to say.

He picked up the knife with a firm hand and stood in front of his victim. The old man's head had rolled to one side— that made it easier. Now it rolled back again. The eyes opened and stared Hugh McRidden full in the face. There was no recognition in the eyes, but they were full of a lost and hopeless wonder. Somewhere in the wreck of that body, the soul sat prisoner and wondered at being so bound. It could no longer master the body, yet it suffered and endured with an unbearable patience. They were the eyes of a lost dog or a beaten child. Then the lids closed over them again.

Hugh McRidden heard his knife drop to the floor. Then he sank into a chair and covered his face with his hands. He could hear the old man's breathing—it had a quiet sound. After a while, he knew what he must do.

He wondered at his own steadiness as he got the ladder and fixed the rope to the beam of the ceiling. Perhaps this was what they had meant after all, but he did not care very much. It, too, was mortal sin, but the better way. Only he must be quick—he knew that he must be quick. Yes, there was a knocking at the front door, he could hear it echo. But he would be off before they came—it would anger them, doubtless. Only he must fix the rope first—there must be no mistake about the rope—and his hands were so clumsy.

"Forgive me, a sinner," he said, and adjusted the noose. The touch of the hemp at his throat was rough and clinging.

He could hear someone calling his name in an agitated voice —had it come to that, already? He shut his eyes, his lips moved once more soundlessly. Then the study door was flung open, and John Waynfleet burst into the room.

"Thank God!" said John Waynfleet, catching him in his arms. "Thank God, I have come in time!"

"You have come too late. I have met the Accuser of the Brethren and I am his. And yet I meant to hang myself at the end," said the miserable young man, and burst into tears.

When the noose had been taken from his neck, John Waynfleet got him upstairs to bed. He was very biddable but started at any slight sound, and it was some time before he sank into a heavy sleep. Then John Waynfleet returned to the study, the key of the minister's bedroom in his pocket. As he opened the study door, he felt dizzy for a moment. "Pah!" he said, half-aloud. "What has happened to the place? It smells like a fox's earth." He began to throw up the windows—that helped a little, though his spirits felt uncommonly depressed. He picked up the knife from the floor and shook his head at it. For an instant the thought came to him, queerly, how well and easily the haft would fit in his hand—then he caught himself, sternly. "So that's the way of it," he said, and broke the knife, carefully, on the stones of the hearth.

When he had done so, he felt relieved and would have said a prayer, had he been able to think of a fit one. Then his eyes fell upon a small brown book upon the table. He picked it up, his spirits sinking as he did so, and began to examine the bookplate with the minister's reading-glass.

When he put the reading-glass down, his face was very white and grave. His hands beat at the air for a moment. "Yes, this is bad work," he said. But John Waynfleet had never lacked courage and he did not do so now. "Lord, lift this burden from thy servant!" he cried, in a strong voice and, catching up the book again in a pair of iron tongs, thrust it deep into the heart of the fire.

There was flame and a roaring noise—and yet to John Waynfleet, when he remembered it, it always seemed more like a flame of shadow than a flame of fire. Certainly there was darkness about it—a darkness that pressed upon the eyeballs. It only lasted for a moment, but, when it was done, John Waynfleet felt himself panting as if he had run a race. There had been something like the tones of a voice as well—but that he never cared to remember. When he looked once more, the book was red ash, and the room much clearer.

"And now, I suppose," thought John Waynfleet with resignation, "I must get this drunken reprobate of a Danny Murphy back to his kennel before he wakens. Well, well, it has been a strange night. Yet it was Danny who wrote the letter that brought me back here—that may be accounted to him for righteousness—though I could not make head or tail of what he said except that the minister ailed. I must never tell McRidden that—it would break him. Best get the lad to my house."

He did so, but when the minister was well enough to sit up, Waynfleet found himself obliged to answer questions, much against his will.

"Yes," he said. "My dear fellow, you are quite sure you are strong enough? Well—the books belonged to a man named Jacobus van Clootz. It was quite a famous case at the time—I have looked it up since—though I do not advise you to read the testimony. Oh yes, he was accused of sorcery and witchcraft—but he disappeared rather strangely during the trial and the body was never found. Before that he had made some sort of incoherent statement that his soul lay in his books, and woe be to them that meddled with it—the usual rant. I am telling you this just to show you there is not a word of truth in such tales. His effects were sold at auction.

I can only suppose that some cheap-jack bookseller bought them and, finding them hard to dispose of, let them molder in his cellar for years before he finally foisted them off on Dr. McCullough. McCullough must have had them some forty years—I must say I am very much surprised at him."

"Forty years!" said Hugh McRidden, with a bleak look. "And they were with me but a few months—and yet—"

"You must not take it like that," said John Waynfleet heartily, and clapped him on the shoulder. "Even supposing there could be a grain of sense in such moonshine—and as Christians we must disbelieve it—well, well, there are men who can walk through pestilence untouched. My father told me of such, in the days of the yellow fever. And others no less honest and honorable, who—ahem—are not so fortunate. Besides, as you know, McCullough was nothing of a reader. I doubt if he so much as took down a volume from one year's end to another. He was a man of great simplicity of soul. And as for the books themselves—well they're burned now, every one of them. I saw to that myself. Indeed, when you return to the manse, you will find it has quite a different atmosphere about it."

"I shall not return to the manse," said Hugh McRidden slowly, shaking his head. "I have been greatly ambitious since my youth, Mr. Waynfleet—the core of the matter lies there, you see. Had I thought more of God and less of my own ambition, I would not be as you see me. Now I think I must spend the rest of my life in rooting that ambition out."

"My dear man!" said Mr. Waynfleet—"I assure you—the best medical opinion—a breakdown from overwork that might happen to anyone—you are young and able—I'll not hear a word against you—"

"It is not that, though I thank you," said Hugh McRidden. "What manner of man was this Jacobus van Clootz—an old man, with a barren face, rather pockmarked, and singular, searching eyes?"

"Why, he is so described in the records," said John Waynfleet, uncomfortably. "But—"

"You see," said Hugh McRidden. "No, Elder Waynfleet, it is useless. I hope and believe in God's providence, even for the worst of sinners—but my road lies straight before me, and it is not the road I once thought of."

So it came about that the young and beloved minister left Titusville, after so short a stay. At the farewell service, his words were few and simple, yet there was a gentleness in them that moved his congregation as no other words of his had done. Later on, they heard from time to time of his work among the obscurer missions—and every word was of praise. The last letter John Waynfleet had from him was dated two weeks before the Army of the East overran and burned his outpost mission, and it contained the sentence: "My dear friend, I think and trust that my penance is at last worked out, for I see the old man no longer. Wish me joy." And when John Waynfleet, later, read the accounts of that heroic martyrdom, he knew it was with joy and faith that Hugh McRidden had gone to his doom. He muttered a text about another joy promised in the Scriptures, and felt the tears come to his eyes, for he was a very old man.

There have been three ministers in Titusville since—good men, all of them; but Hugh McRidden is a legend. There will never be another like him, say the ladies who were girls in his time—and they used to point to Danny Murphy for a proof. But Danny has some years gone the way of reformed characters and no longer sits in the back pew of the old brick church, attentive and doglike, an example to all the church-going. He sleeps well, no doubt, in the churchyard—but no sweeter than Hugh McRidden in the foreign soil that gave him at last the release and peace for which his spirit craved so long.

THE ANGEL WAS A YANKEE

$\mathcal{D}$ID I know P. T.? Did I know him? My father started in the Museum down on Ann Street; he took tickets the first day they showed the Feejee Mermaid. When I was only knee-high to a grasshopper, I remember P. T. Barnum patting me on the head. So, of course, when I grew up, I went into the business. I never thought of anything else. Well, I might have made more money in other businesses, but I was working for P. T. Barnum, the greatest showman on earth.

There never was one like him before and there never will be again. It wasn't just his reputation—it was him. He was Yankee as a woodchuck and smart as a steel trap, and he kind of grew with the country, if you know what I mean. It's an outsize country and it likes outsize things. It even likes being fooled in an outsize way. And that's what Barnum knew. He fooled them but he gave them their money's worth—he gave people things they'd remember the rest of their lives, from Jenny Lind at Castle Garden to the Cherry-Colored Cat. Pshaw, when he had the elephant out plowing his farm, half the folks who rode by in the train knew it was just a stunt. But it made them feel good to see it—and know it was done by a Yankee. And he loved it, and it was life to him—and folks knew that, too.

Which brings me to the tale that's never been told about him—the tale of the biggest attraction he never got. It wasn't his fault, either, for he bid high for it. I guess I can tell about it, now, for the other folks that saw it are dead, from Barnum to General Tom Thumb. But we did see it, in spite of the fact that we didn't believe it.

It happened around in the 'Seventies when P. T. had gone back to the circus business. And for him, he was kind of in the doldrums, which surprised you in P. T. Barnum. He had his big house in Bridgeport, he had plenty of money—the whole world knew him for the greatest showman on earth. But the only trouble with being the greatest anything is, you've got to keep it up. The circus was a fine circus, but there were other circuses in the country. For once in his life, he was stumped for a new and dazzling attraction—something that would make the whole universe sit up on its hind legs.

He thought about a lot of things—I'd hear him making plans with Father for the spring season. He thought about bringing the bones of Abraham over from Palestine and giving them a refined, religious presentation—but the Turkish government wouldn't be convinced. He went back to his old idea of buying an iceberg and having it towed down from the Arctic to New York harbor, so you could run excursions to it. But when we really went into the proposition, we couldn't find a captain who'd guarantee us against melting, let alone promise delivery F.O.B.

Then he got excited over a fellow who promised him a genuine two-headed man, speaking four languages with both heads, and each head with a University education. But when it came down to brass tacks, there wasn't no such animal. So there P. T. was—P. T. Barnum—and never a new attraction. Oh, he had midgets and giants, he had jugglers and bareback-riders, a blood-sweating Behemoth and a first-class Bearded Lady. But they were just small change, now, to a man like P. T. He wanted something stupendous and unique and shiny. It wore on his mind till he didn't even check the feed-bills for the lions as carefully as usual—and that showed there was something really wrong.

I remember the day the letter came. It was addressed P. T. Barnum—personal—but we got dozens of crank letters a day, so Father opened it in the normal course of business. It was on cheap, blue-lined paper and it said:

March 24, 187—

Pikesville, Pa.
Dear Mr. Barnum:—

Understanding you are in the market for attractions of every sort would say I have the biggest attraction in human history locked up in my barn. Would be willing to discuss a cash offer for same or shares if more agreeable but if no reply received will offer to Mr. J. Bailey's London Circus as am anxious to sell as it's being considerable of a responsibility.

Yrs. respectfully
Jonathan Shank

P.S. It's an angel.

Well, Father passed it over to me. "Do you see what I see?" he said.

"Yes," I said. "It's another crank. Shall I tear it up?"

He thought a minute.

"No," he said. "Ordinarily, yes. But not now. Because Mr. Barnum's in a state, and any help we can give him—even to divert his mind—"

Just then P. T. walked in. He had on his frock coat and he was carrying his gold-headed cane, but you could see the wrinkles of worry and disappointment deep in his forehead.

"Well, Mr. Barnum," said Father, "the cheetahs arrived in first-class shape. Not even seasick, Jim says."

"That's good," said P. T. but he didn't say it hearty. He just sat down in a chair and heaved a sigh.

"I've heard about a new kind of Fire-Eater," said Father. "Going to look him over. Calls himself Lucifer, the King of

Flames, and claims he can't be extinguished by even the latest scientific equipment."

"Umph," said P. T., and Father tried harder.

"The Dog-Faced Boy's been kicking about his raw meat again," said Father. "He claims it's horse—well, now, Mr. Barnum, I go down to the market every morning—"

"Oh, buy him tenderloin!" said P. T. "Give him one of the Circassian Beauties to bite on! Fire them all! Close up the circus! How weary, stale, flat and unprofitable—but you don't know Shakespeare, John. I don't want a second-hand fire-eater or a couple of mangy cheetahs. I want to make the world sit up! I want—"

"Well," said Father in a low voice, for he saw he had to play his last card. "There's a letter from Pikesville, Pennsylvania—" and he passed it over. P. T. read it. Then he read it again. And, for the first time in months, there was a light in his eye.

"An angel!" he said. "An angel! Of all the preposterous humbugs!" Then his voice changed. "How far is Pikesville, John?" he said.

"I'll look it up in the gazetteer," said Father. "But honest, Mr. Barnum—"

"I'm getting old," said P. T. "I'm getting feeble. Nobody would have dared to try to sell me an angel when I had my strength and my youth. And if anybody did have an angel they'd have sense enough not to try and peddle it to Jim Bailey. Have you found that confounded town in the gazetteer yet, John?"

So that's how we went to Pikesville, all four of us. There was Father and me and Mr. Barnum and the General—General Tom Thumb. P. T. brought him along because, in spite of his being so small, the General had a cool, clear head on him and was about as good a business man as you'd find. Well, we had to change cars at Philadelphia and Harrisburg. Then we had to drive from Carlisle because Pikesville was back in the mountains. It took us all day, but Mr. Barnum never complained.

Well, even for Pikesville—and Pikesville was a store and a crossroads—Jonathan Shank seemed to be kind of a recluse. But we got to his place finally, just as evening was settling down. It was a mean little farm, tucked up in a fold of the mountains. I don't know how it is you get an impression of places—but even the rail-fence looked kind of spiteful and sour. The land was all right—good Pennsylvania land—but there were thistles five feet high by the fence. You can tell what a man's like by the way the land behaves for him, my mother used to say.

We hollered the house and Jonathan Shank came out. I don't know what there was about him that reminded you of a gray fox; I guess it was his mouth and his eyes.

"Are you Jonathan Shank?" said Father.

"Mr. Shank to you," said the man. He peered inside the carriage. "You P. T. Barnum?" he said.

"I am Phineas Taylor Barnum," said Mr. Barnum, and swelled just a little, the way he usually did.

"H'm," said the farmer. "Well, your pictures flatter you. Some." He peered again. "That your little boy?" he said.

"Little boy?" said P. T. "That is General Tom Thumb, the unparalleled Lilliputian, as frequently presented before the crowned heads of Europe," and the General stood up and took a bow, because he was always obliging.

"H'm," said Jonathan Shank. "Well, he's pretty small to be smoking a cigar. Well," he said, "if you want to get out, you can."

"Mr. Shank," said P. T., and his voice was impressive, "you wrote me a letter concerning an attraction. I have therefore come from Bridgeport at great personal trouble and expense—"

"Uh-huh," said Jonathan Shank, and he showed his teeth like a fox's. "Well, that's all right. He's still in the barn." He jerked his thumb.

"Is he—living?" said P. T. Barnum in a deep, respectful voice.

"Oh, yes, he's living," said Shank. "He had baked beans for breakfast. Seemed to relish 'em."

"Well," said P. T. Barnum, rubbing his hands, "before we see him—and I warn you, Mr. Shank, that I am a hard man to fool—you might tell us—er—how he happens to be here."

"Oh, he lost his way in the fog, coming over the mountains," said Shank. "Or claims to. Sprained a pinion on that big pine over there. There's a suck of air through the valley —seen it happen to birds, now and then. But the pinion's healed up right nice."

"And is he—is he an angel?" said General Tom Thumb, with his keen eyes boring into Shank's.

"Well, that's what he says. Named Wilkins," said the farmer, in an irritated voice. "I'm a free-thinker, myself—I don't take any truck with those things. But he's got wings."

"Wings!" said P. T. Barnum and, for the first time in his life, I saw that great man struck dumb. For, if whatever-it-was had wings, it didn't matter whether it was an angel or not. It'd be the biggest attraction in the history of the universe just the same. I could see Barnum dreaming over it— and all the posters and the advertisements.

"Aero, the Winged Man," he muttered, softly. "In His Unheard of Feats of Active Agility. For The First Time On Public Exhibition—Is He Angelic or Human? Under The Personal Management of P. T. Barnum—"

"Well," said Jonathan Shank, "are you folks getting out? Or not?"

It was twilight, and the sun was setting as he led us over toward the barn. I don't know anybody I've disliked quite as much at first acquaintance as Jonathan Shank. All the same, I could feel myself holding my breath—and I guess the rest were the same.

He lined us all up in a row by a crack in the side of the barn, except, naturally, for the General, who had to pick a knothole lower down.

"Can't let a whole crowd in to see him," he said, in a whiny voice. "He'd fly out, sure as tunket. But you can get an idea."

Well, we didn't even think of protesting, that's how excited we were. We just glued our eyes to that crack. It was dark and hay-dusty in the barn with a couple of long slants of light coming down from the roof, all full of little motes. I couldn't see anything, at first. Then Jonathan Shank put his mouth to a knothole and bellowed, "Hey Wilkins!" I hadn't expected that and it made me jump.

Then I saw it. Well, I must have seen it. The General saw it, too, and he had a cool head. There'd been something huddled up on top of the old buggy there in the barn—I hadn't paid attention because it looked like a pile of clothes or a droopy sea gull. But, when Jonathan Shank gave that shout, it opened its wings and flew. I heard Barnum draw in his breath.

Well, now, how am I going to describe it? You think of them with white robes but it didn't have white robes. It was a man—or what looked like a man—with wings. They weren't opalescent and shining. They were gray, tipped with white, like a gull's. But I saw them. I saw it fly. I couldn't be mistaken about that.

"Great wonders of nature!" said Father and he said it as if he was saying a prayer. But I was thinking we'd have to get new type for the handbills—bigger type than they'd ever used in the world before.

"Well, shall we go back to the house?" said P. T. Barnum. His voice was cool and composed.

Jonathan Shank seemed taken aback. "That all you want to see?" he said.

"For the present," said P. T. Barnum. He yawned a little. "The truth is, my friend," he said, "we're all of us a little hungry—"

"I wrote Mr. Bailey, too," said Jonathan Shank, dancing up and down. "If you don't give me a fair offer—"

"Delighted to hear it," said P. T. "Mr. Bailey is an excellent showman and a man of honor. But I never do business just before a meal."

"Oh, well, if it's grub you want," said Shank, ungraciously, and he led the way back to the house, still scratching his chin and looking puzzled. I didn't blame him. I knew Mr. Barnum was up to something, but what it was I didn't know.

I've eaten some bad meals in my life but I never ate anything like that supper. Shank cooked it himself—and I began to feel sorrier and sorrier for that creature in the barn. It must have been eating his cooking for a week or so, and no wonder it looked droopy. You wouldn't think a man could take a fresh egg, drop it into a frying pan and make it taste as if it had been specially laid by a buzzard. Well, you've got something to learn.

But nothing fazed Mr. Barnum. He ate that awful grub and praised it and asked for more. He carried on conversation the way he could—and when P. T. Barnum really laid himself out, it was calliopes playing and the circus going by. He rolled it all out in front of Jonathan Shank—the gaudy pageant of his life from the time he'd peddled tinware in Bethel to the time when he'd stood before Queen Victoria.

And all of it, seemingly, just to impress one mean-eyed old nuisance. It seemed to me he was lowering himself, and, though I listened, I can't say I liked it much.

Then, after a while, I noticed the General wasn't with us any more. He could move very inconspicuous when he chose. Then I remembered his lagging behind with Mr. Barnum when we were coming back to the house. And that sort of gave me hope.

P. T. broke off in the middle of one of his best stories.

"But, be that as it may," he said. "After all, business is business and I fear I have been neglecting it. How much do you want for this attraction of yours, Mr. Shank?"

"Well, reckon I'll wait till I see Bailey," said Shank, and snickered. "Sent him a letter, too."

Mr. Barnum looked hurt and innocent. "Is this fair dealing?" he said.

"I've got the biggest attraction on earth," said Shank. "I'll sell it to you or Bailey, whichever bids highest. And if the price don't suit, maybe I'll just clip its wings and keep it in the barn. Show it off myself." He rubbed his hands. "Bailey ought to be along, soon," he said.

"It wouldn't be right to clip its wings. Not a thing like that," said Barnum.

"That's what you say," said Jonathan Shank. "But, if it's my property, it's my property."

Barnum leaned forward across the table and smiled.

"Why, you poor little penny pinching man," he said. "I'm P. T. Barnum. All I've got to do is send one wire to the papers and, in twenty-four hours, Jim Bailey or no Jim Bailey, there'll be ten thousand people around this farm. They'll come with their box lunches and they'll come with their babies—they'll come from all over the Union. They'll bother you out of your life and they'll hold you up to immortal infamy as the man who tried to make a hired man

out of a creature with wings. But I don't want to do that—
not yet. Ah, is that you, General?" he said, as the General
slid back into the room. "Did you get that paper for us?
Thank you very much."

"If that little weasel's been tampering with my property—"
said Shank and he rose to his feet.

"There has been no tampering, I assure you," said P. T.
Barnum. "The General has merely been making some personal inquiries in regard to the gentleman you speak of as
your property—was that board at the back of the barn loose,
General? Yes, I thought it would be—and has reduced his
inquiries to the proper and legal form of an affidavit." He
glanced at the paper in his hand—the General always wrote
very neat, though small.

"Um-hum," he said. "Just as I thought—Elias T. Wilkins,
professional angel, affirms and deposes—h'm—and that on the
morning of the seventeenth instant while engaged in his
proper and lawful pursuits was maliciously shot and wounded
by a gun or fowling-piece in the hands of one Jonathan
Shank—"

"It's a lie!" said Shank, pounding the table. "The buckshot hardly touched him! And anyhow, I took him for an
eagle!"

"And has since been constrained, under force and
duress . . ." said Barnum. "It looks bad, Mr. Shank, mighty
bad. We'll have to call in the law on this, I guess." He smiled
a broad smile. "They mightn't take just my word," he said.
"But this is an affidavit. What's the name of the Governor
of Pennsylvania, John?"

"Well, I guess you've got me," said Shank, sullenly. "But
what are you going to do about it?"

"Me?" said Barnum. "My duty as a citizen, of course." He
looked very stern.

"It seems hard that a man shouldn't get anything for the

greatest discovery of the century," said Shank, almost weeping.

"Well," said P. T. Barnum slowly, "I'll tell you what I'll do. Let's not have any talk about angels—you wouldn't know an angel if you saw one. But you've given me supper tonight, and P. T. Barnum pays his bills. I guess a thousand dollars is about the right price for supper when the man's P. T. Barnum," and he counted out the long green bills on the table. "Now, there's one more thing I have a fancy for—and that's the key of the padlock on your stable. I'll pay another thousand for that and what I do with it is my business."

"It's highway robbery," said Shank, but he grabbed up the money.

"No," said Barnum, "but the next time you try to swindle a Connecticut Yankee—just remember it takes more than one man to do it. We figure it takes six Philadelphia lawyers and a goat. Well, come along, boys, the horses will be getting restless," and he walked out of the door. "And when Jim Bailey shows up, just tell him I've been here," he said.

Well, we got the angel out of the barn and into the carriage. Barnum asked him to walk instead of fly, so as not to scare the horses, and the angel obliged. You couldn't see him plain, in the darkness. But you could see the shape of his wings.

I guess that was the queerest drive I ever had. Father was driving, with the General and me in the front seat; and in the back seat was Barnum and the angel. I heard Barnum ask him to give him his promise, as a gentleman and an angel, not to fly away unexpected, and the angel nodded his head in a grateful way. I don't think any of us said a word for ten miles. But I know I kept thinking and thinking—what were we going to do? I'd been brought up to the business—an attraction was an attraction. And I'd do a lot for P. T. Barnum. But, somehow, this was different. The minute the angel came out of the barn, I knew it was different. But I wondered if Barnum knew.

Finally my father called back, "Where we going, Mr. Barnum?"

"Carlisle," said Barnum. Then he thought a minute. "No, Harrisburg," he said. "We can't take him in the cars—the minute folks saw him, there'd be a riot. Oh, shucks, just drive till I tell you to stop." He turned to the angel. "Would you like to go to Harrisburg, sir?" he said.

"Don't matter to me," said the angel. "Not as long as I'm out of that barn." It made me jump to hear him speak, because all the twang of New England was in his voice, and I hadn't expected that.

I heard Barnum shift in his seat. "Are you a Down-Easter, Mr.—Mr. Wilkins?" he said.

"Truro," said the angel. "And Captain Wilkins, if you like. Born and raised on Cape Cod."

"I should have known," said Barnum thoughtfully. "Well, it certainly is a privilege being associated with you, Captain Wilkins," he said. But there wasn't any certainty in his voice. He tried again.

"It must be a wonderful thing," he said. "I mean, we all look forward to the experience with—I mean, having been a church-going man all my life, this demonstration of—well, how does it *feel* to be an angel?"

" 'Tain't bad," said the Cape Cod voice. "Naturally, it's a change."

"I should think so, indeed," said Barnum. He coughed a little. "Of course," he said, "the advantages of your peculiar position—it might even be made a point of though I don't insist upon it—the opportunities to meet celebrities—er—such as George Washington, for instance—"

"Never seen him," said the angel, and I could hear a rustle in the back seat.

"But surely—" said P. T. Barnum.

"Never seen 'em," said the angel, firmly. "I'm on Coast Guard duty. Me and Elnathan Edwards. Wouldn't be here today, 'cept I hit a storm and she blew."

"But, surely, Moses and the prophets—" said Barnum in a pleading voice.

"Ain't seen 'em," said the angel, definitely. "I'm telling you—Coast Guard duty. Far as the Grand Banks. Can't tell you I've seen 'em when I ain't."

"I hope no impairment—the buckshot—" said Barnum, anxiously.

"Not a mite," said the angel, testing his pinions. "They're good as new." He turned awkwardly to us all. "Well," he said, "I'm obliged and that's a fact." His jaws moved up and down. He looked at General Tom Thumb. "Now *he* don't seem real, somehow," he said. "But you've got to believe things when you see 'em." He turned to Barnum. "Just one thing," he said and his voice was wistful. "Duty's duty. But I'd like to have seen that circus. Never seen one yet."

Then he sprang into the air—into the gold air of dawn. It was queer, at first, and clumsy, and then it was clumsy no longer but beautiful as any bird. I'd been on the Cape and I thought about that and the small, tight-fisted boats that traffic and go down in the waters—the sails of New England. I don't know what Barnum thought about, but he had his hat in his hand.

When it was only a dark small speck in the sky, my father gave a long whistle.

"Two thousand dollars blown sky-high, and the biggest attraction on earth!" he said. "And I'm glad of it, P. T." He shook Mr. Barnum by the hand.

"Well," said Barnum, with a wry smile, "at least it wasn't Jim Bailey." He straightened. "Look what's coming up the hill," he said.

We looked, and there was a phaeton, furiously driven. It stopped, and the slight, active, bearded man who drove it jumped down. He rushed over to Barnum.

"Where is it?" he said, half stuttering. "You can't have it. I've got a legal bill of sale," and he waved a paper.

"Where's what?" said Barnum. "And how much did you pay that Shank fellow?"

"Two thousand dollars," said James Bailey, "and if he can't deliver, I'll have his hide and his hair."

"Oh, no you won't, Jim Bailey," said Barnum, and his voice was gentle. "Because angels fly away, and this one has flew. But you won't lose your money, Jim."

"How won't I?" said Bailey, indignantly. "Tell me that," and I saw the other kind of showman—the cool one—look out of his eyes.

"You won't lose it," said P. T. Barnum. "We'll take account of it in our deed of partnership."

"Partnership!" said James Bailey. Then "Partnership," he said again, in a different voice.

"Partnership," said P. T. Barnum, with his eyes still fixed on the sky. "You've got a circus, Jim, and I've got a circus. We've been fighting each other for years and I wouldn't say which has won. But you put us together and—angels or no angels—we'll have such a magnificent and wandering hippodrome of ambulant curiosities as the world has never seen." He rose on his toes, he expanded, he was P. T. Barnum again. "What's an angel between friends?" he said. "We'll have three rings and two stages! We'll bring over Jumbo from London! We'll have the Greatest Show On Earth!"

AS IT WAS IN THE BEGINNING

*T*HERE is always a price to be paid for the freedom and the name of a people. There is always a price, and it does not pass with one buying. That is why I am telling the thing.

Now, the land we left was a good one. Let none question that. It was not the most beautiful of lands, nor a place where the gods walked every day. Nor was it a land full of giants and dwarfs and demons. Those stories are beginning to be told, but they are not true. It was clean and wind-blown and rolling, the Land of the Short Grass. The winters were colder there and the summers hotter, or so it seems to an old man. But men had lived there for a long time and pastured horses. And the first gods those men knew had the heads of horses. But that was long past when I knew the land and we worshiped Atli, our god.

How to tell of the days long before? They are dim, they are lost in time, like stones in the bed of a river. There was the land, there were men. They lived and died. There were tribes and clans and families and heroes and Old Ones. Out of these came a people—our people. We grew in the land like grass and were one with the land. We did not have all the things that men take for granted today, but we were hardy. It was a good land.

Then why did we leave it at all? Let me tell you of that. In the days of my boyhood the whole land belonged to a great king, but he was far away. In our part of the world we did not see him at all unless, now and then, he fought wars.

We knew he lived because he set governors over us and tax-gatherers. When their yoke was heavy, it was heavy; when it was light, it was light. More often it was heavy rather than light. Yet we lived, as our fathers had before us.

We lived, but we had ceased to prosper, we, the People of the Short Grass. The king's men ate us with taxes and exactions; they took our young men and our horses for the king's service, and these did not return. It was no use talking to the king—he was far away. It was no use talking to the governor—the pleasant, lazy governor who sat in his house and drank his honey beer. When we asked the elders of our villages the reason of these things, they would lift their hands and say, "It is the will of the king, the will of the sky." Yet, years gone by, in the days of the first Old Ones, things had not been so. We had been a free people then. We began to remember that.

It was like an itch and a rash and a sickness among us. It was like a fever in the skin. It was partly because of the taxes and exactions, yes. But we would have paid the taxes to men of our own choosing. And yet there was this fever in us, like the fever of spring. What is it that brings such a fever to a people? I do not know. But at one time no one talked of leaving the land. At another time many began to talk, in secret, of leaving the land, so we could have our own ways. I was one of those many, though I had three horses.

Now, there was Marco as well. They have talked about him already as if he were a god or the son of a god. And there is his image in the square, and the children look at it. But he was not a god, but a man, though he had the blood of the Old Ones in him, to be sure.

Let me remember Marco—not the image in the square, but the slight, dark-haired young man that I loved and followed. He was not the strongest among us, but I have not seen his equal with the bow. He had a quick temper, soon done with, and a dream within him. Sometimes the dream was high and far, sometimes close and near. But always it moved behind his eyes. From his youth, he listened to old stories—the stories of the days before the king, when we had been a free people. But when they came out of his mouth again, they were no longer old stories, but something to be achieved. He was willing to do much to achieve that; he made us willing to do much. And yet, he could have been a king's man if he had chosen, for when he was younger the governor, who liked bright lads, had taken a fancy to him and had him taught many things. But that did not make him a king's man; it made him yet more our man. They talk of Marco's miracles, but that was the miracle, and that was in him. It made him break with the governor, it put a price upon his head. Yet he stayed gay and confident and a man that men would follow. Moreover, he was forehanded. He saw that the bowstrings were made and the strongest horses hidden. He saw to that.

So one night, which had been long prepared, we rose against the king's men and the governor. I remember that night well. It was the first time I ever killed a man, and he died much more easily than I had expected. He was a big fat man with a curly brown beard, and he clenched and unclenched his hands as he lay dying. Also there was more blood than I had thought for, though I had seen sheep killed and horses.

So, when it was over, we all met together and lifted Marco on a hide and made him our chief, as was right. He was glad and proud; you could see that in his bright, dazzled face where the torches lit it. But he was thinking, too, and you could see that.

He said, "If you make me the Old One, then I am the Old One. And I will be that."

And we cheered him for what he said, for now we were

rid of our tyrants and could have our own ways. But we did not know it meant such toil.

It meant great toil and labor, because Marco meant to get us out of the land before the king could gather force and make reprisal, as he must do for the sake of his pride and his kingship. It meant leaving our huts behind and our pastures and many possessions and all we had cherished most but the image of Atli, our god. It meant all that and it took three weeks of time, despite all Marco could do. Yet, in the end, he got us across the river—all the People of the Short Grass who would come, for there are always those who stay behind. It was a wide, hungry river that swallowed men, but he had seen to that with boats and rafts, and only eight were drowned. Then he burned the boats and the rafts, so there could be no returning. As the last boat burned, we saw across the river a tiny picket of king's men on tiny horses. They cried out and made insulting gestures and held up a head on a lance. But it would take them time to make boats and they were no boatmen. So we were safe for a while, and I heard Marco sigh with relief, for I was near him. Then he turned and cried "Forward!" in a gay, ringing voice, and we went forward to the mountains.

That was very pleasant and fine for a young man, that march to the mountains. I can remember it yet—the freshness of the morning and the friendliness of the campfires and the good sleep under the stars. It was all new, all untried. We had staked our whole fate on the venture—we, the People of the Short Grass—and each one of us knew it. That is something to feel in youth—to be part of a great venture. And so, at last, we came to the mountains, huge and grim, and entered their first great folds and were safe from pursuit. And I can remember the look and the smell of that night.

I got myself a skin of wine and sat down to eat and drink, for I had done neither all day, being occupied with the rear guard. You must herd them along and yet not hurry them past strength, and there will always be stragglers, and a man should have eyes in all four sides of his head. But I knew that I had done well and my heart was light with it, for, if things had been left to Grell, we would still have been marching. So I looked up from my wineskin, and there was Marco beside me.

I was not surprised at that—he was never the sort of chief who hides in his tent. He liked to see everything. He asked me many questions, and when I had answered them, I passed him the mutton bone and the wineskin, and he ate and drank.

"That is right," I said. "Eat and drink, Old One! For we have done well and men will make songs of this journey!" My heart was light with the wine and my tongue spoke out.

"You are merry, Karn," he said, and looked at me thoughtfully, and as he looked, I could feel the cold night settle about us, and the smell of the night.

"Is it evil to be merry?" I said.

"No," he said, "it is well to be merry. And you have done well today."

"Then drink of the wine!" I said. "Are we not all here in safety? Have we not shown what we are—the People of the Short Grass?"

"Yes," he said, "we have shown what we are. And yet that is only the beginning." And he stared at the huge shapes of the mountains.

"It is well begun," I said. "And now you will lead us on."

"Yes," he said, "I will because I had the dream and could not escape it. And yet it is not so easy."

"Oh, a few will die in the mountains," I said, in the emptiness of youth, "but after that——"

"After that it will still be but the beginning," he said patiently. "I can see so clearly what might be—and that is why I go on. And yet it is such a long journey. And who pays the price of the blood? I must pay, I think. For the governor was a kind man to me, and yet I had him killed for our escape and our freedom. It is not so easy as you think to be the Old One."

Then he slipped away in the night before I could answer him. That was how I first came to know how a dream may harry a man, and yet how it is through such dreams that men go forward. Yet, at the time, I thought little, but turned back to my wine.

All the same, Marco led us through the mountains. And no other could have done so. He did it in every way. He used praise and force and flattery. He was tireless, coughing and indomitable. He spat blood, but he went on. Yet rest was needed, and he saw that we took it. He was ever cheerful, ever confident. He gathered us in his hands continually, as the rider gathers the reins of a willing horse. Yet I have seen him slumped down with his head between his knees, staring vacantly at the snow and the rocks. And that, too, was part of Marco, though the tales do not tell it.

When I think of the mountains, even now, I think of cold and hunger and the wailing voices of men and women and children come to the end of strength. I think of the look in the eyes of beasts who will go no farther—one gets to know such a look. I think of falling asleep for an instant that seemed a year and yet an instant, and waking with all my bones stiff, and going on. I think of the rags on my feet and the frozen blood on my feet and the roar of the sliding stones as they plunged to the gulf, and the blue and hollow faces of the dead. These and the continual howling of the demons who live in the storms of the mountains. I think of the price paid, and it was a price.

For there was a time when it seemed as if we all must die there, even the strongest. There was no way ahead to be seen and we struggled in the drifts and the rocks like winter flies.

So at last the priests brought forth the image of Atli, our god. And shivering in the cold, they besought Atli to show us the way.

But Atli spoke no clear word. So, at last, Marco stepped to the litter and tore the curtains apart, and the priests wailed. But Marco stared at Atli, face to face. "Now, God Atli," he said, and we heard him, "I speak for the People of the Short Grass. Show us your power, God Atli. Show us the way. Or I will heave this image of yours over the cliff and your priests after it."

Now, we could not see Atli's face or hear his reply, if he made one. But we fell on our faces because we were terrified. But after a space we heard Marco's voice, saying, "Faugh, they call it a god, but it is a fat old image. Shut his curtains, lest he catch a cold and die of it. I will show the way myself, and let who loves me follow me!"

Then he plunged forward unsteadily through the snow. And seeing Marco go forward, some of us followed him. Yet the priests gave the praise to Atli, in the end, as was only right, for he, not Marco, was the god. But after that the priests were not easy with Marco, though he paid them all due observance, and there were those who muttered that Marco was a blasphemer.

Yet all this we forgot as at last the track turned downward and we were through the Great Pass. We forgot what we had suffered, we forgot the dead. When we got to timber line, there were men who hugged the trees and women who kissed the trunks of the fire-giving trees. And when, at last, we reached grass and warmth and running water that did not numb the hand, we were like a people stupefied. Some, indeed, died then who had survived through the mountains. I think they died of joy and nothing else. For here were berries and nuts and fish and game—the end of a summer that we had thought lost forever. We gorged and then we were sick, for our stomachs had grown small in the mountains. Yet even the sickness was good.

And yet that, too, was only a beginning, as Marco had said. I came to see what he meant. For after we had rested somewhat, we made a reckoning. It was not too bad. The weakest were dead and our beasts had suffered greatly. But those who were left were seasoned, though there many men without women. But here we were in a new land. It seemed more smiling, more fertile than the plains of the Short Grass. There was fine fruit upon the trees—fruit such as we had never tasted. All that was good. But around us, as we knew, must be other gods than ours, other shapes, other presences. We did not know how they would receive us; we did not know how the people of the land would receive us. We did not know their tongue or their gods or their customs. And yet there was no way back.

Once I talked to Marco of this, and he said, "Yes, Karn. You drop a stone in a pool and the circles spread. But on what far shore of the pool does the last circle break?"

"I do not know," I said, for I saw that he was talking magic, which is quite proper in an Old One.

"Nor do I," he said, with a smile. "Yet we go on. And yet I could have lived in peace with my wife and my son, and bred horses. Then the dream came and I could not. Yet if we can make a free people, that will be something." Then he touched me warmly on the shoulder and I would have died for him then.

Now shortly there began our battles, of which all the world has heard. I think Marco would have been glad to come in peace. But the people of the land—the People Who Wear Bronze—would not have it so. They told us to go back again over the mountains, but we were not going to do that. So there was war between us and those proud, slender, dark-haired people, so much richer than we, so cunning in all the arts. They were better equipped than we and had cars that thundered on the ground. Yet we defeated them utterly at the Battle of the Two Rivers, for we had no choice in the world now but to go forward, and no land but the land we could take. So we entered the City of Bricks and, having cast out their false images, set up in the chief temple the image of Atli, our god. And Atli smiled upon his children and was content. Though it was Marco's planning and Iron's charge on the left that won Two Rivers, and not, by my reckoning, the god Atli.

It was a great victory, and now we had it all—the houses and the bronze and the women, the goods and the gear. So now, surely, this must be the end. Yet, when I spoke to Marco, he smiled and said, "No, it is still the beginning."

He was tired that night, for the cough he had caught in the mountains irked him. Yet he was friendly as always, and told me to choose a woman, since I had done well in the fight. So I did so—a slender one—but, as I had no house to put her in, I left her under guard for the night, as most of them were left.

Now, in this, I think, there was a certain cleverness of Marco's. Not even he could have kept us from choosing the women. But he saw to it that most of us got our women not the night of the fall of the city, but the next day. And by that time the wine and the fury of victory were out of us, and that was as well. For he did not wish these women to hate us too much. He was the Old One—he always thought ahead.

I know how it was with me when I went to get my woman. I know I did not feel like a conqueror, though I pointed to her and called her in a loud, firm voice. She came biddably enough, and I saw from her walk that I had chosen well, and that pleased me. When Grell took his woman out, the guards laughed behind their hands, but they did not do so with mine. She had such a sweet voice always. That was long ago, that first. I did not know a word of her tongue. I did not know her at all. I was being a very splendid conqueror. Very splendid, but I was young also. When she first followed me through the streets, I strode ahead manfully, and yet, now and then I would turn my head to make sure she was not laughing at me. That was how I was a great conqueror in the City of Bricks.

Ah-hee, that was long ago. I did not know that she had a knife in her garments, and all those first nights she would wake and look at me sleeping. I did not know, until she told me later, that, if it had been any but me, she would have used the knife. That may or may not be true. But I know if she had wished to use the knife, she would have used it, for she was quite without fear.

Yes, at first we did not know a word of each other's language. Yet we learned very swiftly, and when we erred, we laughed. It is a good thing to be young and laugh with one's woman—laugh and be not afraid. And so, in the end, we were neither conqueror nor conquered, but merely woman and man. And when it seemed right, we were married both before Atli and before her gods. And in that, too, there was the wisdom of Marco. For he did not wish us to be conquerors alone. He wished us to be one with the folk of the city, and for both he set up one justice, and it was equal. Had he lived, we would have made more than a beginning at that time.

He did not live, and that was our great misfortune. The sickness upon him wasted him as fire wastes a candle. Some said it was the vengeance of Atli for the time that he blasphemed Atli in the mountains, but I have never thought so, though I think that Marco himself half believed it at times.

He said to me once, "We have done what men never did before. But a price must be paid." He said to me again, very wearily, "Must I have the burden always, the burden of think-

ing and planning? I am very weary of it. It may be as well that
I die. The people must learn for themselves. One man can
never do all." And at the last he opened his eyes and said
loudly and clearly, "I was right. It is still the beginning."
And with that, the look of youth came back to his face for
an instant, and passed, and we knew that he was dead.

So died Marco who set us free. And after we had burned
him in the pyre, we made Marco's three-year-old son the Old
One. But as he could not lead us, we made Iron our chief in
council and he swore to respect the customs and do as Marco
had done. And shortly after that, Iron took his armed men
and entered Marco's house and slew Marco's wife and his
son and all of his household. Then Iron proclaimed himself
the Old One.

That was a very evil thing, and we knew it. Yet Iron was
our best general, and a three-year-old boy was not Marco.
Also, we were in a new land. So, when this was done, it was
done, and we hoped for the best. Myself, I would have fought
for Marco's son, but I was not in the city, but on a journey.
And when I returned, I lived quietly and had little to do with
Iron, except when it was a question of the drilling of troops.
I do not think Iron liked that, but he had to let it pass or
kill me, and I was a man of friends.

Yes, it was an evil time. At first there were some who
praised Iron for the things he brought to pass. They said
Marco had been a great chief, but a dreamer and too soft-
hearted. Now, Iron was a weathered man, as hard and tough
as a nail. He lived without delight and he dreamed no dreams
but those of battle and conquest. There will always be those
who think such a man a good leader for a troubled time. Yet
look what happened.

We had been alive under Marco, for, though he was the
Old One, he was always the Old One of the people. But
Iron was his own Old One and no other's, and under him

we were as dead. As soon as he had the power, it was as if he were drunken with it. He had men hanged for small reason; he pillaged the wealthy of the city and ground the poor. He put away his wife and took other women—well, a chief may do that. But soon there was no woman safe from him or his men. And there was no justice any more in the city or among the People of the Short Grass. There was only the will of Iron and what Iron wished to be done.

That was when we came to know in truth that all we had done was a beginning. For again our freedom was lost and the customs not kept. We had not thought that could happen to conquerors, but it happened. Also many of us had wives from the Bronze People. Now we knew what it was to have the Bronze People look at us out of the corners of their eyes and spit in the dust when we had passed.

That was hard on my wife, my woman. It was hard upon her. "How long shall it be that your people and mine are foes?" she said to me once, and her voice was old for a young woman. "How long shall it be till we have no wars and our sons can grow in peace?"

Well, that was not a question a man can answer. Yet it stirred and rankled in my mind, for Marco had tried to make of us not beasts, but men. Now, it seemed, we went back toward beasts and the old blind, bygone years. Nor would Marco have stirred up the western cities to make war against us or sent back their courtly ambassadors spattered with filth. When Iron did that, I knew he was mad with power. Yet he was the Old One now, and we had no other.

So the western cities gathered their men and we went forth to meet them. And this time we had the advantage of numbers, for Iron had decreed that the men of the City of Bricks must march with us. So they did, but they had no heart in it, as I knew. And of our men, some were rusty with their weapons and some grumbled at this new war and some had

had their wives taken by Iron or Iron's men. So, at the first arrow flight we lost the battle, for the men of the City of Bricks cast down their weapons and fled, and Iron was so busy raging after them that he had no thought for the main fight. Thus we were beaten, and soundly, and had not a certain charge that I know of stopped their horse, it might have been worse than that. But as it was, we got back to the City of Bricks.

Then Iron held a council and talked greatly of the revenge he would have and the dooms he would yet inflict. But after the council was finished, there were five men who went to see Iron in the night. I was one of those men. And but three came out of his chamber, for he was still a skilful man with the sword. But when we came out, we had finished with Iron and Iron's ways.

Now, there were those at the time who would have had me be the Old One. But I knew better than that. I am a good fighter, but a chief must be more. So we chose Char, a freckle-faced, snub-nosed man, a distant kinsman of Marco's.

He was not a conspicuous man, though he had a name for shrewdness and courage. And though Marco's kinsman, he had kept himself alive under the rule of Iron, which said something for his wits.

Yet, as soon as we chose him, I knew we had chosen aright. For he did not pretend to be the Old One at that time. He said, "I will be your chief and lead you. But I am not the Old One yet. The name has been soiled and that is still to be seen." Then he gave orders to evacuate the city at once, before the armies of the west closed around it.

Now, that was a hard thing to do, for we had lived there two years and tasted ease and plenty. It was hard to leave those for the bare uplands. And yet it was right to do so, and we did.

Char managed it very skilfully and when the armies of the

west marched into the City of Bricks, we were already gone. And when we had got to the uplands—the uplands of our first desire—he had us make houses and forts, tracing plans in the earth. The women of the Bronze People who came with us—and one was my woman—he honored extremely. And that was a harsh winter, but he saw that the children were fed.

No, I never knew his heart as I had Marco's. I never knew it. For he would be very frank and candid—that freckle-faced man with the gray eyes—and yet there was something behind that which you could not know. He got on with the priests much better than Marco. He gave all honor to Atli. He guided and cherished the people. And yet, when you came to know him, you wondered whether people were people to him or only pieces on a game board. For Marco looked to his dreams and Iron only to himself, but Char looked to the game and its playing, and it was a great game he played.

We stayed in the uplands two winters and a summer, and often there was grumbling. But Char, the freckle-faced man, neither hanged the grumblers like Iron nor inspirited them like Marco. He let them talk themselves out, and then, when they had wasted their breath, he had a cool and reasonable word to say. Once the people of the cities came against us in great force, but Char did not stand to fight them. He had us retreat to the passes, as he had long planned. And when, without a pitched battle, they had lost many men and we had lost but few, they began to quarrel among themselves and retired to their cities disappointed. And all this Char got to know, and when he knew it, he smiled.

He called me into council one day and asked me what I thought. I told him I thought we should march upon the cities at once, for our young men itched to do so. He listened to me, smiling.

"Yes, Karn," he said, "that would have been Iron's way.

And very likely Marco's. But I am neither Iron nor Marco. I plan and wait. If I had my way, I would keep the people here for the next ten years, gathering strength. But a chief cannot have his whole way against the will of the people. I know that; I am not a fool like Iron. Nevertheless, I will keep them here another winter, if I may—and you will help me, Karn."

I helped him, for I, too, am not a fool. I know a chief when I see one, even if his ways are not mine. And while I kept them quiet, Char's spies and his scouts were busy. Things went ill with the City of Bricks—that we got to know. For the men of the west had put their own ruler over it, and he was as bad as Iron, so that now, as folk will, the people looked back to Marco's days. So when we did move at last, there was but fighting enough to whet the sword. For the City of Bricks itself revolted against its ruler and received us, not as conquerors but as friends.

That was Char's magic, and a different one from Marco's. Well, we were glad to get back to the city again and it was pleasant to see those who had spat at us once come out to welcome us. But after it was all over, Char called for me to come to him. They had put a wreath of flowers on his head, according to the ways of the Bronze People, and it was a trifle crooked. He saw me stare at it.

"Yes," he said with his pale smile, "that will always be the way. My head is the wrong size for wreaths. And yet I am the Old One now, or I soon will be."

"I have never said otherwise," I said.

"That is true," he said. "And that is why you will be general of the armies. For once you have given your faith, you keep it, Karn."

So he gave me the ring and the breastplate, and I was moved, for he might have chosen another, though I was the best man.

"I shall serve you faithfully," I said.

"Yes," he said, "I know you will. And the People of the Short Grass also. Or I would have made Saggoth general. But he would serve me finely for six months and then he would want to be the Old One and I should have to kill him. What shall we do with Saggoth, Karn?"

"Give him a wife," I said. "He is young and single. And give him the mountain passes and a little fighting. That will keep him quiet for a while."

He stared at me curiously. "Yes, that is quite right," he said. "You are not nearly the noble and forthright fool you look, Karn. Now, I had thought of sending Saggoth to treat with the western cities. But I was wrong; he would get us into another war at once, and I do not like wars and bloodshed. They destroy too much. And always I count the cost. Now, I do not think Marco did that."

"He knew there was a price to be paid," I said, and Char nodded.

"A leader must know that always," he said. "Well, Marco was Marco. I would not have risen against him—not for ten years, at least. But if they had made you chief, I would have had your skin, Karn."

"My skin is tough and many have tried to pull it off before," I said.

He laid his freckled hand on my shoulder. "Do not take it amiss," he said. "I am telling the truth for the last time before I become the Old One, and after that the truth shall be between me and Atli. And yet I shall lead the people well, Karn. I shall lead them very well."

"If I did not think so, we would deal with you as once we dealt with Iron," I said.

"Yes," he said, "I believe you would. And that is right. But I shall not rule here as Iron did. Tomorrow I marry the daughter of the oldest house in the city most solemnly before

Atli, our god." And his smile appeared. "Well, I dare say she
will make a good wife and a good mother of Old Ones. And
at all events, it is necessary. The two peoples must mix together, or there will be no people at all. And yet there is still
so much to learn, and women interfere with it. There is only
one who would not have. But I saw her dead in the street,
and that was a long time ago."

Now I knew that he spoke of a pale, brown-haired girl,
with no beauty that I could see, who had tended Marco's
wife and died with her. So I kept silence. He hummed a little,
and, straightening his wreath again, got it crooked on the
other side.

"Yes, Marco led us through the mountains," he said, as if
to himself. "I could not have done that. I would have counted
the cost and stayed in the land. Yet to each man his time, and
now, as things are, I shall do better than Marco. One may
dream of a city nobly, yet the walls are laid brick by brick.
And yet you and most men, although they serve me well, will
ever prefer him to me. Why is that, I wonder? Well, it does
not matter." And with that we went out into the square and
he proclaimed himself the Old One and me the general of
his armies. And next day, as he had said, he married the
daughter of the City of Bricks, and when he stood before
Atli his circlet was over one ear.

Now there followed the days of Char, and those you know.
It was as he said—he did not like wars and bloodshed, though
they were pieces on his game board. But he preferred to rule
peacefully, through treaties and bargains and negotiations,
and in these he was very skilful. So we spread through the
land, and the roads were built, and the bridges, the fields
plowed, the justice dealt fairly, the corn shared in need,
till city after city came under our rule. There was the war with
the western cities, but that was not like the first time, for this
time the men of the City of Bricks marched with us and

fought well. There was the rebellion of Saggoth, but that was a small matter, for he was always rash and it was hardly any trouble to get his head. And Char let the fighting end with the getting of his head, as he let the war with the western cities end, not in burning and pillage, but in treaty and peacefulness, for that was Char's way. And both times he heaped me with honors, and there are sculptures of those wars in the square. Well, that was very pleasant for my woman, and no doubt they are fine sculptures, though I do not set bowmen out in front of light horse, as I told the artist. But each man to his trade and mine is not that of making sculptures.

So we waxed in the land and grew, and the People of the Short Grass and the People of Bronze became one people. And in time Char died, and I was with him when he died. It was strange, for he asked me how Marco had died, very carefully. And when I had told him, he was silent for a while.

"You will not weep for me," he said at last. "One does not weep for the player of a game. And yet it is the same game we play—a game against time and chance and one's own worst, that the people shall live like a people. I would have liked to play longer, for it is a good game. But Marco was right, and this is but the beginning."

Then, later, he died very decently, and his words are often recited by the priests of Atli. And now there is Char Vas, his son, and though he is not Char, he does well. But the young look alike to me now, because I am old.

That is how it was, and the grandsons should remember it. We came a long way, a hard one, a difficult one. You may say that Atli led us—I shall not deny it. But if he led us under the yoke of Iron, then was he a worse god than I have ever thought him. We let that happen, we permitted it. And in the end, we ended it. Let the young men remember both these things.

The gods change, the people change. Even Atli wears a

kinder face than he did. No longer does he scream for the blood and the burnt meat, and the new image they have made of him is calm and stately. And yet he was once but a small and wrathful god. That is something to have seen.

The gods change, the people change. We have the fine things now, the fine houses, the good cloth. In the Short Grass, we knew little of many things—all very useful and profitable and diverting to man. The Bronze People had those things, but their chiefs were bad and knavish, and the hearts of their people not free. Now we go forward together, intermingled. And yet that, too, is but a beginning.

For now there is rumor in the mountains—rumor of how the king of the land we left might move against us, because he has heard of our wealth and our power and our arts. If he does, that will be my last battle, if I live till then. I think now we could hold the passes against any king. But there is always a throw of the dice in war. And, when I speak of it in council, the young men smile and listen as they do to a man who tells a twice-told tale. And that is because I am old.

Will it come? Will it happen? What will happen? Will they, too, sweep down through the passes and into the City of Bricks and tear down the image of Marco and set up their own vile gods in the place of Atli, the one god? I wish I could know. I wish there were a man to tell me. The priests have the woven record and the storytellers their stories, and there are the images also. But if Time and another people should lay hold upon them, who will then remember the People of the Short Grass? And yet we did as I have said, and it was not a small thing.

It may be that we shall make a great defense and be sung of. It may be that the son of Char Vas shall be another one like Iron. Or it may be Marco will rise again in new seed. Many things may be. Or again, there may be the blotting out of all. That, too, may be, though the grandsons cannot think of it. And yet I remember Marco and how he spoke of the stone and the ripples in the pool. We came from the Short Grass boldly, and, though we did ill at times, yet our hearts were free. Let that be the thing to remember!

I do not know, I cannot tell. We are the men and the people—surely we are that. We know the ends of the earth from the mountains to the sea. And yet, two seasons ago, a craft was wrecked on our shores and a man came ashore wearing different metal from ours and speaking in no known tongue. Then he died, ere more could be known of him, but he was shaped like a man and there was the image of a sea horse tattooed upon his breast. Did he come from the sea itself? Are there lands beyond? Are there still other peoples, still other gods? Someday, perhaps, we shall know, as our sailors push out more boldly. And for that there will be a price, as it was in the beginning. It is all a beginning, yes. That is what I would tell. It is all a beginning, Marco. It is all a beginning, Char. It is all a beginning, sons of mine and grandsons. Though it be stamped out and cut down, though the people of the Short Grass fail and Marco and Char be forgotten, it is yet a beginning. We have spent a long time with gods and demons. But now at last we are men, with the choice of men. And the journey goes on.

PART TWO

IF THIS SHOULD CHANGE

*I*F THIS should change, remember the tree and the brook,
The long day's summer, the voices clever and kind,
The true verse that burned on the page of the book,
The true love, body and mind.

Remember the tulip in the pinched backyard
And how it asked for nothing except to grow
And that was enough to do. Remember the hard
Country earth, under snow.

All tastes of food and water, of salt and grass,
A bird flying, a cat asleep in the sun,
The hard-paved street where the faces pass and pass
And never get done.

Huge-flowing Mississippi, under full moon,
The giant landscape where the great rivers crawl
And the shabby apartment and the last year's tune,
Remember, remember all.

They all made something, from the wine drunk with friends
In gaiety, without care, without hurt or shame,
To the faces of the dead that a strangeness attends,
The same, not the same.

They all made something. They made eyes and ears,
A country, a time, work, all that is hard to say,
And behind them were many bodies and many years
And night and day.

There was the sight from sea of the straight-backed town
And the old graves, deep in the grass, where the grass is wet.
Though the wind blow and the stones of the walls fall down,
Remember, do not forget.

Though the sky crack and the heart crack under the sky,
There was all we knew. It is not to be finished yet.
There was good bread, well eaten, in company.
Remember, maintain, remember, never forget.

Not in the great inscriptions, but in the blood.
Not in the able words, but under the hat.
These things were freedom. That is why they were good.
Remember that.

TO THE PEOPLE OF FRANCE

*I*T IS not you that we fight. Our own dead lie in your earth,
The boys called Buck and Shorty, from the plains and the
city-street.
You know how they looked and talked. You know what the
blood was worth.
You know how they went ahead through the machine-
gunned wheat.

The record is there and written, from the Aisne to the
Argonne,
In the slope of the river-lands, in the cold stones set on the
hill,
Where your men and our men fought, and knew anguish,
and yet went on.
It cannot be blotted out. It is not forgotten, still.

It was one cause then for us both. It is the same cause today,
The old cause and the new since first our freedom began,
The cause so stubbornly fought from Yorktown to Seiche-
prey,
The cause of the Marseillaise, the cause of the rights of man.

People of France, great France, people of the good wine,
The lovely land, the clear thought, the bells of God on the
wind,

The France that rang like a sword, the France that grew like
a vine,
The France whose cities are books, the France that was
Europe's mind.

We have forgotten nothing, from the aid that Louis gave
To the look of the Seine at evening when the blue twilights
fall.
We know no France defeated. We know no France of the
slave.
We know the France of the great. It is on that France that
we call.

It is not you that we fight but the little and crawling clan
Who sold their souls to a tyrant and their country for twenty
sous,
The white-tied rat of the Chamber and the sad, old, senile
man,
And you know them as well as we, and we know them as
well as you.

It is you that we call upon, for our dead lie deep in your dust,
People of France, great France, and them we shall not betray.
We know how they died, and when. We know that this
cause is just.
And we greet you as comrades still though the guns speak
for us today.

We are not foes for this War. To the end we shall not be foes.
When the despot's chain is broken and his shackles rent in
twain,
We shall stand by your side in friendship, as your men stood
by those,
And France, great France, and her children shall rise and
flourish again!

SONG FOR THREE SOLDIERS

OH, WHERE are you coming from, soldier, fine soldier,
In your dandy new uniform, all spick-and-span,
With your helmeted head and the gun on your shoulder,
Where are you coming from, gallant young man?

I come from the war that was yesterday's trouble,
I come with the bullet still blunt in my breast;
Though long was the battle and bitter the struggle,
Yet I fought with the bravest, I fought with the best.

Oh, where are you coming from, soldier, tall soldier,
With ray-gun and sun-bomb and everything new,
And a face that might well have been carved from a boulder,
Where are you coming from, now tell me true!

My harness is novel, my uniform other
Than any gay uniform people have seen,
Yet I am your future and I am your brother
And I am the battle that has not yet been.

Oh, where are you coming from, soldier, gaunt soldier,
With weapons beyond any reach of my mind,
With weapons so deadly the world must grow older
And die in its tracks, if it does not turn kind?

Stand out of my way and be silent before me!
For none shall come after me, foeman or friend,
Since the seed of your seed called me out to employ me,
And that was the longest, and that was the end.

REMARKS FROM A BACK-ROW SEAT BY AN AMATEUR PROPAGANDIST

CIVILIANS hate. Civilians yell "Get tough!"
Civilians gripe about "a happy war."
Civilians say there isn't blood enough.
Civilians always seem to want some more.

Soldiers are slightly different about blood.
It gets spilled out of them, and on the spot.
And they find certain kinds of hate a dud.
And they know whether men are tough or not.

Ask the dead sergeant in the broken stuff
Just how he'd like some cutie to explain
The war he fought was "soft" or "just a bluff,"
And, if he doesn't answer, ask again.

That's all. Oh, yes, I know. In various lands
Civilians stood and took it by the millions
And propped the leaguered State with their bare hands—
But, boy, not these civilians!

TUESDAY, NOVEMBER 5th, 1940

*W*e remember, F.D.R.
We remember the bitter faces of the apple-sellers
And their red cracked hands,
We remember the gray, cold wind of '32
When the job stopped, and the bank stopped,
And the merry-go-round broke down,
And, finally,
Everything seemed to stop.
The whole big works of America,
Bogged down with a creeping panic,
And nobody knew how to fix it, while the wise guys sold the
    country short,
Till one man said (and we listened)
"The one thing we have to fear is fear."
Well, it's quite a long while since then, and the wise guys
    may not remember.
But we do, F.D.R.

We remember some other things.
We remember the home saved and the crop saved and the
    courage put back in men's faces.
We remember you said from the start,
"I don't expect to make a hit every time I come to bat."
We remember that.
And sometimes you've struck out and we know it

But we know the batting average, too.
(Not we-the-Wall-Street-people but we the people.)
It's written in our lives, in our kids, growing up with a chance,
It's written in the faces of the old folks who don't have to go
    to the poorhouse
And the tanned faces of the boys from the CCC,
It's written in the water and earth of the Tennessee Valley
The contour-plowing that saves the dust-stricken land,
And the lights coming on for the first time, on lonely farms.

Now, there's another election.
And they say you went to Groton and Harvard.
And they say you don't know the people.
And they say you want to be a dictator
(The same bunch of dignified penguins who were yelling
    and howling for a dictator in '32,
And you gave them their self-respect back, instead, and
    they've never forgiven the gift)
The professional dispensers of snake-bite and poison ivy
In syndicated columns;
The air-conditioned boys from the big slicks, wrapped up in
    their latest serializations
(Yes, you can frequently tell them from the canned-soup
    advertisements.
They get illustrated differently)
These, and others, are Viewing with Alarm.
In fact, to tell you a secret, they say you're terrible.
And, if I may speak from the record, we know them, too.
And that's jake with us.

It's jake with us, because we know.
And we know you never were a Fuehrer and never will be,
Not a Fuehrer, just a guy in pitching for the bunch of us,
For all of us, the whole people.

A big guy pitching, with America in his heart.
A man who knows the tides and ways of the people
As Abe Lincoln knew the wind on the prairies,
And has never once stopped believing in them.
(The slow, tenacious memory of the people,
Somehow, holding on to the Lincolns, no matter who yelled
   against them . . .)

A country squire from Hyde Park with a Harvard accent,
Who never once failed the people
And whom the people won't fail.

PART THREE

THE THREE FATES

*T*HEY said they were women, in the old days—and perhaps they were right about it. Not always right, of course, for Fate may be anything from an earthquake to a pebble you kick out of your path. But, at the moment, I am not thinking of that sort of accident—the missed train that would have carried you to glory, the road untaken that might have led you to a hangman's rope. I am thinking of the sort of people who are fate to others—and of my friend, John Tenterden. Because what happened to him began to happen at sixteen. And it certainly wasn't at his own volition. He didn't even fall in love—he was fallen in love with. And yet that was the first of the things that changed his life.

A quietish, dark-haired boy with a thin, pleasant face—up till then, he had jogged along the normal paths of adolescence in an average American suburb without particularly bothering himself as to the whys and wherefores of existence. His father was one of the suburb's four doctors, with a good, busy practice; his mother, the daughter of an economics professor at Cornell. They were vigorous, hard-working people with a great deal of common sense, and the five children—John was the third one—had an excellent time of it in the big wooden house with the untidy foundation-planting in the respectable though not very fashionable section of town where they lived.

It was the sort of family that believes in fresh air and cold baths and family jests and councils—they were all rather good at games and practical jokes, and a stranger in their midst was instantly made at home. That is to say, if he or she were "their sort"—if not, the Tenterdens agreed in private that the stranger was a stick or a queer duck, but redoubled their attentions, politely, nevertheless. If you looked at all old or frail, you were practically certain of having a knobby cushion put at your back by a hard-breathing young Tenterden and getting a coddled egg for breakfast whether you liked it or not. The anemic were given iron-tonic, the sturdy exercised, the despairing diverted and heartened by humorous stories in dialect and a common-sense philanthropy. It was a bracing atmosphere, and most people enjoyed it—the Tenterden house was popular, especially among the young. You could make as much noise as you pleased, for nobody minded noise there—there was always a screen door slamming somewhere, and a child or children running in, hot-faced, from a game, for a bath or a meal or a spare tennis-racket or a bandage.

Proverbially, in such a house the mistress is pale, overwrought and given to sick headaches—but Mrs. Tenterden was a wiry, brown-faced woman, much in demand for every sort of community activity from mixed doubles to charity-drives. She looked a little like an intelligent horse, just as Dr. Tenterden reminded you somewhat of a trusty, large-pawed dog—the kind of dog you forgive for barking because it does so with such a reasonable air. The combination was agreeable in the children—they inherited their father's fresh color and their mother's deep, equine eyes. The girls, indeed, might have been remarkably handsome, if they had ever taken the trouble—but taking that particular trouble is an art like any other. The Tenterdens were not very fond of art—they were well-informed and doughty at pencil-and-paper games, but art itself, art unaccredited by teachers and public opinion, they considered, quite sensibly, a little queer.

I was a nervous, rather sickly child, given to attacks of asthma, and I stayed for two weeks in their house, once, when my parents were away. It was very kind of them to do it—Dr. Tenterden was our family doctor, to be sure, but they took me in out of pure generosity. "We'll soon get the roses in his cheeks!" said Dr. Tenterden. The first few days of my stay, I enjoyed myself hugely—I thought I had never seen people who led so fine and tumultuous a life. After that, the glamor faded, insensibly but definitely. I do not think it was envy on my part for not being able to join in their games except feebly—after all, like most active people, they liked an audience and I was a most willing one. I missed something very much and did not know what it was.

I think now that they were two things: privacy and thought. There was no privacy at all in the Tenterden household; they were never happier than when all collected in one room doing different things at once; even in the bathroom, with the door locked, you somehow felt that the urge and surge of Tenterden life was waiting in the corridor and, at any moment, might rap brisk knuckles on the door. As for thought, that is probably a question of definition. The children always got excellent marks at school, and Mrs. Tenterden, as I say, was the daughter of an economics professor. No doubt Dr. Tenterden thought about his cases—I know he worked like a bull-dog to keep certain people alive. But thought, genuine thought, demands a certain amount of quiet for its flowering —and quiet was the last thing the Tenterdens, as a family, liked or enjoyed. Perhaps I am exaggerating the effect of a sudden dip into the life of a large family on the temperament of a rather thin-skinned only child. But I know that when I returned to my own room, in my own house, at the end of the visit, I sank into its quiet as one sinks into a bed.

Such was the environment in which John Tenterden grew up. As I say, he was quietish, for a Tenterden, but otherwise unremarkable. He had the darkest eyes in the family and the sort of olive skin that must have harked back to some distant

Latin ancestor. That made him rather an ugly baby, and once
you started as anything in the annals of the Tenterdens, that
thing you remained. Gwen was the beauty and Richard the
scholar, and so it would always be. They were kindly and
seldom twitted John about his looks, even when he became
distinctly handsome—they simply saw no change.

As the third child, younger than Richard and Gwen but
quite a bit older than Bob and Sally, he filled an inconspicuous though definite place in the family system. They
would have missed and mourned him if he had been drowned
in a pond, but he was neither a senior to be consulted, nor a
junior to be disciplined and petted; he was merely John.
It was also agreed in the family that John was rather lazy;
perhaps because he had a naturally good temper and no ap-
parent specialties, except a butterfly-collection. This showed
a scientific interest, and the Tenterdens approved of it,
though it was hard to keep any collection undamaged in the
swoop of Tenterden existence. However, when John's speci-
mens were accidentally destroyed, he never seemed to mind
particularly. He merely collected others. As for what he was
to become, Richard would naturally succeed to the practice,
but John might very well be a doctor, too, unless he chose
to be an economics professor like his grandfather. There was
nothing queer about him, and Richard had hopes of him as
a baseball-player, though, being an elder brother, he tried
not to puff John up.

When I was staying with them, John Tenterden showed
me his butterflies, at his mother's request. People wandered in
and out as he did so, and, being three years younger, I asked
quite a few silly questions. They did not seem to bother
John. He showed me his butterflies politely but without ap-
parent enthusiasm, though his eyes grew darker as he did so.
They were arranged with scrupulous neatness; many were
beautiful, especially the moths. I said, "That's a peachy one!"

several times—each time he gave me a quick glance. I had already got into trouble with the use of the word "lovely" at the Tenterdens and was trying to avoid it—they considered it slightly effeminate, except when applied to a sunset or a dish.

Finally he showed me an enormous silvery creature, so beautifully mounted that it still seemed alive, in spite of the pin. The great pale wings were full spread, it seemed as if it had settled on the cardboard for a moment, and in another it would rise and fly to the lamp. I was a child but a sensitive one. I said, in a voice of sincere conviction, "Oh, that's lovely, John!"

"Lunar moth—*neostera pallida*," he said, rather severely. "It's fairly common. Except for the size, of course—it's a fairly big one. They're quite easy to find." But I saw his finger go out to touch the spread wing very gently, and then draw back without touching it. He put it away, with careful carelessness.

"Come out, some time, and you can help me catch them," he said. "It's quite easy."

"Are they all as lovely as that?" I said, imprudently, for the second time.

He gave me an odd look. "Sure—they're all like that," he said. "I mean the lunar ones. They must have fun, flying at night, though they're silly about lamps. I like watching them, but you have to collect, of course. It's scientific."

His eyes altered, as Gwen and Richard came bounding into the room.

"Showing off your bugs, you old bug-hunter!" said Richard, heartily. "Well, get it over with—the Collison twins just came and we're going to 'nitiate them into the Ugliwugs. You can come too, if you like," he said graciously to me. "It's a terrible 'nitiation—we didn't give you half of it because Mother said you'd be scared and yell all night."

"All right," said John obediently. Something had clicked shut in his face, and he was all Tenterden. At the initiation, which I watched with sycophantic dread, it was he who thought of the glue. He didn't repeat the invitation to go moth-hunting, and I was too shy to ask him. Indeed, he rather bullied me after that—which I felt, obscurely, was a pity because I wanted to admire him. When my parents asked me, later, which one of the Tenterdens I had liked best, I said Robert, who was nearest my age. So they had Robert over to play with me several times, though it never worked very well.

As a matter of fact, I detested Robert—he was younger than I but much stronger and liked to hit me in the wind. I used to hope, secretly, that John would come sometime instead of Robert. I could see him coming up the steps with the lunar moth in his hand. But it never happened, of course. Then we moved into the city. I began to go to school regularly; and suburb and Tenterdens passed out of my mind.

So I wasn't there when the Fates began their game with John Tenterden, six years later. But nothing had changed very much in the Tenterden household. Dr. Tenterden was a trifle grayer and the youngest children made most of the basic noise. But Sunday night supper was even more of a bracing hullabaloo than ever, especially when Richard and Gwen were home from their respective colleges with their friends. They had many friends, all the right, healthy, fun-loving sort, yet serious-minded—young earnest giants who hit the line hard for their college and strapping girls who were as little afraid of a ten-mile hike as they were of a hard exam in Chemistry. Gwen was tentatively engaged to one of the young men, but on the most aseptic basis; their caresses seemed to consist in each pushing the other a good deal when they were in the same games. As for Richard, he knew that he could not honorably marry for at least five years, so he was not engaged. He did exercises with Indian clubs instead.

Now and then, John made harmless sport for the visitors—sixteen is always good sport to youth in the twenties. But not often, for, as they generally agreed, he was a good kid—well-liked at school and center-fielder on the baseball team. And yet, oddly enough, he had no intimates, or, if he did, he did not bring them home. Perhaps it was not so odd. If he had brought them home, he would have had no place to put them—the house was always so full. The Tenterdens noticed, vaguely, that when he came in, he did not bring a crowd whooping behind him. But life moved too fast for such details. And then the impossible thing happened—the first of the things that changed John Tenterden's life.

There was a girl named Mona Gregg in the class below him at school; a sallow, straight-haired, narrow-eyed little girl with very red lips and a nervous habit of chewing the ends of her pencils. Her father had been an unsuccessful vaudeville actor before he got a job as night desk-clerk at the Myrick Hotel, and she had many of the faults of the theatre and hotel child, the sharpness, the precocity, the pertness. Her classmates considered her queer and something of a sneak, though they envied her familiarity with elevators, railroad trains and different kinds of ice cream. And she fell in love with John Tenterden as devastatingly as if she were eighteen and he twenty-five.

At first, of course, he didn't notice it. Two years' difference in age is a yawning gulf, in the 'teens. Then he began to notice that he was always meeting her in the corridors of the school. He would say "Hello, Mona"; she would say "Hello, John," and stare at him. He was popular enough, as I say, to be used to certain occasional looks of admiration. But this was different, from the first. He found himself noticing Mona more than he wanted to, without either in-

terest or pleasure. She wore ugly plaid dresses in the winter—
the collars were not quite clean. She did not try to fall into
conversation with him, but somehow, he felt that she wanted
to, and it affected him unpleasantly. Pretty soon he found
that he breathed easier when he was in a classroom that she
could not enter. But sometimes the grades were together
in the same room. Then he would look up from his book
and feel her eyes upon him—if he turned, he would see her,
chewing her pencil with sharp small teeth and nervously
looking away.

Such things are ridiculous, of course. I have often considered how ridiculous they are. Other times, other manners,
and some of the Renaissance great ladies would still be in
the schoolroom today. But there is no doubt as to the effect
upon John Tenterden. He felt both furious and humiliated,
and yet there was nothing he could do. You can kick an unat-
tractive dog that fawns upon you—it is harder to kick a girl of
fifteen, when you have been politely brought up. John Tenterden discovered that he was meeting Mona outside the
school, in streets where she had no normal orbit. They would
pass, he would say "Hello" politely, and she would meekly
watch him depart. It got so that he went by the Myrick
Hotel on the other side of the street, or kept away from it
entirely. The look of the dingy entrance with its faded canopy
reminded him inevitably of Mona, with her sallow face and
red lips.

There was no one he could turn to for aid—for, if a grown
man is a figure of ridicule in such circumstances, how much
more so a growing boy. Once, she hung about in front of
the Tenterden house for an hour and a half—fortunately, at a
time when everyone else was out of it—and John, reverting
to barbarism, had serious thoughts of peppering her with
an air-gun from a window. But the Tenterden children had
been taught how to behave with guns. Finally, when his pa-

tience was exhausted, she went away. Oh yes, it was very funny. It was not so funny, too.

It was a bad winter for colds and influenza, and Mona Gregg had always been a sniffling little girl. Nowadays, the people who dabble in amateur psychiatry might say that she developed pneumonia as a gesture of unrequited love. We were not so complicated, then. John Tenterden, when he heard that she was ill, had the entirely natural and boyish wish that she would die. But, unfortunately, he was too old to wish it without prickings of conscience. As the case went up and down—Dr. Tenterden always talked about his cases to his family in his bluff, hearty way—the stings of John Tenterden's conscience became acute. Only once or twice he dared ask a direct question; that would have shown too much interest. But, by all the circuitous means known to adolescence, he tried to keep up with the progress of Mona's illness.

Sometimes it was very easy—his father would say, without provocation, at breakfast, "Well, the little Gregg girl's coming along nicely." Or, "How I hate cases in hotels! That Gregg child would have a fifty per cent better chance in the hospital if we could only move her." In either case, John's heart would give a jump of relief. He made a pact with his conscience—if he heard about Mona before he went to school, he would not have to worry again till after dinner. But once, at the height of the influenza epidemic, he did not hear for almost two days, and his agony became intense.

I say "agony" with justification. By that time he had come to believe, you see, that if he could honestly wish for Mona's recovery, she would get well. And yet, if she did get well, he looked forward, with the bleak and limited gaze of boyhood, to a future perpetually haunted by Mona. Also, though the Tenterdens were hardly a prayerful family, he had heard, in the breezy Sunday school they all attended ("Doesn't do the children any harm to get a bit of religion") that God is not deceived by false prayers. It is the letter that killeth and the spirit that maketh alive. Suppose he prayed, and God knew he didn't mean it, and Mona died instead, just to show him. An abnormal problem? Look back in your own childhood and see what you see.

His life split in two. It says a good deal for his character that, at school and at home, he still made a fair show of being John Tenterden. But, within him, the struggle increased. School ceased to be a refuge—he remembered that when Pudge Perkins died, they had announced it at a special assembly just after noon recess. So now, when each period ended, he waited tensely—and, when work was resumed, he felt little relief. It hadn't happened this time but it might next.

One morning, he gathered from his father that the crisis of Mona's illness was at hand. The knowledge weighed on him, horribly, all day. The Tenterdens were not Catholics but, that evening, after supper, he slipped away to the Catholic church in the poorer part of the town. He felt shy and ill at ease in the district beyond the tracks—the small stores, still indecorously open, had a different air to them, and people wheeled perambulators, fought, lounged and gossiped along the sidewalks. A couple of boys jeered at him and he carefully paid no attention—no Tenterden could, with honor, decline a fight, but these were not normal conditions. When he finally got to the church, he walked around the block twice before he was able to go in.

It was an ugly church with a garish altar and puttyish stations of the Cross, but to John Tenterden there was something foreign, mysterious, and powerful in its dimness and strangeness. He could not approve of it, but it was obviously strong magic. He tried to remember what little Catholic boys had said about their religion. You had masses said and burned candles. He looked around for candles, but, to his horror, could not see any. Then he saw, in front of a plaster statue, what seemed like a lot of small night lights, each in a red glass. They were not his idea of candles, but they must do. He watched till he saw a woman light one to be quite sure.

Then he went over, himself. There was a money-box near the statue—yes, you paid for the candles, of course. Here and there, about the church, there were grown people, praying—the sight made him less shy and deepened his sense of magic. He lit a night light in front of the statue and sank on the prie-dieu before it, repeating, in a whisper, "Oh God, spare the life of Mona Gregg—don't let her die." After he had said this a sufficient number of times, he looked timidly at the light. It was still burning, and he felt better.

He then went to the next statue and repeated the process. Fortunately, he had money enough for all the statues. At first, he did not notice their names, then, as he began to feel more at home, he became more curious. He even thought for a moment of omitting St. Patrick—Mona Gregg had once called a classmate a dumb mick—then superstitiously decided that that would break the charm. When he had finished his round, he felt intensely relieved for the first time in many days. Even if the prayers were unacceptable, there were still the candles. The thing had been done professionally, and Mona Gregg must live.

He even felt a little proud of himself for having thought of the Catholic church—neither Richard nor Gwen would have thought of it. As he walked home through the crowded streets, past the flaringly lighted shops, they seemed no longer alien and disreputable but normal and friendly. Mona Gregg had been in a killing-bottle, like a ragged, sickly moth, but now she was going to get out.

So certain did he feel of the future that next morning he did not even bother to waylay his father at breakfast. He set out for school feeling oddly light-headed with relief—he had

slept heavily and hotly. It might be a headache coming on—
he had them, now and then, though he had never spoken
of them to his family. By the middle of the morning, there
was a band around his temples and a dryness in his throat, but
he hardly noticed them. He was too busy tasting the ex-
quisite pleasure of not having been a murderer, of not having
killed Mona Gregg.

Everything seemed bright and vivid and in a high key.
When recess came, he played basketball fiercely and swiftly,
in spite of the headache. After recess, they rang the bells for
a special assembly. John had been a monitor for years—he
found himself marching his file in. After a pause, the Principal rose and the room hushed. The younger children rustled
and squeaked—special assemblies were always exciting—the
older ones looked serious. The Principal cleared his throat.
He had not called them together just to chat with them. He
had an important announcement to make—a saddening
one—

At this point, there was an unusual noise in the room—a
sharp, frightening crack that sounded like a pistol-shot in the
stillness. It was John Tenterden's forehead, hitting the wood
of the desk in front of him. He had fainted.

Dr. Tenterden felt a little irritated and self-conscious that
he had not diagnosed the influenza before—as he would tell
you, he rather fancied himself as a diagnostician. However,
he made his family joke that evening about the shoemaker's
child going barefoot, and the family laughed. He was more
worried than his manner showed—for a day or two it seemed
as though John were going to be seriously ill. Then the fever
dropped and the case became normal. Some delirium was
normal enough, too, with high fever—but it was different,
when it was your own son. Dr. Tenterden was not an imagi-
native man. Nevertheless, at one point in the delirium, he
had leaned forward and said in a steady, convincing voice,

"Stop it, John! Mona Gregg is not dead. She is getting better. Do not worry about Mona Gregg."

It was an incident he tried to forget as soon as possible— he did not like to do such things. Nevertheless, he thought he had got through to the boy—and next day, the fever had begun to drop. He tried to shut out of his mind the harsh, adolescent voice, saying, "Mona Gregg's dead. I killed her," over and over from the bed. And then there was something about an announcement and the Principal. But John had not even heard the announcement the Principal was going to make—he had fainted before it was made, from all accounts— and the announcement had concerned a case of cheating in the Eighth Grade, with which John could not have been involved. Dr. Tenterden gave it up. He had heard religious old ladies swear like troopers under anesthesia—there was no use in a practical man's meddling with such things.

John's constitution was good—on the whole, he mended quickly. Still, as his father said, it had been a sharp bout —hang it all, the boy and his mother might go down to Atlantic City for a week, to the quiet hotel where Dr. Tenterden had sent a number of patients. John assented to this politely but without enthusiasm—he felt weak and depressed, as one usually does after influenza. Also, he couldn't remember if he had talked about Mona Gregg during his illness, and that worried him. But when his father remarked, in an overly casual voice, "Gregg's taking his family out to Arizona—I advised it, if possible. The child's lung is still spotty and it won't do her any harm to be in a dry climate for a year or so," he knew that he had.

John digested the information silently. His illness had set a gap between past and present—it now seemed absurd to him that he should ever have suffered so about Mona Gregg. He could not think of lighting the candles in the church without blushing. Everything had turned out for the best, and Mona was not even coming back to school. And yet, he knew that he must see her before she left, though he did not know why.

He watched his time carefully and slipped out of the house when he was supposed to be resting. It was a raw Spring day with a biting wind, and he felt tired by the time he got to the hotel. The woman who opened the door of the small, stuffy suite looked surprised to see him—he had said "Mr. Tenterden calling" to the girl at the switchboard, and Mrs. Gregg must have expected his father. He explained, noting the resemblance to Mona as he did so—yes, Mona would pluck her eyebrows that way and wear that sort of a negligee with soiled feathers, when she grew up.

"Oh yes," said the woman, staring at him, "Mona's talked about you. She was always so interested in her little school friends—always a popular child—George," she called. A large man with tousled hair and a collarless shirt came out of the bathroom.

"George, this is the doctor's son—one of Mona's little school friends. He came to see how Mona was."

"Oh," said George, and stared at John Tenterden. "Well, your father's a good doctor. Don't know how we'll ever pay him, but he's good."

"Now, George!" said the woman. George yawned. "Sit down, Bud," he said. "Her mother'll see if Mona's awake."

John sat down on the edge of a couch that had been a bed and would be a bed again.

"We're a little crowded, here. Since Mona was sick," said George. "Well, I sleep days, of course, so it hasn't been so bad. So you're John Tenterden. Mona's talked about you quite a lot."

He leaned forward, and his flabby face became suddenly the face of a snarling dog.

"If I thought you'd been up to anything with her," he said

in a flat voice, "I'd break your damn neck. High school kid or no high school kid."

"Now, George," said the woman, coming back into the room. "Is that a nice way to talk? You can see what he's like, George. And you know what Mona's like."

"Oh, I know what Mona's like," said the man. "She's like you. She's romantic." He spoke wearily, but there was a trace of pride in his voice. "She can tell you the whole plot of a picture she's only seen once, and the way she keeps up with the film stars, sick as she is! Excuse me, Bud, I didn't mean anything."

"She's made the most beautiful album since she was sick," said the woman, proudly. "It's called 'My Friends in Movieland.' She's had a letter about it already from Mary Pickford. She told Mary how sick she was. Well, she says she'd be delighted to see you, young man."

John Tenterden got up and followed her into the other room. He had thought about Mona so much that he vaguely expected to find a different Mona, now—a remarkable one. But it was merely Mona Gregg. She was thin, she had on a red Japanese kimono, she was lying in bed, propped up with pillows. The small room smelt of sickness. On the medicine-table beside her was a sputum-cup.

"Hello, Mona," he said gruffly, extending the package he had carried in his hands till the paper had fingerprints on it. "I'm glad to hear you're better. I brought you some candy."

He exhaled heavily, having rid himself of his speech. He had meant to add, "I hope they're the kind you like," but he had forgotten at the last moment.

"Hello, John," said Mona, in a mincing voice. "It was nice of you to come. I'm not allowed to eat much candy, but thank you just the same. How's school?"

"Oh, school's all right, I guess," said John, sitting down. "I've been sick myself—influenza—so I don't know."

"Did you have to have oxygen?" said Mona. "I had to have oxygen and I guess it saved my life. It feels funny."

"No, I didn't have to have oxygen," said John. He cleared his throat. "You must have been pretty sick," he said.

"I was awfully sick," said Mona, with obvious pleasure. "I'm pretty sick still. That's why we're going to Arizona."

"Well, Arizona's a nice place to go," said John, carefully avoiding her eyes. "Your mother said you'd been making a —a scrapbook," he said.

"An album," said Mona. "I call it 'My Friends in Movieland.' It's all about the stars. I've got eleven autographed photographs already. Shall I show it to you?"

"Sure," said John. She showed it to him. It took quite a time. Mrs. Gregg went in and out. Now and then, she would look at Mona. When she did so, John averted his eyes, as from something naked. In the look there was fear and a possessive love, both undisciplined.

It took quite a time but at last it was done. John Tenterden got up. "Well, I've got to go, Mona," he said. "I probably won't see you again before I go away. But I'm glad you're better."

He stood looking at her. A curious, wrenching sob rose to his lips and died there. It surprised him very much. He was infinitely glad to be free of Mona Gregg. He was sorry and humiliated that she should love him. And yet, there was something else—a queer feeling he could never have explained to Richard or Gwen. It wasn't patronage but it was very like gratitude. He looked at Mona's thin, hungry face.

"Everybody at school's talking about you, Mona," he said. "They all wish they could go to Arizona, too. You ought to write some of us and tell us about it."

Mona's cheeks flushed with satisfaction.

"I don't suppose I'll have a chance to write ordinary letters much," she said carelessly. "With my album and everything.

But I guess I could send postcards, anyway. You could pass them around the class."

"Gee, that'd be great!" said John, fervently. "Well, good-bye, Mona."

"Good-bye, John. And I hope," she said, with hauteur and from the distance of one who gets autographed photographs of stars, "that you have a good time, too."

John Tenterden had been able to slip out of his house without difficulty. Returning, he was not quite so fortunate. His brother, Richard, down for a week end, met him in the hall.

"Hello, kid," he said, "you look pretty well for a sick man. Where have you been, this windy day? Out paying a call on your girl?"

"No," said John.

"I believe he has," said Richard, with relish. "He's blushing." He laid a heavy, fraternal hand on John's shoulder. "Sometime I want to have a little talk with you, John, my boy," he said. "You're growing up, you know. And no kid brother of mine is going to make a fool of—oh, well, we won't go into that now. But that's a date."

He waited for some expression of gratitude from John. As none came, he tactfully changed the subject.

"By the way," he said, "I was looking around for my old bamboo rod, thought you might have swiped it. But there isn't any light in your closet and I'm afraid I smashed some truck of yours. Apologies, old man."

He pointed to the hall table. Upon it was a broken box and on the box a crushed lunar moth. The wings were off the body, and one wing had been torn in half.

"Tried to stick it together again but I'm not much good at that sort of thing," said Robert briskly. "Suppose we'd better throw it away—after all, a kid your age isn't interested in that sort of thing—"

"You had no business to touch it," said John, beginning to tremble.

"Hey?" said Richard.

"You had no business to touch it. It was mine. You had no business to come in my room," said John Tenterden. He paused. "You're a stupid fool," he said.

"Kid," said Richard, in a heavy voice, "you've been sick. If you hadn't been, you'd get a licking, here and now. Keep a civil tongue in your head or you'll get it anyway."

"I'm sorry, Dick," said John, in a confused voice, still staring at the moth.

"That's better," said Richard. He paused. Something glinted in his eyes. "And now, let's go back to what we were talking about," he said. "You weren't supposed to go out. Why did you go out?"

"I wanted some fresh air," said John sullenly. Richard regarded him.

"You're a bad liar, Johnno," said Richard. "A darn bad liar. I'm going to ask you once more. Why did you go out when you weren't supposed to go out?"

"And suppose I don't choose to tell you?" said John desperately, recognizing the gambit, a familiar one since childhood.

"Well, then," said Richard, judicially, "we'll have to take other measures, sick or not. Come on, Johnno, we haven't done this for a long time. But if you think I'm going to have any kid brother of mine fooling around with hotel-trash—oh, I've heard things about you, Johnno—"

He laid a hand on John's arm again. "Keep off me, you stupid fool," said John and hit him. It was a beautiful punch, well-timed. Richard went to the floor with a crash and came up raging.

It was, perhaps, fortunate for both of them that Mrs. Tenterden returned just then.

John apologized and was a very docile convalescent in Atlantic City. Nevertheless, John was changed. He had time to think many things over, in the bright sleepy air. He was not sorry for hitting Richard—Richard would never bully him again. He was not sorry, now, for having prayed in the church. There was a whole world beyond the Tenterden cosmos—a world where people died and fell in love. He had suspected its existence with his mind, before. But now, he knew.

A GENTLEMAN OF FORTUNE

*J*HEY'D had better fireworks in the days of his youth, thought Mr. Veery, as he woke up on the last morning of Fair Week. You never saw a set-piece nowadays like Custer's Last Stand. But all the same, the program had said that the Fair would end in a Mammoth Pyrotechnic Display—and he was bound he was going to see it, rules or no rules.

Whenever the Board of Directors paid its official visit to the James Bogardus Home for Retired Boatmen, Mr. Veery was on show. He sat in his immaculate little room as brisk and chipper as a canary in a clean cage, and whatever complaints were made, there were never any from Mr. Veery. Old men in Homes are apt to be touchy and querulous; Mr. Veery was always cheerful. Old men, from the very fact that they are old, are apt to suffer from ailments which remind a Board of Directors all too keenly of the uncertainties of mortal existence; but Mr. Veery seemed always to be in the pink of condition. More than one female member of the Board discovering him in his splint rocker with his silver-mounted spectacles on his nose and his Bible open at the third chapter of Kings, had drawn in her breath with a little sigh and tiptoed away as if from the presence of a saint. "So neat," they would whisper to each other as they passed on down the hall. "So gentle and appreciative—and that sweet little twinkle in his eye! My dear, if only the rest of them were more like Mr. Veery!"

When Mr. Veery was sure that they were quite gone, he

would put his Bible away and take off his spectacles. Then
the twinkle would become even more perceptible. The Bible
was a well-thumbed one, though not by Mr. Veery—and it
opened automatically now to the third chapter of Kings. Mr.
Veery had kept the inscription on the flyleaf, "To dear
Andrew from his loving grandmother, June 1st, 1877," merely
altering the "Andrew" to "Amos" with a few deft strokes of
a pen. "Amos" sounded a little better, somehow, for a retired
boatman. Sometimes he would wonder just who "grandmother" had been. But of that, and of the previous possessor
of the silver-mounted spectacles, he had no definite knowledge, beyond the Albany pawnshop where he had picked
them up. Mr. Veery had been born with a twinkle, and he
had never lacked a keen appreciation of the value of suitable
stage properties.

He did not need the spectacles, except as a property; and
the manuscript which he kept concealed in a cleverly con-
structed little recess in his floor-boards—Mr. Veery was a star
pupil of the occupational workshop—might have given the
Board of Directors some odd sidelights upon his career. It
was romantically entitled, Memoirs of a Gentleman of Fortune, and Mr. Veery wrote upon it every rest period in a copper-plate Spencerian hand. He plumed himself particularly
on the Dedication, elaborately enscrolled in purple ink, "To
the James Bogardus Home, within whose tranquil precincts
this record of a busy life was penned." But the New York
Police Department would have been rather more interested
in such chapters as "The Art of the Con"—"The Spanish Prisoner Con"—"Gold Bricks and How to Plant Them"—"Sidelights on Wiretapping and Other Race-track Cons." For in
these, Mr. Veery had put the results of a lifetime of experience. Like all beginning authors, he often wished for an
audience. But being a sensible man, he had resigned himself,
a little sadly, to a strictly posthumous fame.

Not that he had any complaints to make about the James Bogardus Home. Far from it. Ten years before, he had picked out the dozing, upstate town of Winkelstone with its weedy little canal and its air of comfortable, rather stuffy peace as an ideal spot to retire and enjoy the fruits of a well-earned leisure. True, he had intended to retire in a slightly different way. He had planned on one of the big, rambling houses whose iron-ringed horseblocks and chestnut-littered lawns still lent a shabby grandeur to the Hill. But luck had been against him, and the James Bogardus Home was exceedingly snug. Retired boatmen who fulfilled the old-fashioned stipulations of the Deed of Gift were getting fewer and fewer—indeed, the Board of Directors was hard put to it to keep from fairly pampering their pensioners to death and yet carry out the terms of the Deed. Mr. Veery, of course, had had little difficulty with the stipulations. A genuinely retired boatman might be entirely authentic—but he never could seem as authentic as Mr. Veery.

Yes, the Home was a real haven for the storm-tossed, thought Mr. Veery, sentimentally and in character—he always did his best to live his parts. Food, quarters, workshop, free library, tobacco-allowance—all were of the best. The company, to be sure, was hardly the *crême de la crême*—he had never thought to pass his old age next-door to an ex-captain of a garbage scow; but Crutch was a decent fellow, except for his besetting sin of gluttony, and Mr. Veery prided himself on his broad-mindedness. The only thing one really missed was contact with the busy outside world. And after all, there were places where one might miss that even more.

One read the papers, of course, and tried to keep up with the latest developments in one's profession—one must not allow oneself to rust. Sometimes the developments rather took one's breath away; sometimes, on the other hand, they made one shake one's head. All this bombing and racketeering—crude work, very crude. Very little bore the mark of the artist, from such routine matters as poke-snatching to such higher flights as switching the ice in the old chewing gum stall. Of course, if one believed in mass production and purely mechanical efficiency— But Mr. Veery was a born individualist; and it seemed to him, as it must always seem to the old, that his own tradition—the great tradition of the Con—had fallen on sorry days.

He was content, on the whole, to sit by the fire and let the world spin—or had been, till the notice about Fair Week went up on the bulletin board. He had always loved fairs and fireworks—indeed, a fair and a man with three little shells and an elusive pea had started him on his career. But he had not realized until now how much it meant to him in his quietude to steep himself once a year in the noise and heat and dust of a gaping, good-humored crowd—to smell the hot dogs and the peanuts, roasting and sizzling—to hear the yelp of the barkers as the wheels-of-fortune spun and the brassy tune whanged out by the merry-go-round.

"Oh, Lordy, the suckers, the dear, sweet, lovely suckers!" thought Mr. Veery longingly. They were the world's chosen —you could fool them again and again, and they'd come back for more. They went to be fooled and dazzled, and tickled with feather ticklers, and spun screaming on human roulette wheels—they went to be human and silly—you couldn't stick up your nose at any of it or you didn't have a good time. Mr. Veery knew all about carnivals, from the inside—but he'd throw his ring at the solid gold watch and catch the tin one as cheerfully as the rest of them; he'd pay his dime to see the giant man-eating rats from South America and find they were ordinary muskrats, and never cheep. The fireworks alone were worth all the fatigue of the day.

It was all Dan Crutch's fault—overeating himself at the ice-cream stand last year till he had had to be treated at the emergency hospital tent. The paper had run a little squib about it, and the Board of Directors had not been pleased. So this year the Fair was out of bounds. If you broke out of bounds, you lost your special privileges, including tobacco-allowance, for a period of from one to three months. Mr. Veery had practically all the special privileges available, and he cherished them. But when he read the notice, rebellion stirred in his heart.

Mr. Veery said nothing, but in secret Mr. Veery plotted. The first days of the Fair might be allowed to pass. But when the crowded finale came—and the Roman candles began to scatter their stars—Mr. Veery was going to be there, if he had to do a crushout in the best traditions of Dannemora.

Remained the problem of chastising the errant Mr. Crutch. Dan Crutch, as Mr. Veery knew, was given to the consumption of illicit midnight lunches, washed down with sarsaparilla, when lights were out. Such practices struck Mr. Veery as both greedy and anti-social. Somehow, it would be but poetic justice, if, on this night of all nights, Dan Crutch should suffer the penalties of his gluttony by falling just a little ill. It might teach him a lesson in manners and point out to the Board of Directors that the ill-effects of Mr. Crutch's gormandizing could not properly be laid at the door of the Fair.

"I wonder," thought Mr. Veery,—who was a privileged character in the Home dispensary,—"I wonder if I still know how to mix a Mickey Finn?"

It was a long time since he had compounded one. It was a long time since he had picked a lock and crawled down a fire escape. But when the small side-gate of the Home—the one that nobody used—swung to behind him, he felt a certain pride. Neither hand nor brain had forgotten their cunning, and in spite of rules and Directors, he had made his escape unobserved.

He stood in the sunshine a moment, free, breathless, and a little scared. The Mickey Finn powders still reposed in his pocket—Mr. Veery had had compunctions at the last moment; after all, Mickey Finns were potent, and Crutch was old. Now, for a moment of cowardice, he wondered if he hadn't better go back. They wouldn't have missed him yet—and it was a queer feeling, breaking even a minor rule after years of living strictly. But just then a car whirled by at the end of the street—a car with a streaming pennant, "*Harwich County Fair,*" and three hobbledehoys in the back seat, blowing squeakers. Mr. Veery straightened his shoulders and felt like a man again. "Come on, old-timer," he told himself sternly. "They don't make 'em like us any more."

Half an hour later, however, he began to wonder. In a burst of energy and economy, he had resolved to walk the three miles to the fair grounds. But the road was not the road of everyday, but a crowded and roaring thoroughfare. The crammed buses howled past in a cloud of dust and gas—they could not bother to stop for one tired old man. Leather-lunged little boys bawled, "Ride, Mister? Give us a ride?" and now and then some weary philanthropist paused to take one aboard. But no one seemed to see Mr. Veery's hand, deprecatingly extended. No one, that is, until the green runabout came.

Mr. Veery had noted it from afar—it was going slower than the rest of the traffic liked. But the boy and girl seemed oblivious of shouts and angry horns. They weren't holding hands; they weren't even sitting close; but now and then she'd look at him. Mr. Veery knew that look—it stirred a far memory. This girl hadn't Molly's hair, but there was a little, trusting turn of the head that reminded him. He boldly stepped out into the roadway, picking his moment.

The boy with the nervous mouth jerked brakes expertly. "Listen, Grandpa," he said, "this is no place for picking daisies. What's the big idea?" But he grinned as he said it. People generally grinned at Mr. Veery.

"I beg your pardon," said Mr. Veery with dignity. "I was looking for my son-in-law's car. A green car like yours, and—"

"Well, this isn't it," said the boy, his eyes hardening. "Sorry, Gramp." He started to release the brakes. But the girl touched his arm.

"Oh, Bert," she said in a low voice, "can't you see he's old and tired? He probably just wants a ride—"

"That it?" said the boy. He hesitated for a moment. "Oh, well—"

"I do so hate to trouble you," said Mr. Veery mildly. "If only I hadn't misunderstood Frank's instructions. It was green with a Pennsylvania license, and he told me to meet him at the corner of Elm and Pine, but it seemed so crowded there. I'm sure I had it written down. And then, if we did miss each other, I was to take a bus and find him at the Agricultural Building. But the buses didn't seem to stop and— dear, dear, what *will* Frank think of me?" He fumbled in his pockets with ineffectual hands.

"Oh—glory!" said the boy. "All right. Jump in; the front seat's rather a tight fit, but—"

"I wouldn't think of inconveniencing you—" sighed Mr. Veery, squeezing in beside them.

The girl gave him a little smile, and he felt at ease. He began to talk. He had opportunity, for the traffic-stream moved slower and slower till at last it barely crawled. He talked about Frank, and Frank's business and the grandchildren. It was art for art's sake, purely; but it did good to his soul. And while he talked, his bland eyes probed his companions shrewdly. Nice boy, but something on his mind. Double-breasted coat buttoned up, on a warm day, and slight bulge in inside breast pocket. All right as long as you keep the coat buttoned, but bad place for a wallet at a crowded fair. Nice girl and fond of the boy, but vaguely troubled and puzzled. Girl better dressed than boy—boy not quite at home with car—probably her car. Elopers? He wondered. He'd never heard of eloping to a County Fair, but all young people in love were crazy. He expatiated on little Orinda's tonsillitis, watching the boy touch his breast pocket, as they got out of the car.

They started to walk together toward the clamor and the tents. Then suddenly the boy stopped. "Look here," he said, addressing Mr. Veery, "I don't know who you are or whether your story's straight or not. But I've got a—a business appointment—and I don't want to leave Kitty alone in this crowd. You look respectable, and anyhow you're old. So if you'll just take Kitty over to the Agricultural Building, I'll meet you there in half an hour by the front door. That all right, Kitty? Or would you rather take care of yourself?"

"My dear sir," said Mr. Veery statelily, "I should only be too delighted to be of the slightest service to Miss—"

"L-Lane—" said the girl with a little start; then more firmly: "Katrina Lane. Of course, Bert. Run along. I'll be perfectly safe."

Mr. Veery blinked. He had noticed the monogram on the runabout door and the twitch on the boy's mouth. The young lady's name might be almost anything beginning with an L, for the letters tallied; but Mr. Veery was perfectly sure it was not *Lane*.

"A very pleasant man, if somewhat abrupt," said Mr. Veery, as the boy darted away. He slipped a fatherly hand in the girl's arm. "May I congratulate you, my dear?"

"Bert's the finest boy in the world," said the girl defiantly. "It isn't his fault that my father—it isn't his fault that he— Oh dear!" she said.

Mr. Veery patted her arm. "There, there, my dear," he said. "Tell me all about it."

It was a very simple story, like that of most star-crossed lovers. Bert had worked his way up from messenger-boy to teller in the Eastmouth bank, twelve miles upriver, but the Longfords had been in Eastmouth since 1812. "Though what they ever *did* except sit on their land!" said Katrina Longford irascibly. Yes, she was very young. Yes, Bert was very young. But it was the real thing. It was love.

Mr. Veery clucked and sympathized. But it was going to be all right. Bert had a wonderful scheme. They were going to be rich. In fact, if Bert's business appointment went well to-day—

It was at that moment Mr. Veery's mild gaze discovered, to his amusement, that Shad Pickrey was still working the fairs. Time might alter many things, but not that bulbous, imposing nose, those bulgy, fish-cold eyes, even glimpsed for a moment, briefly, as their owner dived between the back curtains of a tent. Mr. Veery noted the tent for future reference—it was away from the main traffic of the Fair. He felt glad that his own features were entirely normal. It was a great asset to be entirely inconspicuous—even negative in appearance. He'd never really done business with Shad Pickrey, but he'd known him by sight and reputation. And yet he gravely doubted if Shad Pickrey would even recognize him now. It might be amusing to see.

Then his eyes widened slightly. Making hot-foot for the tent, in the manner of one who seeks to avoid observation, was the nervous Bert. Mr. Veery blocked the girl's view as her eyes turned to follow his. "Dear, dear," said Mr. Veery, "we must be getting on to the Agricultural Building. I'm afraid of missing Frank altogether, as it is."

He led her along, chatting; but as he chatted, his mind worked furiously. Shad Pickrey and a nervous bank-teller. The coincidence was not encouraging. Shad had been one of the slickest come-on men of his time—and rough, thought Mr. Veery, very rough. "You know," he said tenderly to the girl at his side, "you remind me of someone who was very dear to me." Dear Molly—the sweetest, cleverest partner a gentleman of fortune ever had. He remembered that little, trusting turn of her head—it had got them out of more bad scrapes than he cared to think of. He wished Molly were with them now.

Suddenly Mr. Veery gave an effective start. "Don't turn around!" he whispered to his companion. "There's somebody looking this way—I don't think he's recognized you, but—"

"Oh, golly!" said the girl. "A big man? Panama hat? Oh, why didn't I change my clothes! A big man who looks—looks as if he rather liked getting angry?"

"Yes!" said Mr. Veery libelously. "Keep your back to him —he's looking away—"

"Father," said the girl. "He'll scalp me if he knows I'm here with Bert. Oh, what shall we do?"

"See that fortuneteller's tent?" said Mr. Veery, pointing. "Hurry. Go in there. Have your fortune told. Several times, if necessary. He won't follow you there. He hasn't quite recognized you—yet. Meanwhile, I will find your young man and apprise him of the untoward circumstances, which—"

She seemed about to argue, for an instant. Then Mr. Veery hissed, "He's turning!" and she fled. Mr. Veery saw her disappear within the fortuneteller's tent.

"Safe enough there," thought Mr. Veery. "And now for Bert." He wormed his way patiently through the crowd toward the end of the roaring carnival-street. But it was not long before he saw the boy coming toward him. He looked jaunty, and as if a weight were off his mind; but when he saw Mr. Veery, his jauntiness disappeared.

"Listen, you old dodo," he said violently, "where's my girl? Where's Kitty?"

"Not so loud," said Mr. Veery portentously; "we are observed." He looked for a nook of refuge and found it in a deserted corner to the rear of the grandstand. And thither he dragged his prey.

"Listen," he said, still clutching the boy's coat-sleeve, "what were you doing with Shad Pickrey?"

Something flickered in the boy's eyes and was gone.

"I don't know what you're talking about," he said. "You said you'd wait at the—"

"Imbecile!" hissed Mr. Veery. "I don't know what you've got in that pocket," and he tapped it; "but if it's still there, I'm a Dutchman."

The boy's hand flew to it instantly, as his face whitened. Then he gasped with relief.

"Of course it's still— What do you mean?" he said.

"Have you never heard of the envelope switch?" said Mr. Veery patiently. "Or the box you seal with your own signet-ring so there can't be any mistake, and then—idiot, look inside!"

He shielded the boy from any observation as the latter drew out a long envelope and tore it open. They both looked inside.

It was, thought Mr. Veery judicially, a very fair job. The strips of paper had just the right weight and crackle. But Shad had always had his points.

"Bank's, of course," said Mr. Veery. "What was it? Cash?"

"No," said the boy, his hands shaking. "Government bonds. Big ones."

Mr. Veery whistled soundlessly. "That's nice," he said. "What was the come-on? Green-goods, borax-mines, or that long-lost Australian cousin?"

"Why," quavered the boy, "you know, when this revolution happened, in Spain? Well, there was a fellow who—"

"Great land of Goshen!" said Mr. Veery reverently. "The old Spanish-prisoner game! I didn't know it could still be worked. But live and learn!"

"But," said the boy desperately, "he had all the proofs— letters—documents. I—I bought a Spanish dictionary and translated some of them. They were all right."

"They ought to be," said Mr. Veery laconically. "Shad was doing very well with those letters in '97. Only it was a Cuban prisoner, then. And you had to show them the bonds, just to prove they could trust you? They weren't crude enough to slug you and grab them. Oh, no."

"Why, yes," said the boy. "He—he said I'd have to demonstrate my financial responsibility. But he didn't *ask* for a cent —and I didn't have the envelope out of my hands for more than a minute—"

"Only somebody stepped on your toe and begged your pardon, and when you looked again, it wasn't the same envelope," said Mr. Veery.

"Why—" said the boy. "As a matter of fact— Say, who are you, anyway?"

"Call me Santa Claus," said Mr. Veery. "How many of them are in it?"

"Three," said the boy. "Mr.—" he swallowed, "Mr. Pendleton and two little sort of well-dressed fellows with kind of hard faces. They don't say much, but he explained they were Spanish."

"They may be," said Mr. Veery. "Or then again they may just be a couple of nice Italian guns. Did they ask much about the bank?"

"Why, Mr. Pendleton—he's quite chatty, you know—he seemed pretty interested in banking."

"Oh, Lord!" said Mr. Veery. "And most of the State cops here and the other cops busy with traffic. And the roads pretty clear north of Eastmouth for a getaway, because everything will be jammed around here just about when the fireworks begin. Why, darling, it's a set-up!"

"But I'll stop it—" babbled the boy. "I'll go right to the police—I'll—"

"You'll go to the cops," said Mr. Veery scornfully, "and tell them, please, you think there's going to be a robbery because you just handed over some of the bank's bonds to a man who called himself 'Pendleton,' and now you're afraid that's not his name and he's a criminal. Or they blow the crib and you say you can help identify because—oh, don't you see, you nitwit? The robbery is your only out, and they're banking on it."

The boy's jaw tightened. "All right," he said, "I can take it. They'll believe me if I go to jail."

"I'm thinking about your girl," said Mr. Veery. "Now listen: We've got to work this out."

As Shad Pickrey opened the little compartment in his traveling icebox—the compartment that didn't have pop in it—a beatific smile was on his face. Manna was certainly falling from heaven. Not only had that poor sap of a bank-teller suspected nothing, but he was so firmly hooked that he'd actually brought his hayseed uncle along to sweeten the Spanish prisoner with a little more ready cash. They'd have to work fast to collect it, because the big blow-off at Eastmouth was scheduled for nine P.M.—but Shad Pickrey had never yet let a bird in the hand escape him because there might be other birds in the bush. Ricci and the Flea could drive Uncle over to Eastmouth while Uncle collected his roll from the hotel safe—and he, Shad, would stay here and keep an eye on the kid. It would be a nice little outing for the boys, and they could give the bank the once-over as they went by. Afterward, another little drink, with the addition of some knock-out drops, would settle Uncle and the kid. They could sleep it off, under a tarpaulin—and if the cops found them in the morning, that would be just too bad.

He had a funny idea he'd seen Uncle somewhere before— but Lord, you met so many suckers you couldn't keep track of them! The old man certainly had brightened up at the first mention of liquor. This job would set him solid with the Bacciarotto gang, but the bonds were his private perquisite and he intended to keep them. They were safe inside the kewpie-doll on top of the icebox—it was his pet hiding place, and it always worked. He did not perceive Mr. Veery's glance at the doll. Nor did anyone except the boy for whom it was intended. Mr. Veery was remembering more and more about his old competitor's habits—and remembering that Shad very seldom changed his spots.

"Well," said Shad, lifting the paper cup, "happy days!" He exchanged a grin with Ricci and the Flea. Uncle had nearly spilled the liquor, trying to help pass it—the old fellow certainly had his tongue hanging out.

"To our castle in Spain!" said Mr. Veery politely. They drank, bottoms-up. They shuddered.

State Trooper Joseph Conoy, in his private mind, put it down to leprechauns. Else how would the stroke of luck have fallen on him, and him so new to the Force? And wasn't the little old man like a leprechaun himself, popping out of a big car, as spry as a rabbit, and calling: "Officer—officer! My friends have been taken seriously ill—will you watch them while I get a doctor?" And then he whisked away in a run-about as green as a shamrock, with a girl with a face like all the angels driving it? No, he hadn't taken the number of the runabout—but one look inside the other car had driven all else out of his head. Sure, he'd captured two New York gangsters single-handed—and they weak as kittens with the desperate sickness that was on them—but that needn't go down on the report. And if he ever met the little old man again, he wouldn't believe it, and he'd as soon think of meeting one of the cobblers of the hills. . . .

Mr. Veery, after he had got rid of the young people, dined lightly on a hot dog, a chocolate bar and a bottle of lemon pop, and felt his soul at peace. It had all been very interesting but a trifle exhausting, and he looked forward to his fireworks with childish pleasure. The administration of the Mickey Finn had been elementary, once he got Shad to produce the liquor; but he had not enjoyed his ride in Shad's car. He had been wary enough to feign illness himself from the first—but even so, there had been some very bad moments. However, gunmen were proverbially suspicious of their colleagues, and they had just been turning the car around to go back and kill Shad Pickrey for poisoning them, when the Mickey Finn had—ahem—come to its full powers. It was lucky the State policeman had arrived so promptly; but there was bound to be someone near that crossroads—and he had timed things as well as he knew how.

The boy and girl had played their parts very well—the girl, particularly, in trailing the big car. But the boy had done well also, to keep Shad quiet, with both of them in the throes of the Mickey Finn. He had given the boy as little as he dared —but there was no doubt it had a drastic effect. Foolish of Shad to hide the bonds in that same old doll—but Shad had always been a person of routine.

Well, well, least said soonest mended, and a penny saved was a penny earned, thought Mr. Veery, as he in his turn patted his breast pocket. The bonds had gone back to the boy —and the boy would do well now, after his scare, but the smaller gunman's wallet, while thinner than one might have wished for, came in very handy. And the trouble had been worth it, for the look on Shad's face when he had finally revealed himself. He'd hardly seemed able to speak, when Mr. Veery had stuffed bills in his hand and murmured recommendation of the California climate. Well, it was an expense; but for old time's sake, he could hardly let the bulls get Shad.

So, having protected lovers, and been an instrument of justice in the courts of the ungodly, Mr. Veery stood and enjoyed his fireworks. The set-piece—"Washington Crossing the Delaware"—was, he thought, particularly fine. The last red fire flared out—he thought, with a little sigh, of transportation home. But as he turned to go, he was jostled—and he felt a slight, unmistakable tug at his coat.

Mr. Veery opened his mouth to cry, "Stop thief!"—and shut it again. He remembered, suddenly, the thin, sharp-nosed woman who had stood beside him—the one with the worn clothing and the beaten eyes. She didn't look like a professional; she looked hungry, and even if she were a professional, it was a hard year. He felt the unskilled, desperate hands fumble and retreat with their booty, and said no word. After all, it was gunman's money—fool's gold—and Mr. Veery had always been a philosopher. He would ride back in the crowded bus, with sixty-eight cents in his pocket, but he would ride content.

But as he made wearily for the exit, it did not even seem as if he would have to do that. For a hand fell upon his shoulder, and a voice rang in his ear:

"Well, Mr. Veery, really! We've been looking all over for you! How could you give us such a scare!"

It was Mrs. Ransom, the matron, come in person to seek him. He sighed gratefully, as he thought of the comfortable back seat of Mrs. Ransom's car. Then he had an inspiration.

"Dear lady," he said, removing from his lapel the limp but still fragrant little knot of flowers that had once adorned the coat of Katrina Longford, "permit me. A little souvenir. No —no thanks, I beg of you. Just a tribute."

"Well, Mr. Veery—" said Mrs. Ransom, uncertainly. "Well, I certainly should be very angry with you. Well—"

Mr. Veery smiled to himself in the darkness. He might not lose his tobacco-allowance after all. But when he got back to his room, he would take from its hiding-place a certain piece of printed matter and burn it. The circular spoke in no uncertain terms of a person sometimes called "*Smiling Jim Atkinson, alias Sir George Rumbold, alias—*" and a list. It contained the phrases, "*Gentlemanly appearance—good manners—dresses well but not flashily—*" and Mr. Veery had always cherished it for that.

But now he would burn it—perhaps even burn his memoirs; for he knew, by the ache in his bones, that that chapter of life was closed. He had joined with the world again today, and the world had been very exhausting. . . . For him, the peace of the Home and the games of checkers—the chair in the sunny corner—the gossip of little things—the life of a duly retired boatman. But at least there had been fireworks, even on this last sally. And it was something, to remember fireworks, even when one was old.

FAMOUS

*I*T ISN'T that we aren't proud of him—anybody would be proud of their father's being Jordan Blake. Why, everybody at school knows the songs from *Random Rose* and *Hey Diddle Diddle*, and the rest of them. And, whenever he has a new show, they talk about Victor Herbert and Gilbert and Sullivan and all the boys. And I've been offered as much as twenty dollars for the photograph of Carolina Clay with "To Jerry Blake, whose father wrote 'Random Rose,' from Carolina." But, naturally, when you're famous, it keeps you pretty busy being famous. It isn't like having the ordinary sort of father, if you know what I mean.

Not that I've got any complaints. I liked school and I liked camp. And if I wanted anything, all I had to do was write Miss Hacker and there'd be a check and a note. He'd always sign the note himself and sometimes he'd stick in a couple of the funny little drawings he makes on telephone pads. The fellows thought those were keen And some awfully soupy fathers come up to visit the school.

I would like to have had him come up when I graduated. But it would have made an awful mess. Because I'd written most of the Sixth Form Show—words and music—and that was one thing Father was serious about. He'd leave you alone about most things, but he'd never even let me take piano. He said one song-writer in the family was enough. And he said it with that cold little smile he uses on managers, sometimes. So I had to pick it up by myself—and get Nub Parsons to put his name on the show. But even so, if Father had ever heard that score, he'd have recognized it. I'd swiped a couple of things from him, you see—little things of his that never quite jelled. Of course I couldn't develop them the way he would have—but they sounded fairly keen in the show. Anyway, he'd have spotted them, in a minute.

So I got Miss Hacker on the wire, and told her I knew he'd be awfully busy and not to bother. And a couple of days later, I got a funny little drawing from him showing me graduating with a sort of halo, and him looking at me from New York with a spyglass. So I knew it was all right, and it took a weight off my mind. Though, when the other fathers showed up, on Visitors' Day, I felt a little different. I guess you're bound to feel that way.

And now I was home, with school done and college ahead, and that was a funny feeling. Though things were always a little funny, that first day home. My school always seemed to get out ahead of Bibs' school; so she wouldn't be there, and it would be just the two of us. And each time, on the train, I'd think that things were going to be different this time. I don't mean anything sappy. And it's bound to be different, with a famous person. But I'd visited the Parsons' a lot— and Nub and his father got along pretty well. What I mean is, they could talk about things, in spite of Mr. Parsons' being a Republican and a deacon, whereas Nub is going to write a big, vital book called *Proletarians, Unite!* as soon as he gets through Harvard and has the real beans on the situation. He wanted to put a song about Proletarians Unite in the show, but I told him they were hard words to set.

But Father—well, he isn't exactly Mr. Parsons' type. You'd pick him out of any bunch of people, in the first place—and he'd be standing a little away from the rest of them, looking dark and keen and a little like a black-and-white sword. He isn't handsome, exactly, because you've seen the caricatures

—but he looks as young as he does in the caricatures. I've seen him after he's been up all night at a rehearsal, and his tie was still tied in the neat, slim knot and there wasn't a speck of cigarette-ash on his clothes. He gives you a very cool impression, and yet people like him a lot. Even managers like Jakie Rosebaum like him—and if you put Jakie in a tank with an alligator, you couldn't tell which eyes were which. In fact, all the people in the theatre like him—though some of them say he's snooty, which nobody can help, and they wouldn't say it to me.

But I think he was different, before Mother died. Bibs can hardly remember that time, but I can. I guess Mother was the only person he ever loved, and children aren't the same thing, though he's pretty fond of Bibs. But he used to play with us a lot then and the house felt different. Mother was a swell person. They ran away when he was in Harvard and trouped in vaudeville for three years. It made a big scandal at the time—both their families came from Boston and were quite Back Bay. Then Father wrote *Hey Diddle Diddle*—and they produced it right after the Armistice when he was still in France—and that made him Jordan Blake and the families came around. So we've met our uncles and cousins socially, and most of them are pretty stuffy, if you ask us. Which is one thing Father isn't, even when he's being sarcastic.

But, to get back to coming home—he'd be waiting when the train pulled in, a little away from the crowd. And we'd shake hands and he'd say, "Hello, Jerry—how's the infant phenomenon?" and I'd say, "Fine." And then, of course, in the car, he'd ask questions and I'd try to tell him about things at school. But it's odd how little you can tell. It's awfully important at the time, but when you come to talk about it, it boils down to Bill Latimer being a good egg and the Latin master a slave-driver and the scores of games and things. I always thought it would last longer but it never did.

And all the time I'd be crazy to talk to him about people like Carolina and Noel Porter and the new show of his and the old ones. But he'd only talk about those when he forgot. I guess he felt we were too young, but we'd have understood. It used to get Bibs awfully mad when she was younger and got sent to bed earlier, knowing people like Carolina and Noel were downstairs while she was having milk-toast with the governess. I was luckier that way, because sometimes when he was sketching a song, he'd forget to send me out of the room. And I picked up quite a lot. But he always remembered, finally—and then, generally, I'd be sent to my cousins the week before camp.

But this summer, I was sure things were going to be different. I knew Jakie wanted him to do a Show for that big barn of a 63rd Street theatre in the fall—and it would be the top, just to hear about that. I even had some ideas for a theatre as big as that.

But when I got off the train, the old spell fell over me, as the books say, and pretty soon I found I was telling Father about Nub Parsons being a good egg and the Science Master being a twirp and the scores of the games. And finally, when Father said he'd taken a house at Blue Point for the summer, it was just like a blow with a dull instrument, it didn't hurt as much as it stunned.

"Well?" said Father, when he'd finished telling me. "Anything wrong? You don't seem to greet the idea with cheers, Jerry."

"Oh yes, I do," I said, prevaricating politely. Because Blue Point is all right, in its way, but it's where Uncle Lambert goes with his family. And not even the presence of the Parsons' could make up for Uncle Lambert—especially as Nub would be away, investigating the proletariat in a coal mine, which is what he was doing.

Then I thought a minute. "Will Bibs be there?" I said. "Or is she going to camp again?"

He looked at me a little queerly. "No, Bibs will not be going to camp," he said. "After all, she's fourteen. I'd like to see something of her."

"Well, that's an idea," I said. I didn't mean to be fresh or reproachful or anything—I thought we were just talking.

"As you so aptly remark," he said, with his cool little smile, "it might be an idea. In fact, we might be a reunited family for the summer. Learn to know each others' hearts and chat around the fireside. What would you say to that, Jerry?"

Well, I could tell from the way he was trying to laugh it off that the very idea was an awful chore for him.

"Okey-doke," I said, because I was rattled, looking at him, and that's another expression he hates.

"How often have I told you, Jerry?" he said, and then he stopped. "Sorry," he said, quite nicely, "I forgot you were grown-up." He pulled on his cigarette and started to say something, but I was thinking.

"Look here," I said. "How are you going to work at Blue Point? The sea-damp's awfully bad for pianos. Or so they tell me."

The little frown came back on his forehead.

"I may not be working," he said. "I may take a vacation."

"But the *Times* said," I said, "that you were doing a show for Caro—for Miss Clay in the fall, with Jakie—and another one for—" I'd forgotten I wasn't supposed to know about his plans.

"Don't believe all you see in the papers, Jerry," he said quietly. "If I do do Carolina's show—and, by the way, I wouldn't call her Carolina, you're still a little young for that —I suppose I could commute from New York."

"Why, yes, you could do that," I said, and he said, "Why yes, I could. It might be better all around," in that queer way. "Jerry!" he said. And then he said, "Oh, well, what about those entrance exams, next fall? Do you need any tutoring? The system's changed since my time—"

So I told him, and it took quite a while and couldn't have been very interesting. At least, it wasn't for me—I wanted to ask him if he'd seen Jimmy Manistee, the new comedian, and what he thought of him. But it got us along to bedtime.

But when Bibs came home the next day and I broke the news to her, she said, "How perfectly foul! I was going to be a group-leader at camp, this summer. And now I'll have to tag around Blue Point with that slat-eyed Cousin Lucy of ours for company—and she's a human meat ball if I ever saw one."

"Is that the English they teach you at Miss Foster's?" I said.

"Oh, don't talk like Father," she said. "If we've got to, we've got to. But I bet somebody eats snakes before the summer's over."

And I could not but feel that her prognostications were likely to be justified. It was all right the first week, while we were still getting settled. But after that, the grimness set in.

He didn't even bring down our regular servants or Miss Hacker. He got a special bunch straight from Boston that were about as cozy as iced codfish. We joined the Blue Point Club, which is highly select and quite as much fun any day as a first-class mortician's, and we swam at the right hours and played golf at the right hours and took the sand out of our toes at the right hours, the way you always do in a place like that. I didn't particularly mind—I'd been places like that before—and now and then, I'd sneak some fishing with Mr. Parsons. And Bibs, who's a devil, spent most of her time trying to break down our Cousin Lucy's morale, in a quiet way. But the whole thing simply seemed like an awful waste. And when I heard Father talking to Uncle Lambert about the gold standard and agreeing with every word he said, I knew something was terribly wrong. Uncle Lambert looks like a walrus and he thinks that civilization fell when women got the vote. I got up nerve enough to ask Father if nothing could be done about him, and he just remarked coldly that Uncle Lambert had put us up for the Club.

And yet, I knew that he wasn't enjoying it. I was next to him once, when we entered the Blue Point Club at the proper bathing-hour, and I heard him mutter, "Oh God! Oh Montreal!" And once, when I was going out fishing with Mr. Parsons, I looked back, and he was standing on the porch with the funniest look on his face. Naturally, Bibs and I pretended we were having a good time, but it was hard work. There wasn't any life in the house, somehow, with Miss Hacker away and long-distance never ringing and Father never coming out of the study in his black-and-silver dressing gown and telling us, quietly but snootily, to go and drown ourselves in bathtubs if we had to but keep out of his way for the next eight hours because he was working on a song. Nowadays, he hardly touched the piano at all.

"In fact, if this is life with the famous," remarked Bibs, one day, when we were on the float alone, "give me old Camp Owatchee any time. At least there, you knew you could live through it because you always had. I'm writing a novel called *Rumble Seat Romance* and reading the snappy parts out loud to Cousin Lucy, in deadly secrecy. They make her say, 'Oh, Bibs!' But even that doesn't help much. Do you know that Father told me not to roll my stockings, this morning?"

"That's nothing," I said. "He asked me not to smoke in front of Aunt Susan. Said she didn't approve of the deadly weed for the young."

"As a glittering and sophisticated parent, Father is a flop," said Bibs. "Before, I thought we were going to have a nice time knowing him. Now, every time he looks at me, I wonder if he's going to send me to a nunnery. I don't think he approves of his daughter, Barbara. Or maybe it's both of us. Though Uncle Lambert said you were a fine, clean, manly boy the other day. Jerry—ouch, leggo of my arm, you fool!— And, if Uncle Lambert thinks that—all right, go ahead and drown!"

By that time we were both in the water and after we scrapped, we felt better. Only then we went back to the house and it was grim. Bibs went to bed early, as usual—I suspected her of writing *Rumble Seat Romance* when she was supposed to be asleep—and Father and I sat up. But you couldn't have called it conversation—we'd both start to talk at once and then we'd both say "Sorry" and then we'd neither of us say anything. Till, finally, I said I was going to the movies. They only change the bill twice a week at Blue Point and I'd already seen it. But anything was better than just sitting there, making him uncomfortable because I was around.

And driving over there, I thought of the times I'd brought people like Nub Parsons back to the apartment and how, maybe, they'd hardly see Father most of the time, but when they did see him, they'd be pretty impressed. Because they knew he was famous and yet he never treated them like kids and sometimes, if he wasn't busy, he'd do songs. And people like Carolina and Bill Fields and George Kaufman would be coming in and out. And the fellows used to kind of envy me and ask Father to come up to school.

And now, I just didn't get what he was about. Or why we were at Blue Point or anything. I didn't know if we were there because he wanted to build up some social stuff for Bibs —or because it was what he really wanted, instead of being friends with us—or what. And each time we sat down to talk, we got politer and farther apart. It had me jumping. And I couldn't help feeling that, whatever it was, was my fault.

Then, across the aisle, in the movie theatre, I heard two

old rock-ribbed dowagers talking. And one of them was saying, "Well, I did think the Jordan Blakes would bring something a little new to Blue Point. And the children are passable enough. But the man seems just as stodgy as his brother."

The second dowager made a reproving noise with her tongue, and the first one went on.

"Oh, don't click at me, Harriet!" she said. "I've known Lambert Blake since he wore short coats and he's always been as dull as ditchwater. But I went to *Random Rose* four times —yes, Harriet, I did!—and I always wanted to ask the man who wrote it where he got the idea for that screamingly funny scene in the perambulator. But when I did, the other night, at the Hayes', he just muttered and looked shy. I hoped at least he'd have some of his interesting friends down —I'm dying to see Carolina Clay. But I suppose he thinks they're too good to waste on Blue Point."

"Oh no, it isn't that," said her companion, quickly. "Don't you *know* why he's here? He's trying to get over the drug habit—that's why he's so nervous and shy. I got it all from Maisie—and that's why he never touches the piano—it brings the craving on. That nice boy of his is dreadfully worried about it, everybody says—"

"Oh, is that it?" said the other old sea horse. "Tsh, tsh! Well, that explains the other night. I knew it must be something that—"

Then their voices dropped and I didn't hear any more. But I knew I had to do something. For it was all too plain. If people like that could notice that the Blake family wasn't itself, affairs were serious. And, somehow or other, I must be the false card in the deck.

It must be me, for there wasn't anything else to explain it —Bibs was too young. This was the first summer he hadn't done a lick of work—and it was the first summer I'd been home. So, obviously, I hadn't turned out the way he expected or wanted—and it was getting him down. I even re-membered a line I'd seen in one of the gossip-columns, "Whispers say the new Jordan Blake show is off for the fall, Jick Blake's having family trouble or something."

Well, it's pretty serious when you have to think a thing through like that. But I'm modern. I know there's no reason you should like anybody, just because he's your son. They prove that in books, these days. And if you're famous, why, naturally, grown-up children tie you down and get in your way. I didn't feel bitter about it—I tried not to. It was probably something pretty psychological that Father couldn't help. With one of those Greek names, maybe. But it all boiled down to the fact that things had been all right for him when I was at school—and now they weren't all right. So what was I going to do?

Of course it would have been pleasant if we'd gotten along and could talk like Nub and Mr. Parsons. Because Bibs, after all, is a girl and you can't talk the same way to a girl. But Father was a famous person—and he'd supported me pretty darn well for seventeen years. St. Henry's isn't a cheap school. And all I was doing now was to get on his nerves so he couldn't work and make people think he was a dope fiend. I hadn't meant to do it, but it made me a good deal of a heel. Well, nobody likes to have a heel for a son.

It shook me up pretty badly—for you don't like to think of yourself as a heel, even when you have to. And I don't remember much of the road, coming back. But, when I drove up to the house, I noticed the piano was going—and a nice, tricky melody, too, a Jick Blake melody. But it stopped as soon as my headlights hit the window. And that made me surer than ever. He didn't even want to play when I was around.

I didn't sleep so well that night—I was too busy thinking whether I ought to pull out and join Nub in his coal mine or

whether it wouldn't be better, on the whole, if I just made
for the South Seas. You get crazy ideas sometimes. But we
simply couldn't go on the way we were going. And the move
was up to me. I had to get out somehow and I didn't quite
know how. He'd be all right, alone with Bibs—after all, she
looked like Mother. Or maybe I wasn't even their son—
maybe they'd adopted me and never told me and now he
was scared to, because I hadn't turned out well. But if they
had, I wished that he would tell me. It would be some sort
of relief.

And then, darn it, when I did get to sleep, I overslept and
came down to find that Father had been called to New York.

Well, in one way, of course that made things easier, because I could just hike out and leave a note on the telephone
desk, the way they do in the movies, if I had to. But I didn't
like to leave Bibs alone in the house with those frozen-faced
servants. And yet I didn't want to hash the whole thing over
with her—it felt too sore. She didn't think I was a heel, but
probably she was wrong. And I was stewing the whole thing
over in my mind—and jittering—when the telephone rang
after lunch. And it was Carolina Clay, of all people.

"Oh, hello, Carolina—Dad's in New York," I said. I guess
my voice sounded stiff.

"Are you telling me?" she said. "I've just seen your respectable father and he's breaking Jakie Rosebaum's heart
because he hasn't got a score in his left-hand pocket. But I've
invited myself down to your house for the weekend—so just
run up the flag and be ready to pass me through Customs. I
understand you need a certified blue-blood test to get into
Blue Point."

"But, Carolina!" I said. "But Dad—is he coming down
with you?—But—"

She laughed her wonderful laugh over the phone.

"He thinks he's bringing me down tomorrow," she said,

"but he's not. I'm starting now, with Mother. We're just in from the Coast and we're covered with dust and yes-men and I'm aching for fresh air. I'm bringing the monkey, by the way. Get some anchovies for him, will you, darling? He loves anchovies—the sinister little thing."

"But Caro—" I said and she just said, "Kisses, darling," and rang off. And I went and held my head in my hands. Because it would be swell, of course, to see Carolina again, and she was more fun than anybody. But I didn't much want to see anybody. And what she'd do to Blue Point I couldn't think. And Father would hold me responsible, if she did. I thought of giving it all up and leaving for the South Seas right away. But that would have been cowardly.

She had the monkey on her shoulder when she got out of the car. And about 400-gauge stockings. And nineteen bags. And the kind of dress you don't see on anybody else. And she's older than Father and she can be as young as Bibs. And the servants nearly fell dead. And within five minutes we were all of us talking at the tops of our voices—Bibs and me and Carolina and her mother—and it seemed like old times.

Then we went for a swim at the Club and Uncle Lambert was there. And Carolina had her arm in mine when I introduced him to her and I could see in one brief glance that my reputation was gone, and probably Father's too. And I didn't care—I felt swell. Because it was like old times. I even forgot about Father and what I meant to do. When she's gay, she can make you forget anything except being gay.

And then we were back at the house and her mother was upstairs showing Bibs six new ways to do her hair—her mother's a grand old sport and Bibs always has been crazy about her—and Carolina was asking me what I'd been doing. She knew about my writing songs—she always had. And I felt so good that I started playing some of the numbers from *Sixth Form Follies* and she picked up the hot number and started to go to town with it and it really sounded keen—as keen as I'd hoped it would.

"Gee, that's grand, Carolina!" I said. "I mean the way you sing it."

"I'd be a fool if I couldn't sing it," she said. "It's a real blues. Has Jicky heard it? He ought to."

"Oh, gee, Carolina!" I said, and before I knew what I was doing, I was crying on her shoulder. I hadn't cried since I was eight and I felt terribly ashamed.

She didn't try to be motherly or anything like that. She just said, "That's okay, sport," and let me use her handkerchief. And then we talked. We talked a lot. I suppose she meant her mother to keep Bibs upstairs. She may have. But I don't care. She's a pretty wise woman. If I'd talked like that to anybody else, I'd have felt like crawling into a hole in the ground.

About in the middle she said, "I always told Jicky he was a raging idiot, but the man wouldn't listen to reason." And then we talked some more. And when we'd finished, she said, "Blue Point is right. Nobody could have named it more fitly. Now do you know what we're going to do?"

"No, Carolina," I said.

"I am going to have a highball," she said. "I need it. And you are going to sleep for half an hour on that couch. Now don't argue with Carolina."

Well, I wouldn't have believed it, but as soon as I lay down, I was off, and I slept for an hour. When I woke, it was time to dress for dinner and I felt a lot better. I suppose it does happen to you, that way, when you're tired.

Then we all went to the Waldens' party—Mrs. Walden was the old sea horse I'd heard talking in the movies, and her Saturday night suppers for young and old are one of the more gruesome features of Blue Point. I won't describe what Carolina did to that. She didn't have to do anything, really—she was just Carolina Clay. She wasn't a bit vo-do-de-do—she can do that too, when she wants, but she didn't want. She was sweet and she wore a little cotton dress, with her hair done straight at the sides. But before she'd been there ten minutes, Uncle Lambert was telling her the story of his life, and male and female alike were fighting to bring her lobster salad.

I don't know how she got the whole party maneuvered over to our house, when they asked her to sing. It was just one of the things she does. She started off with some old things, "Roses of Picardy" and "Poor Butterfly" and even "Swing Low, Sweet Chariot" for the old folks. Then she went into *Random Rose*—I was playing her accompaniments, of course. And just as she was in the middle of "Love's A Dangerous Thing," I looked up and saw Father in the doorway.

His face was whiter than I'd ever seen it and his eyes were frowning and he looked like a black-and-silver sword. But I wasn't afraid of him a bit—I wasn't afraid of him. I went on with the accompaniment and even put in a couple of tricks with my left hand.

She didn't give him time to protest—she didn't give him time to do anything. As soon as she'd finished the song, she said, "And now, nice people, we're lucky. Because there's one song in *Random Rose* that needs a man's voice—'Silver Stars.' And we've got the composer himself to play it for us.— All right, Jordan Blake."

Well, nobody could have helped himself when she spoke in that voice. Or almost nobody. But Father wasn't looking at her, queerly enough. He was looking at me—I'd swung round on my stool. And there was something funny in his face. It wasn't as if he were angry, even. It was almost as if he were frightened.

"Come on, Dad—please!" I said, and, for some reason, they all laughed and started to clap. I saw Father stiffen a little at the laughter. And then he walked over to the piano, like a man in a dream, and sat down.

He went through the first verse and chorus. It's an old song, as songs go, but they still make records of it. And, on the second verse, I felt Carolina poke me, and I joined in. My voice isn't anything much but I know that song.

He looked up at me while they were clapping.

"You didn't look at the music," he said.

"I don't have to," I said. "Not with your songs."

And then they were clapping and clapping and, all of a sudden, his fingers were easy on the keys. We did "Nice Pair of Eyes" and "Roaming the World" and Carolina did "My House in Yonkers" and all three of us did the trio from *Harum-Scarum*. Then Carolina made me do "Sixth Form Blues." I felt scared, doing it, but they seemed to like it all right. I looked at Father, in the middle. He didn't say anything, but his left hand was picking out the tune.

We could have kept them there all night if we'd wanted. But Carolina knows how to break up a party, too. They didn't know they were being broken up—they thought it was their own idea. And when the last of them were gone, Carolina turned to Father.

"You'll excuse me for borrowing your house, Jick," she said. "And Jerry and Bibs. But, at any rate, we showed Blue Point a real Bohemian revel." She glanced around at the room and the empty glasses. "And on nothing stronger than ginger ale and chicken sandwiches. It's a miracle."

"Blue Point flows with ginger ale," said Father. "It's about the only thing it does flow with. But I don't understand about the sandwiches. I didn't think it could be done."

"Oh, Mother went out and bullied those Mayflower descendants you have in the kitchen," said Carolina. "Mother can be a terrible bully when she likes."

"I've never dared," said Father. "They know I'm not a Cabot. It's something in my left eye. But I'm glad your Mother did. I hope it means they're leaving tomorrow," and he looked relieved.

"If they do," said Carolina, "Mother and I will cook up the famous *spaghetti a la Clay*, and we'll take the children on a beach picnic. We might do that anyway."

"We might," said Father. "Try and keep us from not."

"Shall we ask your brother Lambert?" said Carolina. "He's such a dear man. Such a sprite. He told me all about his liver and tried to hold my hand in the pantry."

"I guess there's no use trying to establish a good social position with you around," said Father, but he didn't seem to mind.

"The best authorities are agreed on that point," said Carolina. She turned to me. "Good night, Jerry," she said. "And thanks to you and Bibs for your charming hospitality. I've been trying to marry your father for eight or nine years now, but he doesn't seem to think I'd make a good stepmother. Maybe you could convince him. Or maybe I'll just turn around and marry Lambert. It must be wonderful to have a husband with a liver. So convenient when you run out of cornflakes."

Then she laughed her marvelous laugh and ran upstairs. "Good night, Toots, you maniac!" Father called after her, and his eyes were crinkly and amused. Then he turned and looked at me, and for a minute we didn't say anything.

"Carolina's kidding," he said finally. "You know that."

"I wouldn't mind if she wasn't," I said. "She's a grand girl."

"She is," he said. "We both knew your mother." He hesitated a second. "Let's go out in the garden," he said. "It's smoky in here."

We went out and walked up and down for a little while. It

wasn't hard, not saying anything, it was easy. Like not saying anything with any of your friends.

I was thinking about the drawings Carolina had shown me—the funny little drawings he sends instead of letters. He'd sent her these and they were funny, and not so funny. They were funny enough. But he thought we wanted another kind of father—somebody like Uncle Lambert or Mr. Parsons. And he thought we were right. And it was in the drawings. He'd wanted to see me graduate, but he'd thought he'd better stay away. Of course, that was cuckoo of him. But I could understand it, because I'd felt the same way about him. And then Carolina told me about the file in his office. That's a secret between us and I'll never tell him I know. But it's got everything in it from Bibs' first kindergarten work to that darn fool newspaper picture of me when I got the Raeburn Medal. I never thought he saved those things.

He gave me a cigarette and we both lit up.

"I've never told you much about your mother," he said. "You were young—and she wouldn't have wanted me to go in for the sob stuff. She had what she wanted, you see. She said she'd rather have children than live to be seventy—and she thought you and Bibs were swell. You can ask Carolina, if you like. But that was the last thing she said, 'Well, Jick, I've had what I wanted.' It made it hard to talk about." He stopped a minute. "I won't want you to think she was an angel," he said. "She had a temper like the Irish Free State and she never was on time in her life except in the theatre. And there wasn't anybody like her. It made it hard to talk about—even to Carolina, for a long time. You see, she wouldn't have wanted me to do the sob stuff."

"That's all right," I said. "I understand."

"Do you think Bibs does?" he said, and his voice wasn't like his ordinary one. "She was fond of Bibs."

"If she doesn't, I'll get it across to her," I said.

"I wish you would," he said. "Bibs is rather a problem to me."

"Oh, she's got her wheels in line," I said. "She has, honestly. She'll go a little haywire when she's eighteen and probably write a bum child-prodigy novel. And then she'll marry somebody who'll chase her around the house with a shotgun if she tries any tricks and have eight children and end up as a darn good Indian." And, funnily enough, I knew when I said it that that was going to be true.

"Well, that's some comfort for a worried parent," he said. "She used to scare me stiff when she was younger." I saw the end of his cigarette glow red. "In fact, you both did," he said. "I depended on your mother so much for all of that. You won't understand that till you're married. Well, I had to go on working, afterwards—it was the only thing I knew how to do."

"They were pretty expensive schools," I said.

"Why not?" he said. "Your mother and I used to say that the best was none too good for the Blakes. When we were heating bouillon cubes over a Sterno on the road," he made a little noise in his throat, "I got some things wrong," he said. "I ought to have known. But people keep telling you about the right environment for kids. Where did you pick up the piano?"

"I used to wake myself up at night after you'd gone out," I said. "And then there was a fellow at camp—you didn't say anything about camp."

I could feel him grin through the darkness though I couldn't see it.

"I learned from a cross-eyed German who played in a rathskeller," he said. "And Lambert told on me and I got the licking of my life. Your grandfather always liked Lambert. But *his* father lost a lot of honest Boston money, trying to manage an opera troupe in the Fifties. So that's three of us."

He chuckled and pulled on his cigarette again.

"Carolina said I was an idiot," he said. "And she was right. But I didn't want you to get into anything because of me. And when you're inside the game—well, it doesn't look the way it does from the outside. It's a tough game, you know. And sometimes you get thinking the other thing might be better. Till you try it. And then you know. It works both ways, of course. Do you really want to go to Harvard, by the way?"

"Uh-huh," I said. "I want harmony and counterpoint and all the theory I can get. And work on shows in the summer —the practical stuff. Lord, I haven't done anything yet!"

"We'll get Jakie down for a weekend," he said. "And you can listen in on the new one—you'll be a help. I want to do a real light opera and he tells me I can't, but we'll show him. I'm sick of just working for hit numbers and ringing the same old changes. And I want to have him hear your blues. There's one spot in it that's a little tricky—you've got to allow for the singer, now and then. But the rest goes right to town. I can show the spot, tomorrow, with Carolina. And we'll go through the whole score. Okey, son?"

"Okey-doke," I said.

GOOD PICKER

I WONDER what sound they listen for now at night, in the small towns sunk in the wheat of the mid-continent—the young and ambitious, the ones who mean to get away? The drone of the mail plane, I suppose; and that must be different. In our day, it was the long, shaking whistle of the Limited—it didn't even stop for water at Sapepas then. Tom Allin taught us to listen for it, I think—I don't know about Edie Foster, for Edie was always independent. But I was content enough with Sapepas till he came. Oh, I meant to be a doctor, like my father, but that was because I liked my father. I daresay I'd have made a passable one, and not killed more than the average number of patients. But Tom Allin changed all that.

We heard there was a new boy in town—a boy with city clothes and a stickpin—and we wondered what Butch Malone would do to him. It didn't take long to find out—Butch cornered him in the Townsend lot, the first day, after school. We'd all trailed along to see the licking, and I trailed with the rest. I'd rather liked the neat, cheerful looks of the stranger, and he'd caught Bud White on the ear with a perfectly timed spitball while Old Watson's back was turned, so he obviously wasn't a sissy, in spite of his city clothes. But that didn't make any difference—it doesn't, in boydom. He was a stranger and Butch would lick him—you could tell that from their sizes. And if he ran, we'd all of us chase him home. I admit that for a single moment, when they faced

each other, there was something in his face that made me
wonder if he mightn't lick Butch—an odd, interested quality
that had nothing to do with rage or fear. But things do not
happen that way, except in books. Butch knocked him down
twice and rubbed his face in the dirt, while the rest of us
danced and jeered. It was very easy—so easy that when he got
up for a third time, Butch stood back and waited, con-
temptuously, for him to run. But he didn't run. He shook his
head for a moment and stopped crying. Then he said to
Butch in a perfectly friendly, rather superior voice, "You
fight all right, but you don't put your weight behind it. You
ought to get your weight behind it, see—like this." And he
turned from Butch and delivered a blow at the air, while the
rest of us gaped. He was obviously mad, and we waited for
Butch to abolish him. But instead he advanced toward Butch.
"Put your right foot back. Now hit me in the stummick,"
and he dropped his hands to his sides.

"Aw, say—" said Butch, perplexed, while the rest of us
waited, astounded.

"Hit me in the stummick," said the stranger, with a pleasant smile. "Right here"—and Butch did. This time there
could be no doubt of the weight behind it, for the blow sent
the stranger spinning. But, after a moment, he rose again.
He was, obviously, in difficulties with his breath, but his
voice was quite clear.

"That's better," he said. "Now try it again. You're learning."

Butch's face became very red and again we jeered—but not
at the stranger now. Butch drew back his fist and let it sink
again. He looked around the ring desperately. But our faces
gave him no comfort.

"Aw, run along home, bub, and tell your mother she
wants you. I don't fight babies," he said in a weak, uncon-
vincing voice, and the rest of us knew, from that moment,

that we had a new leader. After that, whenever a new boy
came to town, it was still Butch Malone who fought him.
But that, as we explained to the new boy, was because Tom
Allin knew too much about fighting. We couldn't ring Tom
Allin in on a new boy—it wouldn't be fair.

He was our own man of destiny, and we recognized it from
the first. There were questions enough about the futures of
many of us, but never about Tom Allin's. He was never the
best or the worst at games, but the games themselves were
better because he was there. There is the strength of earth
and the strength of fire. And then there is the strength of
water—and that was something like Tom's—running water,
finding its way with a resistless, laughing motion to the place
where it wishes to be. He wasn't a particularly good-looking
boy, as looks are measured. But you liked his looks, you liked
their quickness and tidiness and the very blue, candid eyes
that looked at the world with a complete interest. I can never
remember seeing Tom Allin bored—if he started being bored
with a game, he changed it or went away. He wouldn't suffer
boredom. And with the world of grown people, where most
of us stumbled and fumbled, he was completely at home.
We would have resented that in another—we didn't, in Tom.
He had none of the "good boy's" tricks and it was obvious
that he did it without effort. Every employer he ever had—
and he must have had a dozen or so when he was a boy in
Sapepas—was glad to have him work for him and sorry to
see him go.

And then there was his background and his family. We
like to think of our Lincolns coming up from shiftlessness,
our Grants from the tanyard. The only son of a brilliant
drunken lawyer, to whom Sapepas was the last step on his
long road downhill, and a vague, large, flustered woman with
as little personality as her favorite rocking chair, he shone
by contrast and character against his mother's triviality and

his father's bitter defeat. It made us all feel better, to think of his coming from that. A little as if we'd done it ourselves, as if we were responsible for his charm.

Of course there were dissenters—there are always dissenters. There were those who pointed to his father and muttered about what was bred in the bone being sure to come out in the flesh. And there were one or two, like old Mrs. Witchett, who shook their heads and murmured darkly that that Allin boy was too clever by half. But such comments only lent a tang to the way the rest of us felt. There is no fun in believing unless there are unbelievers, too. It puzzled and distressed me not a little to find my father—well, not exactly an unbeliever, but unconvinced. There was one time in high school, when Tom got interested in medicine and asked my father questions whenever he had a chance. He talked about being a doctor eagerly and convincingly—he made it seem a glamorous profession, even to me who knew about the long drives in the battered buggy and the pile of unpaid bills. And my father was polite enough, answering, but there was never the rare warmth in his voice which came when he talked to a red-wristed country boy like Ed Freed. I could see Tom, in a spotless robe, performing delicate operations—I couldn't see Ed Freed doing anything more exciting than delivering a calving cow.

I said something of the sort to my father once and he grunted. "Yuh," he said. "Well, there's calves I wouldn't want to deliver—they got more legs than babies. But I reckon Freed could do it. He can carry eggs in those hands of his— ever notice? Of course there's a lot of folks that don't know how to do anything but operate. Oh, sure, I reckon your friend could make a doctor." He smoked a moment. "City doctor," he said. "Still, it was him brought Ed Freed around here. I won't forget that."

I didn't quite understand him, but I was glad, on the whole, when Tom stopped collecting medical knowledge and started getting us all interested in amateur theatricals in Edie Foster's barn. You know her as Edith Edmands, if you've ever been to a theater—they've called her "the American Duse" once or twice. But we knew a stringy, freckled little girl with stuck-up manners and very black eyebrows. The Fosters were the richest people in town, but we'd all rather made fun of Edie till Tom decided she was somebody to be cultivated. And then we flocked after him like sheep.

Yes, I've seen him rehearse Edith Edmands—and I've seen her cry and stamp, at fifteen, when he made her play the villainess instead of the beautiful heroine. But he knew what he was doing, and she played it uncomfortably well. We didn't know it was genius—we thought of them as Tom's plays, not hers. And yet, he wasn't an actor. But, with his boundless enthusiasm, he dragooned and drilled the rest of us into an interest, whether we felt it or not. When Edith Edmands made her first success in New York, the critics were surprised at her range, but I wasn't surprised, remembering the plays we'd given. The Fosters were really pathetically grateful to him—they'd worried a good deal about Edie's not being part of "the crowd." After that, we all thought of Tom and Edie as "going together," and the girls thought Edie lucky. "Humph, s'pose Foster'll take him into the bank now," said my father. But Mr. Foster didn't. He was known at the State University, however, and Tom applied for the Kennedy Scholarship and won it. I know, because I was second—they took appearance and character into consideration as well as marks.

It seemed just and right he should win it, and I felt no jealousy. No jealousy indeed, rather gratitude—wasn't I his best friend and hadn't he called me "Old Persistence" from the first? It is odd what a nickname may do to you when it's given by somebody you admire. I can't remember being particularly persistent as a boy. But if Tom said I was, I must be so, and I tried to live up to the character. And then, halfway through my junior year, when my father died, I discovered I really had it—the power of hanging on. Tom was gone by that time, and I couldn't thank him, but the discovery accounts for any success I have had.

I asked Tom why he called me that, once—and he looked at me in the puzzled way he sometimes had. "Oh, you just look that way," he said. An odd interest woke in his eyes. "You look like a beaver," he said. "You look as if you ought to build dams." I didn't know whether to be insulted or pleased—even my parents didn't know, then, that I'd given up the idea of doctoring and was hanging around the men who were building the new county bridge. "Sounds interesting," said Tom, and I took him down there, very pleased at being able to show him something for once. But it was he who introduced me to the engineer in charge of construction —the best friend I'd made myself was only a gang foreman. We spent most of our time there for three weeks, and it was a turning point in my life. After that, Tom went less than I did and finally stopped going, but the engineer was used to me by then.

Tom and I talked a good deal after that about all that was going to happen when I was a great engineer and Edie was a great actress and he was great. And yet, he was curiously uncommunicative about his own ambitions. But we were vocal enough for him. You had only to look at him and know. I remember Mrs. Allin's saying to me once, in her vague voice, "Tom says you're going to make a name, Harry. So you mustn't disappoint him." It was probably her idea of humor, but my ears reddened.

"Oh, Tom," I said. "Well, you know Tom. Tom's about the finest fellow there is."

"Yes, Tommy's very clever," said Mrs. Allin placidly.

"Even Mr. Allin says so—and Mr. Allin should know. He's never given me the slightest trouble, either," she went on, with almost a sigh. "Even when he was a little boy, people took to him. They'd want to give him candy and things, but after he got sick once, he was very sensible about that. And he always played with the nicest children in the neighborhood—he seemed to know just where they'd be. Mr. Allin says he's a changeling, when he's not feeling well, but I'm sure I don't know what he means," and she sighed again.

But I thought I knew what Tom's father meant, and felt proud of my friend. There was, indeed, a changeling quality to Tom—he played in the mud of boyhood with the rest of us, but the mud never seemed to stick to him. He shook it off as he shook off anything that had ceased to interest him—without rancor and with the most amiable of smiles.

I didn't see as much of him at State as I'd have liked, for I transferred to the engineering side as soon as I got oriented. But I heard about him, as we all did. Freshman year he went out for track and would have been elected freshman captain if he hadn't pulled a tendon just before the big meet. As it was, he only missed out for freshman-class president by half a dozen votes and was automatically taken into the best fraternity. Sophomore year, the tendon still gave him trouble, but he was out in a track suit during the season and the coach spoke of him as a fine example of State spirit. We won all our meets that year, and, somehow or other, most of the college felt that a good deal of the credit was due to Tom. And though he wasn't given the Ribblesdale Essay prize, we all knew that was more of a victory than a defeat, for the barbarian from the Great Lakes who carried it off went around swearing Tom Allin must have written the better paper.

I was delighted to see him on the train going down to Sapepas, and we planned things for the summer that he and

Edie Foster and I were going to do. And then we got home and discovered that Edie Foster had run away the previous night with the leading juvenile of a cheap stock company that played a week in Sapepas. His name was Edmands and he was forty years old, with a removable bridge. We all thought Tom behaved very well about it; there never had been any official engagement between himself and Edie, but the Fosters had come to treat him more and more like a son. All he said to me was, "I hope he doesn't let her play things like Camille too soon. She needs a lot of comedy first." I thought it a profound and subtle cry from a wounded heart at the time. But he had that queer, interested look on his face, and I think now he meant exactly what he said.

He was admirable, however, in arranging a technical reconciliation by letter between Edie and her parents, and in cheering the latter up about the whole matter. George Allin died while Tom was in Europe with them; they had always meant to take Edie one of these days, but now they took Tom instead. And when they got back, they sent him to Yale for his last two years. It is difficult for an outsider to come into a class as late as junior year, but Tom succeeded in it perfectly. I have met some of his classmates since. They all speak of him as one of the class leaders, though he did not go out for track. In fact, it is a little difficult to find out from them what he did do, except acquiesce in being elected to various committees and a senior society. One man told me he had done a great deal with the dramatic association, but I looked in his class book and the only role listed for Tom is that of Owen Glendower in *Henry IV*. I'm sure Tom made an excellent Glendower, but it is a small part.

I had spent the four years at State in a daze of work and I was fairly excited about my own future. But when I saw Tom, the last summer I was ever to spend in Sapepas, the old charm returned and my own future seemed small beside his. He had come from visiting friends in the East and brought a classmate with him—a terrifyingly well-tailored young man named John Cowenden, with shy, spectacled, amiable eyes. He was obviously dazzled by Tom and extremely polite to Mrs. Allin and the Fosters. I gathered that he was a young man of great wealth and extremely rigid upbringing who had done very few enjoyable things in his life. There was a sister, too—Tom showed me her picture—a sweet, unformed face, scared and burdened by family and wealth.

I will say for Tom that he treated the whole visit with utter honesty. John Cowenden stayed in the dingy house where Tom's father had died cursing life and the Republican Party with his bitter tongue; they saw the feed store and the drugstore where Tom had clerked and the raw frame schoolhouse where he had gone to school. And all of it excited and enthralled John Cowenden; you could see him thinking of Lincoln and Grant and the rest. There wasn't a thing Tom did, from his behavior to the Fosters to his behavior to his friend, that wasn't right and admirable. And yet, somehow, I knew there was something wrong.

I knew there was something wrong, because I had grown up, in those four years. Indeed, Tom put his hand on my shoulder and said with his light laugh, "You've changed a lot, Old Persistence. You used to be quite a responsibility. But you're going to astonish them now." The compliment did not please me and I asked him what he was going to do. He frowned a little.

"Oh, John, here, wants me to go in with his father," he said. "The chump thinks I'm cut out for a captain of industry."

"Well, you know perfectly well what father thinks," said John, his shy face eager. He turned to me. "I tell you," he said, "Father isn't impressed by many people. Tom's the only one of my friends who— Oh, shut up, Tom, you know it's true. Tom's worried because he thinks he'll be given special treatment, but I tell him—"

"A nice little sinecure in a good climate," said Tom with a grin. "That's what I really want."

They went on talking and I listened. Presently the name of the sister came in. "She's a nice kid, Lisa," said John with more affection than the words showed. "But, Lord, Tom, I wish you'd talk to Father about her. He's dead set on sticking her in that deadly Swiss school my other sister hated so, and she's too scared to stand up to him."

"She ought to have a year in Europe sometime," said Tom judicially. "But not in a school—and afterward." I saw interest in his eyes.

"Well, she's such a nice kid," said John, helplessly. "And you know Father."

"She's more than a nice kid," said Tom slowly. "There's something about her—well, she could be quite a remarkable person if she had the chance."

"Gosh, Tom, do you really think so?" said John eagerly. "Of course I've always thought she was pretty swell, but—"

Tom was looking at neither of us. He was looking at a distance. He was thinking.

"The way she does her hair," he said. "I mean probably she's been told to do it that way. Or the maid. But for her kind of face—"

Then I knew what was going to happen and I felt a little sick. So it had all been for that. The charm and the interest in others, the self-deprecating modesty and the candid blue eyes. I could see, in a sudden flash, like a flash of lightning, the whole history of his rise. Now it would reach apotheosis —in a little while he wouldn't even have to pretend to be a great man any more.

I muttered something and went away from the porch. Tom waved cheerfully after me, "So long, Old Persistence; see you tomorrow," but I knew it was goodbye. And it was, as a matter of fact, for the firm I was hoping would take me telegraphed me from Chicago that evening.

When I got Tom's wedding invitation, a year later on the top of a South American mountain, there was a line scrawled at the bottom, "Good luck, O.P.! I wanted you for best man!" I stared at the stiff, expensive paper dully and dropped it into the fire. It's hard to lose an ideal when you're young.

After that, there were many years and a lot of work. I kept track of Edie Foster from the papers and Sapepas through Mother's letters; but whenever I came to Tom Allin's name in her letters, I would skip. But I couldn't have skipped as much as I intended, for I gathered that Tom's mother had not long survived her husband—and that was Tom's luck again, I thought bitterly and unfairly, for it severed his last link with his past. The Fosters moved to California shortly after his marriage; they might, having served his turn. And once, in a society column, I saw that Mr. and Mrs. Thomas Allin were opening their house in Paris. But I do not usually read society columns and that item confirmed my distaste.

It wasn't till just before the First World War that I ran across his trace again—in London, oddly enough. It may be immodest to say so, but I had become something of a success by then. At least enough of a one to be given medals and asked about. It isn't always the best engineers who get the medals, as I know well enough. However, that sort of thing can be pleasant, after years in the corners of the world, and I enjoyed it sufficiently. Ronny Frazier-Spykes was more or less my guide and mentor, and a very able one he proved. He told me that one of the people I must meet in London was Mrs. Harley Dunn.

"Extr'or'n'ry woman," he said, in that rather bleating voice that made you think him a fool till you'd been in a tight place with him. "Beautiful in a way of her own—pots of money—everybody goes there. Paints dashed well, too, I believe, for an amateur. American, of course—most of our best hostesses are. And jolly good for old Harley, too, if not quite what the family ordered. Oh, no stain on her character, but divorced, and the Dunns were always strait-laced. First husband an extr'or'n'ry chap, for that matter—chap named Allin."

"Allen?" I said, with a queer tightness in my throat.

"With an *i*," said Ronny. "Allin. Unusual name. Most delightful chap from all accounts, but would run off with a snake charmer. Or that's the story. Anyhow, she had to divorce him; hadn't even met Harley then."

He ran on, but I was thinking. And when I did meet Mrs. Dunn, I thought even more. She was, indeed, beautiful; I wouldn't have recognized her from the picture I once saw in Tom's hand. And when she summoned me to tea with her, to talk about Tom Allin—Ronny must have babbled— it was the nearest thing to a royal command I have known.

I didn't mean to be confidential, but she had the art of the hostess, the art that puts you at your ease. I began to speak of the early days and Sapepas, and every now and then she would say, "Yes, that's so like Tom." Then she, too, began to talk, and the story was not what I had expected. She spoke of Tom without rancor, indeed with a good deal of affection, and yet with an odd detachment. A seed might speak that way of the wind that carried it to other soil.

"Oh, I'll always be very grateful," she said. "And yet, sometimes, I feel as if it never had really happened—being married to Tom, I mean. And yet, here I am, and if I hadn't met him I'd still be in New York, being Father's dutiful daughter and scared to death. He made a person out of me—I couldn't even do my hair properly or say three words to a stranger without looking frozen. And yet—well, he was—"

"A changeling?" I suggested.

She stared at me. "How did you know? But of course you know. He was delightful and fascinating, and I never really felt married to him, even at first." She laughed a little. "When we got to Paris," she said, "he made me throw away all the clothes I'd ever had. That was after our first year—his one year with the company. He'd made a brilliant record, too—even Father said so. But he was tired of it—he said he wanted to write. So we went to Paris. He bought all my new clothes for a year, teaching me—then I knew how." She looked at me very simply and directly. "It wasn't the money, you know," she said. "It never was that. I thought you'd like to know."

"I'm very glad to know," I said.

"No," she said, "it was never the money. Oh, he liked not having to worry about it—he'd worried a good deal as a boy. And buying things, sometimes. But the pictures were Matisses—even Father's beginning to admit they were an investment." She laughed a little again. "I don't love him at all," she said. "I don't think I ever loved him. And he hurt my pride when he—left. But I've no complaints." She smiled deeply. "I'd never have met Harley, in New York," she said. "He thinks we would, but we wouldn't. Or he'd never have seen me, behind Father and Brother John."

I went back to something else, wondering. "You said Tom Allin wrote?"

Her eyes were mischievous. "A dozen poems and three stories, in three years," she said. "And they never were published anywhere. But that was how we met Gide and Proust and Shaw. I wrote him one letter, before I married Harley. Oh, just to say I didn't feel hurt any longer—and, well, perhaps to tell him how happy I was. After all, I'm a woman." She smiled. "And I got a scribble back from him, on café paper from some place in Belgium. Just saying, 'Be sure to

have one white living room. It suits you.' Well, as a matter
of fact, when we did over the house—"

She paused. "And I haven't heard since," she said. "I
don't know at all. But there's just one thing," and, for the
first time, she seemed embarrassed. "If you should hear—
and there ever were a question of money—well, I feel a very
real debt, and Harley would understand."

We left it at that, and a few weeks later, when I was in
Paris, I attempted to find some trace of Tom. It was all true,
even to the snake charmer, though that lady I was, perhaps
fortunately, unable to find. He had kept an extraordinary
salon during his last year as Lisa Cowenden's husband. Then
the path became a darker one. The snake charmer, apparently,
had not been good for him. He had not stayed with her long
and had gone on to worse things. I did not write about them
to Mrs. Dunn, but I heard quite enough.

I felt sorry and yet relieved—sorry for the completeness
of the downfall, and yet relieved, in a queer way, to find that
it hadn't been the money he wanted, after all. I could bear
to think of him much more easily as a wastrel than a mere
adventurer. I tried very hard to trace him, thinking I might
do something, but the trail ran into a dead end—I could not
even find whether he had returned to America or not. And
then the war came and blotted many things out, but every
now and then I would think of him, even through the war.

And when I met Edie Foster again, in New York, in the
jumpy '30's, we commiserated together and shook our heads
wisely. She, too, had tried to trace him at one point and met
with no success. I had to stay in New York that winter and
we became excellent friends. And every now and then we
would talk of Tom Allin, his charm and his promise and
his boyhood and how sad it all was.

"If I'd only been able to marry him," said Edie rather
solemnly one day, "I might have saved him. But—well, Joe

Edmands was a rascal—but, somehow, even when Tom kissed me, it didn't seem quite real. He was a changeling, Harry. His wife was right about that."

"Oh, I'm the person that ought to have stuck by him," I said. "I was his oldest friend. I ought to have taken him by the scruff of his neck and—only, how could you, with Tom? But I hate to think of him going the way his father went."

Then we talked very wisely of heredity and environment and failure and success—we were both successes, and I'm afraid we knew it. And as we buried Tom, we praised him, as old friends will. So it was a very decided shock when my secretary came in the next day with the news that a Mr. Thomas Allin wanted to see me. For one second I felt as if she had announced a ghost. And for a long moment, with the cowardice of middle age, I thought of what I would probably see.

I wouldn't like smelling the smell of old, persistent drink and looking at the soiled cuffs on his shirt and giving him ten dollars. I wouldn't like warning Edie and telling the switchboard girl that I was out if a Mr. Allin called. I could take him out and feed him, but it was after three and the banks were closed. I wondered if there was cash enough in the office safe to buy a man a ticket to Sapepas—it was quite a long way. I'd been going to the third night of Edie's new play, but I'd have to put him on the train instead; if you didn't put them on the train, they turned back their tickets and phoned you later from bars. Still, it had to be got through with. I braced myself and told the secretary to show Mr. Allin in.

He was balder than I, but he looked younger—that was the first thing that struck me. And the eyes had not aged at all. They were precisely the same; blue, candid, clear, and interested. His clothes were not New York clothes, but he wore them with an air. There was no smell of drink and his hands were tanned, steady, and healthy. Then I found myself shaking hands and clapping him on the back and opening my private box of cigars. He seemed genuinely pleased to see me, but not nearly so stirred as I.

"Well, Old Persistence," he said, with his light smile. Then he walked over and looked at a framed photograph on my wall. "The Nyanza locks, aren't they?" he said. . . . "From the West Bank? . . . Thought so. 'The greatest piece of engineering since the Panama Canal.' Well, I'm glad an American could do it. Remember when I told you you looked like a beaver?"

We sat up very late at Edie Foster's house on the East River that night—we sat till the dawn came. I think we were all a little drunk, though not with liquor—with the magic of Tom Allin. We revived our childhood, we told silly stories, we unpacked the load of the years. And always Tom Allin led us and drew us on. Only then—it must have been three o'clock and Edie had just finished the incredible, libelous, and excruciatingly funny story of her South American tour— she suddenly said, "Stop! Yes, I want to hear about the Nyanza locks, Harry—you've always frozen up when I tried to dig it out of you before. And I want to tell—oh, there's everything I want to tell. But there's something I want to know first, and it's you, Tom Allin! How are you, where are you, what are you doing, who are you?"

Her voice rang with its full stage timbre—the timbre that sends little waves through her audiences.

"Oh, there's nothing to say," said Tom Allin. "Except that"—and he raised his glass ever so slightly to both of us, with a sudden and boyish grin—"I was a good picker, wasn't I? Yes, I've been that."

"There was a proverb my father used to quote," he said. " 'Unstable as water, thou shalt not excel.' He meant it for me." There were lines in his face for a moment and he looked much older; then the lines smoothed back. "And he was right," said Tom Allin. "And I knew it. I knew it from the time I was five. We moved quite a lot, you see, and I always did well at the new thing, for a while. Well, any child likes doing well. But the minute I did anything too long—" He shook his head.

"And yet, people kept expecting things of me," he said. "And that fools you sometimes. Especially if you're a child and they're older people—you feel they should know. It's a pressure. And then you find out they're eager to take you at face value if you'll only let them, and it isn't hard to do. I don't know just when it was that I first realized the truth. That I was—well, a pace-maker, if you want to call it that. That I wasn't for the long pull. You thought I was joking, Harry, when we sat on the porch with John Cowenden and I said that what I wanted was a sinecure in a good climate. But I wasn't. You see, I love life," he said. Something burned in his eyes.

"I love life," he repeated in a lower voice. "Most people just love a part of it—you have to love a part of it more than anything else if you want to be a great man. But I never could. There was always something around the corner, something I hadn't tried. And then, the people—good Lord! The people you can just give a little push to, here and there! I don't think I ever really hurt anybody—except Lisa, perhaps. I feel badly about Lisa."

I thought of Mrs. Harley Dunn, her house, her position, her securities. They were secure then. They are still secure, though the house was bombed last fall. "You needn't," I said. "I told you this afternoon."

"Yes," he said. "You didn't see the drawing room? I hope she used a good deal of crystal with the white. Oh, it's not quite true what I'm saying. You couldn't help wanting to rescue her—not after you'd seen her father and the house. But at the back of my mind, I suppose I did mean to live on the Cowenden money. Only, when it came to the point in the end—well, I couldn't. If there'd been anything more to do—but there wasn't. She was completed, by then—she was a person." His fingers had the unconscious gesture of a sculptor shaping clay.

"And then—" I prompted.

"Oh, then," he said, and turned his clear eyes on the two of us. "Then I tried the other thing. I thought that might be really what I was meant for."

"Oh, you poor kid," said Edith Edmands, on a deep note. "Was it very bad?"

"No. That was the bad thing," said Tom Allin. "It didn't touch me really, even the drugs. They say the drugs will, but they didn't. I didn't like them enough. I was in a Belgian jail for a year—oh, quite roughly. Not my own name, no. But it wasn't a pleasant jail. And that scared me."

I looked at him—it was impossible that he should have been in jail; he bore no marks of it. I thought of water again —water that cleanses itself every so and so many feet, according to the old wives' tale.

"No," he said, "I don't look like a jailbird. But it scared me. You see, there were other people there. And one day I realized that I was organizing a prison break. And that scared me. It wasn't a bad plan," he said reflectively. "I'd have to draw you a map of the prison to show you, but it could have worked. It could have worked, or they could have been shot by the guards. Stupid, pliable, ordinary small thieves and swindlers. And if they'd been shot, I'd have shot them. Just as if I'd taken a machine gun. They thought I'd sold them out, of course, when I stopped it. I never stopped anything before—it was hard to do. And it gave me a bad time afterward. But it taught me something."

He drew a long breath. "That's when I resigned," he said.

"They wanted me to go to an officers' camp, in the war." He laughed, with the only bitterness I'd ever heard in his voice. "Can you see me leading troops—after the first days? If there didn't happen to be a lucky bullet— No, I've resigned."

"I was asking you where, what, and why," said Edith Edmands stubbornly. "I think you're ridiculous. How ought I to take that speech with Gerald at the end of the first act?"

"If you took it about three beats slower," said Tom Allin automatically, "and turned—let's see—well, this is the fireplace—no, Edie, hands like this—"

"You see?" said Edith Edmands, turning to me. "And I pay a director—or Wallace pays him. We pay a director large sums. I don't know what you're doing, Tom Allin. I know what I could give you to do."

I merely said, "Fen dubs. We're starting the Colorado job next month. I want somebody to handle people, on certain angles. I don't care if he doesn't know an I-beam from a fishplate. I'll outbid you if I have to, Edie—the job's worth it."

He looked at us both and said, "I can't thank you. But, Edie, how long would it be before I spent all my time teaching the fellow who played the butler to play the perfect butler? And, Harry, how long would it be before I found a young botanist in one of your work crews and wanted to make another Linnaeus out of him? Now, there are two things I've never worked at—botany and butling," he said, and his eyes narrowed. "They must be interesting. Tennis, too—I've never tried tennis.

"And then," he said, "you see, there's Minna and the children." He looked at our stunned faces and a little wrinkle came in his forehead. "Don't tell me!" he said. "I thought I had. But I was so glad to see you two again. We were married ten years ago. We have three children—two girls and a boy."

He drew the picture from his wallet and we looked at it in silence—the picture of the plump, square matron in the bungalow apron, in front of the little house, and the three healthy, solid children, looking quite like Tom in a way, and yet not like Tom. The boy's looks were the closest, and yet different. A sudden and very charming smile broke over Tom Allin's face.

"You see," he said quite gently, "she doesn't think I'm remarkable or fascinating or born to be great. She thinks I'm rather incapable, but she's fond of me—Lord knows why. She knows I was married before, but she thinks it was somebody like a waitress. It took her a long time to decide to marry me, after she found I'd been divorced. She doesn't believe in divorce. When I came to New York this time, she warned me against playing cards with strangers on the bus."

"But what do you do?" said Edie helplessly. "What do you do?"

"We run a gas station and restaurant," said Tom Allin. "We're well thought of in the town—it's about as big as Sapepas—I won't tell you the name. Much the same kind of country, too—I like that kind of country, you know. The second year was the bad time—I wanted to sell out then, but Minna wouldn't have it. I'm glad she wouldn't—they're the two businesses where you're always meeting people, but never see them long. Though we have a good, steady, regular trade. And every year Minna makes me take two weeks' vacation by myself. They're supposed to be business trips, but we both know they aren't. Last year I went to New Orleans—there's a painter down there you may hear of sometime—I just happened to run into him and we had some interesting talks. I'm afraid I told him I was a research chemist—I always thought chemists must lead interesting lives. Still, a week is hardly enough to injure anybody. This year I came to New York to look up spiritualists and mediums. You'd be surprised at the number of practicing ones there are. But they're rather dull as a class—duller than I expected. And when I found that you both were here—well, I couldn't miss seeing you, the last day."

He stopped and looked at us both.

"It was my last chance," he said. "Minna always expects me to bring her a present from my trips, though I've never quite succeeded yet in getting just the present she wants. So tomorrow, or, rather, today, I'll have to shop. The children won't mind what I bring them. Not one of them, even the youngest, shows the slightest trace of precocity, thank God!"

All the same, he stayed with us till dawn. I'd have seen him to his cheap hotel, but he asked me not to. And there was nothing I could give him; least of all, money. When he left me, he was the same, with his candid blue eyes unruffled; and I noticed again that his face was younger than mine.

And then, for a long while, I wondered if any of it was true. But I know now. For I picked up the paper the other day and read a long article on the sports page about the new prodigy in Middle Western tennis. Ned Marlow is only sixteen, but apparently he'll burn up the tournaments when he comes East. The article mentioned the fact that he hadn't started as a prodigy—in fact, a garage keeper in a small Middle Western town where he had lived for a while had taught him his first strokes. It didn't give his name, but it gave the name of the town. So I'm wondering about something else now—about a boy named Allin. He must be pretty well grown, by now, and I wonder what Tom's taught him. Maybe nothing —I wouldn't know. But he had Tom in his face, and yet there was a difference, a stability. I wonder what sound he listens for at night in the small town sunk in the wheat.

THE PRODIGAL CHILDREN

 *T*н е ʏ had been together a great many times, on a great many beaches, in a great many restaurants, looking out over the water. The restaurants had been called by various names in various languages; they had had orchestras and dance bands and juke boxes and a little man who played a guitar and a girl who played an accordion. They had been full of sailors in berets and Futurist painters, also in berets, and women in evening dress and women with monocles and women in slacks, and men in tail coats and women also in tail coats, and men with their bare feet stuck in *espadrilles*. This one was called Mrs. Sims' Clam House and, except for two tanned children solemnly eating strawberry ice cream at the counter, it was entirely empty when they came in.

They moved to the small corner table overlooking the water and sat down. The table was supposed to seat four, but they pulled up the clean hard chairs and made it do for seven. They never minded things like that; they had done them many times. They were not particularly demanding; they merely wanted the best, and the new place was always the best. After a while, it got spoiled and they left and found another place. They left while the crowds were still coming and before the receivers came. But only the local people and a few summer colonists yet came to Mrs. Sims' Clam House. It was as new a place as that.

"It's frantic," said Jinny Crick, taking off her sunglasses and slipping them into the special compartment in the special handbag. "Look at the boats. It's heavenly. Isn't it frantic?"

"It's a nice little place," said Beth Blake, in her rich voice. "We think it's a nice little place." She looked at the waitress. "Good evening, Pearl," she said pleasantly. "Fish chowder, crab buns and the salad for all of us." She smiled. "I won't let them have anything else," she said, "even if they cry and scream for it. They mustn't have another thing."

"Well, that's all right, I guess, Mrs. Blake," said the waitress in a small, indomitable voice. "Tea, coffee or milk?"

"Black coffee, very hot, in very thick china cups," said the small man unexpectedly and deeply. His name was Harry Crandall and, though he had flown from the Coast two days before, the noise of the airplane was not quite out of his head. "But they must be thick china—dinner china," he added anxiously, peering at the waitress.

"I guess we got them thick enough, if that's what you want," said the waitress.

"Splendid," said Harry Crandall. "And that is just what I want." He looked around the small new place. "Thank God, there aren't any curtains," he said. "I was afraid of red-checked ones. And matches that look like little sailors. But it isn't. No offense meant to the Navy," he added to the blond young man in ensign's uniform on the other side of Jinny Crick, "but I just don't happen to like matches that look like little sailors."

"You want some matches?" said the waitress.

"No, thank you," said Harry Crandall abstractedly, "I want no matches. I match no want ads. I just keep rolling along." He smiled secretly.

"How was the Coast?" said Jinny Crick. "Did you see Jimmy and Mike?"

"No," said Harry Crandall. "Jimmy's in the Signal Corps. And Mike was out at Palm Springs, rewriting the story line for Little Dorrit. It's going to be Colossal's new contribution to Anglo-American friendship. They've changed it a little, of course. Little Dorrit is a waif brought up in the Romney Marsh and she takes a fishing trawler over to Dunkirk. If you can believe Mike over the telephone. As a matter of fact, it will probably turn out to be a good picture. Mike has a knack."

"A knack and a promise," said Beth Blake. "A knack in his engine. How's the newest bride?"

"She's the best society of Cedarhurst," said Harry Crandall. "But I like Mike. I always did."

"We all love Mike," said Jinny Crick. "It's just the brides and the clothes that get us down. The last time I saw him he had on a shirt with pores in it. But I suppose that's the Coast."

The ensign, who had been trying to follow these remarks, turning his head politely toward each speaker in turn, now addressed Harry Crandall.

"Were you out there making a picture yourself, sir?" he said respectfully.

"No," said Harry Crandall. "This was a radio show. Propaganda." He bit off the word.

"It must have been very good stuff, sir," said the ensign, again respectfully, and attacked his chowder. The red-haired girl sitting opposite him tried to smile at him, but could not catch his eye. Poor Tom—it was all her fault and she had let him in for it. But his train went at 9:38 and there wouldn't be much longer now. All the same, she was glad that he had seen these people, and seen them as they were. It would make things so much easier to explain later on. Though older people were always hard to explain.

She sat in a little pool of silence, quite contented to be opposite Tom, while around her the swift talk flowed—the casual conversation, full of names and jokes, jumping gaps to the next new thing—the patter and the lingo. She had been brought up on it, she had been brought up on them all. It went back to French sands and the rocking sleep on trains and liners, and all the wonderful people coming in through the garden for cocktails, sitting out on the terrace and talking, coming up the stairs to the studio and making a pleasant noise—Aunt Beth and Uncle Charlie and the nice man they all called Monkey and all the others. At one time, many years ago—nearly five years ago, when she was only fifteen—she had thought them the most wonderful people in the world. Then Mummy and Daddy had finally broken up and, since then, she had been away a great deal at schools and camps and colleges. So since then she hadn't really seen very much of them, though she had dutifully read their books and seen their plays and their paintings and their pictures in magazines—even boasted of them, now and then, at new schools, when you had to boast of something. And they had remembered birthdays and graduations and vacations—remembered them with thoughtful and difficult presents and telegrams from California and offers of trips and week ends that she'd stopped accepting, once she began to build her life for herself. And all of that had been genuine, and she granted it. But it wasn't her kind of life any more at all.

She glanced around the table, seeing them with the hard clear eyes of youth. It was hard to grow up and see them as they were, and yet it had to be done. Aunt Beth and Uncle Charlie; Sid Vining, the stage designer; Harry Crandall, the writer; Jinny Crick, who was always there because she was always there. They looked harmless enough and she had been fond of them all. But they were the generation that had made the trouble, and you couldn't forget about that. They had got the world in a mess, and it was her generation and Tom's that would have to straighten it out. They had got the world in a mess—they and wonderful people like them. They had shouted for peace and disarmament, they had shouted of the horrors of war, then they had turned around and shouted for war. They drank too much, they divorced too easily, they lived by a code of their own; there was no health in them. So they ought to behave as if there were no health in them. And yet, even now, they didn't behave that way—and that was the irritating fact. They were eating, instead, with the serious and absorbed attention they always gave to good food.

"Don't tell me that's saffron," said Sid Vining, "because I wouldn't believe you. But it is."

"They get it from a little shop in Weymouth. All the way from Weymouth," said Beth Blake.

"It could be a mint, you know," said Sid Vining earnestly, "with the food as good as this. Remember the place at St. Tropez?"

"They didn't ration gas at St. Tropez," said Jinny Crick. . . . "That's a song title, isn't it, ensign?"

"I guess it really is," said Tom Finlay, smiling pleasantly.

The red-haired girl felt a sudden desire to touch him, to reassure herself of his solid reality. For Sid Vining was talking now of the things that could be done with Mrs. Sims' Clam House and, as the others threw in their quick, light comments, the little place changed and grew. Quietly but inexorably it grew, and the large cars slid up to the dock and the chattering people flooded in—the tanned men in white dinner jackets, the pleasantly scented women who threw their little fur wraps over the backs of the hard bare chairs and sat on stools at the bar and thought it was quaint and darling. It grew, as places always grew when the wonderful people came and until they left.

She wanted to pound on the table and say, "Stop it! Stop it!"

But Harry Crandall caught her eye and smiled. "What's the matter?" he said. "It isn't going to happen, you know. It couldn't any more."

"You wouldn't understand," she said. "The boats out there are real boats and they catch real fish. It isn't just a—a stage set for—"

"For people like us?" he said. "No, the point is well taken. It isn't a stage set any more."

"I guess I'm being rude," said the girl. "I guess maybe I am. But what was the Hotel du Cap like, at Antibes, the last time you saw it?"

"They were quartering Senegalese there," said Harry Crandall, and shrugged. "Well, they had to—I wish they'd quartered more. But it was nice out on the rocks—you must remember."

"I remember all right," said the girl. "I remember those fine old days and the screaming parties and the Russian woman who jumped out of the window. I wasn't particularly old, but I remember."

"You're lucky," said Harry Crandall, "even with that. I didn't get over till I was in the Army."

"If you want the child's point of view—well, it wasn't much fun," said the girl. "We all wanted ice-cream sodas and American clothes and movies that weren't months late. We wanted the funnies and games like the ones we read about, and not to be foreign."

"That's interesting," said Harry Crandall. "Yes, I see how that could be."

The girl stared at him. That was another thing about them that she had forgotten—they were always so open-minded. They'd attack you for a taste, demolish you for a judgment, but not for an opinion, particularly when it was critical of them.

"I suppose that's why I used to be an isolationist," she said. "It hurt Mummy and Daddy. They couldn't understand it."

"Perfectly natural reaction," said Harry Crandall.

"But how can you say that?" said the girl. "Ever since the war first broke out, you—"

He looked at her, and his face was empty and sad. "After the last war," he said, "the one thing I swore I'd never write was propaganda. But this one is for our skins, and the chips are down." He smiled at her. "So no explanations or apologies," he said. "Have some coffee. It's good."

She tried to read the pleasant, lined, empty face. There could be nothing there of importance to her; she knew that when she looked at Tom. And yet the eyes were as alive as a prodigal child's. But the prodigal children were finished.

"And speaking of blackouts, Beth," said Charles Blake, "as we weren't."

"Yes, we should," said Beth Blake, and again, like migratory birds, they collected themselves and began to make gestures of departure. It took a little time, but it was efficient and smooth. They said goodbye, carefully and politely, to Pearl, to Mrs. Sims, to the man at the counter. They looked into the kitchen for a moment, they walked out on the dock and looked at the sunset. It was obvious to the red-haired girl that they should lower their voices on the dock and be less themselves than they were, but they did nothing of the sort. It was obvious that the other people on the dock should hate them, but that did not seem to happen either.

When, at last, she and Tom were in the small car together, the girl gave a sigh of relief.

"Let's drive back by the Point, Tom," she said. "It's only half a mile farther and we needn't be back right away."

"Well, they're very interesting people," said Tom a little later. "They certainly give you something to think about." He laughed a little nervously. "Was I all right, darling?" he said.

"You were fine," said the girl. "Just fine. And you don't have to be polite."

"Well, they were polite to me," said Tom, and she saw the stubborn line of his jaw.

"They always are while you're with them," said the girl. "Oh, don't let's quarrel," she said.

"I wasn't quarreling, beautiful," said Tom, and they both stared out over the darkening water. He was there and solid and the way she wanted him to be. And they should be talking a great deal and they were not talking at all. The wonderful people had spoiled it.

"Oh, damn them!" she said with sudden violence. "Damn them from hell to breakfast! Damn them all!"

"Why, honey," he said. "Why, honey, what's the matter?" Then his arms were around her and she should have felt safe and secure. But there was neither safety nor security anywhere any more. The wonderful people had seen to that long ago, when they first set a match to the world.

"Oh, it's all right," she said. "It's all right, Tom. But we've got to get to your train."

When she returned to the house the blackout shades were already drawn and the highball tray was waiting. Beth Blake was explaining about the blackout shades.

"It's just dim-out, really," she was saying, "but we thought we'd do it rather thoroughly, since we had to." She gestured at the gay, bright flower patterns on the inside of the shades. "Jimmy Bender thought they ought to be much more Dali," she said. "He said he'd do them over, but I don't think Dali's very cozy for a blackout. I'd hate to look at eyes and watches while I was being bombed. So we just made them pretty-pretty, and now Charlie says it's like living inside a seed catalogue." Her rich laugh rang. She turned to the red-haired girl. "I hope your young man got a seat on the train," she said. "They're so tiresomely crowded now, especially on week ends."

"Oh, he got one all right," said the red-haired girl. . . . "No, thanks, Uncle Charlie, not a drink right now; I just want to powder my nose."

And there goes a very nice youngster who's just seen a ghost, thought Harry Crandall, watching her stride from the room. *But the young are so hard to reach. Were we as hard to reach as that? Well, yes, I suppose we were.*

He removed himself unobtrusively from the group and sat quietly in a corner, listening to the phonograph, his highball on one knee. Charlie Blake was playing a new calypso—he always found them, somehow.

"Telling you about the Battle of Midway when those Japanese ships went down," went the strange, effective voice. "Telling you about the Battle of Midway when the U. S. Navy fleet went to town—"

Harry Crandall listened, glad for the fact of noise. He'd talk, if he had to, in a minute, but right now he didn't want to talk, even to Charlie or Beth. And Charlie and Beth wouldn't mind; they had been together long enough.

He tried to remember when he had first met the Blakes— '21? '22? But it was hard to remember when you were tired. He'd met them with Steve Searle, who was dead of a heart attack, and Mimi Post, who wouldn't get out of her sanitarium now, and a lot of the old crowd. But it had been a new crowd then—quite new and shiny. In the days of the Dôme and the Rotonde and Marta's down in the Village and the start of many things; the days of the fierce bursts of work and the quick trips on liners; the days when Paris was Mecca and there wouldn't be any more wars. Yes, a new crowd— quite new and shiny. And everybody had been poor at the start, except the Blakes. But nobody minded the Blakes' not being poor.

Well, he thought, *we've had a good run for it, money or no money. We've had what won't be again—the food and the talk and the wine. But France fell, dammit—France fell. She couldn't fall, but she did. And that handsome youngster probably thinks it happened because they liked good food and things in proportion. But that's part of what you want to preserve. Not all, but part.*

He looked around the room at the good faces—the faces of his friends. They had been together so often and so long and through so many happenings. The work was a different thing, that, in time, could be assessed. Not such bad work either, on the whole, though no doubt it could have been better. But he was thinking of the people, not the work. For nobody was going to be able to put in a book what Charlie Blake was like twenty years ago or why Jinny Crick, for all her mannered folly, had both charm and heart. It couldn't be put in a book or explained to the young. *But these are my friends, my colleagues, my generation—the people I have chosen to live and die beside. And we went on a queer adventure—very queer when you come to think of it, for it brought us back precisely, and in twenty years, to the things we had left behind, and now we must fight for those, if anything good is to live. And after that, we'll be old. But we've seen some things.*

He noticed that the red-haired girl was back in the room again, on a sofa beside Sid Vining. *Well, here goes for a rescue,* he thought. *She won't get on with Sid—not in whatever mood she's in, and Sid's pretty much on edge himself.*

He approached them amiably. "Nice drinks? Nice picture post cards, gentleman and lady?" he said. "Nice guide for the conducted tour?"

"Don't give her a drink," said Sid Vining sourly. "She thinks it's the Demon Rum." He rose and bowed. "I have been rebuked by infants," he said. "I shall go get myself stinking in comparative peace." He stalked away.

"Well," said Harry Crandall, and sat down.

The girl said nothing.

"He won't, you know," said Harry Crandall. "In case you wanted information."

"Who cares if he does?" said the girl in a low fierce voice.

Harry Crandall considered this. "Oh, some of us, in a way," he said. "It isn't particularly good for his work. And he's about the best scene designer we've got. But he's been mostly on the wagon for quite a while now."

"Then why doesn't he do something," said the girl, "instead of talking about putting little bars in restaurants? Why doesn't he do camouflage?"

He stared at her and laughed. "Poor Sid," he said. "He's got a trick knee. And bad eyes. The Army's turned him down twice. Now he thinks they may take him, but he isn't sure. So he's a little touchy."

"Oh," said the girl.

"Yes," said Harry Crandall. "And now I'd really better get you a drink. You've had a white face all evening, and I don't like girls with white faces. Also, I need one myself. You get tired on planes; it's the monotony, I guess."

He mixed two drinks expertly, thinking, *Harry Crandall, the rescuer, Harry Crandall, the lifeguard. Aren't you proud of yourself, Mr. Harry Fix-it Crandall? But Howdy and Ella Martinson were friends of yours, and swell people, so the least you can do is to get their daughter a drink at a party. That will help so much.*

When he brought them back, the girl looked at hers doubtfully. "I don't really like it," she said.

"I am not attempting to inebriate you," said Harry Crandall patiently; "I am recommending for shock. And don't tell me you haven't had one."

"I haven't," said the girl, but she sipped at the very light highball.

"Of course not," said Harry Crandall. "Your generation doesn't. You drink milk and cokes and grow to be six-foot-three. Which is perfectly fine, and I'm for it. But nobody's shock-proof these days. Nobody at all."

"It wasn't anything at all," said the girl, but the color began to come back to her white face.

"Of course it wasn't anything," said Harry Crandall.

"It was just driving back through the blackout," said the girl. "I mean, it takes quite a long time. I—I didn't realize it would take so long. It was spooky," she said, with hurt.

"That so?" said Harry Crandall. "Yes, that must make tough driving." He did not say, *In the last war, I remember the first time we moved with lights, after the Armistice. I remember that because it hit you right in the face; it scared you for a minute. And I remember how London looked at the start of this one.* He did not say any of those things.

"And then I came back," said the girl, "and I'd just seen Tom off, and Aunt Beth was talking about blackout shades and being silly, and I went upstairs to powder my nose in her bedroom, and she's got a very bright tin pail full of very white sand, and I guess it matches the bedroom, and—oh!"

"Nobody will notice it if you cry," said Harry Crandall. "Or we could go out in the kitchen. People often do."

"I'm not going to cry!" said the girl. "But it suddenly got rather horrible. And Aunt Jinny—Mrs. Crick—was in the bedroom. She was sitting there in a chair and she was crying. But she wasn't making any sound—just the tears coming out of her eyes. And I stood there like a fool and didn't know what to do!" Her voice rose sharply.

"That's quite all right," said Harry Crandall carefully. "You see, Jinny has a boy in the coastal patrol. You played with him once, but you probably wouldn't remember him—his name's Sam Langley and he's even taller than you are.

Red hair too," he said reflectively. "Well, you see how that
might worry her. And then Toby Crick's in London for lend-
lease, and she's rather fond of Toby."

"If you're trying to make me feel like even more of a heel,
you're succeeding very nicely," said the girl.

"Oh, no," said Harry Crandall. "No. I'm not claiming
the higher maternal virtues for Jinny—in fact, I'd hate to
be mothered by her myself. But I'd hate not to have her
around, with her silly square make-up box, making up her
silly face and worrying about it. You get to be that way about
people after a while. And it's been a long while." He sighed
for a moment. "So you fought with your young man," he
said.

"I didn't fight with him," said the girl. "It was just—it was
going to be wonderful—and then, suddenly, it didn't mean
anything."

"You can't go entirely by one week end," said Harry Crandall, remarking that the girl's color had now returned to normal. *And, Old Mother Hubbard, how did you pull that well-
worn advice right out of the hat?* he thought.

"You don't understand," said the girl. "You couldn't possibly! It's got to be right for me—after Mummy and Daddy
and the way they broke up! It's got to be safe and secure!
Something's got to be! And I thought Tom was, and I was
counting on that. I thought not even Aunt Beth and the rest
of you could spoil him. And then—"

"And then," said Harry Crandall, "we exerted our well-
known wiles?"

"Oh, it isn't what you did," said the girl. "You never
do. But you made him look dull and ordinary, and he was
respectful to you—so horribly respectful."

"In other words," said Harry Crandall, "he was polite."
He cleared his throat. *I wish I could remember more about
that young man,* he thought. *He was perfectly all right and I*

liked him, but I never could pick him out in a parade. "And as for his being dull," he said guardedly, "I thought he had some pretty solid ideas."

"Yes, that's Tom," said the girl eagerly. She pulled her handkerchief from her handbag and firmly blew her nose. "And they're real ideas too. He thinks there are going to be a lot of changes after the war and we'll all have to be more responsible."

"That's an interesting point of view," said Harry Crandall. *All the same, she'd better meet young Sam Langley, he thought. This Tom may be all she thinks, but he ought to have more competition. And the first time you fall in love you're always so sure it's for keeps.* He cocked his ear to what the girl was saying now.

"But I can't get over being so scared," she said like a child. "Why was I?"

"There's a war on," said Harry Crandall, "and a big one. And you can forget for a while, just the way you can almost go to sleep on a march. But now and then it comes over you, like a wave. It isn't a question of courage and it doesn't affect your doing things. You drove the car back all right, didn't you? You didn't drive it into a ditch? Well, that's all you have to know."

"Yes, that's so," she said gratefully. "I didn't drive it into the ditch."

"Remember that," said Harry Crandall. "Because there was a big car and it got in the ditch. And now we've got to get it out. Not just your generation or mine," he said carefully, "but all of us. That's the difference. Do you hate us all very much? You might, you know. After all, we did have the parties."

"I don't know," said the girl. "I don't know."

"As for me, I'm entirely vulnerable," said Harry Crandall. "This is Charlie's last leave and Beth's going to shut the house. But I'm everything you think. I'm a nasty little civilian propagandist, and will the new crowd make hay of that, in ten years' time, when it's all over! Remember the fearsome tripe the established names—or most of them—wrote about the last one, and how it retched the bowels of my generation? Well, they'll retch at me just the same way. But somebody had to do it." He spoke without heat or pride.

"I don't understand you," said the girl. "I don't understand any of you. I don't know that I want to."

"It doesn't matter a bit," said Harry Crandall. "Only maybe you'd better. If you're going to make a new world—and I gather you are." He looked at her, glad to see her so stiff and uncompromising. "Well, we were, too," he said. "And it wasn't a bad one. It had freedom and pleasure and good food and truthful art. But we had to make our own rules and we couldn't see around the next curve. So that's that, and what happened happened." He stared at his drink. "And you'll do it very differently," he said.

"I should hope so," said the girl.

"That's all right," said Harry Crandall, "but remember that freedom means freedom, not bossing other people—and your friends, in the end, are your friends. With which profound remark," he said, "your cracker-barrel philosopher will now sign off." He finished his drink and stood up. "Let's go outside for a minute," he said. "Charlie's got a perfectly devilish blackout arrangement on the terrace door, but I think I know my way through it."

When they were outside in the cool darkness, the girl took a deep breath.

"It smells nice," she said. "It smells good. Even in wars."

"Yes," said Harry Crandall gently. "You'll sleep, of course?" he said.

"Why, of course I'll sleep," said the girl. "Why shouldn't I?"

He chucklod faintly to himself. "No reason," he said. But you're over your jitters, he thought, and you won't have the same kind again. You'll sleep like a baby and wake, and tomorrow you'll write to Tom, or he'll write to you. And you'll marry him or somebody, but it won't be me, thank goodness, for I've chosen the friends I must live and die beside. And we're getting on, every one of us, but we've got about one more kick in us, and those that are left are tough. No, we won't be easy in your Zion. But we'll try to behave. We're trying.

"Born and bred in the brier patch, Br'er Fox," he said, half to himself. "Born and bred in the brier patch, and now we're back there again. But we did take life with both hands; we weren't cautious about it. And that's still something to do."

But the girl was still standing there, breathing in the night, a tall, confident figure beneath the calm sky that sometime might hold the planes. He smiled, nodded his head and went back to the house and his friends.

THIS BRIGHT DREAM

*N*ow sit down, dear, and take off your hat. I'm not a bit tired and we'll have a nice long visit. The doctor said, "Well, Mrs. Blake, I'm not going to tell you not to give luncheon parties. But just remember there is such a thing as Anno Domini." And I do, of course. Or, if I don't, Carrie reminds me. But the queer thing is that I don't feel old. I know I'm eighty when I think about it, but sometimes, when I lie in bed in the morning, before Carrie brings me my breakfast, I feel just as young as I ever did and I wonder why I can't get up and run out into the garden like a little girl. That's a foolish way for an old woman to feel—now, isn't it? You needn't raise your voice, dear—I'm not deaf.

The time does mix, that's the curious thing. I can't explain to you just how that happens, but it does. It's like seeing a road you've climbed from the top of a hill, all the curves and windings—and some parts of it are very plain and some parts are blurred. Your Aunt Florence sent me a silly book the other day—I shouldn't say it was silly, because it was kind of her to send it, but it was. The woman in it was only sixty-five, but she cried a great deal and kept seeing her twin sister, though the poor little thing had died of cholera years before. Well, of course, these things sometimes happen, but much more often in books, dear. If I shut my eyes I can see my mother in her lavender dress, and your grandfather coming back from market with a fine fresh shad in brown paper, or a basket of fresh strawberries with big green leaves at the

207

bottom. But that isn't seeing ghosts. I couldn't reach out and touch them, though I'd like to. And I'm sure your grandfather wouldn't approve of being a ghost—he was a very particular man and he loved his own way. But he'd walk home, just the same, with the market basket over his arm, when he felt like it. There were patients who didn't like it, but he paid no attention. I remember his saying to one of them, who was always complaining, "Madam, you have been granted three great blessings—a good husband, an excellent liver, and a republican form of government. If you cannot accommodate yourself to life with these, I have very little hope of you, either here or in the hereafter." She was very angry and flounced out—but of course, when she felt sick, she sent for him again.

I wish you could have known him—he died before you were born. He wore a top hat till he died—a stovepipe, we called it in those days—and every now and then mother would give the old ones away. It used to vex him, but she was quite firm about it.

"Flora," he'd say, "Flora, my dear, what the devil has happened to my hat? Don't tell me you've given it away to one of your infernal beggars."

Then she'd say, "Well, Henry, he seemed such a deserving man, but I've gotten you a beautiful new one from Mr. Vincey."

"I don't want a beautiful new hat, Flora—I want my hat!"

Of course he always gave in, in the end—she knew that he would. He would carry his stethoscope in them and it made a bulge on one side. It got to be quite a joke eventually —I remember Mrs. Thurston's saying, "Why, of course I had the man cut the grass—he had one of the doctor's hats on, so I knew he must be respectable." She lived on Larch Street, too—it's very much changed, though it was such a nice street then.

I can see the whole Larch Street house, too, just as plain as plain, and the lilac bush in the yard. How sweetly it smelled! I can see my mother's work basket, and the carpet with the big, soft flowers. But that doesn't mean I'm seeing ghosts either. The person who wrote that book didn't seem to understand that—it must have been a clever young man. I thought I'd write a letter and give him a piece of my mind, but Carrie dissuaded me and Carrie's usually right. After all, why would he like to hear from an old woman? But they make old women such bags of bones, in their books. Oh, I know what I look like now. But they never tell that you might have had pretty hands. I was never really vain of mine, but your father admired them. And I must say, I had a good carriage and good shoulders. Your Aunt Florence was the beauty, but she didn't have shoulders like mine.

I remember that silly old general—General Cranston. I was singing at the piano and he was turning my music and before I knew, he had leaned over and bitten me on the right shoulder. Not hard, dear, but perceptible and difficult to explain. Then he said:

"I apologize, Miss Sophy, but it was just like biting into a peach."

Well, I was only sixteen but I drew myself up and said, "You have taken a very great liberty, General Cranston. I think you had better leave the house," and he bowed and left without saying another word. Then I ran to my room and cried all afternoon because I was afraid, after that, he might ask to marry me and I'd have to. You wouldn't think your mother could be such a jay! But I must say, he behaved himself afterward, though I couldn't bear your Uncle Robert's calling him my beau. And when I told your father about it, years later, he only laughed and teased me. Well, I'd never have married a man who dyed his whiskers, so I suppose your father was right.

There are so many things I want to tell you and the children. I keep thinking about them and then, of course, I forget. It mightn't mean much to them now, but sometime it might. They're just little things—they happen in every family. But if nobody cares, they get lost. A family's like a country—it takes so much living and dying to make it. Then the children go off and do new things, and that's quite right. But something stays.

That's why I sent your Ellen the little scent bottle. It's very old-fashioned, of course—she may not have any use for it. But it was Great-Grandma's—it came from Shamrock Hill. There were only twenty houses in Pittsburgh, besides the fort, when Great-Grandpa came there—he was a trader, you know. He came over the mountains with his pack horses, and Great-Grandma had to pin up her long skirts with thorns. I was only a little thing when I heard her tell about it. She had a great deal of spirit and she used to brush her hair two hundred strokes every night. It fell below her waist when she took the pins out, even when she was old.

It must have been a wild, rough life for her at the beginning. She'd been brought up like a doll till she married Great-Grandpa—he came from the County Tyrone—and she cried when the little red trunk with her wedding dress in it was lost at the ford. She could always remember it floating away downstream, but there wasn't time to stop. The men had heard there was a Wyandot war party, cutting off travelers. But when they found the poor scalped man, still living, beside the trace, she made them put him on her horse and tore up her petticoats for bandages. Do you know, he got well and lived to be quite an old man? They did, sometimes. When he was well enough, she made him a wig out of tow—I've often heard her describe it. It must have looked queer enough, but he said it suited him better than his own hair because, if anyone tried to scalp him again, he said, they'd find it was all done for them, and what more could be asked for? He got a real wig, later on, but he always kept the tow one. Charlie O'Grady. His daughter married one of the Northrups—the steel family. I believe they live on Long Island. I wonder if they've kept the tow wig.

It can't have been just what Great-Grandma expected when she married—to end her wedding journey in a log hut, at the end of nowhere, with a scalped man to care for as well as her own husband. But when people have to do things, they do them. And twice she was flooded out—that's why Great-Grandpa built Shamrock Hill on the high ground. He'd made a great deal of money then, for the time—people used to say that he had a lucky hand. But it all went after he died —the boys were thoughtless and careless, except for your Great-Uncle Willie, and he died very young, at Natchez, of the fever.

Great-Grandma never forgot that—he'd been her favorite child. She carried his hair in her locket—a little child's curl of pale, soft gold. But it was the girls who held the family together and took care of her—it happens so often. Well, money isn't everything and I don't suppose we were meant to keep it. She wasn't a businesswoman and the trustee robbed her—I believe they're very wealthy people now. But your father used to say, "You can see what the Lord thinks of money by the people He gives it to." And I don't envy them.

I wish you could have seen Shamrock Hill, though—it wasn't the money there. It was all the aunts and cousins and friends and relations and their beaus and suitors and the children running up and down the wide stairs. They'd sit down twenty at table, with another table for the children, and strangers were always welcome. They had the rosewood piano brought over the mountains—they had barrels of oysters shipped from the Chesapeake; there was always the fruit and the game and the big loaves of sugar in their blue paper, the cream rising, thick and yellow, on the pans in the dairy, and Dutch Anna baking twenty cinnamon buns at a time. Well, they were open-handed people—and, of course, it helped to ruin them—but no one ever went away hungry from Shamrock Hill. And the visitors—the visitors! There was a cousin and his wife from Virginia—they came for a two months' visit and, my dear, they stayed a year and a half and had a dear little baby too. People died and people were married; they came and went; they moved away; there was so much life there, so much life going on. Then it was all put up at auction. My mother remembered that and Great-Grandma at the auction, dressed in her black silk dress, receiving the people as if they were still her guests. She didn't cry one tear —it was the girls who cried. There's a look of her in your Ellen—a certain look.

The girls worked, sewing and dress-making and working for the women's exchange, and mother taught school. That's how she met your grandfather—he hadn't a friend in the world, poor boy, for the uncle who brought him over here had died right after he came. They'd meant to take up a farm, but there was some swindle about the papers. So he went to work in a livery stable—a boy of fifteen—and the man let him sleep in an empty feed bin, but he'd lock him in at night because he was afraid he might steal. And once he woke up, in the moonlight, and there was a big rat sleeping on his chest. But he opened his eyes and thought, "Well, brother rat, it's a cold night for both of us. But as long as you keep me warm and behave yourself, I don't mind keeping you warm, in this queer foreign country," and he went to sleep again. He always liked to tell that story, though mother didn't like it.

They called him Dutchy, at first, and made fun of his clothes and his ways—it must have been hard on a boy. Then the livery stable changed hands and he lost his job, and there was a time he didn't like to talk about, before he met Doctor Gray. That was the last house he tried—he'd always been interested in medicine.

"I went there with my pockets full of stones," he said to mother once. "I thought, if this man did not take me, the stones and I would go to the river together." Then he laughed and said: "But all the time I knew I could swim like a fish, stones or no stones." But there was something about him that Doctor Gray liked and he let him take care of his horse. "Then," your grandfather said, "the first time I saw him with a lancet in his hand—well, it was a very small affair, but I knew from then what I wanted to do."

Of course, when Mother met him, he was a young doctor in his first top hat. He spoke beautiful English, even then, but he wanted to improve it, and they read the British poets together that winter and were married in the spring. I used to have the little copy of Pope he gave her: "To Miss Flora Shand with the respectful good wishes of her friend, Hendrik Schouten." But those books were burned in the fire.

There are so many ups and downs, so many people, so much I wish I could tell you. There was the way people lived and the things they said. It wouldn't mean much to strangers —oh, I know that! But I don't think it could have happened anywhere else—in any other country. I don't think it could. I'd like the children to know that. Though just as interesting things happen nowadays.

Well, the people who came in the *Mayflower* were free people too. No matter how some of them turned out. And I'm sure I don't grudge them. But it seems to me, it's always been a *Mayflower*, for all the people who came. Though naturally, as Ransom would say, the first ones got the publicity. If you just live along, they don't write books about you. And yet there must be so many of us, all over the nation. Your father used to say, "Well, there's one thing about the family. We've been here quite a while and nobody's been hanged for a horse thief—at least as far as I know. Well, of course, there was your Cousin Myron." Not hanged, dear, no. But he always was such a responsibility.

We never knew quite how it happened and he'd been such a dear little boy, though spoiled. He got into bad company, but I'm afraid it was his own fault too. Your father went to see him, out in that place, and took up the pardon with the governor. I shall always respect your father for doing that— after all, Myron was my relative, not his. Sometimes it's harder for a man to do those things—a woman wouldn't mind as much. I've had your father say to me, "Really, Sophy, for someone who's married to a lawyer, I think you have less respect for the law than anyone I know." Well, now, that wasn't quite just. It was only that I kept thinking of Myron as Myron —such a dear little boy in a white suit. They let him work in the prison library—he'd always been fond of books and your father said he did it very well.

Then afterward, I'm glad to say, he married a nice, plain woman and they went to live in Florida. It was lemons first and then pecans, but his son made a go of it and belongs to the Chamber of Commerce. Your father saw him on one of his trips and said it was perfectly all right. He said the boy looked like Myron, but he'd left his watch out on the table and nothing had happened to it. I think that was one of the few really unkind things your father ever said. Poor Myron! He did so want to be popular with the other boys—and when he took six of them to the circus, it was your grandmother's purse. I could have told them not to trust him with money! But it's all over now and the son has grandchildren of his own. They write very friendly letters and I hope I can see them sometime.

It works out in a very queer way, often, but it does work out. At least, that's what I've come to believe. There's a sort of rough justice. Now, your Grandmother Blake—she was a very fine woman. I always respected her and I think she came to respect me in the end. But your father and I were young when we married—and he was her favorite. It's a difficult relation, dear—you'll see, when young Henry marries—and I hope you'll be more sensible than I was. Why did I want to hold on to you all so closely? And yet, I let you go when you wanted to go.

We were visiting your Grandmother Blake once, and she said something to me—I won't tell you what it was, but I went upstairs to pack. I said I wouldn't stay in the house, and then, of course, I did. She loved you children, she was devoted to you. It must have been very hard for her to apologize to me, but Grandfather Blake made her do it. I didn't know what that meant to her at the time—I was too young and too stubborn—but I did later, with Bertha. Bertha used to say things that would cut me to the heart—but Bertha was Ransom's choice and she's made him a good wife. I wish she wouldn't smoke so much—just like a chimney—but that's none of my business. When the crash came in 1929, she stood by him—and it worried me so terribly. There wasn't a thing I could do but take the children for the summer—and I knew that Ransom was drinking, though I never talked to Bertha about it. My son, my fine son!

Well, thank God, that's all over and done with and they got back their home. But she came to me once and talked to me very simply—I didn't care, that day, how many cigarettes she smoked.

She said, "Mother Blake, I love Ransom, but I guess we're about washed up. And I'm so tired, I don't care—I don't care what happens."

And I said, "Bertha, I know I've made mistakes. I know you think I wanted him to marry Sally Forbes. But if I did, I was wrong. I'm not asking you to stay with my son—I'm asking you to do your best for your husband. If you can't, you can't, and I won't blame you, but I hope you can. Now I think we ought to have a cocktail—I feel tired."

So I made her mix one for both of us, though I've never liked them, and she said, "O.K., Mother Blake," and I knew things were going to be better.

Only then Ransom came in and was very angry with both of us. He said he'd been looking for a job all day and then, when he came home tired, Bertha was over drinking cocktails with me. In fact, he practically accused me of thinking more of Bertha than I did of him, and he talked about the cocktails till you'd have thought I drank them for breakfast. And then, in the middle of what he was saying, it suddenly struck him as funny and he wiped his face with a handkerchief and said, so seriously, "I apologize, I'm sure, ladies," and we all began to laugh.

Well, it was all very silly, but things began to go better for them after that. I don't think Ransom even remembers it now—but I do, and I'm sure that Bertha does. He's done very well with the company, and they're both so fond of the little grandchild. I wish Bertha Junior wouldn't call him "Butch"—that doesn't seem right for a baby, but I suppose it's the modern way.

I'm not going to complain about that, though. Bertha Junior and Frank came over for Sunday-night supper a week ago—they were asking me what I remembered and I think Frank was being polite. But they seemed quite interested, though I know that I talked too much. I was telling them about Great-Uncle Jim—my young uncle—coming back to the Larch Street house in his blue uniform at the end of the Civil War. I couldn't have been more than five but I remember him, because he tossed me up to the ceiling. He used to sing a song too: "I'm a snolleygoster and we'll all jine the Union!" And I learned the tune and copied him, though I didn't know what a snolleygoster was.

And then there was something very sad and, everywhere you went, the houses were hung with black and bells were tolling and tolling. That was Lincoln's death. I wasn't old enough to know what it really meant, and yet I did know. I remember the sadness, the mourning, as if part of the sky had fallen. And yet we went on. We didn't do as well as we'd have done if he'd been alive—and yet we went on. My brother John heard him speak—he was ten years older than I. He said he was a plain-looking man, but the minute you saw him you knew that he was a good man. We've had so many good men. We've had bad ones, too, and cruel ones, but we've had good men. We've made so many mistakes, but we've done some good things too. I think sometimes we forget about the good things—the ordinary things we're so used to.

When your father and I went to Europe, it was such a wonderful trip. I was so glad to see all the things I'd read about in books—I was so glad to see them all. I think about them all sometimes, at night—the Tower of London and Gray's Inn and the Sainte-Chapelle and the nice, hot dinner we had on the boat train to Paris. Your father was just like a boy again and we met such interesting people. And yet, I was glad to get home. I could have stayed there for years, but I was glad to get home. When I saw the Statue of Liberty, I could have cried, like an old fool. Your father said, "Now, Sophy, save your tears for the customs inspectors—you'll probably need them." But I noticed he was glad to get back and sit in his own chair.

There was a very nice man at Mrs. Banks', the other day. He'd traveled a great deal and he was very interesting. But I kept thinking all the time, "Well, I've traveled too." And I have, though it wouldn't have interested him—he'd been to Egypt and Arabia. But when I went West with your father, there were antelope still on the plains. I could drive a horse but I'd never learned to ride one—I learned there. I learned to shoot, too, though at first I was afraid of the noise. But when your father had to be away, I slept with a loaded Colt .45 where I could reach it. Well, dear, it was only sensible—there were some very rough people in the West then. There was one boy who worked for your father—a Southern boy with shallow blue eyes. He was very polite and soft-spoken while he was with us, but afterward he killed eight men. Well, I've told you that story. And yet what I remember about him is how nicely he ate and how pleased and shy he was when I gave him a blue handkerchief for Christmas.

It's such a big country, our country. I was brought up in the East but I'm glad I know more of it than that. I'll always remember the clear air and the stars so big and near that you felt you could reach up and touch them. Your father got me a horse called Billy Baxter—a pinto with three white stockings. It seems queer to me now that I've ridden thirty miles a day on Billy Baxter, and the mountains just as far away when we ended as they had been when we began.

The ranch never paid but it saved your father's health, and I was willing to stay. I'd gotten to love the country and the quiet-voiced people. We were poor for a while, but we didn't care—we were young. The first time I helped a woman have her baby, I was afraid that I'd faint, in spite of being a doctor's daughter. But I couldn't faint with Mrs. MacPherson there—she was a big, red-haired woman with hands like a man's, and so kind. She'd had her first baby all alone in a frontier fort—her husband had been a captain in the cavalry. But he'd never been well since they shot him through the lungs—he had to retire, after that. I'm afraid he drank a little more than was good for him, but May MacPherson was very good about that. She'd say, "Captain, is that your first toddy or your second?" and he'd say, "Now, light of my life, can you expect a military man to walk on one leg?" Then she'd take the bottle away and lock it in the cupboard and he'd grin like a naughty boy.

Your father was very fond of both of them, and so was I. They were good neighbors—good neighbors. I remember how shocked I was when I found he was an infidel—I must have been a rigid little thing. But he just smiled at me very kindly and said, "Did you ever hear of a division of labor, Mrs. Blake? It's like that in our family—I do the swearing and May MacPherson does the praying. And if she can't pray me into heaven, I'll think the worse of the place." He said it so I couldn't help smiling too. When we left the West, I kissed him—it surprised your father. He said, "Sophy, I didn't know you approved of kissing infidels." And I said, "Stop joking —you know he's a good man."

That was after your Grandfather Blake died. Well, there was no one else to take on the business, and your father never ran away from a duty. But his heart was never in it, though he'd work till eleven at night. I was glad when they made the offer and he could give it up. He talked it all over with me and he was willing to go on. But he'd always wanted to study law, and I knew it. So we took the chance. He was

eight years older than most of the other students, a married
man with children, and they used to call him "Pop" and "The
Two-Gun Kid," because we'd lived in the West. But we had
good times, all the same, in that little house on Bradford
Avenue. The boys were shy, at first; but when they found we
were just as poor as they were, they came around. It was
Sunday-night supper and beans—I made a bean hole out in
the back yard, and when the landlord complained I asked
him to supper and he never complained again. A very nice
man named Levy.

And if the baby waked up—that was Ransom first, and then
you—the boys would help me. It isn't every baby that's had
its bottle heated by a justice of the Supreme Court. Poor Will
Laird—he came early one Sunday and your father was out
and I was very busy. So I gave you to him to hold while I attended to the beans and he handled you as if you were glass.
I don't think he'd ever been that close to a live baby before.
I got a very nice letter from Will Laird the other day—remind me to show it to you. I still remember the little speech
he made, when your father retired as dean. He was very
anxious for your father to come to Harvard, years ago. But
your father felt his duty lay here.

Then you children—and life going on. A quiet life—yes,
I suppose so. And yet it seems so full and crowded, when I
look back. All the boys in your father's classes, and sometimes their boys after them. It sounds quiet enough. But he
loved the teaching—he loved to try to make them think. And
some of them remembered the things he taught them, like
Will Laird. He used to say, "Gentlemen, this country is made
out of people. The law that doesn't remember that is an ass.
And so is the lawyer." It was considered very radical talk for
those days.

But your father could be very obstinate when he chose.

It's hard to put down in words—some of the things you know. He used to say, "Well, we aren't remarkable people, but we've done our share of the work." And he never could stand pretensions. Your Aunt Florence has some sort of diploma showing that she's a Lineal Descendant of King Arthur—I remember how that used to amuse him. He was always polite, but he did say to her once, "Well, Florence, if we'd had to depend on the Lineal Descendants of King Arthur, this country would have stopped at the Allegheny Mountains. I think I'll form a society of the Lineal Descendants of Job's Turkey, and I bet it beats yours all hollow." Well, he said it laughingly, but he meant what he said.

It's a long road from Great-Grandpa to the little new great-grandchild. I wish I could make a picture of it—I wish a picture could be made. We've been Democrats and Republicans and Populists and Whigs and Federalists. We've gone in wagons and airplanes, on horseback and afoot. We've built things and torn them down and built them again. And then there was the war. And the war before it, the war that kept the Union. That seems very far away, I know. But when I was a young girl, there were scars on some of the houses still—scars where the shells had struck. And Mrs. Jenkins' rosewood dining table with the brass plate where the solid shot had gone through. Just a house like your house or my house—an ordinary house where ordinary people lived. I keep thinking of that—and yet we had to keep the Union. And I've been in the hospitals, too—I've heard them breathing, in the hospitals, in the flu epidemic. I don't think anyone forgets. I know that a woman doesn't.

And yet, there was a long time, when your father and I were married and afterward, when it seemed as if things were getting better, not only here but all over the world. That's what I can't explain to Frank and Bertha Junior—that feeling we had. They'd think it was just a dream, but it was real, it was true. Oh, we worried about bad times, we worried about all sorts of things. But we felt we could get through them, all together. We felt there was a greatness to come.

Oh, I know—there was the hate and the meanness too. They called your grandfather "Dutchy"; they yelled "Shanty Irish!" at Grandma; they had signs in the West, "No Irish Need Apply." But when one of your father's boys called a classmate of his a sheeny, I gave him a talking to, and he listened to me, I can tell you. We can't have that sort of thing—we can't let it grow on us. It's just like those nasty beetles—it eats the leaves off the tree.

I'm old but I know what I think. If we aren't going to be proud of some things and do our best to keep them, who's going to be proud of them for us? I said to your Uncle George, the other day, "You won't talk against the President in my house—not that way, not the things you're saying. I'm proud of my country, and the President's part of my country. I don't care what you think about the man—though you've been a bad judge of men ever since I've known you— but you'll respect the office when you talk to me. I've washed out your mouth with soap, George, when you were five years old and, old as I am, I'm ready to do it again. I think you need it."

Well, perhaps I was a little sharp, but you have to be, with your Uncle George. He puffed and blew at me a good deal— he eats too many starches for a man of his age—but I gave it to him straight.

"I'm an American," I said. "I believe we were created free and equal. I believe in the people—the good people I've known all over. I believe in this country. If that's being senile, then I'm senile."

He puffed and blew and said, "I never said you were senile, Sophy. I never said anything of the sort. But that man—"

"Don't you talk about 'that man,' " I said. "Go home and

get down on your knees and thank God you've still got a country, and a President who's elected by the people, and freedom to talk like a fool if you feel like talking like a fool. You're not grateful enough for what you've got, and there are too many people like you. We didn't buy this country ready-made in a department store—we built it up, all together, and it was a long, hard road. Now go home and take your digitalis—you probably need it." Well, you know, he was as meek as Moses when he went out of the house. If Lucy had only stood up to him, once in a while!

But I believe it. I believe it. It's terrible news from over there. Sometimes I just can't bear hearing it—I turn off the radio. But you can't shut your ears and your eyes, not even when you're old. It's a new, strange world we live in—a bitter world since last year. It may be we're in for hard and bitter days—the world's so small now. But we made ourselves a free nation. It wasn't handed to us on a platter—we made it and suffered for it. And, what we made, we can keep.

PART FOUR

WILLIAM RILEY AND THE FATES

THERE are quite a few proverbs and such about a young man going out to meet his fate. But the only one I ever heard of who did it was a boy named William Riley. And he didn't really intend to. It just happened to him.

He lived in a town called Snapperville, in the days when Big Bill Taft was President, and he worked for the *Snapperville Gazette*. That is, he did so summers and after school —next year, when he'd graduated from high school, Mr. Slater was thinking of hiring him regular. He'd started out by delivering papers and worked up to local items and odd jobs around the plant. And once or twice a year, because he intended to be a real journalist and a power in the community, he'd get his nerve up and write a slam-bang editorial about civic corruption or how Wall Street preyed upon the farmer or some new subject like that. He never got them printed, of course, because Mr. Slater wrote the editorials himself, but he had the satisfaction of writing them.

Once he did show Mr. Slater the one on civic corruption, and Mr. Slater read it and grunted and said, "Well, William, I'm getting on in years and I'm sure I've seen worse. I must have. But next time you talk about flinging the gauntlet in the teeth of an abysm, just hold yourself in and count ten. Because an abysm with teeth is a pretty unusual object for Snapperville." This encouraged William and he bought a dictionary next day, to find out more about abysms. He had a great respect for Mr. Slater's opinion because, as everybody knew, Mr. Slater had once worked for Dana on the *Sun*.

Of course, if you looked at it one way, William's job wasn't very important. And yet it was to him. To be sure, the *Gazette* came out only once a week, but it covered the whole county, and they had one subscriber who lived as far east as Chicago. And over Mr. Slater's desk hung the framed front page of the extra he'd gotten out for McKinley's assassination. William used to look at that often and hope something like it would happen in his time. He could see himself dashing into the office with the news. And sometimes on make-up night, when the cranky old press started wheezing, he'd shut his eyes and imagine it was the *Twin City Standard* or the *New York Times* or some big paper like that. Then he'd usually get yelled at by Mr. Slater. But other times Mr. Slater would grunt and allow that he might make a newspaperman yet, and William would be pleased.

Often and often he wondered about the future. Of course, he felt pretty sure how some of it would be. He liked Mr. Slater a lot, but he didn't intend to be just like Mr. Slater. He intended to go to New York and be a great journalist and make a million dollars and reform society and marry the handsomest girl in the world and vote the straight Republican ticket and have his name printed on the front page of the *Snapperville Gazette* as "our leading citizen." At least these were some of his intentions—they didn't include the times he was going to be President or the times he was going to be a world-famous ventriloquist, but they covered most of the ground. The only thing that really bothered him was what to do first. For suppose he started after the million dollars and missed the girl—or started after the girl and missed the million dollars? He wished he could get a little guidance on that—but he knew if he asked Mr. Slater, Mr. Slater would just grunt and ask him if there'd been any new arrivals on the

5:30 train. And yet William wanted to know. You generally do, when you're young.

He was thinking about it one make-up day—maybe that's one reason why things turned out as they did. He'd about decided that, sensible or not, he'd have to have a straight talk with Mr. Slater about his prospects, if any. But when he got back to the office, after covering the registrations at the Palace Hotel (there weren't any), Mr. Slater was in a stew. Mr. Slater was generally in a stew on make-up day, but this one was something special. He looked up as William came in.

"Do you know what a man is, William, when he tries to edit a small-town newspaper?" he said. "He's a fool, that's what he is—a congenital, Billy-be-damned fool!"

"Yes, sir," said William, respectfully, for he knew that only meant that Mr. Slater was having dyspepsia again.

"And to add to that," said Mr. Slater, "to add to the congenital Billy-be-damned foolishness of the world, we're short all the way through the paper. I never knew such a dry week for news in my whole life. Our special correspondent at Goose Creek—the dear old she-buzzard—writes in that she's suffering from summer complaint and hasn't been able to supply her usual string of fascinating information on Goose Creek society. Our special correspondent at Fernville—that's the new girl—sends me in a story I can't make head or tail of. She says it was a festive occasion, but I can't make out if it was a progressive euchre party or a popular hanging—she writes the worst hand in seven counties. The tax commissioners were going to meet, but they didn't. The Spanish War Veterans were going to parade, but they haven't. The mayor's off fishing. T.R.'s in Africa. Nobody's died, nobody's been married, nobody's in jail. Not even a local hen has laid an egg with 'Bryan' on it. I don't know what's happened to the world. Oh, God, if they'd only send me a couple of massacres and a tornado! Then they'd find out I used to work for Dana's *Sun!* As it is," and he tossed a scrap of copy paper over to William, "there's some Billy-be-damned organization from nowhere having a basket picnic at Snapper's Grove. Ted Jenkins was supposed to cover it, but he's got a lame back again, and I can't spare Hod from the press—it's acting up. So go get the story, William—it'll fill up the paper."

"Yes, sir," said William, feeling excited and pleased, for he'd wakened up that morning thinking "Something's going to happen today," and now, sure enough, it had. "How much space can I have, sir?"

"Space?" said Mr. Slater and yawned. "You can have the whole paper as far as I'm concerned—there's no news in the world or the universe. String it out, William—string it out—it's good practice for you." He glanced at the scrap of copy paper again. "Call themselves the United Sons and Daughters of Destiny!" he said. "Lodge, I guess, and a new one on me—but if they're a lodge they've got members, and they like to see their names in print. You can step by the window and get your trolley fare and twenty-five—no, thirty cents' lunch money—I won't have it said the *Gazette* isn't a generous journal. But come back with something or I'm liable to skin you alive."

"Yes, *sir!*" said William, and put out from the office as if he had wings on his feet. But, after he'd drawn his expense money, he decided to jump on his bicycle instead of waiting for the trolley. He'd never had an expense account before and he didn't mean to waste it.

II

It was a five-mile ride to Snapper's Grove and a hot August day and William was sweating when he got there. But the ride gave him a chance to collect himself and put his ideas in order, which was a good thing. Because, even when he first touched that scrap of copy paper, there'd been a queer little shiver in his mind. Of course, as Mr. Slater had said, the United Sons and Daughters of Destiny was bound to be just another lodge—though it sounded like a queer one. But that didn't prevent his wondering and speculating about it.

A little while before he got to Snapper's Grove, he stopped and put on his nickel-plated badge. It said "Press" on it and he'd never dared wear it around the office. But this was an important occasion and he felt he could.

It was a big shady grove of trees by the river—Snapper's Grove—and the whole town was proud of it. There were picnic tables and rustic benches and a stone fireplace and a bandstand, and picnic parties came there from all over the state. It was well kept up, too—the town saw to that—and, if parties didn't behave as parties should, those parties never got another permit. There were trees in Snapper's Grove that had been there before there was a Snapperville, and you could still find Indian arrowheads down by the river. It was a pleasant place and people enjoyed themselves there, but always, to William, there was a great sense of Time in it—Time flowing by like the river, rustling and flowing by like the wind in the trees. You could look at some of the trees and see initials cut there by hands that had long been dust. You could lie by the river and wonder how things had been when the first settlers came.

When William got to the gate—sort of rustic entrance it was, beyond the trolley stop—Hi Summers, the caretaker, stopped him.

"Sorry, Willie," he said. "No private picnicking today. Grounds rented to a party."

"Oh, that's all right, Hi," said William in an offhand way.

"I'm here for the paper," and he swelled out his chest so Hi could see his badge.

"Paper, eh?" said Hi Summers. "Does Ed Slater know about it?" But he grinned, just the same, and let William leave his bicycle by the gate.

"Say, Hi," said William, "you might kind of start me off. Want to make a statement or anything?"

Hi thought for a minute. "Well," he said, "if you put anything about me in the *Gazette*, just remember the name is Summers, spelt with a u. And of course you might say something about our popular custodian of the grounds. Not that I've got much time for reading, myself," he said, "but Mrs. Summers subscribes."

"I'll certainly do that, Hi," said William, for he'd done enough work by now to know how people were. "But I mean about this particular picnic."

Hi thought some more. "Well," he said, "they've got a permit and they're well enough behaved. They got ten gallons of cream from Ike Schaefer's and I've got nothing against them. But I'm not mixing in any of it"—and his mouth got thin and set.

"What do you mean by that, Hi?" said William, feeling rather excited.

"I mean what I say," said Hi, and his voice was stubborn. "They may be foreigners, and then again they mightn't be. They may be just what they say or they might be otherwise. But I'm not mixing in any of it. There's a little wizened-up fellow who claims he knew my great-grandfather. Well, everybody knows my great-grandfather died before the family moved West. And there's three ladies in an oxcart who say they came from Wisconsin. Well, maybe they did, and they look to be respectable ladies, but the ox has flowers on his horns. Decoration, probably, but there it is. I'm not mixing in it at all. And if you had the sense of a June bug neither would you, Willie—paper or no paper."

That was a pretty long speech for Hi, and William thanked him politely. But, as he tried to explain, the Press was the Press and not to be hindered. So he went in and left Hi scratching his head. But as soon as he entered the Grove he began to get the feeling.

III

It wasn't anything he could put his finger on, just at first. He'd seen the Grove crowded, before—and naturally, with any lodge meeting, some people would have regalia and badges and such. But there didn't seem to be any rhyme or reason to the regalia these people wore. A good many of them were dressed like anybody else—and then there was one old man in a leather suit and moccasins who carried a long, old-fashioned gun in the crook of his arm. William rubbed his eyes at that, for he knew guns weren't permitted in Snapper's Grove, but nobody else seemed to be paying any attention.

The three ladies with the oxcart were there all right— very handsome they looked in their bright costumes, with their long yellow braids of hair and their icy gray eyes. They seemed to be knitting all the time, but you couldn't tell where the knitting began or finished. Then there were the people who looked like pictures out of old books—and the conjurers and the sleight-of-hand men and the pitchmen. William couldn't see how they got in—games of chance and such weren't usually allowed in Snapper's Grove, but there they were. Only these were different, for as soon as one fellow had finished some sort of trick somebody else would step up from the audience and do it better. He'd never seen that done before, and it bothered him to see it now.

And yet, at the same time, he felt a queer exhilaration. He couldn't make head or tail of these Sons and Daughters of Destiny—he couldn't even find anybody who seemed to be in charge. And yet, in spite of the oddness of the occasion, there was something exciting about it. For some reason the light seemed brighter and the air sweeter and the sky deeper than he'd ever found them before, even at Snapper's Grove. There was something in the air that reminded him of spring and fall—and yet it was neither fall nor spring, as he knew. "It's outside of Time," thought William Riley, though he couldn't have said how the words came into his mind. And suddenly he felt a little afraid.

For, if these people were outside of Time, then he was outside it, too—and he couldn't see a soul around that he'd ever seen before. For a minute he wanted to run out of the Grove as fast as he could, jump on his bicycle, and pedal back to town. And then he remembered the badge on his coat and that he was there for the paper. "Well, whoever they are, they can't intimidate the Press," said William to himself, and he looked around for some reasonable citizen to interview.

There weren't many who looked just like that. But he finally picked on a wizened little fellow because he had merry eyes. He had a sort of booth rigged up between two big trees and he was spinning a dingy old wheel-of-fortune.

It seemed to be mostly for his own amusement, for nobody stopped by to take a chance. So William stepped up to the counter.

"Excuse me," he said, "but I represent the *Snapperville Gazette*, and—"

"Fortune—try out your fortune—step up and try it—everybody gets a prize," said the wizened old fellow in a singsong voice. Then he stopped and looked at William.

"Great Jumping Jehoshaphat!" he said. "Where on mortal

earth did you spring from? I haven't had a customer like you in a hundred years."

"I told you," said William, patiently, "I represent the *Snapperville Gazette*, Lincoln County's Foremost Newspaper. And if you'll just stop whirling that wheel for a minute—it makes me dizzy—and give me some first-hand impressions of this highly interesting gathering—"

"I told them!" said the old man, nodding his head. "I told them it was bound to happen! But they wouldn't pay attention. Of course, I'm only a third-degree man, myself—never could pass through to the fourth degree, though I've studied and studied. But I told them just the same. 'If you want to have the convention in a grove,' I said, 'that's right and fitting. But for goodness' sake pick a grove that isn't all tied up with human living and dying. Otherwise,' I said, 'somebody's likely to walk in without an invitation and then there'll be a pretty kettle of fish!' But they wouldn't listen, of course, and so here you are."

"Well, that's very interesting," said William Riley, who hadn't understood a word of it, "but—"

"Don't interrupt me!" said the little man. "The Rileys always were great interrupters. Why, your great-great-great-grandfather, Theophilus—fleshy man, he was—interrupted a cousin of mine, just because he didn't like the fate that seemed to be laid out for him. And what was the consequences? Well, he had to emigrate anyway—that was laid down for him—but he had to do it as a bond-servant instead of a moneyed man and he didn't like that at all. On the other hand," said the little man, thoughtfully, "if he had come with money, *which* was possible—you'd now be named De Lancey Fayerweather Riley III and look quite a bit like an educated codfish. So that turned out all right, on the whole. But in general I don't advise interruptions. Our work's hard enough as it is."

"It must be pretty interesting work," said William, "and if you could just give me an idea of—"

"Oh, you'll see that," said the little man, and chuckled. "And you'll get what you came for—yes, you're bound to get that. You've come at the one time you could—the time between boy and man. So you'll get more and less than you bargained for—and what it will do to you, I don't know. But we might as well start with the wheel. Pick a number!" he commanded.

IV

Well, William Riley didn't much feel like doing it, but he picked a number all the same and the little old man spun the wheel and spun the wheel till William felt dizzier than ever. Sure enough, in the end, William's number came up.

"There," said the little man, triumphantly, as if he'd done something extraordinary, though William knew about wheels and how they could be fixed. "You see—that's your number, first crack out of the box! And now you get a prize —a prize"—and he scrabbled among a lot of little boxes.

"There," he said, and gave one to William. "Now open it." So William did, and inside there was a nickel-plated badge, just like the one he had on his coat.

"What does it say on it?" said the old man, eagerly.

"It says 'Poultry Inspector,'" said William, and he didn't sound pleased.

The old man looked terribly crestfallen. "Dear, dear!" he said, clicking his tongue against his teeth. "There must be some mistake—some mistake—I can't imagine how that happened. Daughter!" he called, and a girl came out from the back of the booth. And, after the crowd and the dizziness and the talk of the little old man, William felt very glad to see her, for she was a nice-looking girl. She had brown hair and brown eyes and she looked like all the girls he'd known and liked in high school. She even had two little golden-brown freckles on her nose.

"Daughter," said the old man, "this is William Riley and there seems to be some little mistake about his future"—and then his voice dropped as he mumbled to her and scrabbled among the boxes. But the girl, apparently, was used to her father's ways. She picked out another box, while he was still scrabbling, and gave it to William Riley.

"Don't mind Father," she said in a low voice. "He gets a little mixed, sometimes. But this is the right one." And she pinned the new badge on his coat. This one said "Editor and Publisher" and William felt better pleased.

"There, I told you so!" said the little old man and beamed. But William Riley turned to the girl.

"Do you go around like this all the time?" he said. "Excuse me—I didn't mean it to sound that way."

"I don't mind," said the girl and smiled. "Why, we travel a good deal—yes. But Father's work is really quite light."

"Oh," said William, rather disappointedly, and fingered the badge with "Editor and Publisher" on it.

The girl smiled again.

"He always talks about wishing he'd passed the fourth degree," she said. "But, honestly, he likes this better. A new town every week or so, and new people, and a little good luck or bad luck to pass out along the road, because that's the way of the road. And sometimes Father cheats just a little—he's so kind-hearted—and gives out more good luck than the invoice calls for. That's really why they've never let him take the fourth degree. Well, I suppose it does make trouble with the accounts. But there have to be a few of us like that."

"I'm glad to hear it," said William, but he fingered his

badge uneasily. "You mean, if your father wasn't kind-hearted —well, maybe I *was* intended to be a poultry inspector, and of course if that's really so—"

The girl looked at him with wide brown eyes.

"Good heavens, young man," she said, and her voice was sober, "don't you ever think about anybody but yourself?"

"I'm sorry," said William humbly, for the more he looked at the two little golden freckles on her nose, the more he wanted her good opinion. "I guess I am pretty selfish and pretty heedless. But, well, I always wanted to know how things were going to turn out for me. And now—"

"Don't I know!" said the girl. "Why, that's just the way I often feel myself!" And they stared at each other.

"But you—you can't feel that way," said William Riley. "Because, if you are what you are—you're bound to know!"

The girl shook her head.

"Not a bit," she said. "I'm new. I'm young. I'm beginning. I was born in this country. I'm not very wise, but I'm growing. I don't know all I can do yet, but I want to try. I'm not like one of the Eastern Seaboard destinies—not that they aren't very fine stock—but I like all kinds of people." She hesitated a moment. "You see, it's this way," she said. "All sorts of different people have been coming to this country for years and years—and of course, as they came, they brought their fates and their destinies with them. That's reasonable, isn't it?"

"As you say it, it sounds reasonable," said William Riley.

"Well," said the girl, a trifle impatiently, "they couldn't very well leave them behind. And some were weak and some were strong and some were wise and some were silly—just like the people themselves. But, weak or strong, wise or silly, they had to learn American ways. They couldn't sit around in damp caves and wait for people to come to them. They had to take care of their people and grow up with the coun-

try. But it's too big a country for any one of us to decide
about all by ourselves—that wasn't the idea of it—and, as
old destinies die and pass away, new ones are born. And so,
every few years, we meet—but I've kept you talking too long.
Father's packing up the booth."

"All packed, daughter," said the little old man, and, when
William looked around, there wasn't any booth or any wheel-
of-fortune—just a pair of battered black sample cases stacked
under a tree.

"You aren't leaving?" said William Riley, with a pang at
his heart.

"Oh, no," said the girl, with a laugh. "But we always like
to have things neat and shipshape before the meeting. But
there's time left for you to get your story. Come with me."
And she took his hand.

v

William Riley followed her and her father, half in a dream.
As they passed through the crowd he heard queer names and
queer words. He heard every language and accent that people
use in America—the clipped New England speech and the
Western drawl, the lilt of Italian and the lilt of Spanish.
He'd never realized the country was so big and various before. He heard words that were meaningless to him; he heard
people talked about as important whom he'd never heard of
in his life. He realized, of course, that it was bound to be
so. But it dizzied him and confused him, try as hard as he
would to keep up with it. He tried to make notes on his
copy paper, but he knew the notes didn't make sense. Finally
he drew the girl aside, while her father stopped to chat with
the man in the leather suit.

"What's a preview?" he said. "And a tabloid? What's

something called insulin—does it insulate things? What's *spurlos versenkt* and strict accountability? Oh, well, you don't have to tell me. I wouldn't remember."

The girl smiled at him but didn't say anything. He tried again.

"I don't understand anything," he said. "Those two men over there—and they look like sensible men—are just as worried as can be. And what are they worried about? Well, they just got news that some youngster named Schicklgruber back in the old country is growing up just about the way they expected. Now—does that make sense?"

"I wish it didn't," said the girl.

"Oh, come on!" said William Riley, and his voice was exasperated. "A youngster named Schicklgruber! It sounds like delicatessen. Suppose he does turn out bad. I can see it might worry his folks, at home. But I'm here in Snapperville. What on earth has it got to do with me?"

The girl looked at him a little sadly.

"Yes, you'll think that for quite a while, William Riley," she said. "But you're not one man alone—you're part of a nation and a time. And that nation and that time are going to be changed and altered by all sorts of things and people. You're going to wake up in the morning and wonder what's happened in China; you're going to lie down at night and wonder what's happened in Egypt. You're going to make efforts you never thought were in you, and be helped and hindered by men you'll never see in the flesh. For Snapperville isn't just Snapperville, William Riley. It's part of the world. And now we'd better be getting our seats for the meeting," she said.

Well, William Riley followed her, still in a dream. He hadn't taken in a great deal of what she said, and what he had taken in was a worry to him. But the meeting itself was like most meetings. There were resolutions and reports and committees and appeals to the chair—and all that helped to steady him down. He took notes about it and hoped he could read them afterwards, when he wasn't thinking about those two little golden freckles on the nose of the girl beside him. Only then they began to throw the pictures on the screen.

He didn't know how they did it—he'd never heard of movies in the open air before. But he always liked the movies and he settled back to enjoy himself. Only pretty soon he was sitting up straight in his camp chair.

For these weren't like any movies he'd ever seen—they were real, somehow, though he knew the things in them hadn't happened yet. The years began to flicker by, on the screen—the years of the future for America and the world. At first William was very excited and his pencil wrote like mad. When the man was shot at Sarajevo, he strained his eyes and his ears to remember the names and the dates. Then the film went on. It went on, year after year, with the tumult and the confusion, the waste and the striving and the hope. And here and there William groaned, and at a couple of places he covered his eyes.

"But they can't do that!" he said passionately. "Human beings can't act that way!"

"Some can," said the girl beside him. "And hiding your eyes doesn't help it."

"But they shot that little fellow over there!" said William. "I saw them shoot him! And he wasn't doing them any harm."

"I thought you were only interested in Snapperville," said the girl, and William Riley groaned again.

Of course that wasn't all he saw. There were places when his cheek flushed and his eye glowed. He saw men stand up against tyranny, he saw men stretch out their hands to help other men. He saw the discoveries and the inventions—

he saw things that touched his heart like music. But the future's a hard load to bear for any son of man.

Toward the end, the film got vaguer and more disjointed. There were shouts and cries and confusion, the drone of planes in the sky, and the struggle of ideas and nations. He didn't know quite where it ended. He just knew he was walking with the girl toward the gate of the Grove—and they two were alone.

"Well," she said, "have you seen enough?"

"Too much," said William Riley. "I don't see how a man can bear it. I don't see how men live through times like that and come out on the other side."

"No one ever sees till he himself has to do it," said the girl. "And then, if he's worth his salt, he finds that he can."

William Riley turned and faced her. "But why does it have to be me? Why does it have to happen in my time?" he cried out, in a cry as old as the world.

The girl looked at him. She wasn't smiling now, but her face was grave and sweet.

"I can't tell you that," she said. "That's beyond my knowledge. But I can tell you this. There's fate and there's destiny —and there's man as well. And too many people make fate an excuse for failure. They're bright and they're tired and they see something bad might come, so they just lie down and let it walk over them. Or else they're all wrapped up in their little concerns and hates and they won't listen to anything till fate grabs them by the scruff of the neck. But you—you stand up, William Riley! Because you were born a free man."

"But what can I do?" said William Riley. "What can I do?"

The girl smiled a little now.

"Why," she said, "you can print the news as it comes and see people's names are spelled right—that's part of your job. But you can do more. You'll hear a lot of talk in the days to come. You'll hear this country is finished—well, we've heard that right from the first. You'll hear things will never be the same—well, they never have been quite the same, to my knowledge, since John Smith came to Jamestown. You'll hear people say that they can't bear to have children with times so unsettled—well, if they feel that way, let them—I don't want their children. I'm young and I'm free and I'm growing, and I want the bold and the merry and the enduring. I want the laughers and the thinkers, the strong-hearted and the daring. I've a need for them and I'll use them and their bones will be dust in the graveyards, but their fate and mine will go on. And now, goodbye, William Riley."

"But—won't I ever see you again?" said William Riley.

"Oh, you'll see me again," said the girl. "But not as you think. You'll see me in the faces of your children and the look of your town, in your dreams at night and in the things you find worth keeping. But those will be what you make them—and it's up to you, William Riley."

Then she left him, and William Riley went out of the Grove and got on his bicycle. He wondered how long he could remember what he'd seen and heard. He knew, somehow, that it couldn't be for long. But the girl hadn't said anything about not printing the story. Not, of course, that folks would believe it—he knew enough to know that. But he wondered just how the Fates would get around it.

VI

William Riley woke next morning and knew that something important had happened. Then he knew what it was—he'd written his first big story for the *Gazette* and it would be in today's issue. So he dressed as fast as he could and ran downstairs to get the paper.

He looked at the front page eagerly. Yes, there it was—and Mr. Slater had given it a nice position. His eyes screwed up as he read it—he couldn't quite remember some things in it, but he knew he must have written it, because he remembered the assignment.

"Destiny Picnic Well Attended," he read. "Sons and Daughters of National Fraternal Body Enjoy Outing at Snapper's Grove." His eyes skimmed down the lines.

Our popular picnic ground, Snapper's Grove, was again the scene of mirth and revelry yesterday. An estimated 150 members of the Sons and Daughters of Destiny, a national fraternal body with chapters all over the Union, enjoyed the social distractions of the Grove and the beautiful weather for which our State is famous. . . . A number of interesting speeches were made, dealing with national and international problems, and an al fresco lunch was greatly enjoyed by all. The long-distance cup for the family traveling farthest to attend the convention was awarded to the Mesdames Norn, of Wisconsin, who also presided over the cake table. . . . Our popular confectioner, Ike Schaefer, supplied ten gallons of ice cream which added greatly to the festivities, and Hiram Summers, our popular custodian of the grounds, performed his duties with his customary tact and thoughtfulness.

William Riley put down the paper and frowned a little. It was a good story, all right, a first-class story, and he felt relieved that he'd gotten Summers spelt with a u. And yet, there was something else that he ought to remember.

"So that's how they got around it," he said to himself, and then wondered what he was talking about. But whatever it was that he ought to remember still bothered him, and after he'd finished breakfast he went down to the *Gazette*.

Mr. Slater was there, as usual, but, this not being make-up day, he had his feet cocked up on his desk.

"Well, William," he said, when William came in, "we ran you on the front page. Nice story, too. We'll make a newspaperman out of you yet, William."

"Yes, sir," said William, and hesitated. "Mr. Slater," he said, "did I turn in any other copy last night? I was pretty tired when I got back and I can't quite remember."

"Oh," said Mr. Slater. "Why, yes, William, seems to me you did turn in an editorial—about future developments in the world and such. That what you're thinking about?"

"Yes, sir," said William, and waited. "Did you read it?"

"Oh, sure," said Mr. Slater. "Read it all the way through. You're improving, William. Why, some of the things you talked about might actually happen. You've got quite an imagination, William." And he chuckled. "Had a European war break out at some place I never heard of—Sarawitz, or something."

"It wasn't Sarawitz," said William. "It was Sara—Sara—" And then he stopped, for he couldn't remember either. "Have you still got it, Mr. Slater?" he said. "I'd kind of like to keep it. It might do for a school composition next year."

Mr. Slater looked guilty. "I'm sorry, William," he said. "If I'd known you set any real store by it! But, as it is—well, I'm kind of afraid it got mislaid."

William stood in front of him silent for a moment, while a chill wind blew against his cheek. He'd forget,—he was already forgetting,—but things had been shown him, all the same. And even Snapperville would be changed by those things. For a moment he hated the thought of it; then his back straightened.

"It's all right, sir," he said. "It doesn't matter. Fate's fate, but a country's what you make it. And we're going to need the bold and the free."

Mr. Slater stared at him. "Why, William, you're growing up," he said.

"Well, I guess it was time," said William, and went out of the office. He knew he ought to feel terribly disappointed about something, but he didn't. Already the last memory of that other story was fading. He supposed he'd have twinges about it the rest of his life, but he guessed he could stand the twinges.

Then he crossed the street, and down by the market square he passed a girl named Ellen Chesney and stopped to speak to her. She was a nice girl with brown eyes and brown hair, like a lot of girls in high school, and he'd known her all his life and never paid much attention.

But today, as they stood there talking, he saw that she had two little golden freckles on her nose.

THE DANGER OF SHADOWS

Coming home from the office that evening, Harbison was tired. They weren't using the car this winter, and the bus-ride was long and smelt of damp overcoats. He was glad to get out and walk the last few blocks to his home. The first snow of the year had fallen that morning—in the heart of the city it was already grimed and slushy, but out toward Pershing Heights it was still innocent, cleanly patterned with black footprints and the tires of a few cars. The indescribable smell of it was still in the air—it quickened his pace and the strain of the day began to fade from his mind.

It was then that he began to notice his shadow. It jogged along with him, now ahead, now behind, as he passed under a succession of street lamps. Now it was long and starving, now short and opulent—and there was an instant when it changed. It amused him suddenly to think for how many years, with what absurd patience, it had followed him—dragged at his heels, willy-nilly, as long as there was sun or light. He stopped—it halted at once and lay there upon the pavement, long and black. He waved an arm—it waved a lengthier one in obsequious mimicry. He stamped his feet —it jigged like a dark marionette. Then his ears burned with embarrassment and he looked around shamefacedly, to see if anyone had seen him. But most of Pershing Heights was already home and at supper. He felt relieved. Of course he had a shadow, everybody had. But a grown man, a business man, the father of a family! He must be coming on for a nervous breakdown, to play such tricks—and that was one of the things they simply couldn't afford.

He resumed his walk, sedately, and tried to think about the pin business. But his mind had been absorbed in it all day and now refused the task. After all, there couldn't be any great harm in, once in a while, thinking thoughts that were out of the beaten track. He had neither a dog nor a hobby—he might be allowed a shadow. It would neither chew up Minna's overshoes nor litter the cellar with shavings. It was submissive, cleanly and silent—and, when you turned the lights out, it tactfully vanished away. Or did it? Perhaps it merely went somewhere else. If one waited up long enough, would one see all the shadows of Pershing Heights slip out through back doors and hurry toward some antic meeting place? He checked himself sternly again. He was walking up his own front steps and yet he had hardly noticed them. He assumed a brisk smile and put his key in the lock.

Minna met him in the hall as she always did, put up her cheek to be kissed, and said, "You're late, dear." Sometimes she said, "You're on time, dear," and sometimes, though rarely these days, "You're early." In any case, the tone was precisely the same, the tone of a just and competent wife after fourteen years of marriage. He wondered idly, as he kissed her, if shadows ever married and, if so, at what point they stopped pretending to their husbands that their husbands were remarkable men, except sometimes in front of the children. Then the children stamped downstairs and he was engulfed.

He played with them, spoke severely to Warren about his report, but authorized the expenditure of a quarter to get his skates mended, admired Janet's composition and Wilbur's new front tooth, ate his pot roast with appetite, and heard and commented upon the deficiencies of Mrs. Bemis the laundress. A short report on the singular slackness of the pin trade, though by no means novel, was received with silent assent. Later on, he took Minna to the movies. It was only six blocks away, and Mrs. Pettigrew promised, by telephone, to keep an eye on the house. Anyhow, Janet was very sensible for her age and would be sure to save Wilbur and Minna's mother's silver teapot, in case of fire. In case of burglars, on the other hand, she would probably use the teapot as a decoy.

Janet was very like her mother, thought Harbison, as he watched the heroine of *Flaming Flames* being pursued through a penthouse by an evil millionaire. Yes, Janet would some day make an excellent wife. And Warren, of course, was his Grandfather Veech all over again—people always agreed on that. It seemed odd, though not distasteful to Harbison, that he himself should apparently have left so little impress on the physical and mental make-up of his own children. There was Wilbur, to be sure, but he had caught a look on Wilbur's infant countenance only the other day that had reminded him strongly of Minna's Uncle August. "I guess I'm what they call a good mixer, in those advertisements," he thought without rancor. "I've got to be there, but it tastes of the other things you put in."

He glanced for a moment at Minna sitting beside him. Her lips were a little parted as she observed the perils of Daisy Delight, but her face was perfectly calm. She had already seen Daisy pursued by Russian generals through snow storms and by Latin bravos through banana forests and she knew it would all come right in the end. Even when Daisy was tried for murder, it all came right in the end. In the last sequence, she and the prosecuting attorney were sailing for Europe and a new life on a giant liner, with a great many bon-voyage baskets, including one from the jury. It was all very satisfactory and the way things ought to be.

"It's a good picture," said Minna, with a pleased sigh.

"She's always awfully good. I liked the dress she wore at the cocktail party. But I couldn't copy it, I guess. I'm too stout through the hips."

"Yes, it's a first-class picture," said Harbison. "One of her best. I'd like to take a trip on one of those big liners sometime. They've got week-end cruises, now, that don't cost as much as regular ones and they say it's just like a real trip."

He settled down to enjoy the travel reel. Bronzed youths and maidens swooped down incredible slopes on skis, their shadows flying behind them. It took Harbison back to his last year at State when he and the gang had talked of bumming around the world. Well, Red Curtis had got as far as Los Angeles. He had a nice little bungalow out there and some handsome kids—sent a picture of them back for the class book.

Red Curtis—Jimmy Flagg—Tod Weiler—the ghosts arose for a moment from the past. He didn't know why he thought of them as ghosts—they were all alive and he saw them, now and then, at reunions. They thumped each other on the back and agreed about the new football coach; they told stories and sang the old songs. But, late in the evening it always got lonely, somehow, unless you'd had a lot to drink. Well, Minna didn't mind a drink or two, but she could always tell if you'd had too much, even the next day.

Perhaps if he had got to France in the war, like Tod Weiler, he wouldn't be so crazy about travel pictures. Tod said the coonyac was O.K., but Europe was just a dump and he wouldn't go again if you hired him. Well, that was all right for Tod, but then he'd been there. Harbison had spent eighteen months guarding stores in two different arsenals, and that had been interesting, too, but not quite what he expected. Then after that, there had been Minna, and the pin business. It was all perfectly natural and desirable and he had no kick. And yet, somehow, something had escaped him, though he couldn't put a name to it. Or, rather, something hadn't escaped—something that wanted to be free. He could feel it struggling now. It was light and quick as a shadow but it was tied.

They walked back from the movies in a comfortable silence, Minna and he, and behind them, he knew, walked their shadows. But he did not allow himself to turn his head around. "Better let them alone," he thought. "Perhaps mine is telling Minna's of an island in a warm sea, an island full of green parrots and scarlet-bottomed monkeys. But she wouldn't enjoy that—she is probably an industrious shadow and the screaming of the parrots would get on her nerves."

He locked the doors, put coal on the furnace, ate an apple, and put the peelings neatly away. Minna had already gone up, the house was quiet and yet alive, for he knew that sleepers lay in it though he could not hear their breathing. It was all right, it was perfectly all right, the good ship *Harbison Family* rode on an even keel. No storm or peril would come to it that night, and that was good. He always liked this last moment of solitude, it made him feel like somebody on guard. "My duty is to protect all government property within the limits of my post," he said, out of reminiscence. But his shadow seemed to mock the words. It looked oddly youthful tonight and a little disdainful. "I've got a house and a job. You don't realize how long that takes," muttered Harbison. But the shadow did not seem to hear him. He went upstairs feeling a little abashed.

That was the beginning of a strange time for Harbison. Next day, it was not only his own shadow that he noticed but other people's as well. At first he fought against it like a sensible man, but after a while he gave in. People themselves might not be very interesting, but their shadows always were. Mrs. Popham might pretend she didn't gossip, but her shadow was exactly that of a hen who clucks over every egg in the barnyard, and the shadow of Bunce, the baker, was a round loaf topping a long one with two little French rolls for ears. And who would have suspected that Mr. Whicker, at the bank, was really nothing but an old and pompous sea lion? Harbison had always been a little afraid of Mr. Whicker, but now that he had seen his shadow in profile, it was hard to retain that fear.

There were horse-shadows and deer-shadows, the shadows of fish and apes and plants, but, curiously enough, not many that were really men. He rearranged his desk and the chair for visitors so that he could see them more clearly. It seemed to disturb Miss Pickett, his secretary, but he could not help that. Only for Minna's shadow could he find no likeness. It was like Minna herself, too near and familiar to describe.

For some time, Harbison reveled in a new-found sense of companionship. Business might be dull and clients tricky, but, at the worst, he and his shadow could always exchange a silent nod. Sometimes they even did so about Minna and the children—though, on Harbison's side at least, with no real sense of disloyalty. But gradually, as the days wore on, a doubt began to gnaw at his mind. In spite of his efforts to please it, the shadow was not really contented. The little events of daily life that had seemed to amuse it at first amused it no longer. And then, one evening in January, he caught it in open rebellion.

He was even wearier than usual, and it may have been only a flicker in the eyes. But as he turned in at his own front steps, he was sure that he saw the shadow jerk back for an instant. The tug at his heels was almost imperceptible—no stronger than a spider's thread—and yet he felt it. It did not want to go in, it wanted to go somewhere else.

He reproved his shadow for this, when they were alone together in the furnace room that night. It was always very tall in the furnace room and it liked to crouch and waver in a hundred impish postures while he shoveled the coal. Sometimes he would put on a couple of extra shovelfuls, just for the pleasure of seeing it so playful. But tonight he did not.

"Look here, old man," he said, in a friendly voice just barely tinged with severity. "It won't do, you know. You might as well realize that."

The shadow sprawled across the wall, huge and silent. It looked sulky but absurdly like Warren when he was scolded. Harbison relented.

"Oh, come," he said. "You've been in this world as long as I have. You know what's allowed and what isn't. Come, let's shake and forget about it!"

He offered his hand. The shadow raised its own great paw automatically but there was something both lackluster and defiant in the gesture. Harbison felt annoyed.

"Oh, well, if you'd rather have it that way!" he said, and shrugged his shoulders. "I'll have to keep my eye on you—that's all."

He went upstairs and the shadow followed obediently, its head drooping. "Discipline—that's what's needed," he muttered to himself. But as he undressed in the dark, to the sound of Minna's breathing, he smiled. The poor thing had looked so ridiculously discouraged after its scolding. Well, he had shown it who was master, and tomorrow was another day.

But on the morrow, as he started to enter his office, he felt that light, almost imperceptible tug again. This time it prickled the hairs at the back of his scalp. Things were bad enough anyway, without having to deal with a discontented shadow. He plunged into his correspondence to forget and did the best day's work he had in a long time—anything to keep the shadow out of mischief. Towards the end of the day an impressive caller came, a stranger in a fur coat. He produced references from the Chamber of Commerce and Mr.

Whicker; he spoke in large terms of large orders. Harbison listened and quoted figures, but it was half in a dream, for, beneath his desk, he could feel the slight, insistent tugging of his shadow. It was bored with all this—it wanted to get away.

"And now, Mr. Harbison," said the stranger, leaning forward—Harbison noticed, without curiosity, that the shadow of his profile on the wall was exactly that of a fox—"I'm sure we can reach some mutual basis of—"

"No," said Harbison, suddenly. "No."

The stranger looked astonished. "I beg your pardon?" he said.

"No," said Harbison, more loudly—his shadow was tugging gently but inexorably and he must get it away—"there's nothing to be done."

"You have a very strange way of doing business!" said the stranger, rising, obviously aggrieved. "I assure you, my references—"

"It doesn't matter about references," said Harbison, wearily. "Oh yes, good night and all that—Miss Pickett, will you show this gentleman out?"

Miss Pickett looked strangely at him but obeyed. He slumped in his chair. The shadow was very tiresome. Just because it had been bored by the stranger's conversation—

Miss Pickett re-entered, still with the strange look on her face. Harbison straightened up.

"Yes, Miss Pickett," he said. "Take a—" Then he passed his hand over his forehead. "Did I ring?" he said.

"No, Mr. Harbison," said Miss Pickett in a shy voice. "But you told me, some time ago, to remind you about our note at the bank. It falls due the end of this week." She paused.

"Oh yes," said Harbison. "Of course." He was looking at her shadow—it was a great relief after the stranger's. "Well, that will be all right," he said, hardly knowing what he said.

Miss Pickett looked intensely relieved and rather young. "Oh, I'm so glad, Mr. Harbison," she said. "I—I mean it really isn't my business but you've been so decent to all of us—and I think Mr. Whicker was simply horrid about—"

"It'll be all right this time," said Harbison firmly. He was absorbed by the fact that now Miss Pickett's shadow was in the room, his own no longer tugged. A horrid suspicion crossed his mind and he stole a hurried glance behind him. Miss Pickett had noticed nothing but his shadow was gazing at hers with obvious approval. He blushed to the tips of his ears and dismissed her hurriedly. Things could not go on like this.

So it was that when the shadow tugged again, in a definite direction as he left the office, he let himself be guided where it wished to go. If he humored it in one way, he thought desperately, it might be more docile in others—and he simply could not have it upsetting his office force. Nevertheless, as he followed, he felt greatly disturbed.

It was as he had feared. The tuggings led him to the brightly lighted window of a travel agency. Harbison stared at the gaudy leaflets and the model steamship, the special rates to Calcutta and Genoa. "No," he said to himself in a violent whisper, "*No!*" The shadow did not even bother to answer—it had won its point. He tried the door of the agency —it was locked, but the shadow seemed to understand that. Next day, during the lunch hour, they went back.

It was all so much easier, thought Harbison, once you had given in. He was no longer tired and his mind felt clear as a bell. He had an astonishing capacity for work and the figures of the business crept upward, week by week. The shadow only tugged now and then, by way of reminder, for the shadow understood. It was agreed between them that the shadow must escape from this life it hated to that green and tropic island that had always been its desire. But to do so it must necessarily take Harbison with it—and that meant money and tickets and other things. And there was only one way that one could get those.

Harbison wondered, sometimes, that more people did not plan to loot their own businesses. It could be done so simply, provided you had a shadow to consult on matters of detail. Of course, the business must be built up first, to be worth the looting. But that was simple, too, as simple as renewing the note at the bank.

Mr. Whicker had been difficult at first, and Harbison had grown impatient. He was suddenly tired of being catechized by people like Mr. Whicker—what business had a man with a shadow like a sea lion's telling him what to do? "Don't bark at me like that or I'll never give you another piece of fish!" he said, abruptly, to the sea lion shadow on the wall.

Mr. Whicker goggled. "What, what?" said Mr. Whicker.

"I said there were a lot of poor fish in this town who got taken in by that fellow in the fur coat. But he was too foxy for me—I mean I was too foxy for him," said Harbison. "I hope he didn't stick you for any of his paper."

"He had the impudence to use me as a reference. Quite unauthorized—quite unauthorized," said Mr. Whicker, but his eyes were uneasy. "Now, as regards this renewal—"

"I don't merely want to renew it—I want to double it," said Harbison promptly. "We're expanding all along the line and the Little Goliath Clip is going like wildfire. As for the safety-pin side of it, we've got a campaign mapped out on 'Protect-Your-Baby-From-Wounding-Old-Fashioned-Pin-points—Babykins, the Scientific Modern Fastener, Will Solve Your Diaper Problem' that's going to sweep the country. The big fortunes of the next twenty years are going to be made by the people who have courage and vision enough to go ahead now—and that goes for the pin game, too. Now, just take a look at—" He went on, quoting facts and figures.

The strange words seemed to pour from his mouth without volition, and yet, as he spoke them, he knew somehow that they were true. They had been at the back of his mind for years, these ideas and plans, but he had never had the courage to put them into action. He had thought of Minna's disapproval, of Mr. Whicker's scorn. But these things seemed little, now that he and his shadow were at last on the way to their goal.

The telephone was always buzzing these days—the office had a different look—a look of success. He was asked to speak before the Chamber of Commerce—it was a trial, but the shadow carried him through. Of course, it wouldn't last—it was all for a purpose—but now and then he almost forgot the purpose in the excitement of the work. Now and then, as well, he had wild moments of rebellion. He spent an evening in the city library, looking up the subject of shadows, but only one book seemed to have any bearing on his case, and that was the story of a man who had lost his shadow and so no help.

There were moments when he would have been glad enough to lose his shadow—but how? Perhaps a priest—an exorcism—but Minna and he had always been Methodists. He could see the note in the paper: "Mr. and Mrs. John Paul Harbison gave a small exorcism at their residence yesterday for a few intimate friends. Father Duffy officiated and, following the ceremony, light refreshments were served." No, it wouldn't do at all—there was no help anywhere. For an instant Harbison had a timid thought—if not God, then perhaps, the Other? There were historic precedents and a tradition of efficiency, at least. But no. Such visitants, even at their most gentlemanly, would be likely to frighten Wilbur —he had always been a nervous child. Harbison resigned himself to his fate.

After all, it wasn't his fault. He would have been glad

enough to take Minna and the children, but anyone who knew both Minna and shadows could see the impossibility of that. Afterwards, he supposed, Minna would go to live with Uncle August—she had always been his favorite niece. Later on, she would marry again, but Harbison felt no jealousy thinking of that. It was natural that Minna should be married —so natural that it did not much matter to whom. The children would miss him for a while, but she would be very sensible about it, and they would soon forget. And, meanwhile, the shadow seemed to whisper to him, meanwhile— they would be running races with the wind on the golden sands of that far island, his shadow and he. He could feel the heat already warming his bones.

"You are not looking like yourself these days, John Paul," said Minna firmly one evening.

"Well, my dear," said Harbison, automatically, "you know what business is."

"But it is doing very well," said Minna unexpectedly. "You have given me more house-keeping money, and Mr. Whicker stopped me on the street the other day. He said you are one of the coming men."

"That's interesting," said Harbison. "But we have heavy commitments." He liked the sound of the phrase. "Heavy commitments," he repeated; then, dismissingly, "Oh, I'm all right. Don't worry about it, dear."

But Minna, astonishingly, stood her ground. A faint pink showed in her cheeks.

"It is right that I should worry if you are worried," she said rather didactically. "A wife must take care of her husband and see he does not do foolish things."

Harbison stared at her, with a terrible surmise in his mind. Behind him, his shadow seemed to crouch and shrink up into nothing. It could not be possible that she suspected. But, if she did—

She turned and produced something from a sewing bag.

"Here," she said. "Here is a muffler that I have knitted you. It is cold, these March days, and you have a long walk from the bus."

Harbison took it from her—it was gray, warm, and sensible. But at the end was a little scarlet fringe.

"It brightens it up," said Minna, apologetically. He stooped and kissed her, feeling like Judas as he did so—but a Judas whose betrayal was not yet discovered. That night in the furnace room the shadow was very threatening. They could not risk delay—they must act at once.

When Harbison stole into his office at night some days later, he had a sensation of being followed. He put it down to the shadow, but it did not please him. The shadow had seemed to grow more corporeal with each day of the last two weeks. At times it was no longer entirely flat, to his eyes. He wondered, with a sensation that was beyond fear, if this would continue. If one grew, the other must diminish, that was evident. He could see on the sands of the island a tall, running figure, shaped exactly like his own, but black and comely. The shadow it cast was singularly pale and dim; it complained at times in a small voice like the piping of a sea bird, for it still had the gift of speech, but the words were barely audible. Yet, even if this were to be so, Harbison felt that he did not care. He desired nothing so much as an end to the struggle, a peace.

He took the money from the safe and put it on the desk to count it. It was a great deal of money. You could pay off a note at the bank with it—or do other things. The tickets were in his billfold—he had been clever about those. They wouldn't look among passengers on a West India cruise for a man whose shadow was stealing him away. And at some port, they would simply be left behind. After that, it would be time for the shadow to plan—he had done his best.

"Working late again, Mr. Harbison," said the watchman respectfully, as Harbison passed out of the building.

"Yes," said Harbison, "working late." He turned the corner toward the station—it wasn't far and he might as well walk. His bag was at the station, a new bag, with everything in it new. Behind him, his shadow fairly seemed to skip. It was all right now and everything was attended to. Then a horrible thought struck him. He could not remember whether he had stoked the furnace since morning.

If he had not, the fire would die in the night and Minna might wake up with a cold. He was leaving her behind, to be sure, but that was a different matter. For twelve winters, the last thing at night he had put coal on the furnace. He would never have to do it again but he suddenly knew that, this last time, he must.

He looked around for a cab. There was plenty of time—the train did not leave till one. He had planned to get aboard at eleven and be sure of a good night's rest. But that did not matter, now.

Harbison dismissed the cab at the corner of the street and waited till it had gone away. Then he walked forward, quietly, the brief case crammed with its treasure in his hand. There was the house, still and dark. No stranger could have picked it out, even in daylight, from any other of the houses in the row, but he knew every chip in the paint. And yet, tonight, he looked at it, as if he were seeing it for the first time, and that seemed strange to him.

He prowled soundlessly toward the rear of the house—best go in by the kitchen door. There was the gutter that Warren had stopped up with the baseball and the mended railing where Janet had fallen and cut her lip. He had always meant to do something with the back yard but he never had. Once Minna and he had bought some cheap rosebushes, and he'd meant to put up a pergola. But he wasn't handy with tools

and the rosebushes hadn't lasted. Next time, he would go
to the library and read a book on gardening—only there would
be no next time. Great, vivid flowers bloomed on the far
islands—flowers with magic odors and petals smoother than
cream. The scent must grow oppressive after a time, thought
Harbison suddenly.

He stared up at the windows and saw, with a queer shock,
that one was lit. Wilbur must have wakened in the night
with a bad dream, as he sometimes did, for on the blind was
the shadow of a woman bending over a bed. Her hair was
down her back in two childish plaits and the dim light made
the profile soft and quite young. He had not really seen
Minna's profile for a long time.

The light went off as he watched, and he held his breath.
After a moment, the light in the bedroom would go on, and
she would go back to bed. But it did not. Instead, the window
of their room opened and she looked out.

He thought for a moment that she must have seen him,
and shrank further back into the shadows. But she had not.
She was not looking at him, she was not looking at the yard.
She was looking out at the frosty stars. There was weariness
on her face, and the starlight could not give it back its youth,
but there was a certain content as well. It accepted life, root
and branch, without rancor, it would not seek far horizons
but it would not run away from shadows. Harbison remembered trying to tease her, when they were first married. She
hadn't quite known how to take it, but she had enjoyed it
in spite of herself. He remembered many things, from a pink
dress she used to wear to the fact that she had always wanted
him to be more like Uncle August but had never complained
because he was not. There was a great deal that he remembered, in a very short time. They had come new, to the new
house, now both were worn. "It's not such a bad house,
either," murmured Harbison.

Now she shivered, crossing her arms like a girl, and turned away from the window. But as she did so, there was a slight smile on her face. So there were times when she, too, was glad to be alone. He had not suspected that.

Harbison found the old key on its place on the nail and crept silently into the house. He left the brief case in the living room—he did not wish to be encumbered. The fire in the furnace was low, as he had suspected. If Minna did hear him, she would think nothing of it—in all probability she was already asleep.

Harbison bent and straightened, shovel in hand, and on the wall his shadow bent and straightened too. Harbison nodded his head. "Enjoy it while you can," he said softly. "It's the last time." His overcoat made him hot and he flung it off. "No, there's only one way to settle this," he said.

He stood up panting. Then, slowly he took the tickets and the check for the bag at the station from his wallet. He weighed them in his hand, for a moment—they were parrots and monkeys and an island. Then he flipped them through the furnace door. They did not catch at once, but they caught soon enough.

There was only one way in the world to get rid of a shadow. But it must look like an accident or little boys and girls would be hateful to Warren and Janet at school.

The second step on the stairs going down to the cellar had always been shaky. He loosened it still farther with the furnace-bar—now it would give under weight. They were steep stairs, steep as a ladder—he had always been afraid of tripping and crashing headfirst to the concrete floor. Well, that did not matter any more. He must remember not to throw out his arms.

His shadow was huge, as he stood at the top of the stairs. But, like the huge bullies in stories, it was a coward. It shivered on the wall because it knew what he was going to do. Harbison felt both triumph and sickness. It would never run on golden sands now—and that was a pity. But when it came to the pinch, a man must think of his home.

The muffler that Minna had knitted was still loosely slung over one shoulder. He thought of taking it off, but he was too tired. He switched off the light, now shivering a little himself, and stepped firmly forward through the darkness. As the stair gave, he plunged. Then he was flying, as one flew in the good dreams. There was a sudden wrench at his body, and a sparkling crash.

Harbison woke, and stared with mild interest at the shadow of a tree on a window blind. He waited for it to change into something evil, but it did not change. He made a sound in his throat.

"Drink this," said a voice. He turned his head with difficulty and saw a woman in a starched cap.

"It won't put me to sleep again, will it?" he said, after he had drunk. "I want to be awake for a while."

"You can be," said the nurse, with a smile. "It's all right, Mr. Harbison. You're out of danger."

"Danger," said Harbison. "Yes. I was in danger."

"Well," said the nurse, "those stairs are something fierce in those old houses. It's a wonder people don't break their necks every day. But that muffler you were wearing saved you."

"Did it?" said Harbison. He was observing her shadow with curiosity—it was neither the shadow of magpie nor chattering squirrel, but merely the shadow of a girl in a starched cap—and he felt an intense relief.

"Uh-huh," said the nurse. "It caught on a nail or something and kind of slewed you around. Broke the fall. Things mightn't have been so pretty except for that. But you're dandy now." She smiled a gleaming, professional smile.

"Now you'll be wanting to see Mrs. Harbison," she said.

When Minna had told him about the children and the weather and the events of the town, he lay back with his hand in hers and they both were silent. There was one question he wanted to ask her but he did not know quite how to put it.

"They got the money all right?" he said. "I suppose I was silly to bring it home but I got worried about the office safe. There's only old Cooper—"

"Yes, yes," said Minna soothingly. "It was all in the brief case. I telephoned Miss Pickett and she knew it was to pay the bank."

"She's a nice girl," said Harbison. "I hope she gets married." He paused again.

"Minna," he said, in a low voice, "I got tickets for a cruise."

"There was a letter from the steamship company," said Minna, placidly. "I opened it. I thought it might be important." She patted his hand for a moment. "It was to be a surprise, wasn't it, John Paul? You were always a man for surprises."

"Yes," said John Paul. "It was going to be a surprise." He looked intently at her calm eyes. They were deeper than he remembered—deeper and more comprehending.

"You didn't think I was running away from you, Minna?" he said, suddenly, in a low voice.

"Why, no," said Minna slowly. "You are a good man," she said. It was something not to be argued or controverted. "Besides, there were two tickets," she said, with a little smile.

"Yes, of course there were two tickets," said Harbison, shivering a little. He raised his head. Upon the wall lay his shadow. He saw it clearly—the shadow of a middle-aged man with the hair already thin. It was neither magic nor dreadful, merely comfortable. The bandages on his head gave it a Turkish appearance. He nodded to it, as to a ridiculous old friend.

"You will be disappointed about the cruise," said Minna. "I am sorry."

"Oh it doesn't matter," said Harbison. "We can take one some time when the children are older. They ought to see something of the world."

His head had ceased to throb now, and he felt at ease. When he left the hospital he would still notice shadows, but they would no longer be the shadows of goat or ape. They would be human and follow their owners obediently, even to the last extremity of the flesh. "We're all tied by the heels, in a way, but I don't suppose it matters so much," thought Harbison. "Not as much as we think, at any rate."

"Well, anyhow, we can go to Big Lake for the summer," he said.

THE GOLD DRESS

Rɪɢʜᴛ from the first we had trouble with Louella Weedon. Trouble was, she wouldn't stay put.

What I say is, if you're going to be a ghost, you ought to act like a ghost. That's reasonable. If you want to—well, haunt a place and feel upset enough about the troubles you've had to do it—that's to be expected. But Louella Weedon was different.

They were always strong-minded, the Weedons—especially the women. And Louella, being the last of them, was a kind of institution with us. We'd seen her grow up from a child—plain child she was, but stubborn; we'd seen her take care of her father and her mother and her Aunt Minnie. As long as they lived, she did her duty by them, as New England women will. And when she was left alone, she kept on doing it.

She did only one really peculiar thing that I recollect. Once a year she'd spend two weeks in New York City, and, though there were plenty of women she could have asked to go with her, she always went alone. We thought that was pretty bold of her at first, but after a while it just got to be a custom, and part of Louella.

She never married. I don't mean that she didn't have offers—she did. But while they lived, her family always persuaded her that the suitors weren't good enough. And afterwards it was too late. Of course, there were some who said it drove Sam Owlett to drink—her turning him down—but you never had to drive Sam in that direction. He went on his own two feet. And if the town laughed a little about her and Monroe Taylor, we didn't mean any harm.

Monroe was teller in the bank, but he came from Northport, and nobody knew much about his folks. Well, Louella took him up, as you might say, and he called on her every week or so, that last year. It says a good deal for Louella that even that didn't give rise to any particular gossip. After all, she was a leading citizen, and the boy didn't know many folks in town when he first came. I call him a boy, but of course he was older than that—middle twenties and more. But he seemed young to me, and it's hard to refuse a kindness when you're young and lonely. He advised Louella about some things in the house and checked on some of her investments for her, but that seemed to be all it was. All it could be, too, for it seemed sort of written in the book that Miss Louella was bound to be the last of the Weedons. I know it surprised me a bit, when I read her death notice. I'd been thinking of her as an old maid for as long as I could remember. And yet she was only forty when she died.

After that, we got used to the Weedon house being shut up and empty except for the caretaker who came in once a week to dust and wind the clocks. Louella had directed in her will that things were to be that way till the house was sold or disposed of. So there it was, and the first time in a hundred years that there hadn't been a Weedon in the house.

Only, coming back from the funeral, Ettie Rodgers made a curious remark to me. She'd lived next door to the Weedons all her life, and she knew Louella better than most.

"Well, Louella's gone," she said, with her black eyes snapping, "but I wonder if she'll stay put."

"Now, Ettie," I said, kind of soothing.

But she looked square at me. "No, I'm not crazy, Cy Marshall," she said, and sniffed in her handkerchief. "I'm just wondering. Louella was stubborn enough, but she never got much of what she wanted. She should have had marriage and a family—yes, even if she'd had to marry that Taylor boy. But she was a Weedon, and nobody ever let her forget it."

I didn't think much of it at the time, because Ettie always had notions. But I thought of it later, when the talk about Monroe Taylor began.

He'd acted very proper at the funeral—everybody said that. And everybody felt kind of sorry for him. But when he started taking Jean Moffat home from the library, evenings, people started talking. I couldn't see anything wrong in it myself—seemed suitable to me. She wasn't one of your horn-rimmed-spectacles librarians; she was pretty as you could ask for, and with lots of gumption, too. But the way people talked, you'd have thought Louella was the love of his life and he was bound to spend the rest of it mourning over her memory. That's the way towns are.

I stood up for him all I could—I don't hold with gossip. I liked Monroe—always had—and I liked Jean Moffat. I'd seen her stand up to her Board of Trustees on one or two things, and I'd seen how she handled the children and the young folks in the library. And she certainly did wonders for Monroe. He'd always been the serious kind; but now he began to smarten up and take an interest in the kind of neckties he bought. And Jean began to look sort of happy and proprietary. I was expecting their engagement to be announced and was all ready to have a little talk with Ed Parsons about raising his salary—I'm a director of the bank—when the thing happened.

I'd been down with influenza that April—got it one of those raw, sunshiny days that fool you. Took me almost a month to get on my feet again, and when I did manage to get downtown and set eyes on Monroe Taylor, I was shocked.

I thought at first he must have had the influenza too. Then I saw it wasn't that. He looked just the way he always had, sober and overworked—but there was something more. Now and then he'd have a look you don't want to see on anybody's face—the look of someone who's being pushed to the wall and knows it and can't help it. I tried to jolly him along and told him to come around and see us—and bring Jean, too, if he felt like it. And he thanked me very politely, but you could see he wasn't listening. It wasn't till a couple of weeks afterward that he came.

Meanwhile I'd seen Jean Moffat, and there was something wrong there. She looked cool and fresh, as she always did, but the warmth had gone out of her smile. Well, that wasn't the way it should be, and I felt sorry. But I put it down to an ordinary kind of lover's quarrel. I did for a fact.

I work nights at the office sometimes; it's quieter then. And this was one of the first fine May nights—kind of night when you think you can smell lilacs even though you don't. I had the window open, and it was after nine o'clock. Then I heard the steps coming up the stairs. You can tell when it's a person in trouble when you've lived as long as I have. It was Monroe Taylor, and I knew the minute I saw him that the trouble was a deep one. He sat down when I told him to, but he had his hat in his hands, and he kept twisting it.

"Judge," he said finally, "might I consult you about a personal matter—very personal?"

"That's what I'm here for, Monroe," I said. "Though I'd better say first that if it's anything about the bank—"

"It isn't," he said wearily. "Though I don't blame you for thinking it. Oh, God, if only it were the bank!" he said. "If I'd only stolen money and could go to jail for it—why, I'd be as happy as a clam."

Well, I thought that was just one of those high-flown speeches that younger folks make, and I'd better straighten him out.

"Now, Monroe," I said, "if it's this town talk that's worry-

ing you—well, I was born here, and I've lived here all my life.
And it's a good town. But there's a few ladies that would
gossip in the New Jerusalem—yes, even with wings on. It
oughtn't to worry you, and it oughtn't to worry Jean Moffat.
If you've had a quarrel, make it up. And let them go hang."

"Don't you suppose I want to?" he said, and his voice was
hoarse. "But I can't, Judge Marshall. I just can't. I don't dare
to—not for Jean's sake. You don't understand. It's Louella."

"Louella?" I said, kind of taken aback.

"Yes," he said. "You see, I've seen her. Since. I—I see her
about every week now, just the way I used to. I go up to the
house and call, and she's there. Sometimes she's sewing.
Sometimes. . . . Oh, well, you wouldn't believe me, and
what's the use?" He stood up. "I guess I'll be going, Judge,
and thank you for listening. But it's no use telling me to
go and see Doc Robinson. I know what he'd think about it,
and I don't care to do that. If I have to go to State Asylum,
I'll go on my own feet."

"Sit down, Monroe," I said. "Sit down."

And I got the bottle out from behind the Statutes of the
Commonwealth and poured him a hooker. I made it a stiff
one, too, for I thought the case justified it. But even so he was
jumpy as a scared horse, and it took time to get him settled
and the story out of him.

Well, of course I didn't believe him, even at that. But
there was something about the way he told it, sitting there
in my office, with his gray hat twisted in his fingers and the
warm May air floating in. You see, he wasn't the kind of
person a thing like that ought to happen to. Just a nice,
steady, likable citizen—in his bank teller's clothes, talking
about something that couldn't possibly have happened, with
the sweat pouring down his face.

It had started that same day that I got the influenza—late
afternoon of that day, with that queer false spring in the air.

He was going to have supper with the Moffats and take Jean to the movies. But as he went past the Weedon house he thought of Louella Weedon, which was only natural. She'd given him his start in the town, in a way, and, now he was in love with Jean, he felt grateful to her. He remembered little things she'd done and little things she'd said. Now I'm not excusing him at all. It would flatter almost any man to have a woman like that take an interest in him. And he'd say the pleasant little things that a man would be apt to say under such circumstances. Especially a stranger. He wouldn't even think of Louella as an old maid, necessarily—he'd treat her like a human being. I told you I wasn't excusing him. But you see the way it could be.

All the same, when he thought of Louella, he thought of her with sadness but with a sort of relief. For he had a suspicion that it mightn't have been so easy, bringing Jean around to call on her. And yet he'd have had to do it. It was just about then that he noticed the Weedon gate wasn't shut.

Well, he thought the caretaker must have forgotten, so he stopped for a minute to latch it. And as he did so, he saw a curtain move inside the house. He said he was sure of that. He said it gave him a queer feeling—that and the smell of false spring you could feel in the dusk. He said that's why he went in. But he said the queerest thing was that he knew the door would open the minute he put his hand on the knob.

He used to call on Louella in the back parlor—nobody ever sat in the front one. He said, once he was inside the house, he felt he had to go there. And he went, and there she was.

He said it wasn't till he left the house that he began to realize what had happened to him. And then he groaned aloud.

He was late at the Moffats', and Jean didn't like that very well. Then they went to the pictures together, and it was a good picture—but he just couldn't keep track of it. He'd keep seeing Louella, the way she'd been in the back parlor, and hearing her voice instead of the voices on the screen. She'd had her sewing basket on the little table in front of her, just as usual, but she'd been different. And he knew what the difference was. He knew it now that he was in love with Jean.

Well, Jean practically had to nudge him when the picture was over and the lights came on; he was still looking straight ahead and wondering if he was damned or crazy or both. Oh, he explained to her, of course. About having a headache and working late at the bank. You know how well most men explain when they're put to it. It left a sort of coolness be-tween them. And when he went back to where he boarded, there wasn't a more miserable young man in the state. He didn't go back past the Weedon house—he went the long way. But he knew he'd have to go back there, at his regular time. Louella had let him know that, and she'd be expecting him. Well, ever since then it had been going on.

I tried to get him to explain why, granting it was true, he couldn't break loose, and then he got sort of incoherent. He kept saying nobody could understand who hadn't been through it; or know what it was like to be tormented by two women at the same time, and one of them not of this earth. Well, I guess that would be hard to explain—but I knew the Weedon stubbornness. When they reached for anything, they closed all five fingers down on it. I'm not saying whether I believe the boy or not, but when I finally got him quieted, I felt sorry for him. I really did.

Next morning I went around to see Ettie Rodgers. I've known her a long time; and if she's got notions, she's got sharp eyes, too. We talked along for a while, and finally I asked her if she'd noticed anything queer at the Weedon house.

"Nothing except Louella Weedon," she said, with a snap

of her handbag. She looked at me straight. "I told you at the cemetery she mightn't stay put," she said. "Well, she hain't."

I laughed, of course.

"Laugh all you like," she said. "I'm her next-door neighbor, and I know what my eyes see and my ears hear. And I've seen Louella Weedon, just as bold as brass, walking up and down in her garden in the cool of the evening. She's got a new hairdo, too, and a bare-necked dress. Bare-necked and bare-armed," she said with a sniff. "Heathen, I call it. Well, I believe in keeping yourself to yourself. But if she ever comes over here, I mean to give her a piece of my mind." She looked at me, sharper than ever. "Monroe Taylor ought to have more sense," she said. "Or somebody ought to."

Well, I knew by that the fat was in the fire; for, in spite of what Ettie said, she'd keep a thing to herself only so long. I didn't want a lot of smart city reporters in town, making wisecracks about a ghost hunt and telephoning fool stories all over the Union. It isn't fitting or respectable. And from the way Monroe Taylor looked, he was just about on the ragged edge. So I got the key of the house—I'm executor under the will—and I went around.

Of course I didn't need the key, for when I turned the knob, the door was unlocked, just as Monroe had said. I held it in my hand for a minute, making a mental note to blow up the caretaker about leaving it that way. Then I opened the door and went in.

There's always something creaky and strange about a house that's been shut up, no matter how you dust it. The light isn't quite the same, and the rooms are dim. Yes, even if it's your own house, that's true. I knew the Weedon house almost as well as my own. And the minute I got inside the door I began wishing I'd come in the morning instead of late afternoon.

I wasn't afraid of Louella—naturally not. I went straight

to the back parlor and looked around. And, if the back of my neck prickled, that might happen to anybody.

There wasn't anything peculiar in the back parlor. The vases that Captain Abijah brought back from China stood on the mantelpiece just where they'd always stood. And there was the high china cupboard, built in the wall. It all looked the way I remembered it. There was the sewing basket on the table with some half-finished work in it—but naturally that would be there. Everything had been left the way it was when Louella died. I was going to look at the sewing, and then I decided not to. If I had, I'd have started wondering if any of the stitches were new, and that would have bothered me.

There weren't any flowers around, but there was a smell like strawberry shrub. Louella had always been very fond of that scent. I tried to remember when we first got strawberry shrub—I thought it was early for it. But I couldn't remember.

Then I did a pretty foolish thing; I don't like to think of it yet. I stood there in the tidy back parlor of that empty house, and said, "Louella—Louella Weedon." As if I was calling her. I said it low at first, then I said it quite loud.

There wasn't any answer right away; just the scuttlings and creakings of an empty house. But after a while I got an answer.

It wasn't what I expected; it wasn't words or sorrow, it was just a laugh. I knew Louella's laugh—it was dry and sharp. This one wasn't. It was full and rich, the deep laugh of an exultant woman. But it was Louella's all the same. You can't mistake a person's voice when you've known it. And this was mocking past description—mocking and exultant. But it was Louella's still.

I stood hearing it, while the hairs at the back of my neck prickled. And then I got out. Yes, I even locked the door behind me, though I knew that wasn't any use. If there'd been any sense in staying, I'd have stayed. But there wasn't, and I knew what I'd better do.

You don't take that kind of thing to a brand-new minister —I don't care how many degrees from Union Theological he's got. But Minister Henderson was still living up at North Center. He'd been with us forty years before he retired, and I felt he was the right man.

Well, I felt like a fool on my way up there, but when I did explain it to him, he took it very calm. Come to think of it, there can't be much you could surprise a minister with when he's been forty years in a town. And of course there was plenty of authority for similar cases. He showed me one out of *Wonders of the Invisible World*. That was in Cotton Mather's time, but New England's still New England.

Then we got on to the more practical side of the matter. There were various things you could do and wear and say, according to tradition. But he said this was a neighborhood matter, and he meant to treat it as such. And if there was a spirit to be dealt with and exorcised, he was still a minister of God, and he'd do his part. I wouldn't have felt right if he'd said anything else.

He agreed that Monroe Taylor would have to be there. But it was me that insisted on Ed Parsons, too. I knew he was bound to hear about it sooner or later, being president of the bank, and I didn't want what he heard to work against Monroe. Ed's a hard-headed man, and what he doesn't see himself he doesn't believe in. So I wanted him to see.

All the same, I felt queer when I let them into the Weedon house that particular night. There was Monroe Taylor, white as a candle, and Ed Parsons, grumpy and grumbling, and Minister Henderson, old and white-haired and calm. I took them into the back parlor and lit the lamp. The curtains were drawn—I'd attended to that—and you couldn't see a thing from outside. Everything was just as I'd seen it, and the smell of the strawberry shrub was very sweet and piercing. I could see Ed Parsons notice that and not admit it. Well, we had a little prayer. And then I felt queerer than ever. For we sat there quite a while, listening to the rustlings and the creakings, and nothing happened at all.

Finally Monroe Taylor broke the silence. "It's no use," he said in a low, strained voice. "It's only for me, you know. If you'll all go away, she'll come. And I guess that's right. She'll come, and we'll talk the way we used to. I didn't know she counted so much on it. Oh, God, my punishment is more than I can bear!"

I saw Ed Parsons slue his eye on him at that, and I wouldn't have given much for Monroe's chances at the bank. But just then we heard the laugh.

It came, low and rich, low and mocking—the laugh of an exultant woman. You couldn't tell just where it came from —that was the queer part. But it pulled Monroe Taylor out of his chair as if he'd been drawn by cords.

"She's calling," he said. "I'd better go to her." And his eyes were like a sleepwalker's.

But Minister Henderson laid a hand on his arm. "No, my son," he said. He raised his voice only a little, but it seemed to fill the house. "Louella Weedon," he said, "I am speaking to you. Why do you torment this young man?"

"Monkeyshines," grumbled Ed Parsons; but he grumbled it under his breath, for the minister was going on.

"I am speaking to you as a minister of God," he said. "And if you are evil, I bid you begone to your own place. But if you are otherwise, I bid you manifest yourself and say why you torment us."

"Monkeyshines," said Ed Parsons again, but louder, as if he wanted to hear the sound of his own voice. And then he jumped and sat still.

For there was another laugh, and after it a voice, very clear and distinct and recognizable. And the voice said: "Monkey-shines, Ed Parsons? That's all you know."

No, I don't expect you to believe it. Looking back, I hardly believe it myself. I remember staring at the glass lampshade —it had a kind of pattern of leaves and flowers on it—and wishing that anything would happen to make the voice go away. But it was Ed Parsons who spoke.

"That's Louella Weedon's voice," he said. "And she's dead, so it can't be. And whatever she wants, 'tain't my business. So I guess I'll go home."

He made a motion to move, but he didn't, for the laugh came again, low and vibrant, and we all sat as still as mice. I'd never thought Ed Parsons was a coward and I don't think I'm one. But, when the laugh came the third time, I saw his hand begin to shake, till he stuck it in his pocket. The smell of the strawberry shrub was very strong, now—stronger than I've ever smelt it.

"Louella Weedon," said the minister, patiently, "I charge you by the dreadful day when all secrets shall be unlocked—"

But, right then, I put my oar in. I didn't want to, but it came over me, all of a sudden, that things weren't to be done that way—at least not yet.

"Excuse me, Minister Henderson," I said. "But—well, I'm an old friend of the family's and maybe if I said a word." I didn't raise my head any—I just kept looking at the lamp-shade, but all the same, I knew there was something in the room.

"You see, it's this way, Louella," I said. "We aim to be reasonable and we don't mean to interfere in what's not our business. But, all the same—well, to put it plainly, can't you let the boy go?"

There wasn't any answer to that, just the echo of my own voice, so I tried again.

"All right," I said. "I won't even mention Monroe here.

But, as I figure it, these things happen when a spirit wants something done that hasn't been done on earth. Or so they say. So, if you'd just tell us, Louella, what you want and how we could fix it—well, after all, we're your neighbors—" and I stopped, for I thought I'd made my point.

Then the laugh began and, with the laugh, the voice.

"Want?" it said. "Why, what more could I want? I'm back in my house where I always lived—I walk in my garden, evenings—I don't even have to go to the post office to know the town gossip. And I've a fine handsome young man to call on me once a week and hand me my sewing basket. What more could I want—and me a New England woman? What more could Louella Weedon want out of life and death?"

I didn't dare look around but I heard Ed Parsons give a sort of reproving "Tch-tch" between his teeth. And the voice went on, very still and clear.

"Don't cross me, Ed Parsons," it said. "Do you want me to tell them what you keep in the second drawer of your desk at the bank—the one with the special lock?"

"Oh God, no!" said Ed Parsons, quite loud, and the red came up to his ears.

"Then don't cross me," said the voice. "And you, Robert Henderson, minister of God. Shall I go back fifty years in the past and tell these men, who sat under you, what was in that past?"

"My child," said the minister, tranquilly, "if there was sin in my youth, it is between my God and me, now. You cannot make it bitterer in the mouth nor the repentance more anguished. So speak, if you will."

"No," said the voice. "I've heard tales enough in this village—tales enough. And, as for you, Cy Marshall, well, you always were a meddlesome old busybody and you ain't changed a mite," said the voice, with venom. "So you know what I think of you all."

I kept on looking at the lampshade, but I heard the sob in Monroe Taylor's throat. Then the minister spoke.

"If you are an unclean spirit," he said steadily, "I charge you, by the words of the Gospel, to begone to your own place. But, if you are otherwise—"

He had risen now, and his hand was lifted. They talk about the spirit of God being in a man. I guess it was in him, then. For after a long moment, the voice came again, and it wasn't rich or mocking but low and sort of pitiful.

"I am not an unclean spirit," it said. "But I am perplexed and bound. I wanted so much. I wanted so much to be gay— and I never could be. I bought the clothes to be gay—and I never wore them. I wanted love and warm things. Is it wrong to have wanted them?"

"No, my child," said the minister, gently. "And you must forgive us all, for we did not know. But now you must have rest."

"There were so many tongues," said the voice. "All gossiping. They made an old maid out of me while I was still young. It happens a lot, I guess. It was my fault, too. I used to cut pictures out of the papers—pictures of ladies in fine dresses. I always wanted a gold dress—I always wanted gold slippers. Well, folks would have thought I was crazy. But I got them all the same and hid them in the closet. Because they meant everything I'd missed. If I'd worn them, once, I'd feel different. But nobody knows about them. So what's a woman to do?"

"My child," said the minister and hesitated, "my child—"

And then there was another voice in the room. We hadn't heard the door open—we hadn't heard anyone come in. But Jean Moffat was there and her eyes were blazing. She must have been there for longer than we knew.

"Oh, you big, stupid lumps of men!" she said. "Can't you see what's keeping her restless—can't you see what she wants? As if any woman wouldn't mind! Where's the key to that closet, Judge Marshall?"

"Jean!" said Monroe Taylor, hoarsely, but she didn't hear him. She was listening for a moment to a whisper we couldn't hear—the whisper of a woman, talking to another woman, about things man can't understand.

I didn't know there was a key in the potpourri bowl, any more than I knew that high china cupboard was just a false front and there was a closet behind it. But Jean Moffat seemed to know. I always said she had gumption.

I don't know what the rest of us expected to see when she opened that closet. Most anything, I guess. But it was just dresses. All kinds of them, hung on hangers. And some were the latest style and some went back twenty years. But there was one thing about them all. They came from New York and Paris—places like that. And each one would have done for a duchess and not one had ever been worn.

Jean Moffat was sort of murmuring over them and talking to them—not cool and efficient, now, but a woman, sharing another woman's trouble.

"Oh, so pretty—" she said. "So pretty— Of course you couldn't leave them behind, dear—of course you had to come back and wear them. Because you never had, in your lifetime. So that's all right. But now we know about it and you can rest."

"Rest," said another voice that was like an echo and, just for a minute, there seemed to be another woman in the room, standing right beside Jean Moffat and smiling at her. Of course, it was a trick of the light. But I'd have sworn that I saw Louella Weedon—only not the one I knew, not the one that was bound to be an old maid. This one was gay and splendid, black-haired and bare-armed, in a dress that glittered in the lamplight. There were sparkling things on her shoes and a sparkling thing in her hair.

Then she wasn't there any more, and there was just Jean Moffat, crying queer tears as she smoothed the dresses with her hands.

Well, that was all there was to it, as far as I know. Though we had a little discussion about the dresses, afterwards. Ed Parsons was all for burning them, but Jean Moffat knew better and she got her way. Some of them went to folks that could use them—young concert-singers and such that have to make an appearance without much money. And others went to the museum. Jean Moffat figured Louella would be satisfied with that, and she seems to have been. At least the summer people who bought the house haven't complained. They think the china closet's quaint. Well, I'm not telling.

Yes, I guess Louella must be satisfied. That was quite a while ago, of course—the Taylor children must be five and three. They've nice children and their father's fleshed up a bit—lost his looks, some folks think, but Jean doesn't seem to mind. Just a decent small-town couple—you'd never know what they'd been through, to look at them. Well, I'd be liable to doubt it myself. Except for one thing.

You see, there was a kind of little notebook in the closet with the dresses. Where Louella put down where she got them and what she paid—she would, of course, and, I must say, some of the prices turned my hair. But there was one dress we couldn't find—the gold one. Well, I think I know where that is—and so does Jean Taylor. But I say, let the departed rest. After all, Louella bought it and paid for it. And, if she wants it with her, that's her business.

THE LAND WHERE THERE IS NO DEATH

*I*t w a s not very far from Hilda's house to John's house—just three and a half streets and a corner—and it seemed to the children as if they had always known each other. They were always running back and forth—you could hear the light patter of their steps in the street like the patter of rain. Sometimes it was Hilda's mother who caught them and washed them—sometimes it was John's mother who looked up from her baking to see the door open and the children slip in, quite quietly, plump down on their stools and watch her with eager eyes. John was the elder of the two by about six months—he had a merry face, a short nose, and a lively imagination. Hilda had yellow pigtails and round cheeks—she looked solemn and healthy but she was a good playmate. They had known each other since they were born and expected to know each other all the rest of their lives.

The town in which they lived was an old town, even for the land, and a pleasant one. It was big enough so that it felt like a town, not just a collection of houses—it was small enough so that it was easy to get out beyond it, into the fields. There was the gray old church with its stiff stone angels and the city hall with its carved ceiling, the square with its fountain and its statue to a long-dead hero, the running river and the cemetery on the hill. Hilda and John knew all of them, as children know, by exploring. They were the provost's girl and the minister's boy—most people knew them and were friendly. It was not hard to be friendly to the children—no matter in what part of town you found them, they looked as if they had a good time being alive.

Of course, they were not always together. They were part of a whole band of children, running up and down the streets, shouting upon the wharves—part of the river and current of children that streams back and forth to school every school-day—the wreath and garland of children that bring new life to a town. Often Hilda played with other companions, and John too; neither of them was freakish. Yet there was always something that drew them back towards one another, no matter what other friends they had. Even their parents grew used to it—and their older brothers and sisters. They did not bother to say "Where's Hilda?" or "Where's John?" They said "Where's Hilda and John?"

They were able to console each other, too—perhaps that was part of it. Let us take death. That is something which happens and is known. The children knew that it happened and accepted it. Yet when old Ketty died—old Ketty who worked at the provost's house—they were puzzled. Old Ketty, with her gouty fingers and her cross kindness, was as much a part of their lives as the house or the lamps in the street, the fountain in the square or the moon in the sky. She was not as important as some things, she was more important than others. Now she lay in her coffin, with her hands crossed over her breast and her hair very smooth. She looked more important that way, but she was no longer Ketty. The children went to the funeral together and saw her buried. Afterwards, Hilda's mother gave them both a piece of ginger-cake, absent-mindedly, and sent them out to play.

It was good cake and it had a good taste but it did not quite make up for something—for what, the children did not know. They played for a while quite cheerfully at being dead like

Ketty, first John and then Hilda. But there was not much fun in the game, and inside them there was a queer feeling. After a while, they gave it up and sat down on a stone bench by the fountain in the square.

"I guess Ketty must be in heaven by now," said Hilda in a matter-of-fact voice. "I guess she started as soon as they put her in the ground. Is that when they start, John?"

"Oh, yes," said John, who was the minister's son. "I guess that's when they start. They couldn't start before, with people coming in to see them. I wish I'd seen her start, old Ketty!" and he smiled at the thought of old Ketty somehow hurrying and grumbling her way to the door of heaven as she used to hurry, grumbling, to answer the provost's door. "She had on her best dress, too," he said. "That was nice for her."

"Yes, I'd like to have my best dress," said Hilda. "It doesn't matter so much, with boys."

"No, I suppose it doesn't," said John agreeably. He kicked at the bench. "When you held your breath very hard, did you feel dead, Hilda?"

Hilda considered. "No," she said, "I felt funny but I didn't feel dead."

"Neither did I," said John. "I wish I'd asked Ketty how it felt. Now you be Ketty, and I'll ask you."

So Hilda was Ketty, and when he asked her how it felt to be dead, she said it felt very pleasant. Then she burst into tears.

"For goodness' sake, what are you crying about?" said John.

"I don't believe it feels very pleasant," said Hilda, overpowered with grief. "I don't want to be dead myself. I don't want anybody to be dead."

"That's silly," said John. "Everybody's got to be dead some time." But he was moved and made uncomfortable by her tears.

"Everybody doesn't have to be dead," said Hilda. "Tell me everybody doesn't have to."

"Oh, all right," said John, since he was older. "Everybody doesn't have to be dead."

She sat bolt upright, her round cheeks blazing. "Do you mean that, John?"

"Oh—I thought everybody knew that," said John uncomfortably.

"And you're not just talking about heaven? I know about heaven."

"No, I'm not talking about heaven. I'm talking about—" He paused and thought. "I'm talking about the land where there is no death," he said firmly.

The tears were not dry on Hilda's cheeks, but she stopped crying. She fished out a bit of barley sugar from her pocket and sucked on it.

"Tell me about it, John," she said, reassured.

So he told her about the land where there is no death. It was far away, of course, over many roads and mountains, but it could be reached and found. It was a very pleasant land, not cloudy and damp like heaven but green and sunny. As he told about it, he began to believe in it himself and to see it plainly. It was very like the best of all that they knew—the friendliness of the town and the warmth of the fields in summer—except that no creature died there, not even a hare. When he had quite finished, Hilda's tears were dry.

"It sounds wonderful, John," she said. "But we won't have to go there right away, will we? I promised Mother to help her with the ironing tomorrow."

"No," said John. "We won't have to go there right away. But we shall go some time, of course." He felt that he had spoken sensibly, and Hilda was content, for she liked to have things definite and in order. After that, they had a secret— and it was another bond between them.

That is how they first heard of the land where there is no death, and for a long time it occupied their thoughts. Each day when they met, they would add one detail or another to the picture they had of it until it grew very real to them indeed. There were a town and valley, there were streams and forests. They knew it foot by foot, as they knew the streets of their town—and it was a comfort and a consolation to them.

As the children grew older, of course, the land receded farther and farther to the backs of their minds. They would talk of it now and then to one another, half in jest, but it was not a pressing concern. Nevertheless, what is bred in the bone will come out in the flesh. And though Hilda had been the first to raise the question, it was John whose life was changed by it.

It came upon him while he was in the last year of his studies for the ministry—for, with all his merry looks, a minister he intended to be. Perhaps he had been studying too ardently as young men sometimes will—that is hard to say. But at all events, one summer evening he lifted his eyes from the dry page and there it was before him—the land where there is no death, with its wide summer fields and forests and its garland of ageless children who pass continually through the streets of its town. The sound of its streams was in his ears like a calling of voices. He knew that it was but a vision and yet it called to him. Surely, somewhere on earth there must be a land that death did not ravage. He put the text aside and sat by the open window for a long time, with his hand upon his brow.

So when he came before his examiners, they cast him out— for he could not reconcile the goodness of God with the fact that death was loose in the world. He did not complain of their judgment—he had expected no less and no more. For that matter, they treated him kindly enough, except for one or two who called him a heretic. But his heart was unsatisfied by the texts, and he knew that he must go forth and seek what he must seek.

It was hard to do so indeed for by now he was a young man and Hilda a maiden. They had not spoken of love to each other and yet they had taken for granted in their hearts that some time between them there would be love and marriage and the kindly and mortal things. Yet, when they parted at the crossroads, they were gay enough.

"It will not be for long," said John. "Perhaps I shall find it in a month—perhaps in a year. Yet surely I shall find it. We have talked of it so often. And that will be a great thing, Hilda."

"That is true," said Hilda. "And I will not stop your going. Yet the world is very wide. You will not forget me, John? Not even in that land?"

"I could not forget you, Hilda—and would we might go together! But that, I know, may not be. But when I have found what I must seek, I shall come back to you."

"I will be waiting for you, John."

Then she gave him bread for his journey, for he had forgotten that in the exhilaration of his thoughts, and with kisses and sighs they parted as many have parted in this world. How many the partings are! And John took his staff in his hand and Hilda went back to the town, for it was baking day and the rest of her loaves should have been in the oven an hour ago. Nor will bread bake itself, though folk go on journeys.

So John set forth upon his search and it was not a hard journey, at first. He had lived in one town all his life but, being friendly himself, he found the wide world friendly and of passionate interest. The look of each new village was enough to divert him—the sight of each new landscape a discovery and a pleasure. Moreover, where his search was concerned, there he got continual encouragement. For whenever he spoke of what he was seeking, soberly and honestly, with that charm youth does not know it possesses until it has gone, there were those who would listen and reply. Sure enough, they had heard of such a land—or their fathers had. It was not where they lived and died, as John must understand, but it might lie just beyond the mountains—perhaps a little farther—that was hard to tell. But there was a tale and a memory of it in men's minds—let John talk to the schoolmaster or the tavern-keeper or old Agnes, the wise woman, who remembered all the old stories. This excited John and made him wonder why they had not sought for the land themselves. But for that there was always a good answer. This man had his field to plow or the village would get no grain—that man had just been wed, that other had great possessions. They would follow him gladly, were life better arranged—as it was, he must see that they could not—but once he had found the land, he must be sure to send them word. And this John promised gladly, for they were kind people and helpful. Nor could he force them to come with him, though now and then he would have been glad of company on the road.

Here and there, of course, there were those who thought him a fool or a madman. But he had an even temper and was able to bear their scorn. If they threw him in jail, there was something to be learned in jail—if they drove him out of the village, he went from it uncomplaining. He had no quarrel with them—only with death.

Soon enough, the money in his purse was gone and he must turn to a trade to keep on with his journey. But he was strong of body and clever of hand—he would do a day's work for any man, so he got on well enough. Moreover, he found very early that a story or a song often smooths the road for a stranger. They were not hard for him to furnish—he had told so many stories to Hilda when they were children that his tongue was quite in the way of it. When the day's work was done, the folk would gather about him to listen—or, if not the grown folk, the children, and that suited John even better. At first he had but a small enough stock of stories but as time went on and he saw more of the world, it grew larger, and he told them with more art. Some were real and of things that had happened, some were the old tales all men tell, some came into his head as he walked along the roads. He could not tell which sort were the best, though he came to know which pleased one town and which another.

Yet, in all this time he did not forget the object of his search. He was cheerful and gay, but it was continually in his mind, for wherever he went, death ravaged the fields of man. And from death none was exempt, no folk and no nation. It seemed to him once that surely the rich and the proud must have among their treasures some clue to his searchings. So he stayed for nearly a year at a king's court, telling his stories, and the king was well pleased with him. But when the king's son died in the bloom of his youth, there was nought to do. He could ease the king's heart a little by his tales, but that was all. At another time he sought out the scholars—and the wisest of them were most wise. But wise as they were, they could tell him little of the land he sought, though they dragged out many rolls of parchment. For one said that such a land was mentioned in Aristotle the Greek, but another said that it was not, and then there were fierce and angry words among the baldheads. It was all John could do to calm their quarrel with a story—and he left them in the end, happily picking his story to pieces, as men pick bones from a fish.

Now he was no longer young, but a man in his prime; yet the anguish of his search burned in him more fiercely than ever. It drove him across seas and continents, into strange lands, among strange folk. Yet, when he came to know them, they were no longer strange but all children of men. They might live on a bowl of rice under burning suns—they might hunt the elk through the snows—yet they lived and loved and suffered as all men do. Often they broke his heart with their slyness and their kindness, their cruelty and their strange courage, their hate and their sudden brotherhood. He saw great wars flame and cease and the plow go back to the fields— he saw bitter injustice done and yet a few men stand against it, and out of their bones imperfect justice arise. All these things he saw, and of many he made stories and some were bitter. It is bitter to see man blacken the face of man—it is bitter to see him die when he might live. Sometimes it was so bitter to John that it seemed to him that, wherever he went, Death himself followed at his heels, a leering companion, shaking his sides at his endless jest upon man. Then John would brace his heart and put himself in Death's way— but, in plague and famine and conflict, Death passed him by. So he went on.

He went on because, even in the far corners of the earth and the huts of the savage, he would find a hint and a clue and a memory to lead him. Yes, they knew the land he spoke of, though it was many suns away. The great ones had gone there in the past; some time, when the great ones came back, all earth would be like that land. And that night, John would dream and see it very clearly. He would see its murmuring river and its fragrant fields and its fine town, and, with the dream, his hope would be renewed.

You will ask if he thought nothing of Hilda in all these years. He thought of her always and continually—sometimes as the child he had played with, sometimes as the maiden he had left. As the years passed, the memory of her face grew dim, yet he knew he would know her in an instant, once he saw her again, and that was a solace to him. Every child to whom he told a story had something of Hilda in its face and, for that reason, he did his best with the stories. "And, as soon as my search is ended, I shall see her again," he thought.

His search did not end in a day or a year, yet it ended suddenly. For some time he had noticed a difference and a change in the lands through which he passed—the speech was more familiar to him though a speech he had not used for very long. As he struggled one day toward a certain pass in the mountains, he felt burning in his heart the certainty that tomorrow would be the day and with it the long task completed. Had they not said in the valley, "Yes, we have heard of the land, and it is not here. But across the mountains, doubtless—" The mountain air was thin in his lungs as he toiled upwards with the evening, but his spirits rose. And sure enough, at the very head of the pass, he caught a glimpse of it, all as he had imagined first—a fair land with broad fields and bright streams and a good town where men might dwell, all luminous for a moment in the last, golden haze of the sun. Then the sun dipped and the mists of evening shut over it, but John had seen what he had seen. He did not try to go down through the pass that night, for he knew he must husband his strength. But he was content.

Next morning he roused with the first light and resumed his journey. As the road led toward the town, his excitement mounted, for each stone by the way seemed familiar to him and that was a sure sign. Yet it was not all as he had dreamt of it but in some ways changed, and that gave him assurance, too. He noticed that folk looked at him a little oddly as he strode into the town itself, with his ragged cloak around him and his worn staff in his hand—well, that was to be expected when one entered the land where there is no death. He did not stop to converse with them or ask questions—that would be for later. First of all, he must go to a certain part of the town and sit upon a bench by a fountain. He did not know why he must do this, but it was strong upon him.

They were busy with their own affairs, the good people—

he passed among them and smiled. The shopman kept his shop and the housewife came back from market and, all of a sudden, the bells rang and the children burst out of school. How merry they were and lively! He would find the ones who liked stories best later on. So, at last, he came to the square and the stone bench and the fountain.

There was a young girl by the fountain, and as she heard his footsteps, she turned and his heart gave a leap within him, for it was Hilda. He paused for an instant, leaning upon his staff.

"Well, Hilda," he said. "I have found it, as you see. And yet we are together, after all."

Then he saw her eyes change with surprise and knew that it was not Hilda, though very like her. And, with that, his years came upon him and he sank upon the bench. He could see in the waters of the fountain that his hair was as white as snow and his face the face of an old man. Then he knew where he was and what had happened and that he was mistaken indeed.

How long he sat upon the bench he did not know, but after a while he looked up, and Hilda was indeed before him, though not the young Hilda he remembered. Her hair was as white as his own. Yet he knew her at once.

"Well, John," she said. "It is good to see you again. And have you no word for an old playmate?"

"I have many words indeed, Hilda," said John very bitterly. "But they all come down to the one—that I have been a fool. You were right not to wait for me, Hilda—my search has lasted all my life and yet it has been but a wild-goose chase and brought me back to my front door. And now, at the end of it, I have not even children to match with yours."

"Why, it is not quite like that," said Hilda. "Children I have and grandchildren, and that can be. And yet I have always waited for you, John."

She sat down on the bench beside him and took his hand.

"You must come home with me and tell me of your travels," she said. "For even in this quiet place, we know your name, and all children know your stories."

"Some of them are not badly made," said John. "And yet I set out to find the land where there is no death and not to tell stories to children." He looked at her intently. "Have you heard that perhaps one or two of them were not so badly made?" he said.

"I know them all," said Hilda. "Or as many as my children would tell me—no doubt you have more. There was one that you told about old Ketty. You gave her another name but I knew old Ketty at once."

"Yes, that was about old Ketty," said John. "It is not a bad story, though I always meant to mend it a little. But the children liked it as it was." He sighed. "And now I must tell my last story," he said. "I must tell that there is no land where there is no death and that men's hopes are in vain. That will be a hard story to tell, but it must be told. Yet first I would like to look around the town. It has been so long."

"The house where your father lived still stands," said Hilda. "It is town property, but I think the town might grant it to a famous teller of stories. My second daughter's husband now being provost—" she said.

So that was how, after all his journeyings, John came back to his own house again—and matters worked out for him much as Hilda had said. Indeed, at times he was almost happy, for if there were many of his stories the townspeople had heard from other mouths, there were many they did not know, and that is always pleasant for a storyteller. And even the old tales, he found, gained a certain new life from the faces of the listening children—the children not of his loins and yet of his town. They were in and out of his house and

Hilda's house all the time—they slipped in quietly when he sat by the fire and had slid upon stools to listen before he knew they were there—you could hear their footsteps in the street like the patter of rain. Now and then there would be two with their heads together, and John and Hilda would look upon them and smile.

Yet when the dark fit came upon him, John would swear that he must set out upon his travels again and tell his last story—the story that no land exists where there is no death and that death, not life, rules all things. Nor did Hilda attempt to dissuade him. But whenever he tried to frame that story in his mind, the words would not come. He could tell of his own search and his own folly, but that was not enough.

"Indeed, I think I have lost what little wits I had, Hilda," he said to her one day, in anger with himself, as they walked by the river. "For here is a story worth any man's telling and yet it will not come to my mouth."

"It is a grim story," said Hilda.

"It is a true story," he said.

"Are you sure it is true?" she said, and he looked at his old companion with anger and surprise.

"Have I traveled the world for nothing?" he said. "What do you know of all this—you who sat at home?"

"It is true that I did not go with you and true that I am neither traveler nor taleteller," said Hilda. "And yet I have my own ideas, for what they are. I have not found your land, but there are the faces and the bodies of my children. For even though they die before me, I have put life into the world, and though all come to dust in the end, there shall yet be dust of that dust. So I say life rules all, not death."

"You talk like a woman, and they are always bound to have the last word," said John angrily, and flung away from her, for he was annoyed at her crossing him when she was not a taleteller. Yet her words sank into his mind and remained there as he walked further on down the stream, striking at the reeds with his staff.

"Now I wish I could talk to Death himself about this," said John. "For I have neither chick nor child, but only stories. And there are many with neither child nor story." And, even as he argued with himself, his story began to take shape in his mind.

It was a grim story and a sad one. For it showed how vain were the dreams and hopes of men for a land where there is no death—and how, from the cradle itself, behind every man and woman, followed death, a leering companion, at all times ready to play his one monotonous jest. He came to the king and the beggar, and neither might nor humility could ward him away—he touched the strong man in his strength and the fair maiden in her bloom—he tumbled knights from their horses and children from their desks at school. Neither pulpit nor pew was exempt from him; he was there in the crowd at the fair and the roar of battle and the silence of the hermit's cell. Men might cry out against him manfully—they might pray and supplicate and dream—it all came to one in the end, and the end was dust. Nay, the world itself, when it was old, he would destroy in time, having fed his bad heart first with every creature of that world. To no purpose did the sun rise and the moon rise and the sky show its spangled stars—death was in the air and the earth and the waters under the earth—death everywhere, omnipresent, a king of terrors ruling a world of dupes and slaves.

John rolled the words on his tongue, and they were fine words. Let it be his last tale—yet it was truth and his best. He could see the faces grow white as he told it out and he shivered as the wind came raw from the river.

"And yet, that is only Death's story," he said to himself.

Then he thought of the ways of life—not of any one way of it, but of life itself—and how it is renewed each year in leaf and seed and feather and fur and flesh. In the cool jellies of the streams there was life, and in the thrust of the tree-root deep in the earth, in the new-hatched chick and the child curled in the womb. And each year that life was renewed. In the early spring, with the snow still crusted on the ground, there was a change and a quickening as the earth turned back toward the sun. It began with melting ice and the running of the brooks—with the smell of new earth and the cry of the first-come birds and the peeping and buzzing noises of tiny things. It began and swelled through the summer, a great chorus of all the living, and through all the scale of creation Life wandered like a proud husbandman, sowing immortal seed. Though death had been in the world for a million years, yet each new thing came into life as if death had never been—though death slew and slew, he could not wipe life from the world. And, in the thoughts of men—aye, there death was powerless—for, though he could slay the body, he could slay neither thought nor dream. The virtuous he could slay but not their virtue—he could stop the hearts of the bold, but there was a memory and an example to inspirit other hearts. So went the great pageant of life, like an army against its adversary—and ever the battle was won and ever the battle lost, and yet to death, in the end, was not the victory.

"And that is true also," thought John. "And yet—may we not have peace?"

Then he saw his land as it must be, not as he had dreamed it—the land where there is no death—a land without autumn or winter, but all one perpetual spring. Very beautiful it was at first sight, but very strange. For in it, as there was no death, there could be neither change nor time. Forever the waters were untroubled, forever the skies serene. Never could a new leaf grow upon a tree, for no old leaf had fallen to make way for it—never could a child be born, for, with the birth of any child, the mother takes one willing step toward death. The rain might not weather the stone nor the wind blow the blossom nor the sun make folk feel lusty—for these things, too, mean change. There could be no growth in such a land for with growth comes completion and an end, and here there could be no end. He looked upon the faces of those who dwelt there, and they were comely and fair, but not like human kind. Their bodies were unwearied and strong, but upon them was an enormous lassitude and a blankness. For however they toiled and endeavored, their toil must be undone by evening or change must enter their world and, with change, the struggle between life and death begins. They might love, but without the sharpness of brief and mortal love —they might plan, but with all time to plan in, the plan itself had no meaning. They knew not what it was to be safe for they knew not danger—they knew not what victory was for they had never known defeat. On their backs was a huger load than any borne by mortal man—not man's load of a few years or many, but a dark load of endless time, remorseless, absolute. For, in that land, each day was like another day, and every day the same—and, just beyond its borders, Death sat upon a stone, cracking his fingers and laughing. Or was it Life who sat there and laughed, full-throated, for joy of the struggle and the adversary and the way in which his children took Time's harsh odds and yet made a mock of Time? John did not know, for the closer he looked, the less he could distinguish between the figures. Then the vision was gone and he turned back toward his house, huddling his jacket about him, for the bleak wind of spring made him cough.

So after that, he was ill, and Hilda told him what she thought of him for wandering by the river without a cloak. And with all she said he agreed, for she was right, and dear to him. For some days he was in fever, then the fever cleared, and he felt better though weak. Yet he knew, as men sometimes do, that he would not mend. It did not matter very much to him as long as the children still came to hear his stories and Hilda sat by his bed for an hour or so, talking quietly of old times. He knew that they were old but he did not think of her as old.

"I thought for a while that I had been very bad for you, Hilda," he said one day. "But I see that too was wrong."

"Well, John, you were always a little conceited," said Hilda, with the frankness of an old friend. "I suppose that is part of being a storyteller. And I suppose that, in a story, the world might think ill of you for leaving me. But do you not think I had pleasure in a friend gone away to strange lands? It made me quite conceited myself for a time, I assure you. I led Jonas a merry dance because of it—poor man—and it was as well for him—he would not have liked me half as well if I had not. And now it is time for your soup." And she patted his hand.

So it went till John knew that he was dying and that he must tell his last story. There was a child in the room—a child of Hilda's?—a grandchild?—Hilda herself?—he was not quite sure. But its cheeks were tear-stained, and it looked at him with eager eyes.

"Why, what is the matter, child?" he said, though he spoke with difficulty.

"Mother tells me Old John is dying," said the child in a thin voice. "And I don't want people to die. I don't want them to die at all."

"They do not die in the land where there is no death," said John reflectively, for he had his story in his mind. "I shall tell you a story of that land."

"Where is it?" said the child.

"It is not here," said John. "And it is not over the mountains. And yet you shall go there, and I, and Hilda, and all that you know."

He saw Death standing by the bed, but beside Death was Life and both beckoned.

"Yes," he said. "It is only through living and dying that we may get to a land where there is no death. But do not be afraid, child, for you were born to the journey."

Then he rose and followed those who beckoned him. and Hilda closed the eyes of the man upon the bed.

PART FIVE

For Remembrance to R.C.B.

WITH A GIFT OF CRYSTAL CANDLESTICKS

*T*HESE candles are alike, yet they are two,
Take one for the body's worth
Which is more beautiful than rain or spring,
A little body made of sun and earth,
Some flowers (the whitest, these), a cloud, a feather,
The talk of certain birds and certain streams,
The silence of proud dreams,
All living in peace, all held in peace together
By the bright silver penny of the heart
You found long since within a fairy ring.
Take then this candle—not because its art
Can light a path for you along the night
But rather for your hand to give it light.
But stay a moment ere you do depart;
The candlesticks are two.
There is another you.
No flesh however fair
Can bind that fire and air
Nor any night inherit
That lustre, that intense
Thing beyond excellence
And all the tricks of time—

So from your lover, who has made much rhyme
But found few proud enough to match your name
Or your deep steadfastness,
Accept this second toy of glass and flame
And in its crystal read your crystal spirit
And in the flame the love he cherishes.

TODAY I SAW YOU SMILING

*T*o d a y I saw you smiling in your sleep.
I don't know what you dreamt, for good or bad.
I only know you smiled
With all the touching gravity of a child,
Patient and sober, waiting at a door
That it had never knocked upon before,
Or with a gift it was not sure to keep.

My dear, indeed I know that you are more.
How should I not, who see, beyond the grace,
The delicate, secret courage of that face,
So slight, so stubborn in its fortitude,
The Irish laughter in the Irish eyes?
I know enough that you are flesh and blood.
I know you are a woman and distressed,
Subject to mortal comedies and fears,
I know the heart is mortal in the breast,
I know the angry and the fruitful years.
I know all these unnecessary things
And could not love you more if you had wings,
Having once lived with these mortalities.

Yet, then, you slept, and, as you slept, you smiled,
Gravely and patiently and far away
And with such airy peace on every feature,
It seemed to me I must have heard there say

305

A Voice, august and mild,
Rolling down slowly from the cliffs of day,
"How well it sleeps! How well I made this creature!
I am so very pleased with this good child."

Memento Mori

FOR US

$\mathcal{I}$N THE long bed of Time so straitly lying,
Like angels on a shield—
What is this petty artifice called dying?
And when is it revealed?

THIRTY-FIVE

$\mathcal{T}$HE sun was hot, the day was bright,
And all July was overhead.
I heard the locust first that night.
"Six weeks till frost," it said.

FOR YOU

$\mathcal{S}$LEEP in the dust beside me, you
Who never said a faithless word
Or gave a kiss that was not true
No matter how the dust was stirred.

LITTLE TESTAMENT

I HAVE lived. I have thought and labored, I have loved
and possessed my love
To the uttermost inch of flesh, till the deep voice cried in
us both.
I have not cut my coat according to the color of the cloth.
When the world passed by me in the street, it could have
fist or my glove.

My people were soldiers for the most part—they had Spain
and Ireland in their shroud;
I was a coward and afraid, yet I have not shamed them, I
think.
I have not refused the drink when there might be venom in
the drink.
I have written the verse for my pleasure, not for praise or
money or the crowd.

Loving two countries well, sweet France, like a well-sunned
pear,
And this red, hard apple, America, tart-flavored, tasting of
the wild,
I can lie at ease in either, yet may the child of my child
Run the heaps of gold leaves in the Fall, see the red leaf
hanging in blue air.

With the five dull tools of the senses, I have seen great Jupiter
    enskied,
Tasted the buds of spruce, the buds by the lakeside in the
    Spring,
Smelt woodsmoke and snow unfallen, heard the gold horns
    answer to the string
And touched the entire earth, on the mountain, naked as a
    bride.

I have been a traitor and loyal, a fool and the enemy of fools;
Certain friends I would not betray. I have worn ragged over-
    coats for pride.
I shall keep the delusions of my soul a secret until I have died,
Because of a stubborn nothing that would not answer to the
    rules.

So it is. So be it with me. I make my mark and depart.
Children of children of my children, you will yet have a sting-
    ing in your blood,
A dark cell, a hidden laughter, an eye seeing bad and good
That chooses one mask in public but a different image in
    the heart.

Now the mind rusts into madness, the horses run without bit,
The paltry body is nothing but mechanics of bone and skin.
Nevertheless I have spoken. This nothing spoke for its kin
And loved one woman completely. Let her remember it.